Dear Aidan,

Happy, happy 17

Hope you find your life is filled with joy.

Journey to Joy

Anne Perreault

A. R. Perreault

Can she find joy where there has only been defeat and dishonor?

Tricked into indentured servitude, Joy Richards finds herself working for an abusive innkeeper. Her life is so destitute, she feels God has forsaken her. After one last desperate cry to God, a kind stranger steps in to take her away.

Can she trust this new circumstance?

Andrew Lloyd-Foxx abhors injustice. He can't walk away from it. When he steps in on the young woman's behalf, his own life is turned upside down. Burdened with his own loss, he has no room for anyone else.

Will the journey prove too difficult?

Also by Anne Perreault

Royal Skater Chronicles

Skating for Grace

Learning to Trust

Broken

Restoring the Locust Years

Making all Things Beautiful (coming later 2019)

The Cooper Family

Love the Lord Your God with all Your Heart

Dangerous Relations

Rescuing the Weak

Stand Alone titles

Running the Good Race

What if...

Ebooks

An Unusual Adventure

All books are available as Kindle and are free on KU

© 2019

by Anne Perreault

Edited by Lisa DeBartolomao
Cover design by Natasha Perreault
Images by Pixaby.com, and Shutterstock

Printed in the United States of America

ISBN: 9781081522261

Scripture verses taken from the King James Version of the Bible

Facebook: Into the Light Fiction
Webpage: intothelightfiction.weebly.com
Newsletter: https://mailchi.mp/25f04fba2efb/httpsmailchimpintothelightfiction

Trust in the Lord with all thine heart; and lean not unto thine own understanding.

In all thy ways acknowledge him, and he shall direct thy path.
Prov 3:5, 6

To Lisa. We make a good team.

And to Justwouldificould, my beautiful Grace-mare. It was such an
honor to be part of your life for a time.

1

Somewhere in Massachusetts, 1837

G irl! I asked for a pint of ale ten minutes ago!" An inebriated man glowered over his empty tankard.

The *girl* in question spun around, her hands fluttering to her filthy apron, and almost tripped over the hem of her tattered, stained dress.

"Let me teach ya a lesson, wench!"

The man reached forward and managed to yank her hair back, hard. Before he could do anything else, the innkeeper stepped in. He quickly and mercilessly slapped her face. Joy lifted her hands in self-defense.

"Yer more trouble than yer worth!"

The innkeeper glowered at her and went after her as she tried to cower in the corner of the noisy filthy tavern, where the bugs were more plentiful than the paying patrons. Curling into a tight ball against the wall, she protected herself against the brunt of the blows that rained down on her. A kick made it past her defenses and she whimpered, hating herself for the show of weakness.

"Ger-up! Go an' do what I pay ya fer! An' dinna let me catch ya fallin' asleep on the job agin! Next time I won't treat ya as kindly!"

Joy tried to catch her shallow breath. She pulled her hair away from her face and touched her cheek. A sharp pain stabbed through her.

She had neither time nor energy for this.

More fabric ripped as she stumbled to her feet. The hem of what was supposed to be a dress was now hanging down and she was sure to trip on it. She tore it off the rest of the way. What did a little less material really matter to her? It wasn't as though she was going to a ball any time soon.

She *had* attended plenty of lowly barn raisings and harvest festivals. What she wouldn't give to be at one right now, talking to her friends.

Perhaps one of the young men would ask her to dance. Her seedy surroundings vanished as her imagination transported her to a better place. Instead of drunken men groping at her from every side, she was waltzing on the arm of the one man for her. Handsome Jonah. His smile alone could light up the darkest evening.

"Watch it, wench!"

She was ripped out of her reverie and regretted her hasty move as the full tankard she clumsily carried spilled over the filthy man. The one who had apparently been waiting for his drink for ten minutes. Her breath caught in her throat.

Oh, she had done it.

The innkeeper, a man who held her life in his hands, bore down on her, his face twisted in a dangerous scowl.

"So sorry," she managed to sputter, and tried to mop the drink off the table before it did more damage on the man's already filthy pants and tunic.

"Oy, what are ya up to?"

Again, her hair was yanked back roughly, leaving her head no choice but to follow. As for the rest of her body, it wasn't so easily convinced to go along and so she fell. That didn't seem to faze the man dragging her back into the kitchen.

Kitchen was too strong of a word for this place where rats found themselves on the menu as delicacies. The place lacked a certain – refinement.

Joy reached up to keep her scalp attached to her head. He was going to make her regret her daydream, and it was going to hurt. She had been at the receiving end of the man's anger before, many times it seemed, and it was never pleasant. If only he left her with some of her dignity intact.

The look on his face told her that this was not about to happen.

"Dinna I just tell yer ta keep yer wits 'bout ya?" he snarled.

He was inches away from her and she gagged on the putrid breath coming from his partially decaying teeth. She almost lost what little food she had in her stomach into his face.

Joy glanced around the dingy surroundings. If only she could grab a club or something to defend herself with. Or one of the dull kitchen knives.

The thought of taking a club or knife to the man made her withdraw into herself. How could she? Nothing could make her sink that low.

She had to admit that, in the month she had been here, there had been many times when she wished she could stand up for herself and end the torment the man dished out freely. He seemed to enjoy working out his anger on her any way he found convenient. She had been traded by her former alcoholic owner for a barrel of whiskey, and apparently the innkeeper thought he had received the worst end of the deal.

It was strange how calm she felt with him hovering menacingly over her. Was this how she was supposed to die? Beaten to death.

Her parents would be horrified if they knew that their precious daughter had ended up here, in the hands of this man, who had so little regard for human dignity and kindness. They would do anything to get her out of the situation if they could.

But that was the crux of the matter.

They couldn't.

"Yer useless an' not worth the clothes on yer back. 'Ave ya forgotten? I. Own. Ya."

His voice rose and she pressed herself hard into the cold dirt floor, fingering around for anything to defend herself with. The man had murder on his face.

"I won't do it again," Joy whimpered.

She hated how weak her voice sounded. This cowering woman on the floor wasn't even her.

She was yanked to her feet again and the first blow struck her while he cursed her with every foul name he could think of. Pain radiated through her face and her back and, for the first time in a long time, she prayed. It was more like a scream for help and she didn't expect it to be answered.

She grunted as a blow split her lip. Warm, sticky blood gushed down her chin.

"Excuse me, my good man."

The voice sounded like something out of the distance, coming through the thick fog in her brain. It was a clipped, cold voice.

4

The blows stopped and Joy slipped to the ground, the strength she may have had completely drained.

"Sir, ya honor me 'umble abode wit' yer presence," the innkeeper's voice lowered a few decibels and he actually managed to bow.

"Could I trouble you for your time?"

"'Course. Pa'don me while I teach this here wench 'er manners."

Joy managed to open her puffy eyes to see who had postponed the inevitable.

The figure standing in the kitchen door didn't belong. She flinched at her reflection in his tall, perfectly polished, black riding boots. His tan breeches were devoid of any stains. His white shirt and flawless cravat were out of place in this squalor. His red jacket was so bright, it almost blinded her.

A dandy.

There wasn't a speck of dirt in the clean-shaven, aristocratic features. Only a scar across the forehead kept his face from being too handsome. His wheat-colored hair had been gathered together by a piece of tanned leather at the nape of his neck to keep it out of his face. Steely gray eyes peered out from underneath thick, dark lashes and if looks could kill, her master would have given her his last punch.

Apparently, she was the only one in the kitchen who recognized the anger smoldering behind those eyes.

"I say." That crisp voice now cut through the fog, completely. "Could I trouble you for some water for my horse? We've had a long, dusty ride. It is hot out there and my horse is in much need of some refreshment."

"Kin I offer yer lordship a glass o' port or a nice cool pint of me best dark?" Her keeper quickly found his best manners and his diction became less common.

The gentleman flashed a smile that disappeared quickly.

"I think not. What is cooking in that pot on the fire?"

"Ow, sir. It be the best beef stew in the county."

Rat stew was more like it. Joy knew that for a fact because she had skinned the rats only this morning and there were plenty more waiting for tomorrow. At least the meat was fresh.

A look of disgust passed over his handsome face.

"I think I'll pass. A piece of bread and cheese will do. Bring it to me outside."

The man retreated out of the kitchen, glancing her way one last time. Joy shuddered and suppressed a groan when the innkeeper yanked her arm roughly.

"See to 'is needs, ya 'ear! We ain't finished. If I catch yer daydreamin' again, I'm gonna make ya regret the day yer was born!" The hiss was menacing and Joy tried to shove the images that slipped into her mind right back where they had come from. "Go, tend to 'is lordship. Serve 'im some of that cheese."

He turned to leave, then hurled over his shoulder, "Mind, cut off parts the rats chewed on."

Joy worked quickly, cutting the tiny bite marks off the bread. But it proved difficult, with hands trembling so hard. She sliced herself with the dull knife and groaned. Blood soaked into the insides of the bread. She quickly threw it into the fire and wrapped her hand in her filthy apron.

She took a deep breath. In an attempt to steady her hands, she counted to ten, then picked up the knife again. This time, she managed to cut not only the bread but also the cheese.

She stumbled as she took a step outside, tripping over the stoop. Her eyes adjusted to the sunlight and she blinked rapidly. Once outside, she hesitated. Joy's tattered dress made her feel... ashamed. Once she stepped into the light, she wouldn't be able to hide her filth. She would be exposed as to what she had become.

A filthy tavern wench.

But to stay inside was worse. She would find a way to ignite the ire of her owner.

The gentleman reclined against the fat trunk of the oak tree that shaded the front of the tavern. His eyes were closed, his face that had been so taut with anger only moments ago was relaxed. He looked peaceful. It felt wrong to disturb him, and Joy stopped short a few steps away. The horse, a magnificent gray thoroughbred, raised his beautiful head and nickered softly in warning.

His eyes snapped open and for a moment she thought he would go for the musket hanging on the side of his saddle. She took a step backward, stumbling over the root of the oak tree.

"Thank you." His gaze was not unkind. "My horse. Water, please?" His voice, clipped and aristocratic, left no doubt that people jumped to obey his every wish before he finished uttering it.

"I'll fetch it quick," she stammered.

"I shall wait until you have brought it."

He pointed for her to leave the food in front of him.

Joy hesitated. After all, the man had saved her life by suddenly appearing at the door. It would be unkind to let him eat any of the tavern's food.

"Unless you are starving and have a long way to go, I would advise against eating the food. The water is clean."

Did she have a death wish? Her owner would kill her for sure if he heard.

His lips slid into a semblance of a smile.

Joy quickly retreated and fetched a bucket of water from the pump. She carried it back outside and placed it in front of the thoroughbred. She longed to touch his gleaming coat. She caught her hand halfway to his neck and quickly put it down.

"Thank you."

Joy turned to hurry back into the safety of the semi darkness to hide.

"I say. Is there anything I can do to help?"

What?! Joy paused in her steps and spun around.

"I could offer you a better… job."

The gentleman had a look of genuine care written all over him. It hit her in the pit of her stomach. It had been so long since anyone had looked at her in such a way.

She lifted her chin. She was not a victim.

"I'm not free to make that decision." Her voice held a tiny tremor at the end and her statement caused his eyes to widen.

"You - a white woman - are a slave?"

She sucked in a heavy breath. "Yes. In a way." Her bottom lip trembled, reminding her of her injury.

The gentleman recovered quickly from his shock by offering her a crisp handkerchief.

"Your lip is bloody. Perhaps some water to clean it?"

"No, thank you." She shook her head at the proffered linen.

She had successfully managed to serve one customer today.

2

$\mathcal{T}$en minutes later, she lifted her chin and walked back into the hot sunlight. Joy had cleaned her bloody face with some warm water, trying to make herself look at least somewhat presentable.

She knew it didn't matter, really. She was still filthy and couldn't wash it away. Her dark brown hair hung in clumps down her back. No matter how hard she tried to comb her fingers through it, she couldn't.

"It's your turn to brush my hair." Hope. Her sister, handed her the brush, letting her thick golden tresses fall down her back. "I want it to shine like yours. All the girls are envious of your locks. They say that it would fetch a high price."

They giggled and Joy began their nightly ritual.

Tripping on the root system, she was ripped out of her daydream.

Watch yourself, Joy.

When she approached the man, the only thing left of the food on the plate were a few crumbs. Her eyes widened in horror.

"Sir!" She pointed.

A small smile touched his strong mouth. "The squirrels and chipmunks may have become my best friends."

She picked up the plate, swallowing a laugh that begged to be let free.

"Thank you for your service. My horse is much refreshed."

Thank you? She hadn't been shown appreciation in a long time. What was happening to her lips? The left side lifted ever so gently. Was that a smile? How long had it been?

She snapped herself back to the present.

"I'm glad. He is a handsome animal."

"Are you familiar with the Godolphin Arab?" He had gotten to his feet and walked over to his steed.

Joy worked on squashing the excited jitters that passed through her. Why was he still talking to her? This was her kind of conversation. He was keeping her from her dreary duties.

"Yes. After arriving in Europe as a gift for the French king, he was passed off for his small stature and eventually sold to England, where he became the property of the Earl of Godolphin. In the end, he is credited for the improvement to the thoroughbred bloodline with his enormous speed." And why was she even engaging him in conversation?

The gentleman patted his horse proudly, looking at her with a gleam of interest.

Joy withered under his scrutiny. Her lip had begun to swell and there were bruises on her body that had started to fade but told of other incidents of painful treatment.

"This is one of his great great great grandsons." He puffed out his chest as he scratched his horse's head.

Joy gaped at the magnificent animal and reached forward to touch him. Her hand snapped back before she could.

She was filthy and had a job to do.

"Would you like a tankard of water? It is the only thing I would ingest from here." She snapped her mouth shut. She shouldn't be so bold.

"Yes. The day is hot."

Joy scurried through the tavern with the empty plate and worked the pump again. Sweat beaded on her forehead from the heat of the afternoon. The muscles in her back burned before the cool water began gushing out. The well was low because along with the cool water, dirt swirled in the bucket.

Back in the kitchen, she poured the water through a piece of cheesecloth, getting rid of most of the unsightly debris.

"What yer doin', little wench?" the innkeeper snarled. "There be customers to be served."

She felt his hot, putrid breath on the back of her head. It sent chills down her spine. She kept herself still.

"Just taking care of the gentleman outside." There was a slight tremble in her voice. The man scared her and he took pleasure in it.

"Jus' see to it that ya dinna neglect the res' of me guests," he sneered and tugged on a tangled strand of her hair. He seemed to enjoy that entirely too much.

Joy averted her eyes as she turned around. "Of course not."

Guests? Ha.

The more she was outside, the less she wanted to return to the smoke-filled tavern. The gentleman was tightening the saddle's girth, making ready to leave, and Joy almost begged him to take her.

Anywhere would be preferable to here.

She wasn't sure how much more of this she could take.

In the month she had been here, she had been subject to the moods of her owner and had been made sport of by his *patrons*. She had more bruises on her body now than she had ever had in her whole life, and she was constantly waiting for more blows to rain down on her.

She handed the tankard over to the customer, who drained it in one draught. He wiped his mouth, un-genteel like, with his sleeve.

"My thanks." He handed her a silver coin.

Joy stared at it. "This is too much money."

"Make change. And fetch me your owner." He left no doubt in her mind that he was used to being obeyed immediately.

"Is there anything amiss?" Her voice trembled.

"No." He lowered his head, a smile appearing on the aristocratic lips. "I just want to commend him for his excellent help."

Joy hadn't expected that and as she hurried toward the tavern, she turned her head to glance at him over her shoulder. She ran smack into the master who blocked the doorway. She hastily scrambled out of his reach. Just being near him caused her stomach to turn.

"Yer refresh'd then, sire?" His eyes gleamed greedily as Joy passed him the silver coin.

The gentleman's steely eyes flashed with heat, then turned as cold as the sun on the shortest day of the year.

"Indeed. I would like to make a proposal. I wish to purchase this maid. Name your price."

Joy stumbled backward a step or two. And here she had thought that perhaps this man was different. She had to learn to read people better.

"Aye, lo'd. She be a migh'y fine additi'n to dem other girls. Ye 'ave good taste, sir." The innkeeper's face lit up with a lecherous sneer as he licked his lips and brushed a hand over her tangled hair.

13

"What?" The customer jerked backward as if struck by the words. "No, you misunderstand. I find myself in need of a companion for my elderly mother."

It was like someone dumped a bucket of ice water over her. Goosebumps covered her from head to toe.

Not again.

Joy's heart began to race, pumping the blood faster and faster throughout her body. Her breathing became shallow and her muscles became taut as everything inside her screamed for her to run as fast as she could, while the two men were deciding her future.

"Ow!" Now the innkeeper's face took on a different gleam. He puffed out his chest and slipped his fingers through his tattered suspenders. Looking at her, he sucked his teeth. "I purchase 'er for a fair price, ya unnerstand. I've grown right fond of 'er." He grabbed her hair again, forcing her to look at him. "She don't cost you much, works 'ard, an' is a customer fav'rit'."

She whimpered and pressed her lips together tightly. Hadn't he just hit her because she spilled the drink?

A thought entered her mind, bringing hope. If she were sold, she might be able to get away. She could easily manage to slip into the surrounding fields, whether the man was riding a fast thoroughbred or not.

"Of course she is."

The customer took out a leather purse and weighed it. He seemed to consider his burden. He threw it toward the innkeeper, who snatched it out of the air with surprising agility.

14

He would. There were few things he loved in life, and money was at the top of his list. Her owner's eyes glinted greedily. He scratched his scruffy face and let his gaze roam over her leisurely.

"Aye. 'Tis a nice chunk of change fer sure, me lo'd. But it got me thinkin'... 'Tis naught 'alf of what she's worth." He licked his lips and drew her against him, holding her tight.

A rancid stench enveloped her and she gagged silently.

The customer scoffed. "Surely, you jest. See this animal here?" He pointed toward the stallion, nibbling on a leaf. "I could purchase him twice over for the price you suggest and *he* has the purest breeding of any of my horses. He is a masterpiece. Take your money. Give me the maid and let's be done with this. The day is getting on. I have a ways to travel."

Joy's legs wobbled and gravity threatened to pitch her forward if she hadn't been held in place by a meaty arm. She had just been compared to an animal and found wanting. A sob burned in her throat and she bit her lip hard, as her heart, the little that was intact, broke into a million pieces. She forced whatever strength she didn't have to keep upright.

No matter what anybody may think about her, she would stand tall. She may not be worth as much as a thoroughbred horse, but she was not going to show any more weakness.

Slowly, she managed to lift her chin up, to meet her new owner's gaze.

"Besides, it's a sin to own another person and to treat them like an animal." The gentleman's eyes narrowed dangerously. "I know a few very influential people who could make your life miserable."

Joy was propelled harshly toward him and stumbled against his horse. Throwing his head as if disgusted at her touch, he skidded away. His owner put a hand on his neck to steady him.

"Take 'er. She's yer trouble now." The innkeeper grinned evilly and tossed the heavy purse into the air and caught it again expertly. "Pleasure doin' business with ya, *sir*." A sneer appeared on his face as he turned back toward the tavern.

"Do you have any belongings you wish to take?" The voice that cut through the fog was not unkind anymore.

Joy stared at her new master. She squared her shoulders, one thought pressing her forward.

"No." The less she carried, the quicker her getaway.

"Then we best leave." Climbing onto his horse, he tightened the reins just enough to keep the stallion from bolting down the road. The horse pricked his sculptured ears. "Do you know how to ride?"

The muscles in her shoulders became as hard as rocks.

"Yes."

She stared at the hand he held out to her, and shook her head once. If she mounted behind him, she wouldn't get away as easily. This way, she could let him get ahead and she'd simply slip into the surrounding brush and vanish.

"We have a considerable distance to cover. It would be advantageous for you to ride. You would only slow us down. I plan on arriving home today. Please."

Something in his voice made her raise her eyes. His face, scar and all, was kind. Gone was the arrogance, the hardness with which he had dealt with the innkeeper.

16

"Oye, ya takin' 'er or not?" The innkeeper leaned leisurely against the door frame, counting his money. "I'm in the mind ta charge ya fer takin' up space. Ya changed yer mind already, me lo'd? May 'ave me a riot in there. Them clients be mighty fond of 'er."

The lecherous sneer caused a violent tremble to crawl up her body and Joy grabbed the offered hand. Placing her foot into the empty stirrup, she easily swung her leg over the back of the sleek horse, and settled behind her new master. More fabric ripped but she didn't bother to give it another thought.

She was leaving this stench-filled tavern behind one way or another. The horse pranced underneath, reminding her of the rides she had taken in the past. The sudden jolt of speed caused her to lose her balance and her arms flailed in the air.

Her lips parted as she sucked in a deep lungful, imagining herself plunging underneath the pounding feet. She refused to put her arms around the man who had purchased her.

"You may want to hold on."

"This is not my first ride" She gritted her teeth together and bit out the words.

"Suit yourself." He didn't seem to care one way or another.

The road was uneven and the stallion tripped over the ruts and divots. Her seat slipped, throwing her dangerously out of balance. Reluctantly, she clutched the jacket of the rider in front of her. She could feel the power in his stride. It didn't take long until she began to enjoy the ride and relaxed.

17

Andrew Lloyd-Foxx focused on keeping his tense stallion from bolting down the uneven ground. The exchange at the inn had caused him to nearly lose his temper. Anger still churned in his gut, making his muscles as tight as a bowstring, ready to let loose the arrow. Perhaps it would strike the innkeeper between his greasy brow. That would be worth it.

His horse was taking advantage of his unease. The stallion wouldn't hesitate to dump both his riders unceremoniously onto the road. As Andrew forced his body to relax, he slowed his breathing down to a more normal level, released the tautness in his gut, and let his corded shoulder muscles loosen up.

He had to get over his fury that this woman had been kept as an animal. He had a problem with men keeping slaves in general. When he had stumbled into the kitchen and had witnessed the near-beating of the slight woman behind him in the saddle, he had come close to exploding.

That anger still remained with him until he consciously released it.

The horse slowed down all by himself.

The stallion threw his head repeatedly as he pranced along the road, anticipating for Andrew to allow his emotions to surface again.

He cleared his throat to break the ice. "I regret the words I used when completing the purchase. I meant no disrespect. I had every reason to believe that the man would try to get more money out of me. I don't like to be extorted. Besides, if he had asked for more, I would have been forced to leave you there as I was out of money."

They had reached the main road, which was much smoother. He slowed the stallion down to a walk and the tiny woman behind him let go.

"You compared me to your horse. I am not worth as much as your horse." Anger and hurt came to the surface with the whispered statement.

Andrew cleared his throat, regretting what he had said. "I did what was necessary. I wasn't going to leave that place without you. I don't like injustice."

She snorted sarcastically. "How do you live, then? There is injustice everywhere!"

Andrew took a deep breath and sent his horse back into a ground covering canter. His unexpected traveling companion exhaled sharply and held on tightly again.

He marveled at his horse's speed, which never failed to take his breath away.

When he slowed the stallion back to a walk, Andrew patted his neck. "Good boy."

The woman behind him – he hadn't even had the decency to ask for her name – shifted uncomfortably and released her grip. How could he have compared her to a horse?

Andrew could hear his mother scolding him even now. It caused a frown to form on his face.

"What do you want with me?" Her question took him by surprise, as did the lack of emotion behind it.

"Uh... What do you mean?"

"I don't think you purchased me as a companion to your mother. What do you really want with me?"

He stretched his neck at the insinuation, his gut clenching tightly. The horse sensed his tension and tossed his head in anticipation.

"I have no use for you. You are free to go. Slavery is a vile practice and I don't have any intention of holding you against your wishes."

He heard a gasp behind him. As the last word left his mouth, he realized how bad it sounded.

"What?"

He cleared his throat and stretched his jaw, searching for better words to convey what he wished to tell her. "I have no need of you."

"Stop the horse."

"Excuse me?"

Joy had been biding her time, waiting for the right moment. Feeling the tension inside mount to a breaking point, she had picked her spot. Swinging her leg over the back of the horse, she jumped down. Regrettably she was not ten years old anymore and, as she landed, she lost her balance. Her rear end ended up in a very warm, mushy mound of animal manure.

Heat made her cheeks burn. The man on the horse turned and his face twisted not with mirth but with concern. Her humiliation would have been easier to handle if he had laughed at her.

Joy lowered her head and hid it in her arms. Tears fell rapidly, mixing with dirt, shame, and scum. She sat in the warm pile of manure, flies buzzing angrily around her.

This was her life. How very appropriate.

Her new owner dismounted and squatted in front of her.

"I mean you no harm."

His kind voice gave her the courage to look up. Warm, gray eyes focused solely on her face. He held her gaze for longer than was comfortable, making her cheeks burn some more. Suddenly even more conscious of her dilapidated state, Joy tucked the remainder of her tattered skirt around her legs and shifted away. The ground beneath her squished and she couldn't quite hold in the groan.

"Here. Take a drink."

She stared at the silver flask he offered and shook her head. No way, no how.

"Go on. It's a hot day. I'm sure you're thirsty."

The way he spoke with a slight reference to British aristocracy, each word enunciated precisely, caused a shiver to travel up her spine and across her shoulders. When he shook the flask at her again, she gingerly took it with her fingertips and inclined it to allow the water to flow into her throat.

"Thank you."

"Do you have a home to go to?"

She shook her head and stared over his shoulder at the handsome horse.

The thought of home caused her eyes to burn. Her parents had sent her away, after all, expecting her to make something out of herself. She wouldn't return to them is such a state of utter disgrace.

"I.. What you see is the culmination of my worldly possessions," she finally said softly.

Her new master gave a swift nod and lowered himself onto the grass she had missed by inches. He roughed his hand over his face.

"Then I propose this. You come with me, rest, and regain your strength. Then you are free to go wherever you want. I will not hold you back."

Joy snorted sarcastically again. "You don't need to pretend. I will work for you, to pay you back the purchase price."

He shook his head. "I have enough other servants who are well compensated for their service."

Ouch. Another put-down. "Of course you do."

Her benefactor grimaced and rose. "I meant to say that if you would like to stay to work for me, you'll be compensated as all the rest of my staff. You don't owe me anything." He offered his hand. "It is time to go. As I said, we are a long way from home."

Instinctively, Joy drew away, leaving his hand hanging in the air. Clearing his throat, he finally let it fall to his side.

"I cannot possibly mount your horse. I'm sitting in manure. I reek." Her nose wrinkled in disgust.

To her surprise, his lips twitched into a bright smile as he gave an exaggerated whiff.

"I have to admit, you do have an interesting odor about you. I doubt it would bother my horse, though. But perhaps you would feel better if we purchased you something to wear in the next village we pass through."

Joy gaped. "Neither you nor I have any money, sir."

"Oh!" Grinning sheepishly, he patted his jacket and slipped his hand inside. He pulled out a small purse, jingling it. "I forgot about this."

"I can't possibly ask more-"

"Stop." His voice and face were tight. He mounted his horse and held his hand out to her. The steely gray stare commanded her to rise. "Get on!"

3

*A*fter a short while, Andrew purchased fresh berries from a farm that was located just outside a small town. The farmer's wife seemed chatty enough, so he inquired as to where to purchase a dress. Her eyes slipped to his traveling companion. It hit him then that he still hadn't inquired after her name.

"The tailor's house is at the end of the village, the yellow one. His shingle is over the door."

"Perhaps he has some ready-made dresses for purchase," he said hopefully.

"He may. Lately, he's been making them faster, with the help of one of them newfangled sewing machines." The woman clicked her tongue to the roof of her mouth, showing her skepticism. "Not sure if the dress will be any good."

Andrew nodded his thanks and remounted his stallion. Not much later, he pulled into the shade of a large willow tree beside a small brook. He turned around toward the girl.

"Wait here while I go into town to find the tailor."

His horse would need some rest from carrying two riders for an extended amount of time. She seemed only too happy to jump off.

He glanced at her. "Please don't run. I honestly don't mean you any harm. I will return with a clean dress."

Her dirt-crusted face softened and she avoided his gaze. "I'll be here."

Andrew nodded and hurried away after making sure his stallion could rest in the shade of the tree.

The heart of the village consisted of ten houses along the main road. People worked in their small front gardens, weeding or visiting with the neighbors over the fence. Suspicious glances followed him as he walked down the dusty road, sweat now beading on his forehead and puffs of dirt kicking up with every step.

When he found the house with the tailor's shingle, he knocked on the door and entered at the beckoning. A slight man stooped over a device. A whirring sound bounced around the room as his feet pumped up and down on a pedal.

Andrew cleared his throat.

"Good afternoon."

The man lifted his head, his bespectacled eyes measuring him up and down. A look of recognition flashed through his eyes.

"You honor my home, Mr. Lloyd-Foxx."

Taken aback, Andrew found himself momentarily at a loss for words. The small man snickered and straightened his back painfully.

"I'm familiar with your dear mama, sir. I recently delivered several lovely pieces to add to her summer attire at your estate in the country."

"Of course." Andrew forced a smile. He spent enough money on dresses for his mother to keep this man, and many others like him, in business. "I'm sure she is enjoying them."

"You didn't just drop by to tell me this news. What can I do for you, sir?" A twinkle appeared in the pale blue eyes.

Andrew exhaled and shuffled from foot to foot, suddenly feeling less than confident about his request. News traveled quickly and far, apparently, since they were still hours from the estate. It wouldn't do to waffle in front of the man, so he firmed his jaw and met the older man's gaze with confidence he didn't have.

"I'm in need of a dress. Nothing fancy. A simple garment will suffice." Heat crept up his neck under the watchful squint of the tailor. Would this news travel faster than his highly bred stallion to reach his estate before him?

The tailor tapped his chin with a thimbled finger. Then he lifted an eyebrow and nodded. "Why, step this way, Mr. Lloyd-Foxx. I happen to have a dress or two I recently finished."

"Just one will be enough," Andrew mumbled.

After purchasing the calico dress and parting without the last of his coins, he found himself congratulating himself on his purchase. He had never been directly involved in obtaining his own clothing. His mother spent hours and hours with the tailor he employed for her own pleasure. He had other, more important things to do with his time.

His mother assumed that he was on another business trip to check their vast holdings to the west and south when, in fact, he had traveled to New Haven to hear the top abolitionists in the country speak. Hearing their debate had been riveting and had left him with the urge to do more. He'd been in prayer of how he could go about this, when he had ended up at the seedy tavern.

God, no doubt, had directed his path there. The thought didn't make him feel warm and fuzzy inside. Quite the contrary.

Returning to where he had left his horse and the girl, he suddenly wondered if he had made a mistake. He knew nothing about her and had left a priceless animal in her care. Hurrying the last couple of hundred yards, he spotted his stallion, grazing in the shade of the tree.

The girl rested next to his stallion, reins looped loosely around her arm.

How does someone like that end up as a- A nasty taste slicked across his tongue.

She was pretty enough – for a woman. He appreciated beauty where he saw it, although it usually pertained to the four-legged kind. If she weren't so ratty, his mother might take a liking to her.

That thought brought him to stop in his tracks, close his eyes tightly, and pinch the bridge of his nose. His mother enjoyed meddling in people's lives. She'd done it before and she'd do it again. It was best to find a suitable position for this one quickly and far away from his estate.

"You're back."

He flinched in surprise as he found himself being addressed by his traveling companion. She jumped up quickly and brushed her wet, matted hair over her shoulder. He wasn't surprised she had taken advantage of the nearby stream to clean up. Her alabaster skin - glistening with water - showed off more bruises he had missed. Her arms had been marked by the rough treatment. He still would gladly take the man responsible for her rough treatment out back to give him a piece of his own medicine.

What remained of her dress hung on her like a limp, sloppy rag.

Finding himself at a loss for words for the second time in the day, he thrust the package he was carrying at her. A blush formed on her pale cheeks and he took a step backward, bumping into his horse. The stallion flicked his tail at him in annoyance.

"Thank you. I will repay you," she said, her voice thick. "Somehow."

Andrew waved a dismissive hand at her and found that his voice had returned. "I'm not keeping score."

Joy found a suitable patch of thickly growing shrubs to change behind. Only upon closer inspection did she discover that they were black raspberry bushes. Her hair snagged on a branch with prickers. The only way to untangle herself was to break it off, leaving part of it stuck in her long, snarled locks.

She couldn't help compare this to her life. One snare after another waited for her. The last one was more costly and would not be easily forgotten. With that thought lingering around, the shame of it casting a shadow on her in the hot afternoon, she let the sopping wet dress slide down. With a disgusted grunt, she tossed it further into the bush, where it caught on more branches, and hung limply.

She quickly slipped into the new dress. Even though it was several sizes too large, she didn't care. The material was soft and so much more comfortable than the rough homespun thing she had been forced to wear.

"The day is getting on. We have miles yet left to cover."

She should have hopped onto the horse's back and ridden as far as he was able to carry her. She had missed her perfect opportunity. If she carefully stole up-river on the opposite bank, would he even notice?

Joy scrunched up her face and lifted her chin. She'd stepped into this trap with her eyes wide open and hopefully would find a way out.

"Ready." It took every ounce of her willpower to come out from the cover of the brush.

"Very well, then." He tightened the girth and placed a foot into the stirrup. Once in the saddle, he scooted forward to make room for her.

As soon as she had found her balance behind him, he urged the horse into a trot. Joy found herself slipping slowly and fastened her fingers into his coat. Better that than to put her arms around him, forcing her much too close to a perfect stranger, whose name still escaped her.

Now that she had scrubbed the filth off her skin, wore a dress that was clean and modest, she was able to enjoy riding such a magnificent animal.

"Are you comfortable?"

"Yes."

He gave a short laugh. "It has occurred to me that I don't even know your name. My mother would be horrified at my poor manners."

"Yes. But it doesn't matter."

He turned his head and she noticed a deep furrow between his brows. "I beg to differ. Everyone has a name. We all matter in some way or another. Besides, names are important when having a pleasant conversation."

Joy struggled to find truth in his words, but propriety demanded she give him an answer.

"Joy Richards."

Was it wrong to feel the need to curtsey?

"Pleasure to make your acquaintance, Miss Richards."

She cocked her head to the side and lifted her eyebrows, waiting expectantly. "If we are to have this conversation, it would be rude to keep it one sided."

He cleared his throat. "My apologies. Andrew Lloyd-Foxx."

4

*T*he horse slowed down to a walk and Mr. Lloyd-Foxx – now
there was a mouthful – allowed him to stretch his long, graceful
neck. The sun crested above the treeline and a slight breeze ruffled the skirt
of her new dress. Birds fluttered to and fro, one starling passing right in
front of the stallion's nose. He tossed his head and snorted.

Mr. Lloyd-Foxx patted him and murmured soft platitudes, which
settled him down immediately.

"We need to dismount. He is tiring."

She did as she was asked and tried not to wince when rocks pushed
through the threadbare sole of her leather boots.

"Where did you learn to ride?" Mr. Lloyd-Foxx loosened the girth
and flipped the reins over the horse's head. The pace was slow and leisurely,
but every step was agony.

Besides, Joy would rather eat a bowl of the rat stew than to tell
him. Silence stretched uncomfortably between them, and she couldn't help
but feel that he expected an answer. She puffed out a breath, hooking a
strand of knotted hair over her ear.

"My father taught me to ride when I was a mere toddler."

"Ah."

They walked for what seemed an eternity. Joy felt his eyes on her from time to time and concentrated on putting one foot in front of the other without wincing.

A particularly sharp rock poked through her boot and she breathed through the pain. *Don't show weakness.*

"You are surprisingly well-versed in horse history to know about the Godolphin Arab. Your father's doing?"

Joy focused on the rutted path in front of her. What was it about this peacock that made him think she wanted to tell him? More silence hung like a thick, suffocating blanket. Her face became slick and beads of sweat rolled past her shoulder blades.

She should leave.

They passed through another sleepy village. Curtains blew in the windows of the small houses that had been built along the road. Perhaps she could find employment in one of these homes? At least then she could make her own decisions and perhaps, in time, she could rid herself of the shame she had suffered.

Joy passed an arm over her face to wipe the thin layer of sweat.

A sharp nudge to her heart made her pause before taking another step. She owed the man. He had purchased her for a steep price. On top of that, he had dressed her. Cheeks flushed crimson at the thought. She couldn't possibly go her own way now.

She owed him.

Her tongue loosened.

"My mother. She loves thoroughbreds. She told us wild stories about racing in England, not to mention the exotic horses of the Berbers and

31

Arabs. That led us to the story of the Godolphin Arab. She painted such a vivid picture, I could almost see it."

The enigma of a man beside her nodded. "Indeed. He was a beautiful horse."

"He must have been."

"His coat was a rich bay. He was a small horse, only fourteen three. Sham was spirited. And the offspring he produced; they were absolutely magnificent. My grandfather used to tell us stories about Sham's son, Lath."

Her breath stalled and her eyes widened. "He saw him run?"

Mr. Lloyd-Foxx squinted into the sunset. "He did as a mere lad of perhaps seven. The Earl of Godolphin was his favorite uncle. He spent a lot of time at his estate in his youth. When I was a lad, my grandfather introduced me to the business of racing, studying stud forms, examining the pedigree of our horses. He was proud to be one of the first to import the Godolphin bloodlines to America."

Joy lifted her gaze to his face. Then she lowered her head quickly. This man's station was far superior to hers. Even if she weren't a lowly bar wench, she'd never be his equal. She was a farmer's daughter, after all.

"You grew up with horses as well?" His voice lifted at the end, as if he were interested.

Joy stumbled over a particularly sharp rock and righted herself immediately. The road stretched in front of them, and so did the silence. When was he going to understand that she was reluctant to share? His glancing gaze began to bother her and she once again forced herself to make smalltalk. Not her favorite past time on a good day.

"Yes, my father trained horses for the farmers in our area. He bred Morgans once upon a time."

He gave a grunt, clearly unimpressed.

Alright, mister High-and-mighty. Just you wait!

"They are extremely versatile. You can throw them in front of the buggy on the weekends, and on Monday they are ready to plow your field. They can even compete with the best-trained thoroughbreds."

"Ha. Not against this thoroughbred." He puffed out his chest.

"You might be surprised. They have the thoroughbred bloodlines of True Brit." Joy nodded in the stallion's direction. "What's his name?"

He flinched as if her question had poked him in the side. "Lad."

Joy pressed her lips into a flat line. "I was under the impression that a thoroughbred with his pedigree should have a high and mighty name."

His face scrunched up before he passed a hand over it.

"If you must know. My father allowed me to name the colt when he was foaled. He was the first one I named." He gave a funny sigh. "And the last."

Joy managed to bite her bottom lip to stop the laugh. She ought not feel at ease. Even though he had rescued her without expecting anything in return, only time would tell if Andrew Lloyd-Foxx was a man of his word.

"You have to realize I was seven at the time."

She concentrated on the road. "Understood."

"His registered name is much more impressive."

Perhaps talking was preferable to noticing every pebble press into the bottom of her foot through the thin boot. She cocked her head and waited for him to continue.

He lifted his chin and pressed his lips into a thin line as he glanced over at her. "His registered name is Magnificent Lad. He was sired by Mystery Moon, out of Lady Godiva."

"That's nice."

He grunted in return and they walked silently until they took a much deserved rest beside a low brook. Her feet were blistered and raw, and she dipped them into the water to cool them. Pain radiated up her leg and she bit her bottom lip to quell her groan.

"Here. You must be famished."

He passed her the fruit he had picked up from the stand and a piece of dried venison. She nodded her thanks. Her stomach growled as she took the first bite. The innkeeper had kept most of the nourishment for the inebriated guests – which explained the rat stew.

As Joy watched the sun dip behind the trees, their shadows lengthening and enveloping her in their cool darkness, she closed her eyes. What had she gotten herself into now?

A desperate prayer had been answered.

Could it be, after so many years of silence, God finally listened to her? Heard her hopeless plea? Help had come in the form of this man and his horse.

But could she trust it?

Hadn't aid come before and landed her in deeper trouble? How could she trust something when she didn't know the outcome? How could she go along with it? In her experience, if a thing looked too good to be true, it most definitely was.

"Miss Richards. 'Tis time to move on."

Move on…

There was nothing to go back to until she had something to show. The only option was to go the same direction as her two traveling companions.

The stallion snorted, having rested and eaten his fill of grass. As she scooted onto his back, she felt the muscles that had once been so well trained scream in protest. It had been years since she had spent any amount of time aboard a horse. And now, those muscles that had laid dormant were being awoken rudely.

This was certainly more pleasurable than spending a day and night in the smoke-filled tavern, surrounded by men staring lecherously at her, enduring their crude comments and sometimes so much more. Shuddering at the memory and once again glad to have been rescued from it, Joy preferred a few sore muscles.

After riding a few more hours in silence, darkness enveloped them in its thick, humid warmth. Lad stumbled over some of the ruts in the road. He almost went down on his knees and they both slid off his back immediately.

Mr. Lloyd-Foxx considered his surroundings and gave a long, weary sigh.

"We'll be walking for a while. Do you think you can manage it?"

He pointed to her boots. Now they were holes with some leather in between.

"Of course." She'd never tell him that every step was agony.

Show no weakness.

"Where are we going?" she asked, more to distract herself from the discomfort of walking.

"Our estate is east of Boston, just along the shore. The stud farm is outside a small village an hour ride from Boston. Where are you from?"

"South of Hartford. A small farming community."

That earned her a raised eyebrow. "You're far from home."

She didn't have the strength to answer him, so she nodded quickly and blinked away a rush of tears at the pain.

"Do you have a family?"

"Mm-hmm. Don't you?" Her jaw tightened.

Mr. Lloyd-Foxx smirked. "I just thought... They must miss you."

Joy drew in a breath. "Perhaps."

5

*N*ight had fallen. They had taken to riding short distances and walking longer ones. Joy's foot snagged on either a rut or a very cruelly placed stone and, stumbling, she bit back a groan as she landed on her knees.

"We're almost there." Mr. Lloyd-Foxx lifted his chin and took in the surrounding darkness. An oil lantern illuminated only so much and the sounds of night beyond what she could see caused a chill to pass through her. "Why don't you ride for a little while? He can carry one person much easier than two."

"I'm fine to walk." No more special favors.

Her companion laughed under his breath. "At this rate we'll arrive for breakfast. Get on."

Apparently, no wasn't in his vocabulary. Joy avoided his gaze and placed her foot into the stirrup while he held the horse's head for her. She shortened the stirrups by several holes and settled comfortably on the stallion's back.

What a privilege it was for her to ride-

Lad tossed his head and snorted, prancing in place. Joy settled into his stride and pulled back as his pace increased. His ears pricked and he glanced ahead.

"He knows where he is. He is as eager to get home as we are."

The horse tossed his head impatiently, giving Joy a hard time about walking. Already, sweat began to run down between her shoulder blades and the muscles in her arms trembled with the strain of holding him back. Lad gave a particularly disgusted snort and shied to the side, making her lose her balance.

Her father would tan her hide if he saw her hanging onto the horse like a sack of potatoes.

"He's as spirited as his great great-grand..." The rest of the sentence was lost to her in a rush of air.

Lad had found enough energy to surge forward, passing Mr. Lloyd-Foxx, and leaving him mid-sentence. Barely within the glow of the lantern, the stallion exploded into the air, sticking his head between his front legs. As he rounded his back, Joy felt the force of gravity.

The buck would have caused her issues in the past, back when she had been well-trained. Now, Lad had no problems tossing her. She felt herself sailing over his head with a very impressive somersault before she landed in the road with a loud thud.

Whoosh!

She lay on the ground, gulping for air as darkness pressed around her.

Now what do I do? I've killed her!

Andrew gazed at the unmoving form on the ground, her eyes closed, mouth opening and closing like a codfish. The sound of Lad's hooves quickly receded into the distance.

And I've lost my best horse.

He bent over her and scratched his chin. This was not how he had planned on returning home after a month's absence. His mother would have a thing or two to say if he arrived with an unconscious, bruised barmaid in his arms.

A cut on Miss Richard's temple drew his attention. He took out his pristine linen handkerchief and pressed it to the wound. It soon turned crimson. He cleared his throat.

"I say. Miss Richards." He poked gently at her and she moaned softly after gasping in a deep breath and coughing. He helped her into a sitting position.

She looked around, confusion puckering the skin between her eyebrows.

"I'm afraid you took a spill. Are you hurt?" Yes, that was a needless question.

Her eyes widened as she became aware of her surroundings.

"I'm... perfectly... fine."

As if to show him, she pushed to her feet and collapsed right back onto the ground. He caught her before she hurt herself even more.

"Take a moment to recover," he said.

Shame and fear flashed in her dark blue eyes. She groaned and shook her head as if reprimanding herself for the involuntary utterance.

His linen was soaked with her blood and he removed it. Her eyes widened.

"I've soiled your good handkerchief," she uttered, cheeks now the color of a ripe, juicy apple.

He arched an eyebrow. "I have another, not to worry. Catch your breath before you move."

He glanced at her footwear, or what was left of it. Holes covered the bottom, exposing the skin. Both feet were covered with bleeding sores and blisters.

Her tongue swept over her dry lips repeatedly and she glanced at anything other than him. She shifted away and drew her arms around her knees, pressing them against her chest.

"I am so sorry about that. I don't know what got into him. He hasn't bucked in the longest time."

Her colorless cheeks deepened to a near crimson and she swallowed visibly. Her eyes filled with moisture and she quickly lowered her gaze again.

"I'm fine."

She rose and stood swaying.

"I can see that. Please, allow me to help you." Andrew offered his arm.

She shook her head violently. When she took a small step, she bit her bottom lip and sank back down onto the road.

"I may need another moment." Her voice was barely above a whisper and she passed her sleeve over her still-bleeding cut.

"Miss Richards. I think you need more than that. You are incapable of walking. Your feet are covered with blisters and your head..." He frowned. "My horse will have to apologize for his extremely ungentlemanly behavior."

"It was probably my terrible riding that made him do it."

He gave her a sidelong glance and shook his head. "I doubt that. But I'm afraid that I cannot allow you to sit here in the middle of the road for the rest of the night."

Joy waited for the wave of dizziness to pass through her and gathered her nonexistent strength.

"Miss Richards, please."

Joy saw nothing but compassion in his charcoal steel eyes. She reluctantly reached for his proffered hand and leaned on his arm. They walked for what were very painful steps for Joy.

"How much longer?" She gritted her teeth.

"It's only three more miles."

Ha! Three miles might as well be a hundred!

Her knees buckled and she was forced to lean on her companion even harder.

You have to do this. One step – ouch – at a time.

"Are you in the habit of praying?"

She glanced at him furtively. "I've been known to beseech the Almighty."

"Now would be a good time, if you don't mind."

"By all means." It seemed that she stepped on every single sharp pebble in the path.

He gave a slight nod and shifted his arm around her waist, giving her the support she needed without her asking for it. Or making her feel cheap.

41

"Lord, please give us strength to make it home, give us help, for our bodies are tired from the long journey. Thank You, amen."

"That was short and sweet." *Ouch.* Her foot touching the road was like stepping on hot coals.

"I wasn't about to give a long, drawn-out address. I'm too tired for anything eloquent tonight. Short and sweet works just as well."

They both stilled at the sound of approaching hoofbeats. Someone sure was in a hurry. They glanced at each other and she forced herself to breathe.

Don't show fear. Don't show anything.

"Er, I suggest you hobble over to the side of the road, out of the way. We never know who is coming."

Joy didn't complain. She limped quickly to the thick brush by the side of the road, and hid herself into the darkness. Mr. Lloyd-Foxx stood in the middle of the road, his arms hanging at his sides. The light from the lamp illuminated his features and he looked fierce. Drawing in a deep breath that lifted his chest, he bunched his hands into fists.

The horses were still coming at a fast pace and a look of panic flashed across his face. Joy pressed into the brush, hoping to become part of it.

Oh, God. Please don't let anything happen to us.

"Master Lloyd-Foxx, sir. Is that you?"

She saw the relief as the muscles in his face relaxed.

"Ben." His voice held an emotion she couldn't quite comprehend. "You're a welcome sight."

At this point, the other rider – leading another horse – blocked her view. "Lad returned without you and we feared the worst. We've heard of reports of bandits preying on lone travelers."

"He threw my traveling companion. You were brilliant to bring another horse."

"Of course, sir. I'm just glad I found you so quickly."

The young man leaned forward and held out the reins of the second horse, a chestnut.

"Miss Richards."

She peeled away from her hiding space and stepped onto the road, her head held high. She knew she looked a sight.

"Oh!" Ben, the young man, flinched in the saddle of his horse, making the gelding shy away underneath him.

Leaves stuck out of her hair. Dirt covered the new dress, which hung off her in a very unflattering manner. Dried blood clung to her left cheek.

"Miss Richards, meet Ben. Ben brought us horses." The left side of his face inched up.

"Yes." Her voice quivered in exhaustion and she chided herself for it.

Ben jumped off the horse and handed her the reins. "Can you ride?"

Joy hesitated. She used to think so. After getting tossed so easily, she wasn't so sure anymore.

"She'll do fine."

Ben's eyes widened with doubt.

"Trust me, Ben. Besides, she can't walk anymore. Get on that horse, Miss Richards."

Joy reached for the saddle and managed to mount without style. Ben's eyes widened ever more. Embarrassed, she turned in the direction the horses had come from.

The saddle creaked behind her as Mr. Lloyd-Foxx mounted the chestnut. He draped an arm around her waist before he picked up the reins. She should have panicked, yet all she felt was comfort. However, she would be loath to lean her back against his chest.

"Let's go."

The horses took off as fast as the dark road would allow them to. The light from both lanterns bounced with every stride they took.

A sudden wave of weakness made her lean into the gentleman behind her.

"Not to worry, Miss Richards. I won't let you fall." His breath tickled the back of her neck, slipped past her ear.

Joy found it best to concentrate on the darkness ahead.

Finally, they slowed down to a walk and entered through a wrought iron gate, with a small gatekeeper's cottage on the side. A gnarled old man sat on a wooden bench, lantern held aloft, and slowly raised a hand in greeting.

"Sir, you are home, safe and sound. When Lad came shooting through the gate, we feared the worst! Glad to see you made it." He squinted at Joy and doffed his shapeless cap. "Miss."

She'd been called plenty of other names, but *Miss*... Her throat closed up and all she could do was stare.

The path they were on was well maintained, minus all the ruts and bumps. Large, stately oaks and maple trees stood sentry on either side of the drive, which was wide enough for two carriages to pass each other.

Her imagination took over and she pictured an extensive park spreading out beyond the darkness. In her mind, she stood in the thick grass, the moonlight shining behind her. She wore a gown fit for a queen and danced with a most dashing gentleman whose face her own imagination didn't let her see. But in her heart, she knew he was handsome and kind, with eyes that laughed.

The change in the horse's gait jerked her back to reality. Her gaze flickered to the man behind her. His face was worn and dust-covered. He shifted in the saddle to flash her a reassuring – if not fleeting – smile.

They rounded a bend in the drive and came upon a stately brick mansion. Joy's breath caught at the sight of lights in the windows of a grand house. This was even more magnificent than she had imagined. She had envisioned Mr. Lloyd-Foxx living in a grand house. Someone with that name didn't live in a hovel.

But this-

The front portico alone was larger than the farmhouse she had grown up in. Servants poured from the oak doors as soon as they halted in front. Both men dismounted immediately and Ben took the reins of the chestnut.

As she slid off the mount, her host reached for her. Irritated, she was tempted to slap his hand away. She could handle herself without help.

6

*A*s soon as her feet touched the ground, fire rushed through them and up her legs, fanning out into the rest of her body. Bile pushed up into her mouth and she fought it back down. Her knees buckled, forcing her to cling to the saddle.

A hand touched her elbow, as if fearing to cause more pain.

"Allow us to help you." The voice was kind and tender, void of condescension.

At his beckoning, two servants hurried over and half supported, half carried her up the stairs through the front door into the main hall and helped her onto a soft divan.

Her jaw went slack. She'd heard about places like this. She had never thought she would actually be sitting in one.

The hall was of polished black and white marble. An oak staircase wound its way to the second floor landing. Oil lamps were lit in sconces along the wall. Soft light brightened the long hall, revealing doors on either side.

The door to the room directly across from her stood ajar, giving a glimpse into the richly furnished room. She had never seen a house with wallpaper. Nobody in her small farming community could afford it. The mayor's wife had painted her parlor a light violet color a year before she left, causing an uproar.

"Master Andrew. You are home at last!"

A tall, bony woman greeted Mr. Lloyd-Foxx with a bow of the head. She waved a nervous hand about and servants appeared to relieve him of his red coat and hat.

"Mrs. Brown, it's good to be back." Weariness sounded in his voice and he gave a long drawn-out sigh. "This is Miss Richards. She is in need of some..." His voice trailed off as if he wasn't sure how exactly to phrase it.

"Say no more, sir."

The woman clapped her hands swiftly, and everyone moved as a well coordinated ballet. Joy found herself ushered up the stairs to a bedroom. The furnishings were elegant, with a large canopy bed standing between two windows, a divan and a small tea table to the side. Once again, Joy felt her inadequacy and her filth as she stood trembling in the middle of the room. Soon, a pair of twittering maids appeared. One deftly removed her dress while the other appeared with hot water for a bath, placed in the middle of the room.

Joy bit back a soft cry when her feet touched the hot water. A hiss came out instead, and the maid tending to her stopped what she was doing to stare at her feet.

"Oh, you poor dear. We'll take care of you, have no fear." Her eyes shone with kindness and understanding.

Soaking in the water smelling of roses and lavender, she let the whole day play back in her mind, Had she honestly been rescued from that life? Or was something far worse waiting for her? What if this was some way-station for women? What did Mr. Lloyd-Foxx do for a living?

Owning and running race horses was not cheap.

Her imagination took her to a dark place and once the maid returned to help her wash her long hair and help her out of the bath, Joy was ready to defend her life to the end.

"Let's look at those feet." The same maid came to her side and helped her into a simple shift.

Then she guided her to the divan.

"You poor thing. I can't believe Master Andrew didn't stop to get you proper footwear. I'm shocked, aren't you, Marie? He's usually so observant. I'll have to speak to him on that matter."

The other maid nodded solemnly.

They would speak to their master about letting her walk in her worn boots? What kind of a household was this?

Both maids now busied themselves. The one that seemed to be more senior was applying a salve onto her feet. Every touch produced intense agony to snake its way up her leg. The other started to comb out her snarled wet hair, which proved equally painful.

"I'm so sorry." The maid flinched when she snagged on another thick knot.

Between the feet and the hair, tears blurred Joy's vision.

"It's fine. No trouble," she breathed through clenched teeth.

Closing her eyes, she transformed herself to a better place – where a fiddle played lively music and the farm boys lined up to have a dance with her. In her imagination, her sister twirled and laughed along side her and her heart clenched tightly with the memory.

To finish everything off, the maids rubbed sweet-smelling lotion into her sore and bruised muscles. Although the result was very pleasing, the discomfort now almost gone, it was another agonizing process.

In the end, the maids had managed to not only make her feet and muscles ache less, but they had combed through her clean but knotted dark brown hair. They even sprayed perfume into it as they braided it into a thick braid.

Exhaustion made her eyelids heavy as they massaged her skull. As she drifted on a cloud of lavender and roses, her mind once again traveled to the last time she had seen her family.

Her father's face had a certain stiffness about him when she had hugged him good-bye, while her mother's eyes had deepened with held-back tears. Her sister had nearly refused to look at her or bid her farewell. But Joy's future seemed so bright and promising as governess to three children in Boston.

"You must be spent."

A voice drew her back to reality and she shifted. The room was unfamiliar to her and yet, she felt it in her heart. This was a good place.

"I am," she replied and yawned, covering her mouth with her hand.

"Why don't we turn down the bed for you. And I'm sure the cook will be happy to heat up some of that delicious venison stew she made earlier." The accent was definitely Boston but the way the maid spoke made Joy wonder if she weren't born into a highly bred family.

Both maids hefted her onto the feather mattress and Joy swallowed the moan that threatened to escape. Never in her life had she sat on something so soft and comfortable. Her mattress at home had been stuffed with hay and over the past years she'd become used to sleeping on the ground, no matter how hard or cold.

Sleep took her within seconds.

49

Andrew collapsed onto a soft chair and stretched his tired legs in front of him. This trip had taken a lot more out of him than he realized. The meeting in New Haven had been riveting. Charles Finney and the members of his *Holy Band* had been among the speakers, and had once again spoken with fiery passion concerning the Lord and slavery. He had spoken about the need to get right with the Lord, to surrender to His will in everything. He had left the meeting with a lot to consider.

He had prayed for God to lead him and He apparently had. Straight to a seedy tavern. Andrew hadn't planned on coming home with a beaten-up bar maid, even if she had some horse knowledge.

Lord, You placed me into an awkward situation. What am I to do with this new girl? She knows horses, can ride as well as a man, but where does she fit into this estate? Is she even to stay? I submit to Your plan, Lord. I do not want to run my life my way. It is Your way, all the way. Please help me figure it out.

Sitting here, in the luxury of this home built by his grandfather, he felt safe. He thought of the countless slaves who were not. His own station made him feel guilty.

Journalist William Lloyd Garrison, whose editorials in his magazine were both inspiring and inflammatory, had thundered on about the sin of keeping slaves and the need for good men to stand up against it. Andrew felt compelled to do something about this problem plaguing his country.

The disease of slavery was one that had plagued mankind for centuries. And then there were those slaves nobody talked about, those who were hidden, still forced to do the bidding of masters. They were indentured servants or lower and had no voice of their own.

"You - a white woman - are a slave?"

"Yes. In a way."

Did that mean that Miss Richards had been one of those nobody wanted to acknowledge?

It was one thing to feel remorse and another to do something about it. Andrew wasn't a man who sat back. He took action.

So, he now had another mouth to feed, for as long as she was his guest.

Rubbing some ointment into his tired cramping calves, he pursed his lips. Traveling was exhausting.

He hadn't chosen this life. If it were up to him he would have been a preacher, inspired by the great Lyman Beecher, whom he had the pleasure of hearing preach during his time of studying at Yale University.

And he would have traveled only to see his horses running.

His father's death and that of his older brother a year later had put an end to that. Andrew now oversaw not only the horse business, but also that of the estate – something his brother enjoyed so much.

Nowadays he understood and accepted – most of the time – God's path for him. He ran the business to provide for his mother.

No matter how hard he tried, however, he couldn't turn a blind eye to the plight of those less fortunate. He was in a position to help others. And, being a man of action, he did.

Most of his staff had found themselves in bad situations at one time or another, out of which Andrew had rescued them. Instead of preaching, he lived it. His staff consisted of ninety percent born-again believers.

"Sir. Your milk and cookies." His man-servant, a man who had been in his father's employ, placed the tray on the table. His expression never faltered, even though Andrew, at twenty-six years old, was too old for this nightly treat.

"Thank you, Bruce. That will be all for tonight."

"Yes, sir." His man bowed and Andrew dipped his molasses cookie into the milk, grinning sheepishly.

His mother would chide him for this childish ritual.

"When you finally find a wife, she is going to laugh you right out the door when she finds you having cookies and milk before bed."

Her sharp tone bounced around in his head as he dipped another cookie. He was not in a hurry to find a wife. He was comfortable as he was. Women caused trouble. And they were expensive. The cost of his mother's wardrobe alone could bankrupt a small country. But after their past stormy relationship, he tried to make her happy.

Popping the last cookie soaked with milk into his mouth, he slipped into bed and sighed in deep content. After spending the month on the road, sleeping in his own bed was heaven.

I ask You to watch over the slaves and move the hearts of men. Nobody need be owned by another man. Make this country stand not only for independence but also for freedom of all men and women, no matter their color or status. His mind wandered. *And please watch over Miss Richards. And Ben, and Laura, and...* He named his servants one by one, not forgetting anyone.

Before he succumbed to sleep, he remembered how Miss Richards had tumbled through the air after that incredible buck Lad had given. That horse, even though he was special, had always had a temper. Just like his great great grand-sire, who had supposedly only tolerated a grubby cat named Grimalkin as his stablemate.

7

*J*oy floated on a cloud of lavender and rose. When she became aware of her surroundings, she blinked to focus her eyes.

The room had looked elegant in the soft light of the oil lamp the night before, but in the daytime it looked regal. The furniture was exquisite. A tall dresser stood along the opposite wall, with ornate carvings on the doors. A sitting area provided a thickly upholstered lounge chair and settee. A low table with delicate legs stood among them.

The vanity held mysterious instruments to improve the female body. There were various apparatuses to tease the volume into fine hair, to straighten curly hair, to curl straight hair. There were creams, combs and pastes that Joy had no idea how to apply nor what they did. A farmer's daughter didn't have much time to spend on looking like a doll.

Wincing, she moved her stiff, aching muscles. The room spun momentarily and she closed her eyes, willing for it to still. When she stretched her legs to the floor, she remembered.

Her feet were covered in soft bandages to prevent further injury. Everything that had transpired the day before came rushing at her. Her cheeks burned when she recalled tumbling off the stallion, Lad, like a novice rider.

Groaning as if she had aged overnight, she rose from the soft, heavenly mattress, and hobbled over to the door to peak out. From the sounds of hushed yet hurried voices coming from downstairs, the household servants were awake.

Joy contemplated her options as she leaned wearily against the door. First of all, her feet felt as if she had been walking on burning coals. Heat slowly and painfully throbbed up her legs. If she hid under the covers all day long, perhaps she could recover and slip out the door by night. Nobody needed to be the wiser to her absence.

She had almost reached the bed, when the door opened and one of the maids who had so tenderly cared for her the night before entered.

"You're awake." The greeting was so cheerful that Joy felt bad that she wanted to hide herself away. And then a delectable aroma from the kitchen filled the room and caused her stomach to growl. The maid smiled even brighter. "And you're hungry. I have just the remedy for that. Before you eat, we'll bring you water for another nice, hot, soothing bath."

"But..."

What a waste of perfectly good water. At home, they had bathed once a week in the old cracked tub - a ritual for Saturday nights. It wasn't that she was filthy anymore. The thought of another bath made Joy wonder what else these people wasted.

But to linger and feel her muscles relax... A soft sigh slipped from her lips.

"I brought you a spot of tea to get you going. Her ladyship is stirring and I am sure she would love to have company for breakfast, since Master Andrew is already out and about. That man never sits still for longer than a second. He's always going somewhere, doing something."

Her senseless chatter was soothing.

Joy took a whiff of the tea as steam billowed into the air, and sipped. Warmth sloshed around in her gut, adding to the feeling of comfort. The maid carefully unwrapped the bandages from her feet. Some cloth stuck to the oozing sores and sharp flashes of pain traveled from her toes to her knees.

"Those feet must hurt like the dickens. What in the world did you do to them?" Hands on her hips, the young maid looked at her with her great big chocolate eyes shimmering with tears.

Tears for her?

"I- didn't have the appropriate footwear for a long walk."

"Oh," the maid looked down and pointed to a pair of sorry-looking boots. "You mean those things? We should have thrown them into the fire last night. No matter. It will be done right now."

"No. Please, let me." She shuddered involuntarily.

A soft chuckle escaped the girl's lips and she nodded. "Very well. You may do the honors. Now, let's get you into the bath and let you soak in it."

As the maids carried in heavy buckets of hot water, Joy found that she felt guilty She ought to be doing this work. When she hobbled forward, the young maid shot her a scowling glance.

"You are to rest, Missy. No helping, no matter how hard it is."

She could get used to this.

But she shouldn't, because she, Joy Richards, didn't belong in this world. No matter how much she longed to change it, she was a farmer's daughter. Her family made a living out of working the ground, taking care of the animals that helped them, and they had done so for generations.

Except... Joy always wanted more.

It was why she had gone with the gentleman who had offered her a life in the city, a chance to reach beyond the sleepy town and her family's farm. Her parents had trusted him to tell the truth when he had offered Joy a position as governess to his three children. The very generous amount of money he had given them would have seen them through until they had another harvest.

Joy's younger sister Hope – the good girl – had been content with the small-town existence.

What had happened to her after Joy left?

Not for the first time, a jolt went through her heart. A longing to see her family began to burn. What if Hope had met the same fate or worse as she had found herself because her family was destitute?

"Miss Richards? Are you ready to come out?"

Water sloshed over the brim of the tub and she drew in a sharp breath.

"N-no. I..."

Joy bit back a groan. She needed to go home. Even if she didn't return with riches and glorious stories, she needed to see them.

"I'm coming in, Miss Richards."

The door to her room inched open and Joy flinched. Water from the tub slopped onto the spotless floor. Would she be driven off?

She snatched up the towel hanging on the chair next to the tub, and soaked up most of the wetness. An explosive exhale behind her made her stop and turn around. Her cheeks burned and her stomach churned nervously.

The maid from last night stood in the door frame.

"What are you doing? Let us take care of you. Take this time to rest up. You look like you need it. Besides, this towel is no good for soaking up this mess." She winked and handed her another towel, just as soft as the first.

Joy blushed and wrapped it around herself.

More waste. Joy's family had one coarse towel per person. The maid placed a thick stack on the chair near her.

"No, I... I need to earn my keep!"

The maid's hands slipped onto her hips and she pursed her lips.

"Trust me. This is your time to heal. I know how hard it is to accept help, but we're here to take care of you. And your poor feet." A look of deep compassion penetrated her face.

Oh, yeah. Her feet began their dull throbbing, something she had managed to ignore.

As the maid pressed her into the soft sofa, salve and bandages in hand, Joy's mind wandered again as it usually did.

It would take her days to walk home. She couldn't afford anything else. As of now, she was in no shape to travel.

What do I do?

A tiny thought lodged itself in her mind.

Ask for help.

Joy's lips twitched into a smile all by themselves.

She hadn't asked in a long time. Help was never available when she needed it. It hadn't come when her father had been injured, nor when the family had fallen on hard times. The solutions that presented themselves had *looked* good, but they had been the exact opposite.

Except yesterday, her plea had resulted in being rescued by a perfectly normal person.

The man lives in a mansion and breeds thoroughbreds. What's normal about that?

As she continued her musing, her heart began to soften. Even though she had expected the innkeeper to drop dead from a lightning bolt, he hadn't. She had still been rescued and taken to this beautiful place.

The maid's nonsensical twitter was a comfort to her because she didn't have to pay attention. Instead, she turned to the inner longing of her heart. She wanted to pray.

She longed to feel the reassurance that God was still there, somewhere. She wanted to be taken care of by Him.

I... need... I'm not the same young naïve girl I was when I left home. I know we've had words of anger – mostly my anger and Your silence. I need You, God. Help me find my way home.

"There you are. All bandaged up." The maid rose to her feet.

Joy's thoughts returned to the present. "Thank you."

The young woman smiled tenderly and squeezed her hand. "I know how you feel, Miss Richards. I had trouble adjusting in the beginning."

Joy cocked her head. "In the beginning?"

The maid nodded solemnly. "Yes. I came here three years ago."

"Oh. I... I don't even know your name."

"It's Laura, Miss Richards."

Heat traveled to Joy's cheeks. "Please call me Joy. Did your family send you here?"

Laura laughed under her breath. "I have no family. I grew up on the streets of Boston until one day I came upon a beautiful horse tied up outside a home. I jumped on its back and tried to ride away. I don't know what happened, but I woke up in a cozy bed – much like this one – with a physician attending my injuries and Master Andrew watching his every move like a guardian. Apparently, Lad had a different idea than I did."

Joy's lips formed an *O*. "Yes, he seems... particular. He probably knew you were trying to steal him."

Laura now laughed out loud. "Don't I know it. To this day, he pins his ears at me."

Joy grinned, her imagination filling in what the spirited horse had done to the maid. Suddenly, she didn't feel as bad a rider. "What happened next?"

Laura helped her into the chair by the vanity. "Instead of having me arrested, Master Andrew brought me here. At first, it was to recuperate. I felt like I had died and gone to heaven. And I tried to help out wherever I could. I was reprimanded very sharply. After a few months, he asked me if I would like to stay on as a servant." Her cheeks blushed prettily. "I had made friends among the others and... stayed on. I'll be getting married this summer. It all worked out in the end, the Lord be thanked."

Joy nibbled on her bottom lip as she thought about that last statement. *It all worked out in the end! The Lord be thanked!* The Lord... be thanked. She wasn't ready to go that far. Experience made her wonder if God was interested in taking care of her. So far she was not too impressed with the way He was going about it.

As Laura set to work administering more sweet-smelling salves to her tired muscles, Joy's attention turned to the person staring back at her from the vanity mirror.

So thin. So pale. So- sickly.

She had been tanned and fit, with muscles that could put some men to shame.

She had lost a lot more than muscle in the two years she had left the farm. Abuse and so much more had taken its toll on her once trim body and left her cowering in – fear. Joy felt it now, waiting to rear its ugly head when given a chance.

"... you'll love it here, Miss R- Joy. This is a good place. Master Andrew always finds a place for the people he brings home. I'm sure you'll fit in like the rest of us, in time. Then you have a chance to live a happy life, here at The Downs."

"The Downs?"

"That's what the stud farm is called. It reminded the old Mr. Lloyd-Foxx of the place where they train the racehorses near his home in England. So he called it that, because the family is in the horse business."

8

*L*aura carefully brushed her hair that now reached down to her hips. When she snagged on the knots, Joy gritted her teeth. The young maid picked up several ornate combs and started to twist and roll and manipulate Joy's locks onto the side of her head so that it circled like a crown. Laura fussed some more, stood back from her and cocked her head, her fingers drumming on her lips.

"Ah..." She added a pin here, another comb there. "That'll do."

Joy's stomach twisted uncomfortably.

"I've taken the liberty to lay out a selection of dresses that might fit you."

Laura spread out three gowns on the bed. They were fancier than anything Joy had ever seen in her life.

"I... can't..." Joy gasped.

Laura actually rolled her eyes. "They are dresses the mistress has discarded because they are either out of fashion or – most likely – she doesn't wear them anymore. You need something other than that thing you came in. Don't worry, Joy. We all went through this." She touched her hand gently.

Joy's heart thundered in her chest.

"I think this one." Laura picked up a dress the color of maple leaves in autumn and held it up. "Yes, this one will be lovely." Her eyebrows danced a merry dance.

Laura expertly and quickly fastened the corset, something Joy had never had the displeasure of wearing, and helped her into various underthings. As soon as the dress was laced up, Joy began to feel trapped. The high neckline, the long sleeves made it hard to breathe. Not to mention she was confined by all the undergarments.

How did they do this every day?

By the time Laura had finished dressing her, sweat already beaded on her forehead and she was exhausted. No wonder rich people needed maids and menservants.

And for what reason?

"Now, I suggest we leave your poor feet out of slippers today." Laura tsked and shook her head. "Even though it's not entirely proper, I'm sure the mistress will excuse this oversight."

Laura went to the door and turned before she opened it.

"Follow me. And if I might give you the slightest piece of advice: Don't let her intimidate you."

Joy hobbled after her, suddenly feeling even warmer in the dress. She suppressed the urge to run a finger under the high collar and swallowed the lump forming in her throat.

By the time they were standing in the dining room, with its long, dark mahogany table and sideboard, chairs and paneling, Joy was exhausted and sweating.

The morning sun spilled into the room through the tall windows, which were open to admit the breeze. Elaborately crafted crown molding decorated the ceiling, from which hung a small but luxuriant crystal chandelier. A beautiful mural of racehorses on race day had been painted on one of the shorter walls.

On the sideboard was a selection of mouth-watering dishes. Her stomach growled loudly as the smell of bacon reached her nostrils and more heat traveled to her cheeks.

A tall woman entered behind them. "Good morning, ladies." Her voice was stiff and the words clipped. She settled in the seat at the head of the table.

Cool, blue-gray eyes steadily measured Joy from top to bottom, the regal mouth forming a stiff line. She daintily placed her napkin into her lap, nodding to Joy.

"You must be the young lady who returned with my son last night."

Joy trembled.

She had known some intimidating people, even women, who treated her cruelly. The woman's frosty gaze continued to roam over her, making her feel like she was being measured.

Would she be found wanting?

A maid dressed in a dark skirt and perfectly white blouse placed a dish in front of her, earning her a curt – not altogether unkind – nod. The woman pointed an elegant hand to the only other prepared place setting next to her.

"Please, join me. I enjoy the company. I doubt it very much my son will grace me with his presence this morning. I believe he is already out there." She waved her hand toward the window, her smooth face turning into a scowl. "Somewhere."

Joy shuffled from one painful foot to the other. The air in the room was so thick, it was difficult to breathe. Sweat slicked her face.

When she didn't sit down, the mistress of the house turned the scowl onto her.

"I would like to start eating, but if you insist on standing all morning it would be impolite for me to start. Please." She emphasized the word. "Sit! The food is getting cold."

Joy allowed her knees to give and she slipped into the chair being held out for her.

"A spot of tea for you, ma'am?" A tall, elderly man with twinkling eyes appeared at her side, making her flinch.

What did she know about etiquette? What if she slurped, or banged her spoon against the dainty teacup and broke it?

"This is where you say, *Thank you, I would love some.*" The skin around the man's eyes crinkled with even more lines.

She nodded, the heat in her cheeks not from the temperature in the room.

"Very good, ma'am. And how would you like your eggs cooked?"

What was the proper answer?

"Any way is fine, Miss." Again, the voice came out soft and kind, void of condemnation.

"S-soft, please."

It seemed to satisfy him because he disappeared through the door as silently as a cat. Joy stared at the teacup in front of her. A noise as if someone cleared her throat came from her left. A look of understanding appeared in the older woman's eyes and she lifted her teacup to her lips, pinky pointing out, and sipped daintily.

Exhaling very slowly and softly, Joy imitated her to the letter.

Who could have thought that drinking tea was a challenge?

"Are you well rested?" The mistress picked up her fork and knife and cut into her food, bringing it to her mouth as if it were a dance.

Joy nodded and feared she would spill her tea in the process.

"I understand you and my son arrived well after dark. And there was a problem with the horse? I hear it threw you?" She shook her head in disgust. "I stay away from those spirited racehorses and prefer my gentle mare. She is as ancient as I and we get along perfectly fine." A smile formed on her face.

"As you have most assuredly surmised, I'm Camile Lloyd-Foxx, mistress of this estate. Now, girl. What is your name, and who are your people?"

Joy swallowed hard.

"Joy, ma'am. Joy Richards. I'm only a farmer's daughter."

Cool eyes narrowed. "There is nothing wrong with that. We all need to eat. I have the utmost respect for people who work the land."

Joy exhaled again and fought the urge to tug on her long, frilly sleeve.

"You must have had a time of it." The blue-gray eyes misted over upon another quick inspection, then the woman blinked. She reached out her elegant hand and touched Joy's. "You are safe. Andrew will find a position for you here if you like. When he was a child, he continually brought home stray cats and dogs. He even brought home a parrot once. We ended up having to find a different placement for that one. It knew some very inappropriate words. Andrew started repeating them and his father had to wash his mouth out with soap."

Joy's lips formed a smile and she quickly forced them into a thin line again.

The woman next to her had noticed and nodded. "I'm attempting to put you at ease. It's quite appropriate to smile. And please, eat."

Joy peeled the hard shell of her soft-boiled egg. The tall man reappeared and placed a plate full of food in front of her. She ate until she felt she would explode.

The older woman smiled benignly and nodded.

"Come, my dear. Let us convene on the veranda. It is such a lovely day, I would be remiss if we didn't enjoy it while we still can."

The woman gathered her skirts and swished past her. Joy hobbled after her in a very unladylike manner. Oh, to be able to walk so gracefully.

"Oh, my dear, you are injured. Please sit." Mrs. Lloyd-Foxx pointed to a soft chair and shook her head. "What happened?"

"I wore the wrong footwear, Ma'am. I didn't expect to be walking through the country yesterday."

"Where did Andrew find you?"

Joy felt her heartbeat in her ears and refused to make eye contact. How could this woman understand the nightmare that had been her life?

"Please." The soft, cool hand covered hers. "You will find that nobody judges you here."

If only that were true. Swallowing, Joy lowered her head.

"I... was a... I worked... in a tavern last. Before that..." Her cheeks turned crimson. The hand on hers squeezed and understanding shone in the blue-gray eyes. "I found myself in various places. Some were better than others but they were all unbearable. None of them treated me or the others with any human decency."

67

She turned her face away.

"I'm sorry, child. But you are young. You have your life in front of you. And you've come to a good place. Recover, regain your strength, and you are free to go anywhere you like. Good things happen here."

Joy exhaled heavily and blinked away the tears in her eyes.

"But I must say, we will simply have to find a place for you here." Mrs. Lloyd-Foxx examined her again.

It was pleasant out on the veranda. A luscious oak spread its majestic branches over them, providing shade. A breeze kept the heat at bay for now. Beyond them, the lawn spread out around them. Not a blade of grass seemed to be out of place. Joy imagined an army of gardeners with tiny scissors in hand, snipping away. Instead of grass, she envisioned tiny green men with long, grass-like hair.

Her imagination had always been very impressive and it was something nobody could take away from her.

She allowed her fancy to take her to the castle under the blooming rose bushes. Here, a beautiful queen ruled with a gentle hand. She was the most beautiful woman in all the land, and suitors came from everywhere to bid for her hand in marriage. Except, she waited for that special someone to capture her heart.

"...would you?"

Joy's heartbeat ratcheted to high speed. Caught daydreaming again.

"I'm sorry, ma'am. What did you say?"

"I asked if you were in the habit of reading the scriptures?"

Joy bit her bottom lip. How long had it been?

"M-my mother and I used to read at night." Joy twisted her fingers together.

"How lovely. We used to do it together as a family, too. But the boys grew up and my husband died. Shortly after, Andrew's brother Peter passed away also. Andrew and I..." The blue-gray eyes misted and blinked. Sniffing, the mistress of the house sat straighter. "I'm sure the Lord has His way with us, after all."

"Isn't that the truth," Joy murmured.

"Would you, please? I so enjoy listening. I find that scripture chases away our troubles."

Mrs. Lloyd-Foxx handed her an old, leather-bound bible. From the looks of it, someone was still reading often.

"Of course. It would be my pleasure." Joy took it with trembling fingers.

Mrs. Lloyd-Foxx inclined her head and settled into her seat, eyes closing.

"Is there anything in particular you would like me to read?" Joy's voice quaked slightly.

"I love the Psalms, don't you?"

Joy nodded and found her place. She cleared her throat and started to read. Her voice, trembling at first, became stronger as she heard the once so familiar words.

David.

Now there was a man who had seen his share of trouble. And yet, he never turned away. He ran to the Lord in bad times. When misfortune had come to her and she had done the same, nobody cared.

I will lift up mine eyes unto the hills, from whence cometh my help. My help cometh from the LORD, which made heaven and earth.

69

9

*A*ndrew entered the cool front hall of the manor. This house was always a constant temperature. In the winter, they were warmed by the many fireplaces, in the summer it provided a nice retreat from the brutal heat.

"I take it the horses had their morning exercise, sir?" Bruce helped him shrug out of his jacket.

Perhaps he should just forgo etiquette and wear a shirt when watching the morning exercise. At least he wouldn't boil to death.

"They ran well. And it's a good thing too, with this weekend's races approaching quickly. How many have accepted our invitation so far?"

Andrew took the offered water and downed it in one draught.

"So far we have three hundred guests coming for the ball on Friday night. Have all the entries been filled, sir? It should be a good day of races."

"Yes."

Andrew thumbed absentmindedly through the stack of letters Bruce handed him. Today was the last day to enter and it seemed that there were still a lot of people who wanted a part of the very large purse.

"How many have accepted our personal invitation to spend the weekend?"

"Mr. Houghton and his family have accepted your invitation, as well as the Northampton Morgans and the Billings. We were waiting on a reply from the Jacksons, but the Missus is ill and therefore Mr. Jackson has decided to stay at home this time around."

"That is unfortunate. Send our regards to Mrs. Jackson and let her know she is in our prayers. Please inform the servants to pray for her."

Bruce bowed. "Very well, sir." He was about to retreat when Andrew caught him.

"I assume my mother is finally up. Where would I find her?"

Bruce hid a smile. "She is resting on the veranda, taking in the summer breeze."

"That woman does nothing other than rest and retire." Andrew bit his lip and recalled that he was trying to mend fences between him and his mother.

What happened to them?

They used to be able to laugh and talk. Now, if she laughed at him, it was usually a put-down. Their talk centered around how much money his mother had spent on her dresses and her entertainment. It usually ended up with him stomping out and his mother leaving for Boston the next day.

He entered the veranda through the ballroom and paused when he heard the soft, feminine voices. It was only ten in the morning and already she had a visitor. The young woman sat with her back to him, but her voice was familiar.

"Andrew." His mother raised her hands, beckoning him closer. He took a double take and stepped out.

Strange.

"Come and join us, dear. You work too hard."

Who is this woman and what has she done with my mother?

"Mother, I didn't know you were entertaining so early. I won't interrupt."

Her face twisted in confusion. "What are you talking about? Who in their right mind would come around at ten on a Monday morning?"

"But.." He slowly turned to the visitor sitting on the other lounge chair. There was something familiar about her and when he saw the bruises on her face, he remembered. A feeling of unusual warmth rushed up his neck.

"I beg your pardon, Miss Richards. I take it you slept well? My staff has seen to your needs?"

She certainly didn't look like the lowly barmaid he had rescued yesterday.

"Thank you, sir. Yes. Everyone has been most kind to me. And I have enjoyed visiting with your mother."

Andrew's eyebrows shot up but he quickly trained his expression. His mother could be kind, if she chose to be. Just not to him.

"I'm glad to hear that. I'll leave you to it, then."

Best to escape back to the barn where the horses didn't change their appearances overnight and he was surrounded by men.

"Andrew! You will sit and talk to your mother! I haven't seen you in a month and it is doubtful that I will see you in the next few days, with the races this weekend. I wish to talk to you, now!"

I knew she'd be back. Feeling mollified that this was still the woman with the sharp tongue, he turned back with a sigh.

"I will leave you two." Miss Richards rose to her feet and stood, swaying. She paled further and reached for the back of the seat to steady her. He made to reach for her, then changed his mind when he glimpsed two shrewd eyes watching him.

"Nonsense." His mother's soft tone drew the young woman to a stop and she fell back into the chair. "Stay. If we can't be civil to each other for a few moments, there are greater issues here than either one of us are willing to admit. And this will be a good test for this weekend. How are preparations coming for that, Andrew?"

Andrew settled into the lounge chair. So, she wanted to make nice in front of the new girl.

"It will be an exciting day. I just have to see to it that every horse will be accommodated. We seem to have more entries than we have stalls. I've commissioned a team to make some temporary housing for some of our mares."

"How *do* you do it?" Sarcasm laced her words. "Who are you running, Andrew?"

This was a first. Since when did she care which horse was doing what?

"In the two year old race, I entered Grandpop and Ladiesman. For the three-year olds we have Minuteman and for the mares I entered your favorites, Mother. Cleopatra, Justwouldificould, and Midsummer Dance. And then, of course, there are the older horses. I thought we could let Justletme run one last time. He's about to be put to stud, and I hope he will be in the money."

"Andrew, you did well."

"I beg your pardon, Mother?" Andrew blinked.

"You picked excellent horses." His mother leaned back in her chair.

Breathing a laugh, he brushed his hand through his hair. "How would you know?"

His question made her flinch. "Do you not think I would concern myself with the horses we have at the stable? They are part of our livelihood. I'm quite looking forward to this weekend. We are watching from the roof, are we not?"

"Where else would you want to watch the races?" he managed to ask.

Every year, since his grandfather had established this stud farm, his family had held races in the spring, summer, and fall. He had built a flat track just beyond the park that surrounded the mansion. It's beauty was well-known in the area and throughout New England.

In the spring, they held their annual horse sale, with as much pomp and pageantry as possible – not to mention some exquisite racing. The summer races were popular because of the ball his family, as sponsors of the race, held. The fall races closed the season until they did it all again in the spring.

The guests of the family had the extreme pleasure of watching the races from the private widow's walk on the roof of the house. His father had designed it for the purpose of watching the horses do what they were designed for.

Run like the wind.

Anticipation surged through him.

"Have you ever been to a race, Miss Richards?"

Andrew turned toward her and found himself staring. With her hair up and out of the way, her face was so pale and... delicate, her bone structure was like a-

With a quick mental shake, he faced away only to find his mother watching with interest.

Now, that was unfortunate.

He rubbed his hand over his chin and gave her a shrug of his shoulder with his most roguish grin. Her eyes narrowed calculatingly and she turned her attention back to the girl. She really wasn't a girl anymore. She was more like a graceful gazelle. Andrew blew out a breath through his nose and attempted to join the conversation. After all, he had asked her the question.

What did I ask her, again?

"... around the village green on Saturday going to the races, then yes. I have gone to the races." A soft twinkle of amusement showed in Miss Richard's incredibly blue eyes. Eyes that seemed to suck him right in.

He shook the woozy feeling from his mind.

"Nothing compared to our highly bred thoroughbreds, then." Did he have to sound so haughty? "You are in for a treat."

Miss Richards lips formed a smile, transforming her face, and Andrew found himself lost.

What is going on?

She twisted her hands into the soft fabric of her gown. Which, if he had to admit to himself, looked quite fetching on her.

I'm losing my mind.

"Sir, I appreciate what you have done for me. I need to be on my way as soon as my feet are healed."

Andrew flinched and the chair he had been lounging in seemed to pitch him forward – resembling a bucking horse.

"I beg your pardon?"

The maiden's face turned away and he found that the veranda had suddenly become less bright and cheery.

"There are things I must take care of, sir. I have a sister... I don't know what happened to her. And my parents... I really should make sure they are well. Last time I saw them- Things haven't been well for my family in a long time."

"You're leaving us?" The question was stupid, he knew it. Even more stupid was the way he said it.

"I have to."

Andrew frowned and the day looked dark and dreary. "How are you going to travel all the way from here to just outside Hartford?"

She drew in a long breath. "I don't know yet. But that is not your concern. You have done so much for me already. I couldn't impose on you any longer than I have to."

"Nonsense, Miss Richards. You will stay here." His mother sat up straight in her seat, determination in her face.

Oh, you poor woman. My mother is going to set you straight.

"I will not hear of anything else. I would like to employ you as my companion. I have enjoyed the way you read. Your voice is very pleasant."

"I beg your pardon, ma'am?"

"I will pay you a handsome fee to stay on as my companion." Mrs. Lloyd-Foxx lifted her chin, daring anyone to defy her.

"I... I can't. I need to see if my family is well."

Andrew's eyes bounced back and forth between them. "One moment, please! Mother, what are you saying?"

"Never mind, my boy. You sort it all out. I am going to retire for a while. The heat is getting to me. We will continue to discuss this later."

"Wait!" Miss Richard was half way out of her seat before his mother entered the house. She turned to him with panic on her face.

Andrew pinched the bridge of his nose. His mother had sunk her fingernails into his affairs yet again. A companion? Did she really need another one? The last one had-

"I'm sorry. I didn't mean to cause you any problems. You have been so kind."

Miss Richards' velvety-soft voice drew him back to the present.

"It's not you," he sighed. "My mother can be difficult. If you stay, you would be well taken care of, Miss Richards. What do you say? About the employment, I mean."

Miss Richards sat back down and twisted her fingers together, a look on her face that caused his heart to clench. What about her made him feel this unsettled?

"I can't." Her voice trembled. "I have to go home, first. Do you think your mother would allow me to return once I've seen to things?"

"It depends on how much she liked your reading." He smiled and her cheeks turned the color of his mother's favorite roses – pink.

"It wasn't that spectacular."

"My mother has taken a liking to you." He ignored the wild race going off in his gut. "I'm sure she'd let you go for a few days, see to your family's well-being, and return. How long would it take you?"

"I don't know. Things were- I left because we had some financial problems. The harvests had been terrible and we had other set-backs."

"When was the last time you saw your family?"

Why did he even care? She had been a barmaid and he had rescued her. That was as far as it went. He never felt this level of concern with any of the other people he had brought home.

What was it about her that made him want to help her? Made him want to protect her?

"I left two years ago." She swallowed hard.

"And you thought you could find employment elsewhere?"

Miss Richards lowered her head. "Something like that. They don't know what happened to me. They think that I'm living in Boston with a good family."

"What happened? Why aren't you?"

Her delicate face paled – making the bruises so much more pronounced – and Andrew regretted prying into her private affairs.

"Apparently, there never was a family." She smoothed the material of her elegant dress and let the sentence hang. "I stayed with the man for several months…" She shuttered. "When he tired of me, I found myself sold to the highest bidder, to a peddler. He treated me like an animal, keeping me in the shed out back when I wasn't working. Eventually, I was passed on to the innkeeper for the price of a barrel of whiskey."

Andrew's breath caught in the back of his throat. He'd heard of this happening to girls from destitute families. How they had been tricked and forced to work in the streets, selling their bodies to the highest bidder. Thankfully that hadn't happened to Miss Richards. Or had she been forced to perform 'favors' for her owners? By the looks of her shame written over her face, he began to wonder.

Anger passed through him in a red-hot fury before he could control it.

Why did he care?

"So, you see. I have been gone from home far too long. You've been so kind and if I may allow my feet to heal for a day or two, I'll be on my way. I can always find work as I travel."

He narrowed his eyes and leveled his gaze with hers. "I would advise you to be cautious. You may find yourself in worse shape than before. A woman traveling alone is always easy pickings. Besides, my mother has taken to you." He flashed a smile to put her at ease. "Her last companion was with her for five years until she had the misfortune to marry."

Curiosity flashed across her features. "The misfortune, you say?"

"She married my older brother."

"Oh?"

"Yes," he said softly. Not willing to elaborate, he shifted away.

"Where are they now?"

"Dead."

Silence sliced through the thick summer air.

"Well, that's past." Andrew rose. "Think about my mother's proposal. You will be taken care of, Miss Richards."

He nodded and strode off the veranda in an attempt to shake the thoughts that were beginning to haunt him again. His brother's shining eyes when he married his wife, the note that informed them they had been shot and killed by highway robbers. By the time he reached the stables, his mood had slipped to melancholy and not even watching last years foals chasing each other in the field lifted his spirit.

Thinking of his brother was painful and he still blamed his mother for introducing him to her companion. If Peter hadn't married that woman, perhaps he'd still be alive, helping to manage the estate.

10

$\mathcal{S}$itting on the padded seat by the window in her room, Joy examined her feet. The salve seemed to be working wonders and already her feet were less sore than this morning.

Why shouldn't she stay here?

In her heart, she felt this was a safe place, a good home. She wasn't afraid of hard work. Whatever a companion did, she was sure she could handle it. And perhaps then she could send some money to her family, like they had agreed when she had set off on her adventure.

That had turned out to be worst mistake she'd ever made. Worse than the time she had trapped a skunk in the cold storage without realizing.

And who knew? Perhaps she could find a good man who would marry her.

A sharp pain snapped through her gut.

Who would marry someone like her? Certainly not a man of any standing. Not a good man, either.

A tear slipped down her cheek and she brushed it away quickly before anyone was the wiser.

It looked like her destiny was to be an old maid, without children or husband. Joy bit her bottom lip and prevented more tears from flowing.

I should go home.

She longed to feel her mother's soft arms around her, telling her that it was all over, smell the scent of hay and outdoors on her father. At least, that is how she liked to remember him. She wanted to whisper and giggle until late into the night with her younger sister and watch the stars from the roof of the porch. Perhaps she could reconnect with Jonah.

Please let me go home, Lord.

The air vibrated with heat, as it usually does on a hot summer day. All around, birds chirped and sang.

But nothing came in terms of God having heard her. And He certainly didn't answer her. The only difference was that a deep, comfortable peace swept away her questions and doubts.

Before she could think of anything else, a knock on the door sounded, followed by it being deftly opened. Joy's heart slipped into her gut and she rose quickly to greet Mrs. Lloyd-Foxx.

"Ma'am..."

The mistress of the house swept in with swishing skirts and stood in front of her, hand poised upon her hip.

"What is this I hear? You intend to leave before the summer ball?"

Joy's mouth opened and closed.

Her would-be employer scanned her face and let out a long sigh.

"Child. I understand your longing to see your family. I don't hold it against you at all."

Joy gasped and blinked away the emotion making her eyes tear up. "Ma'am. You have no idea-"

Mrs. Lloyd-Foxx waved an impatient hand at her. "I would like you to be my companion. I feel you and I are of the same mind and heart." She paused for a moment. "That being said, I by no means mean to hold you against your wishes. If you need to return, you are free to do so. However, think of the fun you would have attending a real ball."

Joy closed her eyes and immediately she found herself surrounded by twinkling candle light, soft music, and the gentle hum of voices. She wore an elaborate gown and danced with a charming young man, who complimented her.

"If you attend the ball at my side, you could return to your family sooner with the wages you have earned."

"I beg your-"

Again the hand was held up.

"This ball is the most important event for this family and let me be clear. I generally get my wish." A sheepish smile touched the woman's lips. "Look at it this way, Miss Richards. It's going to be a splendid time. I would love to see you in a gown."

The blue-gray eyes twinkled with mischief and Joy felt a twisting of her gut.

"But-"

"It's settled, then. You'll attend the ball and the races, then hurry home to take care of your family. After, you will return to me and serve me as my companion."

She had been swiftly and simply bamboozled. If she said *no,* she looked ungrateful. "But you have already done so much for me."

Mrs. Lloyd-Foxx raised her well sculptured eyebrows. "What have we done for you, dear? Other than to feed you and give you a bed for the night. I like you, Miss Richards."

"Very well," she finally whispered.

Mrs. Lloyd-Foxx clapped her hands in excitement. "Wonderful. We have much to accomplish! As my companion, you will need to look the part and act accordingly. From the way you behaved at breakfast, I can see you have much to learn. Hurry. We can't let the day slip away! It's time to get to work." Eyes twinkling in excitement, Mrs. Lloyd-Foxx waited for her to rise, which she did so slowly and carefully. Her employer slipped a hand through her arm. "Oh, how does four dollars a month strike you as a salary?"

Joy's mouth dried up and all she could do was gawk. Mrs. Lloyd-Foxx closed her jaw gently.

"First lesson of the day. Close your mouth, child. Gaping is not becoming." The mistress sighed and draped a hand to her brow. "Come, come. The work awaits."

The work would be the death of her.

They were gathered in the seamstress' room, several gowns spread out in front of her. These were the fluffy, puffy, yards of material kind of gowns she had always heard of. Laura had been summoned to give assistance and the women set to undress Joy down to her shift. Three ladies stood in a row, inspecting her as if she were a prize filly. Heat crept into her cheeks. The fluffy pastry she had hurriedly consumed not moments ago churned in her stomach.

"She has lovely long limbs." The seamstress drummed her fingers on the table in front of her. "I suggest, ladies, that we go with something delicate for her. Definitely low shoulders and cut bodice."

Whatever that meant, Joy didn't have a good feeling about it.

"Oh... Yes." A look slipped into Mrs. Lloyd-Foxx's eyes and she winked at the two other women in the room. "That will draw attention."

Don't want to draw attention. The muscles in Joy's gut twisted into a tiny knot.

Laura nodded thoughtfully. "That delicate neck needs to be shown off."

Joy's jaw went slack and she felt the sharp gaze Mrs. Lloyd-Foxx reprimanded her silently with. Snapping her lips tightly together, she forced herself to breathe.

This was certainly NOT what she had expected. Her idea of work was schlepping tankards of beer and serving drunk customers. Her day had consisted of hours and hours of bone crushingly hard work.

This was a completely different form of torture.

While the women talked about how to show off her *assets,* she allowed her mind to wander. Yes, attending a ball would be fun. But she would rather be riding in the races. She recalled a time when she had been only eight or nine years old.

Her father had owned a Morgan stallion and he had entered him into the local once-around-the-town-square-race on Saturdays. Being hard up for cash, he had dressed her up as the jock. They had stuffed her long hair under a felt cap, smeared dirt on her face, and she had been told not to speak. Feeling the wind in her face as Brownie had passed all the other horses, hearing the cheers from the crowd... A smile slipped onto her face.

"I see the idea appeals to Miss Richards," the seamstress said.

She stared at the three women and lowered her lashes. Mrs. Lloyd-Foxx sighed and picked up her hands, turning them around this way and that.

85

"Laura, we need to do something about her hands. They are entirely too rough! She needs to soak in that delightful concoction of yours every day. And her nails! Goodness, I have never seen such a sight. It's a good thing she will be wearing gloves. The hair will be lovely once all the dried ends have been cut."

More excited discussion followed and Joy was beginning to feel that this was a very bad idea! She had just become their prize experiment.

Laura grinned and clapped her hands in delight. It took Joy all her strength to keep her face placid. "Isn't this so exciting, Joy?"

Exciting wasn't what Joy would call this prospect which filled her with dread.

For the rest of the morning and early afternoon, she was in Laura's tender care. The woman scrubbed her, pummeled her and primped her. When Joy thought she could not stand it any longer, Laura attended to her hands in earnest, soaking her in something sweet smelling.

"While those are soaking, let's cut your hair." Laura shook her head and picked up a pair of scissors.

Joy bit back the tears as she watched her hair fall all around her. When it was all said and done, Laura had hacked off a good five inches.

"Well," Joy mumbled, her voice shaky and weak. "That was unexpected."

"How is our patient doing?" Mrs. Lloyd-Foxx entered and gave her a thorough examination. She pursed her lips and nodded. "Much better. Those bags under the eyes, Laura. We must simply do something about them."

"Of course, ma'am. We are going to work on that. God made the world in seven days. We have a mere four days to work on this. It's going to be close."

Joy couldn't help but snort in response.

"When you are done, Laura, I need Miss Richards in the ballroom."

"Yes ma'am."

11

*T*wo hours later, Joy hobbled down the stairs, smelling like a flower garden in high bloom. Her skin felt as is it would slip off her bones any moment now. Her muscles had been kneaded like dough. Her face had been covered with a soft cloth which had been soaked in water infused with herbs and flowers.

"Miss Richards, you are starting to look much improved," Mrs. Lloyd-Foxx crooned. "Now, let us discuss the ball. When you are asked to dance, you will want to make some silly comment over the weather or the upcoming race. Do not talk about anything else, other than those topics. Your dance card will be filled in no time." She pursed her lips and narrowed her eyes. "I assume you know how to dance?"

"Of course, ma'am. I've attended festivals and barn dances."

Once again, Jonah's ruggedly handsome features came to mind.

Mrs. Lloyd-Foxx's eyes opened wide. "Barn... dances? How- how lovely." She shuddered. "This is a ball. Let us see if you can waltz."

Apparently, the dances she had learned did not meet the specifications for this elaborate ball. For the next hour the woman moved her about, instructed her how to hold her hands, her chin, and her tongue. According to Laura, Joy's habit of pushing her tongue out of her mouth when she concentrated very hard did not look very lady-like.

Andrew entered through the side door and hoped to retreat directly into his room. His mother's commanding voice coming from the ballroom stopped him in his tracks. He poked his head around the corner and sucked in a surprised breath and drew his head back.

Miss Richards and Laura were waltzing through the room. Laura did her best to keep a straight face as Miss Richards stepped on her foot. His mother stood on the side, counting out the beats to the music.

"No, Miss Richards. You must watch your tongue! You simply cannot stick it out. I can see it in your cheek. And don't look at Laura's feet. *Feel* the movement." His mother threw her hands up in the air.

"I need a moment," Miss Richards gasped, her cheeks flushed.

Andrew hid an amused smile behind his hand and stepped fully into the room.

"Mother, what have you done to poor Miss Richards? She looks... I don't know. Are you alright?"

Groaning, Miss Richards collapsed on one of the chairs.

"Andrew Francis Lloyd-Foxx! How dare you? Have you no decorum? We don't tell you how to prepare your horses, you don't dictate to us how we prepare ourselves for this ball. Unless you wish to become Miss Richards' dance partner while she learns to waltz properly, I suggest you leave and keep your comments to yourself."

A shiver passed over him and Andrew took a large step out of the room. His mother was in her element and he knew that she meant business. Her face was flushed with excitement and her eyes shone merrily. He hadn't seen her like that since-

He wasn't going there.

"I apologize, Miss Richards. I would have gladly come to your rescue, but alas. The price my mother extracts is too high."

He shot his mother a cheeky grin and retreated to the solitude of his own rooms.

Joy lay on her bed staring at the ceiling, trying to ignore the throbbing of her feet. Learning to dance the *proper way* was proving to be hazardous for her health. The primping wasn't her cup of tea, either. She endured both because she needed the job to get home. And she had a good feeling about this place. It prevented her from dashing into the stable to 'borrow' a horse to ride home.

Laura, who had left her alone for an hour, appeared in the door. "It's time to dress for dinner, Joy. The mistress is expecting to test your knowledge of your lesson today."

Joy shifted on the bed and rolled over to glare at Laura.

"I can't," she moaned. "I hurt."

Laura laughed without much compassion and mercy, and pulled her by the arms. She helped her into the chair in front of the vanity and began to work her magic.

"You've heard of the story of Cinderella, yes? She went to the ball, even though she was not exactly prime material. She even ended up with the prince." Laura grinned evilly and brushed her hair vigorously until it shone and her scalp hurt. She tightened the corset, making it difficult to breathe.

"What are you doing?" A bead of sweat appeared on Joy's forehead when she struggled to take a breath.

"Maximizing all your assets."

"My what?"

"Your long limbs, your tiny waist, and your incredibly lovely dark hair. Not to mention those baby blue eyes of yours. What a contrast. Think of it as a dress rehearsal for the ball."

"I'm not ready for that. Please, let me breathe. I don't think I would do anyone any good if I faint because this contraption around my waist is too tight."

Laura waved a dismissive hand. "You won't. We're going for the maximum effect."

She slipped a pale blue dress over Joy's head. This time, the puffy sleeves left most of her arms uncovered. The low neckline was simply shocking, making her feel naked.

Laura gave her a once over and smiled a strange smile. "Yes. Very nice."

Feeling completely out of place, Joy hobbled to the door. The skirt of the dress made a swishing sound. When she passed Laura, the maid had a gleam in her eyes she didn't find encouraging.

By the time she had made it to the dining room, nausea was her companion. As if a heavy weight sat on her chest, she could only draw in small gulps of air. Wearing such a fine dress drove home one thought. She was completely out of her element and would never really fit in here. The stable was a proper place for her, and she had a feeling that even that was probably much too fancy for the likes of her.

91

Joy limped to her chair under the watchful gaze of Mrs. Lloyd-Foxx. With a silent nod from the hostess, Joy sank into the seat, gulping at whatever air she could manage. Swallowing repeatedly only made her feel worse and more sick to her stomach.

It seems that You and I are now on speaking terms, Lord. I... need to be able to breathe, please. She took another gulp of air and sipped from the crystal glass in front of her. It tasted sweet, yet left a funny feeling on her tongue. Apparently, this family drank red wine for dinner. *I feel out of place... and pray that I can return home soon.*

Another sip and a fuzziness invaded her mind. Perhaps it was the lack of oxygen.

"Good evening, mother." Master Andrew entered the room, looking very dashing and dandy-like. Once again, his attire was flawless. His gaze slipped past her and bounced right back to her. Then they passed to his mother, who was watching like a cat about to spring on a particularly juicy mouse.

"Andrew. How was your day?"

"It was a lot less exciting than yours. I didn't play with live dolls." He grinned and sat down on the opposite side of Joy. His attention was focused on his glass of wine.

"I meant no disrespect, Miss Richards." He cleared his throat.

Mrs. Lloyd-Foxx still had a very smug look about her when she lifted her crystal wine goblet to her lips.

"None taken."

Talking was difficult because of her unsuccessful attempt to inhale. The room became terribly stifling and Joy had to force herself not to wipe her moist forehead. Another unsuccessful attempt to draw in air made her brain feel woozy and disembodied from the rest of her. The voices in the room became distant and a dull throbbing began in her temple.

Master Andrew glanced in her direction for a fraction of a second, then focused on the flower arrangement behind her. "I'm sorry about that. I didn't expect my mother to transform you into a society belle. I assume you enjoyed the treatment?"

Joy couldn't prevent the look she gave him. Since she couldn't tell him how much she *didn't* delight in it, she tried to convey it in a glance. He must have seen it because he passed his hand in front of his mouth, the corners of his eyes crinkled in amusement.

Joy tried to follow the conversation during dinner but it was becoming increasingly difficult to concentrate. The more she tried to breathe and found that she couldn't, the less she actually could. A wave of panic began to build inside her, waiting to crash over her at the right time. At last it came, and Joy found the edges of her vision darkening.

"Would you excuse me?" She managed a mere whisper. "I... need to... retire."

"By all means, my dear girl," Mrs. Lloyd-Foxx crooned. "It has been a tiring day for both of us. And we'll do it again tomorrow."

"Can't... wait."

When she rose out of her seat, the room spun violently. Dark spots danced in front of her. The need for air became so all-consuming that she tugged at the low collar of her dress even before she had taken a step. Her lungs were exhausted from working too hard and gave up the fight. Joy's vision darkened completely and she heard a surprised gasp from the other people in the room as she slipped to the floor.

"What?!"

Andrew's lips parted as he stared at the unconscious woman on the floor. He beat his mother to her side and began to check her. He had studied medicine for two years at university, thinking he'd become a doctor, and knew a thing or two about the human body. Such as its need for oxygen.

"Mother, what have you done now?" His voice was harsher than he had meant for it to be. Her heart was pumping but she wasn't breathing.

His mother, hovering beside him, gasped. "What do you mean? I had nothing to do with this."

Andrew gave a disgusted grunt and sat back on his haunches. He knew what the problem was and the remedy was easy.

"You cannot blame this on me!" she whispered.

"Wanna bet?" he hissed. "If it weren't for you and your endless dress-up..."

His mother drew in a sharp breath.

If Miss Richards didn't take a breath soon, she would die.

"Hand me the knife, Mother." Andrew pointed to the sharp utensil on the table. His mother jumped away in jerky movements and handed it to him.

Within seconds he managed to cut the tight strings of the pesky corset and watched, willing her paralyzed lungs to work. The chest didn't rise and fall miraculously.

Andrew pressed his fingers to his temple.

"Pray, Mother, because if she doesn't take a breath soon..."

His mother's face paled and she closed her eyes. Andrew stared at the limp form.

Come on, Miss Richards!

A memory flashed in his mind. During his semesters at medical school, one of his fellow students had shown off a technique he had learned overseas. Another student had stopped breathing and he had simply breathed for him. It had worked.

Wonderful.

He squatted next to the unconscious body and tipped her head back just enough to clear the airway. Then he breathed into her lungs and felt her chest expand.

He repeated it again and again until he felt a shudder go through her body. Andrew scooted onto his heels as Miss Richards coughed. She brought up chunks of food she had only moments ago consumed.

She slowly came out of the daze. His mother stood next to her, a horrified expression on her face.

"I'm so sorry!" Miss Richards' eyes became misty and her bottom lip quivered.

"You deal with this." Andrew rose and rushed out of the room.

12

omen! What motivated them to go to such lengths to make themselves look more attractive than they already were? Couldn't they just leave well enough alone? No. they had to catch the attention of every available male around with their...

Andrew shook his head and rushed over the pristine lawn. Fireflies were out and usually, this was his favorite time of the day. Today, he saw nothing as he rushed toward his maple tree in the middle of the property. His grandfather had planned on cutting it down for firewood, but his father had insisted that this particular tree was the best climbing tree available. His grandfather had reluctantly relinquished and this tree had been the entertainment for his father, his brother, and himself.

Andrew leaned against the bark of the old tree, missing his brother and father in this very moment. He longed to seek their sound advice. The silence reminded him of how they would never be able to share it with him again. However, there was One, who was closer than a brother. He would seek Him tonight!

"I am so sorry." Joy stared at the mess on the floor and covered herself with the ripped fabric of her dress.

Mrs Lloyd-Foxx had summoned an army of servants and helped her to her feet.

"Don't worry, child. You aren't the first to fall prey to a corset that was too tight. You are not used to this and so it was bound to happen. My son just doesn't understand the sacrifice we make to look good."

"I don't want to make that sacrifice again." Joy's voice quivered with horror. "I can't do this, Mrs. Lloyd-Foxx. I'm just a farmer's daughter. We go to barn dances, laugh and dance with our friends and the next morning we muck the stalls again because we have to. I don't fit into your world. Besides that I've been a barmaid and-" She couldn't utter the word. "I don't belong here."

"Not yet, but you will. I know it." Mrs. Lloyd-Foxx had a certain twinkle in her normally cool eyes.

Joy covered her face with her hands. "I'm utterly humiliated, madam. I can't ever face your son again."

She heard the smile in Mrs. Lloyd-Foxx's voice. "He's a big boy. He needs to be reminded that there is more to life than horses and business. I hope you help him realize it."

Joy gulped in the air again. Her mouth gaped open. She shook her head. "I..." She opened her mouth again but no intelligible word came out. She managed to get up. "Good night."

Joy dashed up the stairs as fast as she could with her gimpy feet. Never in her life had she felt so used and disgraced. As she shut the door to lean heavily against it, pressure built behind her eyelids.

This isn't the time or place to fall apart.

She swallowed her tears and her humiliation.

Is this how You look after me, Lord? Do You even see what is going on down here? Do You care? How could You put me into this situation? I thought I was safe. I'm far from it. I don't think there is any place on this earth where I can feel secure.

She slipped out of her dress and threw the ruined corset onto the bed. As she donned a soft nightgown, Joy made a decision. As soon as the household was asleep she'd leave.

Waiting for her breathing to still and the soft mouse-like noises to stop, Joy tried to slip to her happy place.

She and her father were training a particularly handsome team of big draft horses for a neighbor. Both geldings were sweet and very eager to learn to pull the weight behind them. One of them, Tom, even liked to be ridden, while Ollie wanted nothing to do with it. One Sunday afternoon, after a long session at church, her family rested. Joy slipped out her bedroom window and stole to the paddock. Standing on the top rung of the fence, she slipped a bridle onto Tom and hopped onto his broad back. Her legs barely fit around his huge barrel, but he seemed to anticipate her thoughts. They spent the afternoon galloping down dusty roads, exploring fields, and cooling off in a nearby pond.

She forced herself to the present and sat up, listening for any noise at all. The slightest creak from down the hall made the hairs on the back of her neck stand up. Slowly, picking up the dress Master Andrew had bought her on their trip, she slipped into it. She'd repay him somehow.

A lone oil lamp shimmered in the corridor and on the stairs. Joy held her breath while she stole to the bottom floor and out the back, through the winter kitchen.

Darkness swallowed her up and she ran. Her feet sank into the soft grass and when she was far enough away from the house, stale air exploded from her lungs. Looking back at the house she felt a twinge of remorse. It seemed like a good place.

I need to learn to read situations better.

What hurt the most was that she had begun to trust the people around her. She even liked Mrs. Lloyd-Foxx. Master Andrew had seemed like a very kind gentleman. Joy felt a kinship with Laura.

Now in the middle of the expansive lawn, she stopped and leaned against a giant tree, panting. Her feet stung and burned. How was she going to leave? A long sigh escaped and she sank down in the soft grass, covering her head in her arms.

"Why can't I count on You? Where are you, anyway, God? What do You want from me? Do You not even care?" She pounded the ground with her fist. "What do You want from me!?" She ground her teeth together in an attempt to keep from screaming at the top of her lungs and thus waking the whole household.

"I can't believe I thought You would come to help me. I guess it was just a coincidence! So does that mean that You don't exist? Would You please answer me?"

Nothing but the crickets and the creaking of the old tree could be heard, until the branch directly above her trembled and a deep, unmistakably masculine throat was cleared.

Please, please let it be a mountain lion – making a swift end of me – and not who I imagine it to be.

God wasn't that cruel, was He?

Slowly, as if her head had suddenly filled with the weight of a thousand rocks, she lifted her chin and spotted the dark figure on one of the fat branches above.

Just kill me now.

Nothing happened except the leaves on the branch quivered.

Andrew would have preferred to be a cricket at this very moment. There had been no time to scramble out of the way when he realized that Miss Richards intended to collapse underneath *his* tree. And then she had gone off on her tirade and he had prayed that she wouldn't spot him. He had humiliated her enough already.

Taking another deep, ragged breath, he slid down the tree. He wasn't getting the answers he searched for tonight anyway.

"I'm... sorry, Miss Richards."

The woman's cheeks turned the color of a ripe tomato and she bit her bottom lip hard, avoiding his direct gaze.

"I would have announced my presence sooner, but you didn't give me a chance."

A very thin smile played on her lips and she plucked up a blade of grass.

"This is your estate. You don't have to answer for anything, Mr. Lloyd-Foxx. I was on my way out. I'm only resting my feet and formulating a plan to get home."

"Ah." Andrew found that he didn't like the idea of her slipping out in the middle of the night. Furthermore, he felt an urging to say something to her.

"May I talk to you?"

"No," she whimpered.

Andrew laughed. "I understand. I sympathize with you."

Miss Richards laughed humorlessly and covered her face with her arms. "How can you, who has everything, know anything about what I'm going through?"

Andrew sat down in the grass near her, keeping enough distance between them not to seem threatening, and leaned his head against the tree. The bark was rough and yet so familiar.

"I was twenty, going through theological training at the university. I was one of the most promising students in my class. My instructor had inspired in me a desire to walk with Christ. It was completely overpowering. I went out into the community with my friends and we tried to evangelize everyone. Even if they didn't want to hear, we talked.

"One afternoon, I came back to the student housing and found myself summoned to the dean's office. I discovered that my father had died. His heart had simply given out. I was devastated. He was my role model, my hero. My father could do everything. And now, he was dead. I hadn't even been there to say goodbye.

"Peter – my older brother – took over for my father, but his heart was not in it. He never enjoyed working with the horses on a daily basis. He liked running the business of the estates, but he had also fallen in love with my mother's companion, a beautiful young woman with connections to British aristocracy. It was a match made in heaven, conspired by my mother."

Miss Richards' gaze lifted and he could see the thoughts zapping around in her brain. She understood what he was talking about. His mother was a force to be reckoned with.

"When they married it was as though Peter had just become the king. When he and Margaret died, it was like God had left me. He didn't seem to care that I had lost my father and my brother. Besides that, He stopped me from being an evangelist, something that was pressing on my spirit. I was willing to go anywhere He sent me. I wasn't prepared to stay home and shepherd what had remained of my family.

"I had to learn that my path wasn't about what I *wanted*. God has something planned for every one of us. And He will do it, too. Whatever He has in store for us, we can trust that it is still good and *for* our good. You probably didn't exactly want to run into me tonight, did you?"

Miss Richards swallowed hard and shredded another blade of grass, her face in the shadows so he couldn't see her expression.

"That would be an understatement." Her voice was so soft, he nearly missed her reply.

"But God knew you needed to hear this. From me, of all people. I don't know why." He closed his eyes to give himself some privacy. Somehow, he always figured if people couldn't see his eyes, they wouldn't know what he was thinking. "To tell you the truth, you are the last person I hoped to see tonight as well."

Miss Richards gave a soft, grunted laugh. "Thank you."

Andrew smirked and slapped at a mosquito on his neck. "Sorry."

They sat in silence, the humidity pressing down on them.

Finally, Miss Richards sniffed. "I'm so humiliated."

102

He cocked his head and opened his eyes. His gaze fell on her and he felt the pressing need to ask, "How is your heart before God?"

She sucked in a sharp breath. Turning her face, Miss Richards picked another unfortunate blade of grass to shred. It seemed a long time before she answered and he saw the emotions playing on her face. Grief. Anger. Hopelessness. It stirred something deep inside him and he clasped his hands together over his knees.

"I don't know. I have been struggling for a while. My father broke his back, falling off a horse. He was riding in the snow and ice and the horse slipped. Fell right on top of him. When we found him, he was barely breathing. He had cracked a few ribs in the process. The doctor couldn't help him, but he made him as comfortable as possible.

"Our clients, our reputation, our business went right out the window. Nobody sent us horses anymore. Of course, with my father bedridden, nobody wanted their horses trained by a girl." A scowl formed on her pretty face. Andrew drew his knees to his chest and waited.

"I still hung on to God. It seemed silly to stop believing in His goodness solely because the going got rough. I prayed, I pleaded, I bargained. And the crops failed, food became of short supply. After three years we were barely making ends meet. My father never improved, and he was in constant pain. All our money went into managing his agony.

"Farming is a rough occupation for three women, who had to chop wood, tend to the livestock in the dead of winter, and look after an invalid. Two years ago, we didn't have enough wood to last the winter. And then came what we thought was salvation.

"A city gentleman stopped by and asked for directions. He asked if he could spend the night and that he would pay for it. God was finally answering our prayers. It was such a blessing because he had to stay another night due to weather conditions. He ended up staying with us for four days, paying handsomely. When he left at the end of the week, he promised to come back through on his way home."

Andrew had a feeling he knew how this story was going to end. She had already shared it with him and he wanted to spare her further humiliation.

"You don't have to-"

She gave him a sad smile and waved his objection away. "He came and proposed to take one of us girls with him to his home in Boston. He needed a new governess for his three children. Everyone knew I should be the one to go. I had dreamed of the wide world out there. My sister was too young and naïve.

"God answered our prayers for provision. My employer, Mr. Gardener, gave me an advance on a year's worth of wages and I knew that God was good. My family's problems weren't fixed but a disaster was abated." Joy closed her eyes. "Tell me this, Mr. Lloyd-Foxx. How do you justify what happened to me? Being sold from place to place, abused and sometimes beaten? My second master used me to entertain his best clients after the shop was closed. Was God in that? Did He make that happen?"

Andrew didn't answer right away. The truth of her words sank in and he fought the anger once again spiking through his veins. Slowly, it was replaced with something completely different. The need to protect her pulsed through him. But first, he had to wipe away her pain.

"If I may, your Christian name is Joy, correct?"

She nodded but said nothing.

"What does it mean?"

Miss Richards frowned and shrugged her shoulders.

"Do you think that God is only with you when the going is good? To be joyful, like your name suggests, is it to be happy? Or is it deeper? *But the fruit of the Spirit is love,* joy, *peace, longsuffering, gentleness, goodness, faith.*"

Miss Richards stared, nibbling her bottom lip.

"Miss Richards, why would our Lord ask this of us, if joy was dependent on our happiness? *My brethren, count it all joy when ye fall into divers temptations; Knowing this, that the trying of your faith worketh patience.*"

Miss Richards shifted.

"My hero from the bible is Joseph. I was my father's favorite, too. My brother was quiet and refined, a lot like my mother. My father and I had a love for horses in common. I can't imagine the prison Joseph found himself in was a healthy, cheerful place. Were you in a good place? Absolutely not. Did God know you were there? Yes. Did He hear your plea? I would gather He did. He brought you here. I would gladly have traded places with you." He swallowed a large lump in his throat.

Abruptly, Andrew rose to his feet.

"I hope you stay at least until the ball and the races. You are free to go, but wouldn't it be interesting to see what God has in store for you here?"

She didn't say anything, so he turned to go.

"Tomorrow is going to be a long day for you. My mother is going to primp you and turn you into a miniature version of herself." He looked over his shoulder with a bit of a grin on his face. "Sometimes I really do thank God that I was born a man."

Miss Richards' lips twitched and she gave a soft laugh.

"I suppose I'm far too tired to walk all the way to Connecticut tonight. And my feet hurt. I'll stay until the ball and watch the races."

Why did her statement send a stampede of horses galloping through his gut?

She rose and fell into step next to him, wincing now and then. He slowed his pace, coming to the conclusion that he enjoyed the company.

"If you would like – and my mother will give you a moment's peace – I could show you the stables tomorrow. It might be more to your liking than the fitting for your ball gown."

Her smile brightened. "You are correct. I would love to see the stables. And thank you for your counsel tonight."

"It was my pleasure."

"I think I'll stay out here for a little while longer."

He paused and brushed his fingers through his hair. "You won't run away?"

Her smile slowly brightened. "Not tonight."

"Very well." He gave her a bow worthy of a queen and turned toward the house. As the mansion neared, he decided that tonight had turned out far better than he had anticipated. His irritation and his anger toward his mother primarily and women in general, was gone, melted by the compassion he felt for the woman left on the lawn.

13

he stars were overwhelmingly bright as Joy lay down on the front lawn, the house looming in the background like a giant guard watching over her.

From the direction of the stable complex she heard the horses snorting. It was a very familiar scene. In the blink of an eye, she was sitting outside her family's farmhouse, looking up at the sky. Her sister was resting in the grass next to her and they were both giggling because they had stolen out of the window of their room.

Just as quick and real was the image of discovering her father under the horse, which had broken a leg and back. The agony of knowing that she couldn't help him, and the dread of waiting for the doctor to get to their house, settled on her as thick as it had on that day.

Had she truly trusted God? Had she really allowed Him to be the sovereign ruler over her life, or had she tried to dictate to Him how she wanted things to play out?

She remembered praying over her father, like the traveling evangelist they had heard at church had preached. When her father hadn't been healed, she had started thinking there was something wrong with her. The evangelist had insisted that if her heart was pure, her father would recover. He had told them that if they had faith enough, God would move a mountain. Keeping that in mind, she slowly realized that she wasn't good enough. She had thought that her faith was non-existent.

That was when she had begun to make bargains with God, with the Lord of the universe. She had thought that if she worked harder in the garden, worked harder with the horses, He would heal her father. Instead, the clients had taken their horses. They didn't want to have a girl training them, especially after her father's fall. It didn't matter that for years they had successfully produced excellent riding and driving horses. All their hard work had been erased in a split second.

After that, her life had become a constant bargaining with God. Nothing had come true. In the end, when the gentleman had come, she was almost overwhelmed when he took her with him, paying her parents for a year's salary. After a while, when she realized the situation she was in, she turned her back on God, officially, and yet deep inside hoping He was still there.

Bargaining had gotten her nowhere.

God wanted to rule her heart. It was just...

I'm not willing to pay the price.

He wanted everything.

I can't, Lord. I can't possibly give You my whole heart, when I can't be sure that nothing bad is going to happen to me.

There was no great revelation, no answer. There was only the sound of the night, the breeze that tickled her face, and the stars that twinkled above her, as though they were in on a great joke. A shooting star streaked across the sky, making Joy smile.

Was this God saying that He had her life in His hand? That even though things may not go the way she planned, nothing surprised Him?

Did Joy mean more than her own happiness?

Grass tickled the skin on her arms and hands. Reluctantly she rose, feeling like not enough had been settled. Granted, she felt more at ease, more at peace than she had been for a long time.

Back in her room, Joy slipped underneath the soft covers and fell asleep easier than she had in a long time. The last thought that crossed her mind was the scripture Master Andrew had quoted.

My brethren, count it all joy when ye fall into divers temptations; Knowing this, that the trying of your faith worketh patience.

The house was just beginning to stir when she woke early in the morning, as it was her habit. She snuggled into the soft pillow, marveling that she didn't have to get up so early to get breakfast ready for everyone. As she rose, Joy stretched leisurely, feeling very much refreshed.

In fact, she hadn't felt this refreshed since before her father's fall.

As she stood by the window, her line of sight went directly to the brick stable. A lone figure was crossing the lawn with long, purposeful strides. His dark blond hair was once again tied with a leather strap, keeping it from falling into his face, unlike last night. He had seemed... vulnerable.

Not the man who had it all together like this morning.

Sitting down on the sill, she watched as he met the first set of horses for morning exercise. He didn't just look at them, Master Andrew patted every one of them and ran his hand down their sleek bodies to make sure they were in top condition.

Watching him with the horses stirred a longing deep in the pit of her stomach.

109

It had been years since she had been up close and personal with horses. Before she thought more about it, she donned the dress she had worn the night before, twisted her hair out of the way, and secured it with a few pins. Quiet as a mouse, she stole down the stairs, where she could hear the servants scuffling about.

Once outside, she sprinted barefooted across the dew-drenched grass. Her feet felt much less sore than they had the previous day. Finding an ancient maple from which she could hide behind to watch the horses, her breath stalled.

The horses were not tall, by any means. But when they ran it was as though they were enjoying a stroll in the park. The pounding of their hooves sent vibrations through her body.

I would give anything to sit on the back of one of those horses, running as fast as the wind.

Before each set of horses ran, Master Andrew patted each and inspected their legs. After giving the riders their instructions, he sent them off. Joy instinctively rocked with the motion of the horse, caught herself, and laughed. Their run completed, the horses returned to where Master Andrew and a young man stood, talking quietly. Creeping out of her hiding place, she hoped to catch a snippet of their conversation. They were too far away.

When the last set had gone through their exercise, Master Andrew and the young man turned back up to the stable, where the horses were being cooled off and pampered. He patted a sleek neck as he made the rounds, checked a thin and delicate leg for heat. He wasn't watching from afar, as some owners might. He took an intimate role in the daily operation of the stable.

Joy found herself smiling for no apparent reason.

Before someone found her hiding behind the tree, Joy quickly returned to the house across the lawn. She had left two sets of footprints on the dew-covered grass – and yet.

Was she alone out here? She blinked rapidly, suddenly feeling that maybe she was not.

Half an hour later, Laura found her awake, sprawled out on her belly across her bed. Her nose in the Bible, her feet, bandaged and grass stained, stuck up in the air. Laura propped her hands on her hips and scowled down on Joy, a twinkle in her eyes.

"You think you don't need me anymore, do you?"

Joy flipped over and grinned. "Not at all, dear Laura. I have no idea how to beautify myself. I need your expertise if I am to be a companion to the mistress. But I have one request. Can we just leave that corset off? Not just today. No corset for me ever!"

"Miss Joy!" Laura started to sputter but was stopped by Joy's hand shooting up into the air.

"It's Joy, remember? You didn't see what happened to me last night." Her face turned red when she recalled Master Andrew cutting the corset off her. With a steak knife, no less. "Please, I don't want to be humiliated like that again."

"But did he notice you?" Laura sat down on the bed next to her, a bright, devious grin spreading over her face.

Joy snorted and shook her head. "Laura! A blind man would have noticed me!"

Laura threw her head back and laughed.

"Why are you laughing?" Joy asked, her voice laced with irritation. "It wasn't you, laying on the floor, half naked." She shuddered and tried to get the picture out of her mind. "Let's not talk about this anymore, please. No corset! Or I'm not going to the ball."

"You can be stubborn. I didn't think you had it in you. You seem so nice and sweet. Very well. We will tie the corset loosely today."

Joy stood up and shook her head violently, sending her hair tumbling down. "No!"

Laura snickered evilly. She grabbed Joy and pushed her toward the waiting tub, smelling of rose and lemon. Joy suppressed a groan.

Not again.

As she soaked, Laura fussed with her hands. When the emery board scraped across her nails, she closed her eyes and recalled the times when her father had filed down the horses hooves. It put a smile on her face and she endured the meaningless administration.

When Laura insisted on washing her hair for the fifth time with a sweet-smelling concoction, Joy dunked her head under the water – putting an end to that. To reciprocate, Laura arranged her hair particularly roughly, making Joy wince from time to time.

The result of all of the maid's hard work made Joy gape at herself in the vanity mirror.

"That's... not me," she whispered and Laura frowned at her.

Once she was downstairs in the dining room, she found that Mrs. Lloyd-Foxx was already seated at the table, reading a newspaper. Looking up at her, a pleased look appeared on her face.

"Joy, my dear. How are you feeling?" she asked. There was concern behind her voice but also something else. Joy swallowed hard.

"Much better, ma'am. And I'm so sorry about last night."

The older woman waved her concern away with a flick of a hand.

"Today, you will be learning table etiquette."

Both women stilled as Master Andrew strode into the dining room, taking his seat across from Joy. He unfolded his napkin and grinned at his mother in a sheepish, boyish manner – as if he had been caught stealing an apple from the tree.

"Good morning, Mother. Miss Richards."

His dark blond wavy hair was once again tied back with a leather strap - in perfect order - his cravat tied expertly. He made a neat and exceedingly handsome picture. Joy lowered her face and focused on sipping her tea without gagging accidentally.

"Andrew." His mother recovered from her shock quickly enough. "You are joining us this morning?"

"I overslept and missed breakfast. I thought I should remedy that while I could. Pass the jam, please, Mother."

He liberally spread his piece of bread with jam and chewed it carefully. His bright eyes carefully avoided looking directly at Joy, something she began to wonder about. He was probably still embarrassed about the incident last night. Even though, when they had talked he seemed to have forgotten about it. Perhaps seeing Joy all dolled up brought it all back.

Wonderful.

He quickly finished his egg and lifted his gaze in his mother's direction, his jaw set.

"Mother, before you continue in your exercise of turning poor Miss Richards into the newest socialite, would you allow me to take her on a tour of the stables? I know she would enjoy that more than the torture that is planned for her."

Joy cleared her throat as something tickled the back of it. She covered her mouth daintily with her napkin, as she had seen Mrs. Lloyd-Foxx do on occasion. The older woman narrowed her eyes at her son.

"If you weren't a grown man I would now put you across my knee, Andrew Francis."

He merely grinned and nodded. "I know. Sometimes being old has its benefits." His eyes flashed in mischief as his mother drew in a sharp breath.

14

*S*ettling back in his seat, Andrew made a very intense study of his scrambled eggs and sausage. If he even lifted his eyes to her briefly, he'd remember... too much. And he'd start to wonder...

For crying out loud! She's just another woman.

Out of the corner of his eye he saw that his mother watched him, her lips pursed, eyes bright. His mother was having too good a time at his expense. He could already see the cogs in her well maintained mind working and scheming, drawing conclusions that were entirely mostly false.

In his musing last night he had prayed for Miss Richards after he had retired. He couldn't sleep anyway and her story and her cry to God.... It had touched him deeply. He could see and feel the pain in her heart.

He wasn't sure if the conflict he had experienced had worked itself out.

Watching his mother chat easily with Miss Richards, he felt that resentment he carried with him for so long. At first, it had been a tiny spark, anger that his mother had introduced his brother to her companion to foster a relationship. Then he was furious at her for suggesting they survey the estates in the south as part of their wedding tour, which caused their deaths.

Women are no good for anyone. All they do is burrow into our hearts and cause our swift demise.

Knowing that his logic was flawed and admitting it were two different things.

"... but not a moment longer." His mother glowered at him over the brim of her dainty tea cup.

Andrew forced a disarming smile onto his lips, grunted a nondescript response, and focused on his food. It wouldn't do to give his mother more ammunition than she already was able to gather. That woman had a sixth sense – especially when it came to her sons.

He finally pushed his plate out of the way and nodded.

"Thank you. If you're ready, Miss Richards?"

Why had he offered to give her a tour? If his mother caught any hint of his growing attraction-

Now I've really lost my mind.

He waited for Miss Richards to rise to her feet and glanced at her from the side. She had certainly changed her appearance. She looked very... elegant.

The dress she wore today was the color of the sunset. He caught a look at her dark blue eyes and found himself lost for a second. Those deep, bottomless orbs were in such interesting contrast to her dark, almost black hair.

"I still can't wear shoes." Her cheeks turned the color of a ripe apple.

Swallowing hard, he offered his arm. Her hand wrapped around it and he was very aware of the warmth that was trapped beneath her touch. Slowly, it radiated up his arm.

"We'll make an exception in your case. Please do watch your feet, though."

That comment caused her to lift her chin.

"I used to go barefoot to the stable all the time."

"Mind the road apples, then." The skin around his eyes crinkled.

Miss Richards flattened her lips in an attempt to keep from smiling. But her eyes glimmered.

They walked toward the stable block.

"Did you enjoy the exercise session this morning?" Andrew asked, his tongue in his cheek.

Miss Richards slowed down for a flash of a second, then resumed her pace. Her cheeks once again began to glow and she nibbled on her bottom lip. Her hand around his arm tensed.

"I don't mind, Miss Richards. I merely mention it to-" *see your cheeks turn the color of my favorite apples.* Andrew cleared his throat. "To tell you that you are welcome any time."

Her gaze lifted to his. "Thank you. I would like that. I watched the exercise and it was breathtaking."

"Yes. We have a good crop of horses this year. I'm very pleased with them."

They walked through the gate, a stone arch his grandfather had constructed in the days when he was still a young and fit man. A few rocks were falling out and needed replacing.

The stable yard spread out before them. Horses had their heads out over the half doors, peering around. His grandfather had designed these stables to resemble his uncle's in England. It was divided into sections, each arranged like a horseshoe.

"My race horses are stabled here. Our carriage horses are in the stable yonder." He pointed to the left. "The breeding stallions are all in their own stable, separate from the rest of the horses. Our pregnant mares are over there."

To the left was a large barn structure, with individual runs. A stallion pranced around – tossing his mane like he was on display. When he spotted Andrew, he stopped his foal-like antics and stared in his direction. His nostrils quivered in a greeting.

A warm, comfortable rush passed through Andrew. Miss Richards seemed to have noticed and gave him a look he knew. She understood.

Clearing his throat, he pointed toward the mares and foals frolicking in the pastures beyond. When she giggled at one particularly new foal trying to keep up with the rest of the herd, he noticed another curious rush of warmth. He swallowed it down, and chose to ignore any more.

"We have ten mares presently with foals. We're waiting for five more mares to foal soon. Most of the foals will be with us for a year, then will be sold as yearlings in next years auction. I try to give my mares a breather in between raising a new family. Thus, you can see them out there among the herd." He pointed to the various pastures dotted with grazing horses.

"How many horses do you own?" Her voice was filled with a touch of awe.

"I own forty horses right now."

She gasped and pressed her hand to her lips.

"That includes foals and yearlings. I have three yearlings starting training. They are doing well. I have seven two-year-olds. Only two will be running this weekend. The majority of the horses are for the breeding part of the business."

"And are all of them descendants of the Godolphin?"

"Indeed they are."

The more questions she asked, the more he realized her knowledge when it came to horses. He found himself enjoying the tour, probably more than he should. Part of him resisted being a pawn in his mother's plans.

As they passed stall after stall, the horses greeted him with soft nickers. Some merely thrust their noses at him, expecting to be scratched.

Joy couldn't remember when she had seen anything like this place. The individual stalls were roomy as if they housed kings and not mere racehorses. Each horse had enough room to move about comfortably and was free to poke its head over the door as well as gaze through a large window on the back of each stall. Thick straw covered the ground, and there was not a speck on the dirt in the courtyards.

Each of the animals seemed to be drawn to their master, wanting his attention even if it was for a split second. Her heart beat faster when he turned back to a gray gelding, whispering something into his ear. The horse nodded, as if he understood and nibbled on an offered treat.

A silver name plate was attached to each door. Joy bent closer to take a peek at the chestnut in front of whose stall they stood .

"Simple Cure? What kind of name is that? What do you call this horse. Simple? Cure?"

"Her name is Mommy."

"Mommy?" She laughed.

"Yes, she is the oldest mare here. She has raised most of these horses and taught them what it means to be a race horse."

"That's why she's called Mommy? You racehorse people have peculiar customs."

Joy shook her head and scratched Mommy between the ears. The mare closed her eyes and leaned into Joy's touch. It was an incredible feeling to reconnect with something she loved so much and a memory flashed in her mind. Her first horse. Her father had a pony that needed training. It had been a devil, but when it left their farm, a tiny child could ride it without problems.

She loved horses.

When she turned back, Master Andrew was watching her closely, keen interest flashing in his eyes. She lowered her head, waiting for the army of spiders to crawl up her spine and across her shoulders as it usually would when a man paid her this kind of attention.

Instead, sadness penetrated her, wrapped her in a cloak. He was so far superior to her and would never accept her as an equal, only as someone to use and discard. Shame slipped under the cloak and joined sadness.

15

$\mathcal{S}$urprised at her thoughts, she took his arm, noticing in alarm that her fingers weren't all that steady. They proceeded to walk through each section of the stable complex. On the way, he stopped to introduce her to a wide-eyed young man.

"Good morning, Miss."

"You're the gentleman who came to our rescue the other night."

The young man's face turned bright red and he laughed.

"Miss Richards, this is Ben, my right-hand man. I couldn't do this without his expertise and help. He's got a touch with even the most difficult horses."

"Ah..." His cheeks became brighter and ruddier. "It's my pleasure. Laura tells me you are staying on as companion."

"You're Laura's fiancé?"

Ben opened his mouth and shut it. Master Andrew laughed and elbowed him.

"He is." Master Andrew seemed to find it amusing that his right hand man had gone mute. The groom bowed and hurried off. Then he took her elbow and steered her away. Joy forced herself not to make anything of any of this. "I have more horses to introduce you to."

He's only being nice to me, his mother's future companion.

They passed stall after stall. Master Andrew had to pause to either pet each horse, or tell her a humorous anecdote about each. Joy found herself more and more drawn in, despite her misgivings.

"And this is Ladiesman. He is running this weekend."

The chestnut poked his head out and examined Master Andrew's pockets as if expecting a treat.

"Ladiesman?"

She scratched his wide forehead and the stallion turned his intelligent eyes toward her, as if he was pondering whether she was worthy of his attention or not.

"Yes, indeed," Master Andrew replied, watching the exchange between the two of them. "And that he is."

Joy snickered when Ladiesman began to lick her hand with great fervor.

"Ah... Let's move on." Master Andrew snatched her hand away from the horse and steered her away. He gave a glance back at the horse and Joy could have sworn that she saw a flash of something in his eyes. Jealousy?

It's all in your mind, child. Someone like him most definitely would not be lacking for female companionship.

"This way, if you please." Master Andrew cleared his throat. "I want to show you the brood mares and stallions."

They walked back into a courtyard, with a large elm tree in the middle. A few of the horses were standing in the shade of the tree, grooms fussing over them. They were mares, some heavy with foal. Master Andrew introduced them as if they were his children. Pride and love lit up his expression.

"Lady Suleika is my most prized brood mare. We imported her from England last year, with great expectations. She's due to have Lad's foal soon." He scratched her withers, making her stretch her neck in pleasure.

Joy bit back a smile. He cared so much for each horse. Walking by his side made her feel a part of something special. He chatted about a storm that had destroyed the stallion's stable, forcing his father to rebuild, as if they had been friends forever.

She longed to soak it all in, like the heat that was penetrating the layers of clothing. He was so absorbed to show her his horses that he seemed to not care that she was a lowly barmaid he had rescued only a day or so before.

Why was he doing this?

Turning toward him, she searched his face as he introduced the next mare. This one was a dapple gray, with a deep forehead and gentle, kind eyes. Andrew patted her and gave her the treat from his pocket.

"Do you reward all your horses when you come around to them? Is that why they love you so much?"

"I bribe them as well as I can. They are incredible and deserve the best treatment anyone can give them. They run their hearts out for me. Why shouldn't I spoil them?" He gave her a quick smile.

The air became heavy with humidity and she felt it for the first time. He treated his horses with honor.

Something inside her shifted.

Suddenly, she wanted him to treat her the same way. She wanted him to light up at her, the same way he did when he approached each of his horses. Only more so.

Her stomach growled and, as a result, Master Andrew drew in a sharp breath. Taking the watch from his pocket, he flinched.

"Oh, dear. I've kept you much too long. My mother is going to lynch me. Before we return for me to receive my punishment, let us visit the stallions."

He took her by the arm and led her away. She was very aware of his nearness, the scent of horses and outdoors more overwhelming than the touch of cologne he wore. It twisted her gut into a knot and caused her breathing to stall.

"Andrew!" Ben's voice was sharp and everyone's head snapped around as he came flying out of the large barn.

Master Andrew stopped in his tracks, his eyes widening in surprise and annoyance.

"Ben! You know there's no running when the mares-"

"Lad's down, Andrew." Ben panted, interrupting him. "It doesn't look good. I just sent Richie to ride for the vet, but..."

Without hesitation, Master Andrew sprinted off. Joy followed, pulled as if by a force outside of herself. Ben passed her, running much faster.

As soon as she stepped inside, she stopped dead in her tracks. The stallion's stable was fancier than her family's old farmhouse. The mahogany paneling on the walls was gorgeous. Thick, varnished oak planks covered the floor. The stallions hung their heads over their stall doors, their attention riveted at an open door. A young groom sat in the thick straw, patting Lad's sleek neck soothingly. The horse lifted his head in welcome at Master Andrew. His body was lathered with sweat, as if he had run for miles and miles at a full gallop. His flanks heaved heavily.

124

"What happened?" Master Andrew's voice was husky. He slowly walked into the stall, his face hard. The groom rose and backed out.

Lad's ears twitched and his nostrils quivered, letting out a snorting whinny.

"He was fine until we checked on him a few moments ago." Ben had removed his cap and was twisting it nervously in his hands. "He didn't have any manure in his stall and we should have taken notice. It's been so crazy here with the upcom-"

Master Andrew raised his head and stopped the groom in the middle of the word with a look.

"I'm sorry, sir. I didn't spot that he was collicking."

Master Andrew's nose twitched and his eyes narrowed. His jaw muscles tensed and for a moment Joy feared he would blow up in Ben's face. After exhaling with a puff, his expression softened and he turned his attention to his horse. He squeezed the young man's shoulder on his way past him.

A sob make its way up her throat and Joy clapped her hands over her mouth.

"Old man." His eyes now filled with emotion and he blinked quickly. He ran his hand over the silky smooth coat of his neck. "What seems to be the problem?" He cradled his horse's head in his lap, smoothing the stallion's cheek and forehead with long, soothing strokes. The horse exhaled softly and closed his eyes.

"You can go, old man. You've been a faithful friend, Lad." He leaned closer toward the stallion's ear. "Thank you, my good boy. For all you have done." His voice cracked badly.

125

It seemed that this was what Lad had been waiting for. He gave another long, shuttering groan. Then the big horse lay still.

Andrew bit back the tears and swallowed hard. A sob came from behind him. Miss Richards stood in the middle of the six stall palace, her eyes thick, tears running down her cheeks. Seeing her cry was not helping him, so he turned away. He scratched his friend's neck one last time and rose.

His feet seemed stuck in thick, gooey mud as he tried to walk away. He even stumbled over the little rise on the floor of the stall door as usual.

As soon as Andrew closed his eyes, memories came flooding in, causing him to lean hard against the stall wall.

Get it together. He gritted his teeth. *He was only a horse.*

Lad had been more than that. He had been an equine friend.

I've lost too many people I care about in the last couple of years.

"I'm so sorry, Andrew."

He lifted his head sharply and stared into deep blue eyes, widening in horror. Even though he felt a heavy weight of grief, he liked the way his name slipped off her lips so easily. As he held her gaze, a funny thing happening in his stomach, her cheeks slowly turned that bright red – a becoming color on her.

"Thank you... Joy."

He hadn't thought it possible, but her cheeks reddened even further and her lips pressed firmly into a thin line. Perhaps he shouldn't have teased her like that. But it seemed the perfect opportunity and he needed a laugh.

He sank down against the wall and glanced up at her. Then he patted the spot next to him. Would she take his invitation?

Hesitantly, Miss Richards – because he needed to keep his mind from wandering to places where it shouldn't – sat down. Her skirt poofed out and the scent of roses filled the small space between them for a fraction of a second. Then the smell of hay and horses soon replaced the fragrance.

"I wish you had known him. He was a special horse." He focused on the grain in the dark wood instead of her nearness.

"Tell me about him."

"Are you certain you want to hear about a mere horse?"

"According to your own admission he was special. It would be an honor." A tiny smile pinched her cheeks.

Andrew swallowed hard. "He was an ornery one, he was."

Talking about this amazing horse in the past didn't seem right. His vision blurred.

A real man doesn't cry. Get back on that horse.

His grandfather's sharp, cold voice brought back a flood of memories and he fought the onslaught.

"He broke my arm. Twice."

"Ouch."

Sitting on the floor in the almost silent barn, the stallions unusually subdued, he opened up about the somewhat ornery, but exceptional horse.

"My father insisted I break him." Andrew flinched. "He bit my forehead. That one left a scar. The doctor had trouble holding me down when he stitched it up. I howled like a banshee." He fingered the scar with a lost look.

Miss Richards smiled. The dreariness that had settled in his heart disappeared for as long as her face was lit up. Andrew had the need to share the loss of his incredible champion. Time became of no consequence as he recalled the good, the bad, and the ugly.

"He took pleasure of dumping me at the most inopportune moment."

A soft laugh came from next to him. "I can relate to that."

She made him smile. Andrew focused on the grain of the wood flooring they were sitting on and continued until a tall, wiry man in his late forties entered. His hair was roughed and his cheeks were sunken. The clothes he wore hung off him without shape.

"Dr. Henderson. Thank you for coming."

After examining the remains of what had been an incredible athlete, the vet apologized for his tardiness and agreed that Lad had succumbed to a particularly vicious bout of colic.

"We see this in a lot of older horses. I'm sorry, Andrew. I know how much he meant to you."

The man gathered up the tools of his trade and excused himself.

Andrew hadn't forgotten about Miss Richards during this exchange. She lingered near, but not so close that she was intruding. After the vet left, the grooms hurried over and began to prepare his faithful companion to be moved to a burial plot already picked out for him. He had no desire to see this process at all.

"Allow me to escort you back to the house. My mother will be on the warpath already."

Miss Richards' eyebrows arched, giving her a very stern look.

"I believe I can find my way back. I'm not blind, you know."

128

"Yes, but my mother would tan my hide if I didn't escort you."

"We won't tell her." A mischievous grin spread over Miss Richards' face.

He found himself drawn in and could have kicked himself. What was he thinking?

I'm blaming Mother. "Very well. I have work to do before..." His voice faded and he didn't want to finish the sentence.

Miss Richards leaned forward and touched his arm. "I'm so sorry."

Andrew found himself unable to move his gaze from her. The tiniest things she did were... fascinating. He rubbed the back of his neck.

She turned to go and everything inside him screamed to stop her, to make her spend more time with him. Where was all this coming from? He didn't fawn over a woman.

"Miss Richards. Would you like to accompany me tomorrow morning to evaluate the string I'll be running for the race?" The question was out before he could do anything about it.

She paused, her face taking on a glow that was hard to miss.

"Certainly. I would be honored."

He couldn't help the grin that spread across his face. "Wonderful. After the exercise I plan on taking a hack with a few that aren't racing. Would... you be interested in riding out with me?" He needed to stop himself before he promised her more than he was willing to give.

Her beautiful blue eyes widened and swallowed him up.

"... handle your horses?"

He averted his gaze and had to wrack his brain of what she may have said. Taking a chance, he answered, "If anyone can, it's you, ma'am."

Her cheeks flushed in that appealing red and, giving a curt nod, he turned around before making another disastrous comment that would cost him much. As he approached his office, he found that his steps weren't as labored as one would expect after having watched a faithful friend take his last breath.

As she neared the manor, Joy spotted Laura coming toward her wearing a deep scowl on her face.

"You had better have a really good excuse for being late. The mistress is ready to lynch both of you. Mark my words, she'll have it in for you this afternoon."

"Lad died." Joy's quiet words made the maid stop in her tracks. Tears filled her eyes.

"Oh..." Laura sniffed and dabbed her starched apron to her eye.

Allowing her emotions to finally catch up to her, Joy leaned against her. "It was so beautiful and yet utterly sad. He waited for Andrew to arrive. And then he died."

Laura's arm tightened around her shoulders. "How awful. How is Ben?"

Joy allowed a smile. "Your fiancé?"

Laura's cheeks flushed a becoming rose color. "Yes." She giggled. "He's nice."

Chuckling, the women walked into the house. Laura came to a sudden halt.

"Did you just call him *Andrew*?"

Joy nibbled her bottom lip.

"I... er... No. Of course not. He's Master Andrew. You must have heard wrong. Being all emotional about Ben and all."

Laura fixed her eyes on Joy and, even though she told herself not to take the bait, she wanted to say something like – *I find him amazingly kind and I love the way he treats the horses.* But that would be her undoing in this household.

"Well. You being with *Master* Andrew must have been a comfort for him."

She could hear the tease in Laura's voice.

Keep walking. Don't react.

16

*T*he mistress had it in for her, no doubt. Joy spent the next few hours with endless instructions on how to properly sit at a table. It was a tedious exercise, especially when it came to learning how to make polite conversation. But it was better than anything she had done in the past two years.

"Never let your dinner partner know that you may be smarter than he thinks, which will no doubt be the case. You must play the demure, sweet woman interested in gossip or the weather."

Joy stared.

"Religion and politics are taboo."

"How about horses," she murmured under her breath.

The comment earned her a sharp look. The gaze relaxed and resembled a near amused twinkle.

"Of course, you may speak about horses. We're having a race, aren't we? But don't be more knowledgeable than your dinner partner about the subject."

Joy caught herself.

During this time of mindless instructions, Joy's thoughts went back to earlier events. Had she been right or had Andrew – *Master* Andrew – not wanted her to leave? Had he taken comfort in her presence?

Of course not. It was only her overactive imagination.

"Miss Richards!"

Her head snapped around and she found Mrs. Lloyd-Foxx had turned into something akin to a fire breathing dragon.

"Ma'am?"

"Kindly focus your attention on the present, if you please. There is much to go through to make you presentable for this weekend. It is important."

Swallowing a huge groan and exchanging a glance with Laura, whose face was a blank mask, she put on a demure face. That seemed to please her mistress well.

"Much better, Miss Richards."

More instructions on flattery and complimenting followed. By the time Mrs. Lloyd-Foxx allowed her a break in the late afternoon, Joy's head was swimming with all sorts of useless information.

Joy chose to take a walk to stretch her tight muscles and to catch a bit of air before she was tested on all she had learned today. Mrs. Lloyd-Foxx had threatened her demise if she didn't do well. Somehow, Joy didn't quite put it past her to make her life even more miserable the next day if she failed. Her stomach soured at the thought. She wanted to make her teacher proud.

Lord, please don't let me make another fool of myself as I did last night. And please, don't let me let them down.

She owed this family a huge debt of gratitude. She intended to pay them back before it was all said and done.

133

Quickly stuffing that thought away, she hid in the shade of the old maple tree just shy of the stable yard. Evening chores were beginning and she heard the whinnies of excited horses coming over the stone wall. Longing to have one more look at the beautiful creatures, she pushed away from the tree and stole to the rock wall, separating this part of the lawn.

Horses hung their heads over their half doors as stable hands hurried to prepare dinner. Already, carts filled with hay were pushed about. Buckets of water were topped off, something important, especially on a hot day like today.

This was where she belonged! She didn't belong in the ballroom, nor in the fancy house.

Her gaze traveled over the scene and she longed to pick up a pitch fork to muck a stall or two. Wouldn't Mrs. Lloyd-Foxx have a conniption if her companion tossed manure about?

Joy bit back the huge smile and allowed her eyes to move beyond the stable yard in front of her to the pastures beyond. Beneath a large chestnut tree stood a lone figure, leaning against it.

Her lips parted as a noiseless sob escaped. Master Andrew was mourning next to a freshly dug grave. Joy averted her eyes, suddenly feeling as if she were intruding on a very private moment. Before she could retreat and un-see all that she had, the lone figure turned toward her. The shade of the tree obscured his expression.

Joy backed away, unable to draw her eyes from him. He stepped beyond the shadows and lifted a hand in her direction, beckoning her.

Oh, fiddlesticks!

Giving a furtive look around to see if he was possibly summoning someone beside her, she drew up her courage and closed the distance hesitatingly.

"Miss Richards."

Feeling even more like a schoolgirl called to the teacher's desk for misbehaving, she cleared her throat. "Master Andrew. I'm sorry. I wasn't trying to intrude on-"

He held up a hand, effectively cutting off her nonsensical babbling.

"Do you know that this spot has the best view of the whole pasture? I thought he would enjoy his children and grandchildren nibbling the grass growing on the grave."

She bit her bottom lip as her vision blurred. He hadn't said it with a melancholy tone, but she sensed his loss, nonetheless.

"Not that it would matter. It's just his body that we buried. He's with the Lord now."

"Do you believe that?"

Having grown up on the farm, she had seen more than her share of death. Her beloved dog Jasper had caught rabies the year before she left and her father had asked Jonah to shoot him.

"Why not? There has to be a horse for me to ride when I get to heaven."

She couldn't help but smile. "Mm."

They stood together, silently. Joy glanced around. A tiny breeze caught a lock and brushed it across her face. She tucked it behind her ear.

"You're right. It's a beautiful spot. If I were a horse, I'd want to be buried here."

More silence filled the air until Master Andrew said quietly, "Thank you for keeping me company."

"I intruded on your solitude."

Master Andrew turned with an expression on his face she didn't understand. "No."

He shifted and glanced at the mansion, a sigh coming from his pinched lips.

"Allow me to escort you back to the house. I believe my mother would murder both of us if you don't return post haste." A tiny smile appeared.

"I can find my way. I haven't gotten lost yet and I've done it three times so far. It might challenge my mind beyond which fork to use where and when and to pretend to be as dull as a spoon when I talk to my dinner partner."

Now, Master Andrew wore a huge grin.

"'Till supper, then." He disappeared into the stable yard where she assumed he spent most of his time.

Mrs. Lloyd-Foxx decided that they'd had enough of table manners. After Joy returned to the house, she dragged her to the seamstress room. Her shoulders still ached from having to sit up straight all day long and now she'd have to stand up tall. Joy longed to lounge on the chaise on the veranda, taking in the slight breeze that had started earlier.

The three women gaped at the creation the seamstress unveiled. It had taken her less than a day to create something masterful and elegant.

Having taken bits and pieces from older dresses, this dress was a dreamy concoction of lace and puffy sleeves. Dresses with bustles were in fashion and Joy doubted she'd know how to even sit down, much less walk and dance daintily.

"I have to admit that this has been enjoyable." The seamstress examined her closely.

Giving a sigh of relief when the dinner bell sounded, Mrs. Lloyd-Foxx turned to her.

"I hope all our hard work wasn't for naught. We shall see tonight."

Feeling a wave of nausea pass over her, Joy remembered to keep her thoughts to herself. She was sure to pick the wrong fork or spill her drink on her dress.

"Shall we?"

To her utmost surprise, Mrs. Lloyd-Foxx took her arm and walked up the stairs.

"I know I've been hard on you today, Joy, but you'll see. It will be worth it in the end."

She touched Joy's cheek almost tenderly and entered her room, where her maid was waiting to dress her in her evening finest.

Laura awaited Joy upon her entry and deftly proceeded to prepare her. The dress she wore tonight was made of a fabric of midnight blue, a tone so dark that it looked close to black. But when the light touched it, the gown sparkled as if it were sprinkled with stars.

"This is too beautiful for me to wear."

Laura pressed her into the chair in front of her vanity and began to brush her hair with care. She caught the maid's hand.

"Thank you for doing this, Laura."

A smile broke free. "It's my pleasure. I'm not doing this entirely for you, Joy. Master Andrew has had a horrible day and he needs something to get his mind off his grief. I think you can do that."

Heat rose up her neck and into her cheeks. True. She felt a connection with the master of the house. They both loved horses. And that was where the affection ended. Master Andrew was a kind man. He was not interested in her beyond that.

"I don't think it's what you're making it out to be."

Laura winked and tweaked a curl she had attached so artfully to the top of her head.

"Time will tell."

Laura finally removed the bandages on her feet and carefully rolled up the stockings. The material was so soft, it didn't hurt the blisters one bit.

"Your dress requires shoes. And these are it."

The slippers Laura carefully placed on her feet were pliable.

"I have never..."

"This is fashion, Joy. In about three months we may be back to those horrid little things with the tips that squeeze your toes together."

"They feel amazingly soft," she cooed and took Laura's hands. Seconds later, the girls were floating around the room, dancing to an imaginary tune.

"I say, Miss Richards, you look astonishingly beautiful tonight. And you dance divinely, like a swan gliding in the water."

"Why, how kind of you, dear sir, whose name I have forgotten. Would you say that the races will be an excitement?" Joy batted her eyelids and both girls collapsed onto the sofa, panting and giggling.

"Out with you. And don't faint tonight." Laura shooed her out the door.

Joy gave her a look that should have rendered her unconscious.

"If you hadn't insisted on this horrible corset, there would be no fear of that." She tugged on the bodice of the dress rather immodestly and Laura gave a suppressed shriek of horror.

"Don't you be doin' that during dinner," the maid giggled.

Joy gave an evil grin in reply.

17

$\mathcal{S}$he entered the dining room and was immediately aware of the attention the two people in the room turned to her. Mrs. Lloyd-Foxx wore an expression Joy didn't quite manage to decipher, nor did she want to. Whatever the woman was thinking, it was obvious that she was pleased.

Joy walked to the offered chair and caught a glimpse of her reflection in the glass of the window. Her hair shimmered when it caught the light from the lamps. A glorious dark bay – like a thoroughbred. Joy wouldn't have recognized herself, if she hadn't been the one looking. The gown she wore was beyond beautiful. She became more and more aware of the glances thrown in her direction.

Oh my. If Hope could see me now. A princess in a gown.

A sharp twinge in her heart made her catch her breath.

Everyone's attention turned sharply to Mrs. Lloyd-Foxx, whose stomach growled. The woman's face became a mask and she busied herself with arranging her napkin daintily in her lap.

"Mother?"

Her eyes narrowed. "I know what you are going to say, Andrew. It's not proper to address bodily functions at dinner. Or any other time."

Joy bit back a grin and lifted her chin. She found her gaze caught in dark gray orbs and fought for composure. Her heart raced as if she had completed a vigorous ride.

"How was your day of torture, Miss Richards?"

Mrs. Lloyd-Foxx gasped and turned her attention to her son. "I beg your pardon?"

"Miss Richards is more at home with horses than she is with teacups and salad forks, Mother. You have to admit that your education can be overwhelming."

Despite the fact that he was right, Joy didn't know if he meant the statement as a compliment. She was more comfortable around the four legged creatures, but- She wanted him to see her as more than the farmer's daughter.

"It was educational. Who'd have thought there were so many different kinds of forks."

"Hear, hear." Master Andrew lifted his water goblet to his lips to hide a smile.

"I had a feeling that that tongue of yours would get you into trouble at some point. This is it." Mrs Lloyd-Foxx lifted her nose in the air and peered at Joy, a dangerous glint in her gray eyes.

They looked so alike, mother and son. One second they were charming as could be, the next their eyes pierced right into her heart.

"I found myself tempted momentarily to give you the evening off from the torture. But just because of that cheeky comment, I am too afraid that you will find yourself in trouble come the weekend. So, perhaps a little light reading would add to your education. Just to make certain you know exactly what to do with the many forks you will find in front of yourself at dinner."

"Oh... Th-thank you so much." A dense fog settled in her brain at the thought of having to learn more useless facts about forks. Reading was a secret pastime, one her father never appreciated her to indulge when there were horses to be taken care of. But reading about silverware...

A smile played on Mrs. Lloyd-Foxx's lips. "You are more than welcome, child."

Joy daintily touched her napkin to her lips and received a pleased nod from her task mistress.

Master Andrew was studying the tableware with great interest, as if he was trying to discern if he knew the functions of all his forks.

"I heard that Lad is gone, Andrew."

He inhaled sharply and Joy saw a brief flash of grief replace any mischief in his gaze. "Yes. It was relatively swift and I was there to say... farewell."

"I'm sorry, Andrew. I know the horse was special to you." His mother sniffed and dabbed her napkin to her eyes.

"It was amazing how the other stallions knew." Master Andrew leaned back in his seat, his gaze going soft. "Don't tell me that animals don't feel emotions."

"Yes," his mother mumbled. "How are the preparations for the race coming?"

"We are finishing up the last minute details." Master Andrew picked up his fork and stared at it. "Is this the right fork, Mother, to eat my potatoes with?"

His mother growled at him and Joy forced her lips into a flat line in an attempt to hide the grin. Once dinner was served, the conversation settled on subjects of utter boredom.

This is a rehearsal of sorts, she thought and answered a question Mrs. Lloyd-Foxx had thrown her way about the weather. Stifling a yawn,

Joy answered in a very demure, soft tone and thought she heard Master Andrew breathe out a laugh.

"Mother. What are you doing to poor Miss Richards?"

His mother's gaze fastened on him with such fierceness, Joy feared for him.

"I'm turning her into a proper lady."

"Mm."

"I think Cleopatra is going to come up as a winner, Mother," Andrew said.

He was thoroughly bored by the conversation. Miss Richards wore a glazed look on her face which disappeared immediately at the mention of the race. He had been right in telling his mother she preferred horses to the ballroom.

"Do you, dear? Well, we will bear it with humility, won't we? Andrew?"

He threw his head back and laughed loudly. "No, we will celebrate it, and thank God for allowing me to have such a wonderful horse in my stable. And then we'll breed her and make more winners. Of course, Minuteman is going to show the rest of the horses how to run like the wind, just like Sham. Nobody can touch him."

"Pride, Andrew, cometh before the fall!" his mother mumbled softly, holding up a finger.

His mouth parted in a roguish grin. "This isn't pride, Mother. It's praising God for what He's given me."

"No, dear. You have this look on your face. It's not a look of praise. It's haughtiness. Be careful, my dear son. You don't want to fall in front of your friends. They will laugh you off the track."

"Mother!"

"Andrew, I will not allow my guests to laugh at me when your precious horse comes in last. You never know what kind of a day it will have."

Andrew's head snapped back toward her, his eyes narrowing dangerously. "I know it's usual for us to talk about racehorses as though they were possessions, but I prefer to call him a *he*. Mother, he is a stallion! How would you like it if our horses talked about you behind your back and called you an *it*?"

His mother shook her head and placed her napkin in her lap. Clearly, this conversation was over. But he was just beginning. Why did his mother grate on his nerves so? Horses weren't objects. They were flesh and blood. The stallions had shown that they mourned the passing of one of their own. His mother would never understand that.

"Andrew," his mother said with a measured, calm voice. "I don't care if your horses talk about me behind my back. They are still *its* to me!"

Andrew threw his head back and laughed. Hard.

The tension that had been building behind his eyes started to fade and he laughed until tears burned in his eyes. His mother stared without emotion. When he had composed himself she rose, her gaze scalding.

The air on the veranda was cooler but the light from the torches were attracting all sorts of pests. Andrew scratched a new welt on his neck and stretched his arms into the air with a yawn. Taking a furtive glance at the clock in the other room, he found that it was nearly time to be able to bid everyone good night.

Miss Richards sat on the settee, a book on her lap. It had been quite some time since she had turned a page. Her eyes were half-closed and her chin rested on her chest.

He bit back a smile. As soon as his mother, who was softly snoring on one of the armchairs in the corner, found out that she was not reading, there would be a price to pay. He found that it was entertaining watching Miss Richards. She had fought so valiantly to stay awake.

And she looks so fetching in that dress. The way the light shines in her hair, catching some amber streaks...

Had he dozed off? He sat up straight and caught Miss Richards gaze. The woman had been startled out of sleep and wore a very charming expression. He grinned and the reaction caused a slight tremor to rise through him. Her smile was genuine and absolutely breathtaking.

Splat!

The book in her lap slipped onto the floor, startling everyone awake. His mother gave a soft snore in surprise, her eyes momentarily unfocused until Miss Richards bent forward to retrieve the book.

"*Ahem.*"

Miss Richards paused, cocking her head in question. His mother's head twitched in his direction several times. It took a while until Andrew understood. He was obligated to give her a taste of what she was in for on the weekend. No doubt, there would be a slew of men vying for her attention, hoping she'd drop something for them to pick up only so that they could prove that they were man enough.

"Allow me, Miss Richards."

He bent down and retrieved the book. While he did so, a curious thought entered his mind and he decided not to pay it any attention. As he handed her the exciting reading material – something about the history of forks – he noticed that her cheeks had lost much of their color and her eyes were darker than before.

"If you'll excuse me. It's been a long day and I believe it's time for me to retire." Her voice was soft and weary.

His mother examined her and nodded graciously. "You may, dear. Sleep well. I know this is boring and tedious, but you are doing well. The gentlemen will be charmed by you, Joy."

A sigh slipped out from Miss Richards' lips and she crossed the parlor to hug his mother. Her arms wrapped tightly around his mother's shoulders.

What would it feel like to hold her-

Andrew stopped the thought right then and there before it became like a runaway horse, taking him on all sorts of sharp turns until he inevitably would fall.

"That was quite unnecessary," his mother said stiffly. "But I thank you, all the same." She cupped the young woman's cheek tenderly.

A smile brightened Miss Richards' face. He, too, moved to his mother's side.

"Mother, good night." Andrew placed a dutiful kiss on her cheek. "I have a long day ahead of me."

He allowed Miss Richards to precede him out of the room, as a gentleman would. But a real man would take her arm and Andrew wasn't going to make that mistake. Instead, he folded his hands behind his back – to be sure they didn't accidentally brush against her.

He recalled how she had allowed him to guide her earlier. Her skin was softer...

Andrew!

They ascended the stairs.

"Will you be up to watching the horses at six tomorrow morning?"

Her cheeks looked less pale and she nodded with a gleam in her eyes. He returned the gesture and entered his room before he did something he might regret.

18

*J*oy lay awake. The night was hot and stuffy, making it difficult to drift off. Kicking the sheets off her, she sat up. The grandfather clock in the corner chimed three times.

The muscles in her stomach tensed and a sick feeling rose. What if she fell off the horse tomorrow? Butterflies flitted about in her gut and she rolled over onto her side, trying to find a comfortable spot.

Please Lord. If You let me fall asleep I'll do whatever You want!

A soft moan escaped.

Was she bargaining with Him again? Was she pleading for things to go her way?

Yes.

Why couldn't she accept what lay ahead?

I don't know what the future holds. The thought locked fear in her heart.

The ticking of the clock gave her imagination wings. In her mind, God was sitting behind a massive desk, papers piled up in front of him. His fingers drummed patiently on the surface, perhaps gopherwood, as he waited for her to make up her mind to stop trying to manipulate Him.

She blinked and focused on the sticky heat surrounding her. This was reality. It was now or never. Swallowing hard and, feeling the weight of what she was about to do press on her, Joy slipped off the bed and onto her knees. Tension caused her eyes to tear up, or was it more?

Oh Lord. Thick tears splattered onto the crisp sheets. *I have been deceiving myself that I can be in control. I'm tired of fighting against You. I don't know if I can accept what happens to me, but I know that You are in charge. I choose to trust You. I may need reminders now and then. Somehow I can count on that. In Your name, Jesus, I choose to trust.*

As she tried to come to grips with where her journey had taken her – to her knees – her eyelids weighed a ton. It took more strength than she had to keep her eyes open. She let them slide shut, welcoming sleep.

Muscles trembled as they approached the large pile of brush. Joy shortened up her reins and urged the horse forward. They sailed over the sticks and-

"Joy."

A soft voice invaded her jump.

"Time to get up."

When it dawned on her that she might only be dreaming, Joy sat up even before her eyes were fully functioning. The room was a blur of vague colors and the person giving her another tender nudge was equally so.

"Laura?"

As her eyes focused, the scene became more clear – as did the person in front of her. She pushed her feet out from under the sheets in a flash.

"I overslept, didn't I?" A stampede of galloping horses was let loose in her stomach. "I knew this was going to happen. Where is my dress? What

149

have you done with that thing I came in? I need boots. I should never have burned those old ones..."

A snicker came from the maid.

"Why are you standing there, grinning? I knew I'd oversleep!"

Her eyes focused on the clock and she let out a breath.

"I may not be as late as I feared."

Laura now patted her head patiently. "All is well. Master Andrew hasn't stopped snoring yet." The maid winked at her. "Plenty of time to make you look beautiful."

Joy batted at a strand of knotted hair. "Why? I'm going riding. All I need is riding attire."

"And a hat, gloves, a form fitting jacket. A riding suit that will make him pay more attention to you than the horses."

Joy's face went blank. "It is far too early in the morning to speak in riddles or in suggestions of things that aren't."

"Ha!"

Laura held up a dark navy suit.

A thought wormed its way through Joy's mind. "Are you suggesting I ride in a dress? As in, side-saddle?" She could, but it would put a damper on her enjoyment of the ride.

Laura clicked her tongue softly to the roof of her mouth. "Sad, silly little Miss Joy. Have we never seen a split skirt?"

Joy cocked her head and nailed her with a dark look. "It's too early for this and I'm famished. Don't tease me."

"Aww..."

Laura tugged her to get her to stand up, then she patiently guided her toward the sofa, where a small tray of food had been placed on the delicate coffee table. Joy let out a squeal and dove at her.

"You brilliant woman, you. I'll take back every dark thought I've harbored about you."

Laura was enveloped in Joy's arms. "I forgive you. You may name your firstborn after me," she teased, her voice muffled by the nightgown.

"I'll do that. If I ever have children."

Joy devoured the food and cold tea, while Laura fussed over her to fit her into the tight suit.

"I think this is meant for a child."

Joy sucked in her breath and Laura grunted. She fastened the buttons on the jacket and Joy feared that if she breathed out, the buttons would pop off.

An evil grin crossed Laura's face.

"Per-fect."

"You're trying to kill me," Joy wheezed. "I know it. I won't be able to move in this."

Laura backed up and tapped her finger to her nose. "You look lovely."

Joy's cheeks turned red from the lack of oxygen. "I know what you're doing. You want me to pass out again and kill myself in the process."

"Not the killing part exactly."

Joy tried to cross her arms over her chest, finding it difficult.

Laura didn't say another word but set to work on pinning her hair up while Joy stewed.

"You are pure evil," Joy growled when they were done.

"What happened to naming your firstborn after me?"

"That was before you tried to kill me."

Laura pinned the hat on top of her elaborate up-do. Then, she backed up. "Mm-mm. Spectacular."

Warmth rushed through Joy and a twinge of anticipation rumbled around inside.

"What if I really do fall off?" she whispered.

Laura patted her arm. "You'll look great doing it. Try not to get too much mud on the suit."

The maid fled the room before Joy could pick up anything to throw at her.

Andrew rested on the sofa in the hall right outside her door, his booted feet propped on top of the banister. His eyes were closed. He had struggled to get a few hours of sleep last night. He blamed the heat but knew full well the real reason behind his sleepless night.

A bedroom door opened and he turned, expecting to see one of his servants. Instead, his eyes fairly bugged out and he had to remind himself to take another breath. A vision stood in front of him.

"Good morning." She spoke.

He cleared his head and stumbled to his feet. He took a bow.

"Miss Richards."

Her cheeks were flushed. He wasn't sure if it was from the early morning heat or...

He offered his arm gallantly, knowing that he needed to do this. He had to touch her, even if it was only a gesture.

Her hand rested on his arm, warmth spreading throughout. What was happening to him? He had vowed, after his mother had manipulated his brother into marriage, that he'd never, ever succumb to love or the thought of allowing another person a glimpse of his heart. He realized, because he was a reasonably intelligent man, that he was in danger of losing his heart.

"I believe you shall enjoy the morning exercises, Miss Richards. And I have picked just the right horse for you to ride. Perhaps this will help you tolerate my mother's instructions."

"I'm looking forward to it."

Her voice was soft, yet a little sleepy. It also held an anticipation.

"I hope you'll enjoy riding the horse I picked out for you."

Now her gaze met his and he found himself doing exactly what he hadn't wanted to. A weightless feeling, followed by an almost overwhelming recklessness, swept over him. He was falling.

The grass was covered with dew yet he felt none of the wetness settle into his boots. All he knew was that he was walking, her petite hand on his arm. Andrew would have given her anything she asked for in this moment.

The stable yard was busy so early in the morning. Grooms were readying the string of horses, others were feeding them, or brushing them. Some horses, mostly the mares and foals, were in the middle of being turned out. Excited squeals sounded all around.

"Mornin', sir."

Ben appeared with his horse, a prancing and head tossing Minuteman.

"Ben. He looks like he is in rare form." Andrew grinned and ran a hand down the thoroughbred's side and legs. The stallion almost kicked at him and Andrew nudged him. The horse stood still for a split second then he proceeded to prance around him again.

Andrew examined the other three horses that were to run with him, just to make this an interesting time for the horse. They stomped excitedly, quivering in anticipation.

"Very well. Take them out."

The riders mounted and walked toward the track. Now that the horses knew what was coming, they were more subdued and docile.

Andrew offered his arm to Miss Richards and couldn't help the bright smile that settled on his lips when she took it. He didn't want this time to end.

"When you're ready."

The horses must have heard his instruction because they all took off at the same time.

19

*H*er stomach clenched as nerves tensed the muscles. Never in her life had she seen such horses of beauty and stamina. They shot past her at high speed. Her hand tensed around the arm and she leaned forward in order not to lose sight of the horses.

A soft chuckle came from beside her.

"Miss Richards. You want to ride in the race?"

She cocked her head, not understanding.

"You're rocking to the motion of the horses."

She closed her eyes for a moment, mortified.

"It'll be our little secret."

"I appreciate it." Rocking back and forth... What was she thinking?

Her attention focused on the exercise again. She wasn't impressed with Minuteman. The stallion was lingering a pace ahead of the others, seemingly going for a stroll. He didn't look like he was trying at all. It was as if he was bored with it.

Joy sucked in a surprised breath as Minuteman slowly increased in speed instead of slowing down. He flew past the others in relative ease.

"That's my boy," Master Andrew murmured under his breath as the horses slowed down and approached them.

They were all breathing heavily, their coats dark with sweat, but Minuteman tossed his head as if begging for more.

"Did you see that?" he asked.

Joy couldn't help but laugh and bounce on her toes. "That was amazing. To tell you the truth, I didn't think he had it in him."

"He'll do his father proud." Master Andrew flashed a quick smile in her direction. "He's Lad's offspring. I have high hopes for him. He is a firecracker and hard to handle, but boy – can he run!"

The riders pulled up in front of them.

"He looked strong out there today."

Minuteman's jockey's grin spread across his dirt-covered face. "He was unstoppable. Once he decided to get in the race, he plowed right along."

The youngest jockey, riding a very promising gelding, laughed.

"We weren't even part of that race."

Miss Richards beamed from one horse to the next. Andrew became even more aware of her as she shared in his elation. Everything about her drew him. How could he possibly shield himself from her?

She was even more irresistible now that her face shone in excitement. The careful up-do of her hair was coming undone, curls of silk snaking along her graceful neck. His fingers twitched to tuck them over her ears.

"Are you ready?"

Andrew swallowed and turned toward Ben. His right-hand man looked at him closely, a small grin slowly lifting his lips.

156

"By all means. Bring the next group."

Miss Richards leaned forward, her face enthralled with the exercise. She did that rocking motion again and he found himself watching her more than he was his horses. When it was over, she dabbed her handkerchief to her forehead.

"Too much for you?" Andrew teased.

She flashed a smile at him. "This is exciting. Thank you."

He nodded and forced himself to focus on the next group.

"You're going to love this," he said softly. "Watch Ladiesman,"

The horses were going at a good clip on the track and he was looking forward to what was about to happen. He couldn't wait to see her face.

"Minuteman is a professional. He knows just how much speed to give and when to give it, without exerting himself too much. He can be lazy if he feels that the competition is not there. Today, his rider let him go and he took to the challenge. Another day, he'll just hang back. But this horse is amazing. Watch what happens when his rider asks for more. It'll make your head spin."

Sure enough, as they rounded the last bend, the jockey asked the horse to produce more speed. He caught up to the other two horses, which were at least three to four horse lengths ahead within seconds. He pinned his ears as he shot past them and finished up with the others coming in way behind.

When they came back to them, Andrew patted his sweaty neck and the cheeky stallion grabbed the sleeve of his jacket, giving it a quick tug. Andrew laughed and slapped his shoulder playfully.

Ladiesman pricked his fine ears.

How'd you like that? he seemed to ask.

"Well done." Andrew nodded to the young horse and the animal snorted, as if he understood and wasn't quite satisfied with his answer.

Andrew gave his rump a good wallop and the horse squealed in indignation. He laughed and turned toward his companion. Her eyes shone with excitement. They tugged him toward her with such strength, he backed away.

This is not happening! I'm not falling for her simply because she loves horses.

"Thank you, sir."

He thought he could resist but merely the sound of her voice did something unique and unsettling to his heart. He gave a weak grunt-laugh, chiding himself.

"You watch that one. He'll pretend not to be interested, but then... He'll leave everyone behind."

The way he joked and talked with his riders and stable boys. The careful attention he gave his horses. He treated Ben like an equal. A deep longing built up inside her and she found herself wanting his attention all to herself. He made everyone feel special, including her. To have asked her to witness this and now to offer her a ride all made her want more of his time.

Lord, if only...

She caught herself.

You're doing it again.

Hadn't she come to terms with whatever God had in mind for her only last night? Hadn't she decided to stop bargaining for his help? Habits were hard to overcome.

She unclenched her hands.

Thank You, God.

It was as if by just saying those three words her world had shifted. No longer did she hang on so tightly that she could feel her fingernails cutting into the palm of her hands. The pressure that had been building inside her chest for so many years began to go away. A peace replaced it, lifting her in a manner she'd never experienced before. It went so deep, she gasped.

"Are you alright?"

Heat traveled up her neck into her cheeks. She nodded.

"Yes. That was spectacular."

Master Andrew nodded, a look of pride on his face. "Yes, indeed. Thank you for accompanying me this morning. I know many people would have preferred to stay abed. Which one is your favorite?"

She cocked her head and tucked a strand of hair that tickled her cheek back into its pin.

"Me? You're asking me?"

He glanced around. "I'd ask Ben, but I already know the answer. Perhaps you'd want me to ask the squirrels over there? Mind, they are quite experienced, so I would think twice about your answer. Yes, I'm asking you."

Her breath was a laugh and she lifted her chin. "I... eh... I think Ladiesman has a lot of potential."

"Good answer, Miss Richards." He sounded much too pleased with himself.

Joy's heart leapt and she took the arm he offered with greater confidence than ever before.

20

*ack in the stable complex, horses were being cooled down and groomed, others were being made ready for an exercise run. A tremor ran through her when a groom led two horses toward them.

"Ready?"

"Am I ever," she said slightly breathless.

"My rule is normally that if you want to ride, you have to ready your own horse." A mischievous grin spread from his lips to his eyes, lighting them up. "I didn't know if you could manage."

He nodded to the groom who handed him the horses.

"I see." She took the reins for the horse he offered her. "What am I to do with these?"

He said nothing but swung the reins over his horse's neck.

"Shall I assist you, Miss Richards?"

She pulled down the stirrups as far as she could get them.

"I've done this a time or two." She patted the pretty mare she was about to mount and paused. "You gave me Mommy?"

A soft chuckle came as he mounted the stallion. "I thought I'd give you an easy ride today."

Sure she had been insulted, Joy swung into the saddle with a few difficulties. It was different, riding in a split skirt. Too much material kept getting in her way. That and added to the fact was that she was nervous.

161

What if she really didn't have it anymore? Could she handle a horse as gentle as one called *Mommy*?

Giving a bored snort, the mare merely pawed the ground impatiently. Once settled in the saddle, Joy shortened her stirrups to a more appropriate length.

"We'll see about that," she murmured and shortened her reins.

The momentary unease was short-lived. As soon as Mommy moved off in a smooth gait, Joy's muscles responded in a well trained manner as if it hadn't been years since she had ridden. The horse moved so smooth, like her hand when she passed it through water. And they were only walking.

Andrew glanced behind him to assure himself that all was well. Mommy, his nurse maid, followed him placidly – her ears twitching front and back in a happy manner. Seeing Miss Richards in the saddle, sitting straight and tall, a look of pure joy on her face, did something curious to his insides.

It was like finding out that his birthday and Christmas fell on the same day and he was able to stuff himself with all sorts of cakes and puddings. That sick feeling, which always followed gorging on goodies wasn't there. Instead, he found that he was... full, content, happy. It tickled his tummy and made his heart beat faster, as though he had just gone for an exercise run on Minuteman.

It had been a long, long time since he had felt anywhere near this happy. He recalled that in the last six years, he'd been downright miserable compared to how he felt today.

"How are we doing?"

He moved his horse to the side so they could walk side by side. Racehorses usually took that as a sign that they would be running, racing the other horse, but he didn't think there would be an issue in this case. Mommy pricked her ears in anticipation.

Or not.

His own mount tensed as they approached an incline. Both horses knew where they were going and he shortened his reins. The orchard lay ahead. These animals knew what happened when they entered the orchard.

"How are we in picking up the pace? Think you can handle it?"

Miss Richards threw him a glance and he liked it.

A challenge. He'd take it.

Both horses picked up a trot. Turning to watch his companion for signs that she might be afraid, he found the opposite. He released the reins further, an invitation for his horse to pick up his speed.

The horses were trotting at a fast pace. Miss Richards' hair was falling out of her pins and Andrew had to focus on his horse, who seemed to take the distraction as an invitation to pick up a canter.

"This is okay, yes?"

Again that look and he decided to let the horses set the pace.

Mommy seemed to take offense that the young upstart was staying neck on neck with her. As his steed increased his speed, so did she.

Andrew decided that they needed to slow back to a more civilized speed. The full-out gallop would come later, on the beach.

Miss Richards patted her mare's neck, a look of pure joy still on her face. "I've never ridden a finer horse. She's quite competitive, too."

"That is why she is the matriarch. She keeps everyone in check."

They continued toward the coast on smoothed out dirt paths. Now and then they crossed a meadow and allowed the horses another canter or trot.

"When did you learn to ride?" she asked as they allowed the horses a breather.

Andrew gave her a sidelong glance and stilled. Her hair had escaped all its pins and hung down her back in a tousled mess. Her cheeks and eyes glowed as she turned to him and met his gaze. He had forgotten her question. Something about riding...

"My father put me on my first pony when I was five. We were here for a visit. My father had a law practice and we lived mostly in Boston. I had witnessed Lad's father run. I was quite insistent that I should ride him – immediately. My father laughed at me like never before. I didn't like it. He picked me up and pointed to a teaser pony. *When you learn to sit on that one, you are ready for the big guys.*

"I practiced on that pony until I couldn't walk anymore. It threw me so many times, I lost count. I think my mother was rather offended that my father would do that to me. They had *words*. In three months time, I sat on that pony as he carted me all the way around his pasture. The next day, my father put me on my first horse, Lad's father. I didn't stay on very long, but at the end of the day, I wore a smile."

He tipped his chin in her direction. "Just like you right now." Her smile warmed him more than the sun ever could.

She quickly turned away and focused her gaze on the path ahead. Andrew regretted his tease.

As they closed their distance to the shore, the horses became more aware. Their muscles tensed and ears pricked in anticipation of what was ahead.

"I have to warn you, Miss Richards. The horses know where we are. This is our exercise ground when we're not preparing for a race."

Mommy tossed her head, covering Miss Richards with white foam from her mouth. The young woman laughed and patted the mare's neck.

"What are we waiting for, then?" Her eyes twinkled in excitement.

"Well, I'm not sure..."

The mare surged forward, spurred on by her rider.

"Wait!"

His horse hopped forward and squealed in indignation at being left behind. *Forget it.* Andrew loosened the hold on the reins and allowed him to catch up.

The wind ripped at her hair and at her face, teasing tears from her eyes. Mommy didn't need much to get her going. The mare was stretched out, her hooves pounding the hard sand underneath.

She hadn't ridden this fast in – ever.

The mare decided that she was going to keep Master Andrew's horse behind her. Every time he tried to pass her, she sped up. By the time they reached a path that led through the dunes and to a small lighthouse, they were flying neck on neck.

"Turn!"

His voice was carried away on the rush of wind. Mommy knew where to go and sped down the path toward the water. Joy flattened herself against the horse's neck and checked if she had anything else to give. The gelding was breathing heavily next to her and she wasn't sure if she really should.

Her competitive spirit had taken over and wasn't letting go.

Mommy stretched her long neck and picked up her pace. Master Andrew gave a surprised grunt as they pulled away from them. They shot past the lighthouse with two horse lengths between them.

Joy let the mare run out, and by the contentedly flapping ears, she assumed that if she were to look the horse in the eye, she would see her wearing an extremely smug expression. As they slowed to a walk, she patted the sweaty neck.

Master Andrew pulled up beside them, looking speckled with white foam and wearing an expression Joy couldn't quite decipher. He, too, patted his heavily breathing horse, who wore an extremely mulish look on his face.

"You beat us." Panting, he wiped his face with his handkerchief.

Joy lips curled up in satisfaction. Yes, she was panting about as hard as the mare, but both were extremely satisfied. Joy's chin shot up a fraction and she stood up in the stirrup.

"I should have pulled her back and not let this develop into an all out race."

He snickered and handed her a clean handkerchief. "It was a good one. You beat us."

Heat traveled across her cheeks and she dabbed at the perspiration on her forehead. "I let myself get carried away."

"You beat us!" Master Andrew repeated, his breathing now steadier. "That hasn't happened in years!"

The horses were content to walk on the path along the shore. The waves crashed into the beach. Mommy's ears flopped happily back and forth while the gelding sulked.

"How did you know that she still had something to give to you?" A touch of awe colored his voice.

Joy laughed. "I may not ever have gone to a fancy race, but we had races in town once a month. I was ten when my father caught me with the plow horse, kicking him into a semblance of a gallop. He pulled me off and gave me my first spanking ever. He said that it wasn't right to ask something of the horse that he wasn't designed for. Then he put me on the Morgan we were training and told me to do that again. I did. He signed the horse up for the races that month, with me as the rider. Of course at ten, nobody was the wiser. We worked on a good disguise."

Master Andrew threw his head back and laughed. "How did you do?"

Joy fingered the mare's mane. "We held our own."

"Miss Richards? Tell me." He searched her face.

"We came in second. My father laughed all the way home and bought us girls some ribbons for our hair. Then he made me swear not to tell my mother. She would have been mortified." Joy smiled at the memory.

They didn't say much all the way home. Andrew found himself much too preoccupied with his own thoughts – centered around the woman next to him. She'd beaten him on his own horse. She was nothing like he was used to. She was extraordinary.

"Would you do me the decency and not mention this in front of the grooms?"

"What? That we beat you?"

Andrew groaned dramatically. Inwardly, he liked her taunt.

"Well, yes. You managed to pull ahead for a few seconds. If the grooms find out, there will be no end to their teasing." He patted the gelding, who was plodding along, ruefully.

"Why do you do that?" she whispered.

Andrew did a double take. "Do what?"

"Treat those around you as if they matter. You are wealthy. You don't have to treat people like they have opinions. You can order them around, if you want. They would still do what you asked them to because they have to. But you treat everyone as if they were your... friends. Why?"

"I suppose... I suppose I'm just following my father's example. He was a man who was much ahead of his time. He believed that people were created equal. He may have had more money than others, but it didn't give him the right to treat them without respect. When he took over the estate, the first thing he did was to set the slaves free. My grandfather was a wonderful man, but he followed tradition.

"He had slaves, which he treated well enough. My father couldn't do it. He set them free and made sure that if they wanted to stay on, they were paid. Not an exuberant amount, but enough to get by. He did that in the south too. It made him have some enemies. He taught me and my brother that our wealth didn't give us the right to abuse our position. We were to treat others the way we want to be treated. You read the scriptures. What's the golden rule?"

168

"Do unto others as you want them to do onto you." Her words were mere whispers.

"There you go." Andrew squeezed the gelding to walk next to Mommy, who turned her head towards him and snorted.

"Thank you," he said softly.

"For what?"

"You gave her a good ride. She hasn't beaten anybody in years. A thoroughbred is born to run. With her age, I've been coddling her."

They continued in silence for quite some time. The horses were no longer lathered with sweat and the air was filled with the heat of the day. The road turned back toward the stable.

Andrew wanted to stop time. Soon their ride would be over and she'd be in his mother's clutches again. And he would have no reason to seek her out again.

They rode into the busy stable complex and the grooms appeared to hold the horses. Andrew waved them off, wanting the few moments more. He dismounted and held Mommy's head while Miss Richards slipped off her horse.

She certainly was worse for the wear. Her hat had slipped half way down her head and her hair was a wild mess of dark, unruly curls. He found himself hard pressed not to reach out to touch one, only to prove to himself that it was silky soft. Instead, he backed up and focused on Mommy's forelock.

"That was an exceptional morning hack. Shall we do that again tomorrow?" The question came out before he even knew he'd speak it.

Her lips parted and her eyes widened. She looked between him and the horse.

"Yes," she whispered breathlessly. "I would be honored."

He nodded and watched her hurry down the path toward the house.

His lips slowly formed a smile when he walked toward his office. She'd said yes without hesitation.

Andrew, my boy. What are you getting us into?

After a few hours of answering the last minute entries to the race, his office door opened and Ben walked inside. He closed it carefully and sat down in the chair opposite.

"Have a good run this morning?" His green eyes shimmered with mischief.

"Har-har." Andrew drew his fingers through his long hair that had come loose from the leather string.

Ben leaned forward. "A new group of runaways arrived this morning."

All jesting was gone out of them and Andrew put down his quill. "You've seen to it that they are fed?"

Ben gave him a curious look and nodded.

"When will they move on?"

"I've had a message that the next guide will pick them up Friday night."

Andrew passed a hand over his face and pursed his lips. "Good. Are they well?"

A sad look crept onto Ben's face. "One of the men was badly beaten. I've seen to it that he is treated. A small child has a sprained ankle and needs rest."

"Should we wait, send word that they should stay?"

Ben shook his head. "No. We can't risk it. Word may get around. Everyone knows you are an abolitionist. We've had a visit from a slaver, hunting down runaways, while you were gone. Thankfully, there was nothing to see. It's becoming more and more dangerous to hide them, Andrew. That old barn is much too obvious."

Once again, the thought of how much he had and how little those slaves had invaded his mind.

"We keep on, Ben. If there is anything they need, let me know."

Ben nodded and moved to the door. When it closed, Andrew folded his hands and prayed for this new batch of slaves, hoping for freedom.

21

He is the most handsome man I've ever known. Joy's heart did a funny thump instead of a lub-dub. The way he'd stood in front of her, looking ever so forlorn, his blond hair mussed about, splatter of horse saliva on his pristine jacket.

If he felt any ill-will toward her because she'd left him behind, he hadn't shown it. Instead, he'd asked her for a repeat. She'd endure the endless torture of baths, nail treatments, hair beatifications, and hours of being measured and fitted for the perfect ballgown if it meant that tomorrow morning she would be on the back of a horse, running with the wind.

"Miss Richards. If you would kindly pay attention. It wouldn't do to have you distracted when you're in the middle of a conversation with your dinner partner."

Road apples! She'd let her mind wander again.

A knowing smile played on Mrs. Lloyd-Foxx's lips. "I take it you enjoyed your morning exercise run."

Had she seen them flying along the beach? Joy's cheeks heated at the thought of being watched.

"It was glorious. Your horses are amazing. I hope they all win."

"Laura reported that you returned in quite a state of disarray." The mistress clucked her tongue. "A lady always keeps some sort of decorum."

Joy felt the soft reprimand. "I'll remember. I tend to let the competition drive me."

Elegant eyebrows rose in a perfect arch. "Competition? I wasn't aware there was a race."

"It wasn't meant to be but it ended with both horses flying down the beach, neck on neck. And then I asked a little more of Mommy and she flew past the gelding." Joy gave a small, satisfied laugh.

Mrs. Lloyd-Foxx's eyes brightened. "Well. Well. I would venture to guess that you won?"

Joy bit her bottom lip. "Master Andrew made me swear I wouldn't breathe a word of this to anyone."

His mother laughed. "I'm sure. The teasing he'd have to endure. Well done, Joy, well done."

"It was absolutely exhilarating! Nothing on earth like it."

Mrs. Lloyd-Foxx watched her shrewdly. "Mm, yes." She smiled. "Would you mind reading to me?"

She handed Joy her cloth-covered Bible. Joy certainly didn't mind. She read the Beatitudes from Mathew. Joy was reminded of how Master Andrew followed his father's example of the golden rule.

"A penny for your thoughts."

She hadn't realized that she had stopped reading. She cleared her throat and traced the embroidered cover with her finger.

"It's hard to live like God would want us to."

"Yes. It is."

Joy nibbled her lip which earned her a look. "Have you ever tried to bargain with God?"

173

Mrs. Lloyd-Foxx leaned back in her chair. "Too many times to count, child. When my husband passed away suddenly, I made so may pacts with God. And when He took my son and his wife home – I was not in a good frame of mind. I still struggle with those events. But I've learned that when we're in difficult situations, God is in control at all times."

Joy nodded.

"I suppose that riding is a lot like learning to trust God. You can try to control the horse, but in the end you have to trust that you won't be thrown. And when and if that happens, you just get up and do it again."

Mrs. Lloyd-Foxx touched her cheek tenderly. "You and my Andrew are a lot alike."

Joy's cheeks turned the color of the curtains, which were a deep burgundy red. The older lady nodded contentedly.

"I thought so."

This was not a conversation she was willing to have.

"Ma'am, I... would rather not... I'm not sure that you ought to be thinking in this way. Your son has been more than kind to me. But that's all." A knot formed in the pit of her stomach.

Mrs. Lloyd-Foxx picked up the ladies magazine. "Mm-hm..."

Someone was sawing wood outside the window of his office. The constant noise was giving him a throbbing headache. The carpenters were busy constructing temporary stalls.

Andrew roughed his hands over his hair for the umpteenth time, resulting in it covering his face. The chart he had arranged on his desk would be the cause for him turning prematurely gray. Housing extra horses

174

for the weekend was always challenging. Changing the routine in the stable could cause some major issues with these temperamental athletes.

He needed his runners to be calm, ready to perform and a change of *modus operandi* would be sure to stir them up.

His carriage and riding horses were already put into the nearest pastures, to be available for use if his mother and her guests wanted to avail themselves of them.

That in itself could create chaos, resulting in possible injury. Andrew prayed they would be spared that. There was so much still to do to assure that the races would go off without a hitch.

He and Ben, along with every available groom and stable boy, would walk the track the night before each race. Tomorrow he would have it dragged again, because the ground was terribly hard right now, which had him concerned. Thoroughbred legs were very fragile.

Then again, Mommy had not cared about her delicate legs this morning.

Andrew stared at the chart, not seeing it.

She had left them in the dust!

Instead, the rosy cheeks and wild hair appeared in his mind. She hadn't held back. Sad thing was, he wanted more. He wanted to see those sparkling eyes again.

What did all this mean? After the disastrous dinner with the wardrobe malfunction that had almost killed her, he had gone to seek the Lord. And not five minutes later, Joy – Miss Richards – shows up and pours her heart out to God.

He liked her...

"Andrew, we have a problem out in the pasture. The horses are running around like crazy. We thought we heard some dogs earlier. Do you want us to bring them in?"

Andrew stared at Ben as though he was talking French, a language he never had the stomach to learn. When he didn't say a thing, Ben was still waiting for an answer.

"Er..."

Ben frowned. "Andrew, you want us to round them up and bring them in?"

"Who?" He lowered his head to stare at his chart as if the answer was right in front of him.

Ben's eyes narrowed. "The horses in the field!"

Andrew's head snapped up. "Of course. Bring them in. And find out if something set them to running."

Ben's face scrunched up and he shook his head.

"And why are you still standing here?" Andrew tilted his chin toward the door.

"Just making sure you want me to go, sir." A touch of sarcasm colored Ben's voice. "Are you feeling well... sir?"

"I have a lot on my mind, Benjamin."

"Is that why poor Gourmet looked so depressed after his morning run?"

Ah. It had taken all day for someone to say something. And here it was.

Andrew closed his eyes.

"Benjamin, I pay you well enough to keep the horses safe, not to ask me questions. Go and make sure they don't run themselves into the ground."

Ben chuckled as he walked out the door. "Did you get up on the wrong side of the bed this morning? Sir?"

Andrew narrowed his eyes and motioned for him to scurry away before something dangerous might befall him. Ben grinned before he exited.

His thoughts went back to this morning and he...

I need something to do.

The men were rounding up the horses and he joined them. Mares and foals were flying around the pasture, tearing up perfectly healthy grass with their pounding hooves.

Stepping into the pasture with a leadrope in hand, he concentrated on one mare bearing down on him. Her wild eyes and flaring nostrils made him concerned for her safety and that of her unborn foal.

He raised his arms slowly. "Eeeasy, girl."

She snorted and shied away. Andrew dove after her and found himself eating dirt. He found himself staring at the horse's retreating haunches. For good measure she kicked at him, squealing as she sent chunks of dirt in his direction.

Well, I deserve that.

Brushing off the dirt on his clothes, Andrew turned to the mayhem around him. Ben was trying to corner a particularly agitated horse and almost got himself kicked in the head. They had to do something before someone was injured..

He locked eyes with another mare and she stalled as she went to barrel through him.

"Whoa!" he said softly.

The mare stopped and trained her eyes on him. There was panic and terror in her normally calm brown eyes. "Easy girl!"

He held out his hand and she snorted.

"What's got you running scared, huh?"

As he lowered his head, talking softly, the terror in her eyes eased. The mare took a step toward him. It was almost like she took a deep breath and sighed. Andrew attached the rope onto her halter and started to lead her away from the others, which were being taken care of one by one.

Finally, the horses were rounded up. How was this weekend going to go, if today was any indication? After making sure the horses were all uninjured – minor scrapes on legs were taken care of immediately – he retreated to his office.

Andrew had to figure out how to keep them safe. Ben leaned against the door frame, studying him, as he bent over the chart of incoming horses.

"Ben?"

His friend cocked his head and studied him. "My question is this. What are you going to do about her?"

"*Her*?" Andrew didn't like the sound of that. Not because he hadn't been thinking about her, but because he didn't want there to be a *her.* "And here I thought you actually had an idea to ease my mind with. Have you gone soft in the head?"

Ben threw his head back and laughed. "You've gone soft on something, Andrew. You've stared at your desk all morning long, sighing and making grunting sounds."

Andrew's eyes narrowed dangerously.

"I have not. If I had, it is because I have the nightmare of trying to figure out where all these surplus horses are going to be stabled for three days!"

Ben smirked and nodded his head. He pushed his cap to the back of his head and sniffed. "It's not really that difficult. You put the mares here," he pointed to the stalls in the main barn. "Then you have the stallions on this side, move our horses, the ones not running, into the carriage house and the extra stalls they are building right now. The rest you put to pasture."

Andrew rolled his eyes. "I thought of that hours ago. And you are only now coming up with that solution? What happened out there in the pasture today?" He was becoming increasingly irritated.

"They were fine. They're horses. Quite honestly, Andrew, I don't see what the problem is."

Andrew nodded. "There is no problem. It's all in your head."

His friend watched him closely and nodded his head, a devilish grin spreading over his face. "Mm, yes. I remember you were very encouraging when I met Laura. I'm just trying to repay your kindness."

"I don't even know what you are talking about."

"Just use your brilliant mind." Ben whistled as he walked back toward the horses.

22

*L*aura was in her element, tugging on Joy's new dress here, straightening a fold there. The maid's demeanor was serious, more so than she had ever been. A shiver passed up Joy's spine and across her shoulders.

"How do I look?" she asked wearily.

"You look... amazing."

"I'm afraid," she breathed. "What if I make a faux pas during dinner? What if I faint dead away again?" She shuddered.

Laura grinned evilly. "Then Master Andrew will come to your rescue, like the handsome prince he is."

She gave her a dark look.

Tonight was her dress rehearsal. Some of the family's guests had arrived early and would join them for dinner. The tension in her shoulders and gut grew as Laura opened the door and curtseyed.

"Off you go, dear. Have a nice time."

Joy felt utterly naked. It had nothing to do with the fact that the dress showed off too much skin. What would the guests think of her? Why did she even care?

Of all the voices drifting up the stairs, she could identify one for sure and it filled her with comfort, giving her the courage to take another step. Soon she was in the hall.

The guests were gathered in the parlor.

I can do this.

A tingle of laughter so pure drifted through the open door and filled her with a strange tangle of emotion. Her heart beat faster, her stomach clenched.

"Oh, Andrew. You are so funny."

Whoever had spoken had the voice of an angel. And it caused her gut to become a tight ball of nerves. When she finally managed to step through the door, all eyes in the room fastened on her.

I'm going to faint.

Her vision blurred. A soft, warm hand covered hers and snapped her back to the present. Mrs. Lloyd-Foxx's gaze was kind, encouraging. She seemed exceedingly pleased with herself.

"Oh, there you are, dear. May I introduce our guest, Miss Joy Richards from Connecticut. She is considering the position of companion. It is time for me to engage another."

"Especially since all your companions seem to find themselves married within the first year."

The tall man, impeccably dressed, peered down his nose at Joy. She felt inadequate and swallowed past the lump in her throat.

Mrs. Lloyd-Foxx touched her shoulder lightly. "I can't help that my sons have good taste." She gave a shrewd smile.

"Mother." The soft growl came from the figure standing next to the angel with the soft, lyrical voice.

She'd felt deficient before but now, Joy knew she would never measure up to any of the society women. The thought Mrs. Lloyd-Foxx had somehow managed to force into her mind that she would find the right man at this ball disappeared into thin air.

The woman's dress accentuated *all* her curves – and there were plenty. Amber strands shimmered in her brown hair, which had been expertly curled and formed delightful ringlets around her exquisite oval-shaped face. Bright red, full lips formed a demure smile as the cornflower blue eyes examined every inch of Joy. It seemed that she found her beneath her and the young woman turned to Master Andrew, who stood by her side as if he were her guard.

Joy swallowed a wave of something she'd felt so often in the past. But why? She was at the mercy of a kind man and his mother. He had never made any advances toward her in the few days that they had known each other. Her gaze slipped to the couple and the flame of gut-churning, red-hot jealousy grew into a roaring fire.

Why was she feeling this strong reaction to seeing him with another woman?

This isn't right. I shouldn't feel like this.

"Good evening, Miss Richards."

Master Andrew had somehow managed to extract himself from his partner and turned to her. The involuntary reaction was for her heart to skip a beat. Would he offer her his arm as he had earlier in the day?

Oh, what has gotten into me?

"Master Andrew."

He bowed his head, his hands clasped firmly behind his back. "I take it that you have recovered from the morning excitement?"

Joy found herself utterly fascinated. His steely eyes drew her attention. She hadn't noticed the tiny specs of blue and golden amid the gray.

"It *was* a wonderful time. I loved it. Thank you again."

His full lips curled into a smile. "I hope you'll be ready tomorrow morning. I think you are ready for a more challenging mount."

Her heart gave a delighted thump. Not only was he was publicly declaring that he wanted her to accompany him again, he had complimented her riding ability. Her smile spread over her face and she felt her cheeks warm.

"I look forward to it."

His attention was snagged by the touch of his companion's hand on his arm. He cleared his throat as she claimed his attention.

"May I introduce Miss Henrietta Billings and her father, Mr. Frank Billings. They are our guests for the weekend." He inclined his head toward the two.

Miss Henrietta Billings inclined her head regally. Joy bit back the urge to undo some of those fat curls, just because-

This is all wrong. Master Andrew and I shared a few moments when his horse passed, had an exciting adventure this morning. He's obligated to make a good match. She's an excellent choice. I'm a farmer's daughter, that's all.

"Andrew, my dear." Henrietta's voice was soft as honey, dripping with sweetness. She slipped her hand through his arm. "Are your beautiful horses going to win every race for me?"

The twinkle in his eyes extinguished when he gave Miss Billings his full attention. "I think not. It would be unfair to the rest of the participants."

Her adversary knew how to play the game at an expert level. She lifted her chin and gave a melodic giggle. She even managed to blush.

"And don't forget. You always dance with me at least once."

Master Andrew inclined his head.

Mrs. Lloyd-Foxx took the offered arm of the older gentleman and led the way to the dining room.

"Frank, dear. Tell us the news from Boston. I have been in the country for far too long. I am no longer aware of any social news."

Andrew stifled a yawn as he lifted his cup to his lips. Out of sheer boredom, he had consumed one glass too many of the wine the steward had brought. The room was hot and humid, something that didn't help the wooziness in his brain. Henrietta's droning voice threatened to put him to sleep.

She'd been a family friend from before he could remember. Their fathers had been partners in the law firm before his father had moved to the country permanently. They had seen much of each other, and were roughly the same age, but that was where the buck stopped.

Henrietta was terrified of horses. She loathed them and wouldn't go near them. She was nothing like Miss Richards, who had dared him to give his best this morning.

He couldn't help the sudden smile when he thought of the way she had looked after the race. His gaze traveled to her as furtively as he could possibly manage.

She looks awfully nice in that dress. Drats and chicken gizzards.

He had no business thinking of her in such a way.

"I say, Miss Richards. Are you of the West Hartford Richards? I do business with them often."

Miss Richards face fell and she lowered her fork quickly. She glanced in his mother's direction for help. None came.

"No. Miss Richards' family lives in the country," he found himself answering.

Eyes turned to him and he cleared his throat.

"Yes," she said weakly. "My father is a farmer and horse trainer."

Someone gasped softly and he could see the humiliation on her face.

"Miss Richards is an extremely good equestrienne herself," he said. He hated the way the smile disappeared from her eyes. He wanted to put it back where it belonged.

Silence stretched uncomfortably.

"Do you train racehorses like Andrew's family?"

She shook her head, her face lowered. "No. We used to train workhorses. We've had a few riding horses also."

Henrietta gave a condescending laugh. "How quaint, Andrew. A fellow rider." There was a dangerous glint in her eyes.

A moment of silence followed. Frank Billings wiped his pretentious mouth with his napkin.

"I look forward to your horses winning the races. What's the name of the one that is winning everything?" he asked in a nasally, bored tone.

"*His* name is Minuteman, by our stud Lad. And I do have high hopes for him. He is fast and he has had a great time this summer. This has been his year."

"Well, I do hope you do well, my boy. It would be nice to see him win. Your mother speaks of nothing else in her letters." Frank's hand rested on his mother's shoulder.

Andrew raised his eyebrows and glanced at his mother, who was busying herself with arranging her skirt. Her cheeks had turned a pretty pink.

"Frank."

"I'm sorry, Camille. Your son should know how much interest you take in the horses."

Andrew glanced in his mother's direction. Their gaze met and he couldn't understand the look in her eyes. Was it pride? No, she didn't believe in it. He inclined his head to her.

"Good to know, Mother."

"Perhaps your equestrienne friend here can win a race or two for you." Henrietta masked her biting words with a sweet smile.

He'd had enough of this. Putting his fork – he wasn't even sure which one he'd used – next to his plate, he pushed it away from him.

"Excuse me for retiring early this evening. I have a morning run to supervise."

Chairs were shuffled back and everyone rose. Henrietta pouted.

"I'm not tired yet. Take me on a stroll in the garden. It is such a lovely evening."

He knew she was playing with him, but anything to get her from treating Miss Richards in a condescending manner.

"Of course." He offered his arm. "Good evening, everyone."

Miss Richards looked like a strong breeze could knock her over.

23

The night was humid, a promise of rain in the air. Joy leaned against the window frame and peered out over the dark lawn. Earlier, her heart had all but broken into pieces and she knew that she had failed. Master Andrew, a nice and generous man, had tried to make an embarrassing situation bearable. That was before he had gone strolling arm in arm in the moonlight with the nasty, ugly Henrietta Billings.

She didn't fit in, no matter how hard she had tried. She had been found wanting. Before, she had envisioned herself living here, being Mrs. Lloyd-Foxx's companion. After tonight's disaster and humiliation, she'd leave before the ball.

Tonight. After the household was asleep. She'd steal away into the darkness and work her way back home, where she belonged.

God...

A lone tear traveled down her cheek and she quickly wiped it away. Coming here had been a good thing. She'd begun to heal from some deep wounds and would have loved to have stayed. It just wasn't the place for her.

She'd fallen in love with the people, Laura, Mrs. Lloyd-Foxx. Her heart pinched painfully.

And the horses. Don't forget the horses.

But her real home was far away. She could cover ten miles a day and she'd be home in... It would take her nearly a month to return.

Thank You, God, for placing me here for a time. She was being thankful. Scripture advised it. *I don't know Your plan, but it's going to be wonderful. I'm not afraid.*

A tingle of fear passed through her and she pushed it out of her mind. She wasn't going to allow it to plant its roots in her heart.

Eventually, the household quieted. Lights were dimmed and Joy picked up the pair of boots Laura had given her for her morning exercise. She would wear the day dress, a very sensible – if not too warm – dress for traveling. She'd be on foot.

I can do all things through Christ who gives me strength.

She heard the soft voice telling her that the verse meant something else, but Joy concentrated on taking one step at a time. She'd walk as far as she could tonight, find a reputable farm to sleep in the hayloft, and continue on tomorrow.

As she crossed the soft grass, she turned back to the silent, dark mansion. It was a good place with good people.

What would it be like to stay? To become one of them?

She realized that she would never be that. She was and always would be a lowly farmer's daughter. She wasn't even one of the West Hartford Richards.

But Andrew and his mother, Laura and Ben have become family too.

Aware that she had thought of Master Andrew as *Andrew,* she dismissed the thought. She had fought the attack of jealousy earlier. Now she determined not to give him another thought. There could never be a *him,* where the master was concerned. His match was the curvy Henrietta, and he seemed pleased with that.

It would have been nice-

It didn't matter after tonight. She turned back to the gatehouse at the end of the property and covered the ground speedily.

"Goin' somewhere?"

Joy flinched at the gravelly voice coming from above. The figure – hidden in the branches of the same oak tree she had sought refuge under before – poked his head out through the leaves. The moon had disappeared behind thick clouds, shrouding the tree in even more mystery.

"I... I didn't... see you there," she stammered.

Master Andrew was crouched like a tiger, ready for his pounce on an innocent victim; Joy. For several labored breaths, she wished he would. Then, she realized that this was reality, not a fairytale. Though, he would make a dashing prince, truth be told.

The way he scowled down at her, looking distinctly disheveled with his shirt unbuttoned at the top. His usually neat hair looked rumpled and there was something about him that drew her like a moth to the light. She blinked herself back to reality.

"I..." Joy gritted her teeth. "I'm going home."

A soft snort sounded from above and the branches of the tree moved as he climbed down. He came to stand in front of her, wearing an expression she couldn't quite decipher. His steely eyes searched her face and she was tempted to step back from the scrutiny.

Then Joy lifted her chin.

"Without bidding us farewell?" he asked. The eyes glinted dangerously.

She gave a breathy laugh. "How fortunate that you caught me, Mr. Lloyd-Foxx. Please give your mother my undying appreciation. She'll understand that I'm needed at home."

"Mm." He rubbed his hand over his slightly rough chin. "I didn't think you'd turn tail and run." He took another step closer, putting himself into her personal space.

She should have stepped back, but she suddenly found this exchange exhilarating. There was something terrifying about it, and yet she wanted it.

"I'm not running!" She crossed her arms over her chest.

He raised his eyebrow. "Of course not. Everyone knows that people who run, don't leave in the middle of the night, under the cover of darkness."

"That's not what I'm doing."

Master Andrew cocked his head. "No? Looks to me like that's exactly what's happening."

Joy looked around for an escape. Master Andrew blocked her way.

"My question is, how are you getting home?" His eyes twinkled ever so slightly.

He's baiting me. Don't respond.

She couldn't stop herself. Joy lifted the hem of her skirt ever so slightly. Then she pointed the toe of her booted foot.

"I have boots. I'm quite capable of walking."

Andrew – she suddenly couldn't think of him as *Master* at this moment – frowned. "Have you lost any good sense I thought you had?"

191

She straightened her spine and lifted her chin. "Pardon me, sir?"

"It would take you a month to walk all the way to Hartford. You can't possibly be serious." He crossed his arms over his chest and narrowed his eyes dangerously. "Joy – Miss Richards. You are going to find yourself in worse trouble than what I rescued you from."

Her good sense, the one she had left in her room, told her that he was absolutely right. And yet, she didn't like to be told what to do by him. Not tonight, at least. He was about to ride off into the sunset with his beautiful Henrietta. And she needed to get home, where she belonged.

"I have taken care of myself before. I'm not as weak and helpless as you make me out to be."

"Ha!"

Oh, now he's done it. She turned. "Give your mother my love. And I thank you for all you've done for poor little me."

Andrew stepped away, a sneer forming on his face. "Have at it. Enjoy. I hope you brought some rain gear. They have predicted rain tonight and from the looks of it, they are probably right."

Joy shook out the hem of her skirt, stepped around him, and began to march purposefully toward her goal, some two hundred miles south-west.

"Yes. I'm sure *they* are absolutely right. I'd better hurry, then."

"Stop – Joy." His voice had suddenly changed. "Why are you really leaving?"

"I... I need to... check on my parents." She found herself somewhat breathless. His tenderness and the use of her given name had taken her completely by surprise.

His gaze caught hers and wouldn't let go. Joy's heart began to race as a batch of butterflies exploded in the pit of her stomach.

"A simple letter would suffice, you know. We have ink and parchment. You have but to ask."

Unable to find a quick enough answer, she stepped around him again. Andrew fell in step with her, walking backward.

"This is not real. And I don't belong in this fairytale," she whispered. Tears burned in her eyes so she averted her face.

Andrew stopped in mid-step. He threw his head back and barked out a laugh.

"You think we live in a make-believe world? Who are you? Cinderella?"

Joy nailed him with a blank look. Andrew placed both hands on her shoulders, stopping her from moving. His eyes never wavered from hers. He pointed to the house.

"This is not some pretty fiction. I believe that God puts people exactly where they are supposed to be."

She shook his hands off. "That's all fine and dandy, but I don't belong among your highly bred guests, your three forks, and your fancy clothes. I belong on the farm."

He rolled his eyes. "Mm, and people accuse us of being snobs. You are more snobby than anyone I've encountered. Just because you were born on a farm, you think you have to die on the farm? Whatever happened to being created equal? How about allowing God to lead?"

"You... you don't understand. I have to go." She curtseyed and passed him.

Andrew stepped away, bowing. He watched her disappear into the darkness and turned toward the house. This wasn't right. He glanced over his shoulder to see if she had changed her mind.

Stubborn woman! So like one to mess with my head.

She was twisting his guts and heart until they were in a tight knot. Right now, all he wanted to do was to fling her over his shoulder and drag her back to the house. Instead, he let her walk away.

His steps faltered.

He couldn't let her go. Tonight of all nights, when the hidden slaves were moving on. What if she stumbled upon them and-

A thick drop of rain splattered on his nose.

This should stop her.

He waited and listened as the rain increased in intensity. No footsteps approached. She wasn't coming back merely because she didn't want to get wet.

Pigheaded... Obstinate... Tenacious... Courageous...

He scratched his head and drew a hand over his soaked face. Then he turned toward the stable. If she didn't know what was right for her, someone had to look after her.

After their surprising run-in, he wasn't going to let her go. He felt God forcing him in one direction. Usually, this wasn't a good feeling. But tonight, he found himself wanting to take that path, to explore where it took him.

Andrew unlatched Mommy's stall and slipped on the bridle. The mare blinked sleepily.

"Let's go and bring that stubborn woman back home. We'll make her see that she belongs here. With us."

194

He swung onto her sleek back and urged her out onto the road.

24

*T*he rain, which came all too soon, was chilly for a summer night. It soaked her within minutes. Her clothes hung on her, dragging her down. Joy splashed through yet another puddle and longed to be back in her room, nestled in her soft feather bed. She shook her head, sending droplets of water in every direction.

It was not her room and she didn't belong.

She stopped splashing through the mud and lifted her head.

Was someone following her? She could have sworn she heard hoof beats. And there were mysterious cracks and sounds in the dense forest on either side of the road which gave her goosebumps. Nobody in their right mind would be out on a night like tonight. She took a shuddering breath.

What does that make me?

Tears mixed with the rain.

She tripped on the dragging hem and fell head-first into the mud. She *was* out of her mind. She should have taken the olive branch Andrew extended.

But no.

She had to be bullheaded and see this through, even though it was a huge mistake.

Besides, why did he care?

The way he looked at me when he asked me why I was leaving... He cared more than she imagined. Joy curled into a tiny ball and sobbed.

"Would you be willing to return to the house now?"

With a yelp, she bolted upright. Rain obscured her vision momentarily, but when it cleared she recognized the horse. Mommy looked downright miserable, water dripping from her drooping ears. Andrew was just as waterlogged as the horse. He shook his head and dismounted, mud splashing on his soaked breeches.

"Please," he said softly and reached out to take her hand to help her stand.

Joy took it and something deep inside her slipped into place.

"Thank you." Andrew lifted her into his arms as though she were a mere sack of potatoes. "I was beginning to feel soggy."

He threw her onto Mommy's back and jumped up behind her. Joy swallowed and swallowed, trying to keep the tears from escaping. It really didn't matter. Her face was drenched from the rain, so nobody would know if she was crying. She trembled, causing Andrew to tighten his arms around her, while guiding Mommy safely around ruts.

"Cold?"

"It's like the flood out here."

A warmth began to glow inside her as she turned her head towards him.

"Have you been following me the whole time?" She asked as his breath touched her cheek.

"Most of it. I couldn't let you go off alone. Besides, it's not safe for you to be out here tonight."

The something that had righted itself in her released a deep, tremor inside her heart.

She knew what it felt like now. Andrew was right. How could she be merely happy? This feeling inside her was all encompassing and didn't come from the circumstance or from her.

God, in His mercy and grace, saw it fit to keep her safe tonight. He had sent Andrew, despite the rainy weather. Joy suddenly understood how much she meant to Him.

"Yes. I think I understand."

"No. You don't. If I tell you something, will you keep it to yourself? It's a matter of life or death."

She drew in a sharp breath. "Of course."

"I help runaway slaves escape into Canada. I have set up a safe place for them to rest until they can be ferried on."

She didn't say anything for a long time.

The mare trudged through the mud, looking completely mulish. Nobody would take her for the prized brood mare she was. Joy scratched her neck, which made her perk up.

"You will keep my secret? There is only one other person besides you who knows about this. I don't know why I told you but-"

"My lips are sealed."

Even though she was drenched to the bone, she suddenly felt as warm as on a hot summer's day. He had shared something so precious with her-

"Thank you for trusting me with it."

He gave a soft laugh. "I thought it might be prudent because you almost ran into the first group leaving the manor for a different station. You were ten feet from running across their path."

"No wonder I thought I was being watched."

By the time they reached the manor, Joy was cold again, her teeth chattering. Her hair hung in soggy strands, rain dripping off her and onto the wet horse.

Andrew slipped to the ground and helped her down. Her knees buckled when her feet touched the ground and his arms came around her. Their gaze locked for a breath before he tucked a soggy strand of hair behind her ear. He gave only a semblance of a smile before stepping away.

"Don't run away again," he said tenderly.

His fingertips grazed her cold cheek, thawing out the spot he touched.

All Joy could do was nod.

In the house, she left a trail of soggy footprints and felt guilty. A puddle gathered as she removed the soggy mess of her dress and undergarments. Laura was going to skin her alive. Then she would give her another bath.

That doesn't sound so bad right about now.

A tremor passed through her, so she decided to step closer to the dying fire in the hearth. They had lit it tonight, with the cooler weather coming in.

"Don't run away again."

Tonight had changed something for both of them. He had let her into his life more than anyone else had. It felt incredible. The thought of leaving became so much harder.

But before she could read more into it all, the door opened. Light filtered into the room. Laura stood in the doorway, her thick hair braided. The expression on her face told Joy that she had guessed right.

The skinning was about to commence.

Without a word, Laura stomped into the room, avoiding the numerous puddles.

"Are you happy now? Running away in the middle of the night like a thief. After all we've done for you..."

That one stung but good.

"I'm so sorry." Joy trembled. She stood, dripping steadily in the middle of the floor.

The maid grumbled as she wrapped Joy in a thick blanket. "... catch your death... nothing less than you deserve... hair a mess... ungrateful... soggy clothes..."

Joy touched her hand. "I'm sorry. I didn't mean to run away. After tonight, I felt like it would be for the best."

"Oh, Joy!" Laura wrapped her arms tightly around her. They stood like that for a while, heat returning to Joy's partially frozen limbs. When Laura drew away, she tweaked her cheek.

"You didn't see what I saw." She winked. "And Master Andrew threatened hell and high water if you were ill tomorrow for your morning ride."

"To-tomorrow?"

Laura shook her head. "Are you really that daft, child?"

Child? She was merely a few years older than Joy.

"You know I can't stay."

Laura made a great show of thrusting her hands on her hips.

"You're impossible!" Laura squatted down in front of her. "Do you know why I serve you?"

"It's your job."

Laura cocked her head. "My job? My job is to help in the kitchen. No. I serve you because there was something about you that touched me, reminded me of when I came to this place. I asked Master Andrew if I could help you. He had this look on his face when I asked. I've never seen it. I serve you because I love you, dear."

"B-but you don't know me." A lump the size of a carriage horse wedged itself in Joy's throat.

"I know enough of you by now. We have become quite attached to you, Joy. You're part of us. Mrs. Lloyd-Foxx does not offer just anyone the position of companion."

Joy groaned and hid her face in her hands. "I feel like such a heel. All because I had a moment of utter, nonsensical weakness."

"Let me guess. Her name is Henrietta Billings?"

She couldn't help the tiny giggle.

"She's nothing but an inflated windbag. And I mean that the way I say it. She comes and throws her weight about. She twists the poor master around her finger and makes him dance to please her. He's always drained when she leaves."

"Oh. I was under the impression they were getting married."

Laura's eyes widened. "What?"

"Well, you know..."

"What did you see, Joy? Or more importantly, what did you think you saw?"

"They took a walk." She sounded like a child caught in the apple tree, an apple in her mouth.

"They took a walk?" Laura imitated Joy's voice to the tee. She turned to fluff up the pillow and blanket.

"Would you like a warming brazier tonight, ma'am?"

Joy gaped at her. "That's it? You aren't going to explain?"

Laura shook her head. "No. I'll let you figure it out. You aren't as smart as you think you are, Joy, if you haven't figured it out yet. Come along. Six o'clock comes early around here."

"Six? I don't think..."

Laura shook her head and covered her with the thick feather quilt. Tonight it felt so good to snuggle into the softness.

"You are silly, Joy. Everyone with eyes can see what is going on."

Joy sneezed for good measure. Laura patted her head like that of a little child. She turned down the lamp and walked out. Although Joy was exhausted, sleep didn't quite come.

Deep down inside, she heard God's voice.

Don't run away again.

Things certainly had changed tonight when she had let the green monster of jealousy take control. A good thing had come out of it. She now knew him much better than she ever imagined.

As she drifted off to sleep, his soft pleading accompanied her into dreamland.

Morning came too soon. A shuffle and someone clearing his throat made Andrew open his eyes. Bruce, his amazing servant was ready with a cup of steaming coffee.

"Thank you, my friend." His voice crackled. "I need something strong today."

He sat on the edge of the bed, stretching and yawning.

Bruce regarded the mess on the floor. Wet clothes left a dank scent. "Pardon me, but I'm curious. What in the world made you go out in that pouring rain last night, sir?"

He drew his fingers through his hair, making it stand in every direction. Andrew shrugged.

"A crazy notion, Bruce. Can we just keep this whole thing to ourselves, please? I don't want my mother fussing over me because she thinks I may have caught a cold."

Bruce nodded solemnly. His father's manservant was nothing if not discreet. He always liked that about him.

Andrew took a deep sip of the hot brew. It warmed a path to his stomach. Another thought that warmed him was how he had shared his deepest secret with Joy. It had felt incredible to tell her.

He dressed and waved Bruce away as the man tried to tie his cravat.

"I don't have time for that this morning." Andrew pointed to the clock. It was about to chime six times.

"Sir!" Bruce bristled in indignation.

Andrew steadied his servant with his hand. "I'm not going to the stable to impress anyone. Well..." Andrew shook his head. "I don't need to impress anyone. It's just me, the grooms and the horses. And... Never mind!"

He gathered his hair to the back.

"Sir?"

Andrew handed him the cup. "Thank you for the coffee. It was needed this morning."

Bruce bowed deep and Andrew entered the hall. His eyes were drawn to a woman sitting casually on the bench. Any thought he had flew out of his mind.

"You're late."

Joy's dark blue eyes twinkled. Not a hair was out of place, nor a fold untucked on her riding attire. Her face was pale and exhaustion was written all over, yet she was waiting for him.

If that's not a challenge.

"We're looking a little rough around the edges this morning."

Andrew remembered the lack of cravat and his unruly hair.

"I'm too old for forays into the night during a summer flood."

She patted his arm, a sympathetic look on her face. "We'll have to make sure to take it easy on you today, then. No crazy racing. You might fall flat on your face."

"Shall we, then." His voice cracked.

How could she look so delicious at six in the morning after looking like a wet dog not even seven hours ago?

"I can see that you are no worse for wear after your late night stroll in the rain." It was a pleasure to offer his arm and an even larger delight when she took it. Once again, the result was very telling.

After the cooling rain, the temperature was more fall-like. Mist rose from the ground all around.

"We had better be on our toes today. The horses are going to be very fresh."

Joy – he couldn't think of her as *Miss Richards* after all they had been through – inhaled deeply and gave him a grin filled with mischief.

"That would be a challenge."

"Yes, especially since I chose to take Minuteman out for a ride this morning. I thought he could use a hack. I like to keep my horses fresh. Too much track time would sour them."

"I see. Why would you do that the day before a major race?" She gave a breathy laugh as her eyebrows drew together into a frown. "He could get hurt."

I knew I liked her for a reason.

Not that he'd admit it to anyone. And this was why. Her love for horses was so apparent, she oozed it with every breath.

"I can't help myself. He needs a bit of fun." He winked and watched her cheeks brighten.

They were greeted by the waiting horses, their breath coming out in white plumes against the mist. It was a breathtaking sight. Today, the horses ran lightly on the track. Andrew gave the riders strict instructions not to let them all out.

Watching her was about as much pleasure as watching his horses run. She enjoyed every minute of it. Once the last horse had run the track, he motioned her to the stable.

"We are going to get our horses ready," he said, watching for her reply.

She drew in a heavy breath but he had a feeling it wasn't because she was offended. She immediately looked around.

"Of course. Show me where everything is."

Andrew nodded and walked into the main stable, busy with the morning rush of activity. He motioned toward one stall. The chestnut was tied to the door, his ears pricked and eyes intent on what was going on around him.

"You are riding Ladiesman today."

Her eyes widened. "You want me to ride him?"

"Yes. Are you afraid?"

Joy lifted her chin and proceeded to groom the stallion with expert strokes. Andrew himself readied Minuteman.

This should be interesting.

Why was he pitting these two against each other when they had a major race to win the next day? He mentally kicked himself but enjoyed the tingle running through his body. They were about to go on a ride for their life.

The stallions would not be easy to handle this morning. Not with the slight chill in the air, nor the anticipation of the race. Both horses were fiercely competitive and he already knew that Joy was.

Once ready, Andrew swung into the saddle of a plunging Minuteman. The animal tossed his head up, the whites of his eyes showing. Next to him, Ladiesman was prancing down the wide path.

"We have to be on our toes today. We may both be walking back." He gave a short laugh and checked his mount sharply. Minuteman wanted to run.

"You could have picked a better day for this, Mr. Lloyd-Foxx. We are both half asleep."

Andrew shot her a glance laced with mirth. "Speak for yourself. I'm wide awake."

"Is that why you aren't wearing a cravat today?"

"I thought it was superfluous. And I ran out of time. Besides, we should dispense with the formalities. After last night, we should be on more personal terms, Joy."

25

*J*oy. She liked the way her name flowed from his lips. As if it was meant to. Of course, that was utter absurdity because she was nothing but a farmer's daughter and a lowly companion to his mother. Not to mention, she had done things that would probably make him turn around and run the other way as fast as he could. Good girls didn't do the things she'd been forced to do.

And in a flash, her elation of riding Ladiesman, no less, was disappearing into the mist.

"Why do you help the slaves?"

He drew in a sharp breath and glanced around, as if he were afraid that someone might overhear them.

"I suppose it's something I can do to help the evil that has plagued our great nation for so long."

Their horses walked along, both prancing slightly.

"I think it's noble."

Andrew gave her a soft smile. "No. I simply chose to use what God has given me to help those less fortunate. But let's not talk about it anymore. Tell me about your farm."

She was struggling with the stallion, who wanted to go much faster than a subdued walk.

"It's not big. We have twelve acres."

"Brothers? Sisters?" Andrew yanked Minuteman's head away from Ladiesman's neck. The older stallion was ready to take a chunk out of the chestnut.

"Sister," she panted. "She's younger than me. I... fear for her safety."

"Is there anything I can say to make you stay here?"

Oh... "I need to go."

"Can you please not run away again in the middle of the night?"

She gave him a furtive glance. "Only if we can pick up the pace."

Andrew grinned and Joy leaned against her horse's pull. Ladiesman was doing everything to make her loosen her grip on the reins, allowing him to shoot past Minuteman. She wasn't about to let him. Not with the race coming up.

Their pace increased to a fast trot. Ladiesman tossed his head and snorted in pleasure. His ears twitched back and forth in the rhythm of his stride. The leather creaked and the metal from the stirrups clinked. All the sounds were absorbed by the mist.

Soon, the horses weren't satisfied with a mere trot. They picked up a canter along the muddy road. Their legs were soon splattered with thick mud.

"Slow down." Andrew tugged hard on Minuteman's reins. "This is going to turn into an all-out race."

The stallion flattened his ears against his head and ignored him. Up ahead was the bend that led down to the shore, past the lighthouse.

"I can't stop him."

Andrew leaned back and hauled on the reins. Minuteman only slowed down for a stride, grabbed the bit between his teeth and pinned his ears.

Joy sat deep in the saddle, using her body to haul Ladiesman back. He obeyed, but only until Minuteman shot past him. Then he shook his head and pinned his ears. He hopped on his hind legs and shot off after the leading stallion. Soon, they were going all out toward the lighthouse. Her hair came free of her pins, tears ran down her cheeks. She tried to rein him in again, but was unsuccessful. Ahead, Andrew was trying to get control of Minuteman.

Once they rounded the corner both horses sped up. There was nothing left to do than to settle in and enjoy. She rose in her stirrups and leaned forward, going with the motion of the horse.

Mud from Minuteman's hind hooves splattered her face. It stung, forcing her to close her eyes.

As they passed the lighthouse, the horses slowed down naturally. They were both snorting, panting from the prolonged exertion. They finally stopped, sides heaving.

"Crazy horses." Andrew growled as he swiftly dismounted.

They both loosened their horse's girths. Both horses stood with their heads low, nostrils flaring blood red. They were coated with white foam and mud.

"They are both in finer shape than they should be." Joy ran a hand over Ladiesman's smooth, delicate leg and found no cuts or swelling.

Andrew gave a sigh as he examined Minuteman. "I had high hopes for this one tomorrow. But after the stunt he pulled today... I suppose he won't be winning anything. I should take this as a lesson not to take out my best horses the day before a race."

"I think they had a grand time." *They weren't the only ones.*

Her heart was still pounding. She was practically pulsing with excitement.

Although they were tired, both horses looked like they were mighty pleased with themselves.

"Looks like we are walking back." Andrew slipped the reins over his horse's head and began to walk toward the stable.

Everyone seemed winded and conversation was unnecessary. Joy splashed through the mud when her feet slipped, depositing her swiftly into the puddle.

Andrew's head appeared before her as he lifted her swiftly onto her feet. His hands remained at her waist.

"Are you hurt?"

She scrunched up her nose and drew a soggy sleeve over her face. She shook her head, too mortified to make a sound. Eyes filled with tears.

His lips twitched and his eyes crinkled in amusement. "You do have an extraordinary knack for getting yourself into trouble."

His hand lifted, then he returned it to his side.

"You have mud on your cheek."

Joy groaned – the only sound that would escape her lips – and hid her face behind her muddy hands, only smearing more across her cheeks.

"I say." He raised up her chin for her to look at him. "That was well done, again. You didn't fall off the horse. You merely fell when your feet were firmly planted on the ground." His lips twitched.

Joy found herself caught in his gaze. His eyes resembled that of a stormy day in the fall, one that swept all the remaining leaves off the branches and usually meant that winter was on its heels. Instead of chilling her to the bone, she found herself enveloped in warmth. Swaying closer, she caught herself.

What was she thinking? Swooning over the boss? That was going to get her nowhere quick.

Andrew let her go, suddenly aware of how near she was. He stepped away to focus back on the horses. Andrew cleared his throat.

"We should move." His voice came out more husky than anticipated.

They walked side by side, not talking. Both were too focused on their own thoughts.

"You miss your family?" Andrew asked, tired of the silence between them.

"Yes. Especially my sister."

"I was close to my brother. We would get into the worst trouble. My poor mother. She had a hard time retaining nannies to look after us. What about you and your sister?"

Seeing the hesitation, he went to assure her that his intentions were not to harm her. She spoke before he could.

"Hope is fair, soft and sweet, the exact opposite of me. She's so sweet that when she speaks, it sounds like rain trickling onto crystal. Her laughter makes you think of a summer night with fireflies lighting up the sky."

212

He paused in mid-step. "That's quite extraordinary. The way you describe her... She sounds like someone very special. I suppose I have no right to stop you from leaving. But, please, when it's time, will you let me help you? You should take Mommy when you go." He reached for her gloved hand before he could stop himself. "And don't leave without saying farewell. It would break my mother's heart... Joy."

"I will remember that... Andrew."

Her voice had a haunted quality to it and Andrew's heart slammed hard into his chest. He was transported away from the thick mist, which was beginning to clear as the sun burned through, into a field of flowers. They were walking hand in hand. As Joy's face tilted toward him, his arms slipped around her slim waist.

He blinked and returned to reality. They were still walking through the mud. Her hand was still in his and something had shifted between them. He quickly removed his hand.

After receiving a solid scolding from Laura, which trickled off her like the drops of rain on her hair, Joy joined the others for breakfast. Her mind was still on the morning's ride, the way Andrew had said her name and how his hand felt in hers. She walked as though in a daze.

The other house-guests arrived mid-morning. During a small luncheon, Mrs. Lloyd-Foxx introduced her as her companion. Heads swiveled in her direction and scrutinized her critically. Andrew was standing to the side with a small group, laughing, when she caught up with him. Clearing her throat to gain his attention, he met her on the veranda.

"I feel like I'm missing something. Everyone is staring at me."

213

Andrew's brows pinched and he brushed a hand over his face.

"Ah... yes. You see... this family has an unfortunate history with companions. They get married."

Joy smoothed down a fold in her dress. "Yes. It would be a natural occurrence."

A pained expression took hold of his handsome features. "My mother, a woman from a wealthy Boston merchant family, became my grandmother's companion, thus meeting and soon marrying my father. My grandfather married his mother's companion."

Joy's stomach lurched pleasantly, causing her lungs to become non-functioning. "I see a pattern. Your brother married one of your mother's companions."

He cocked his head in a bow. "You see what is happening?"

Her heart decided to skip around like a rock tossed over a silent pond.

"Indeed," she said. "They expect you and me... That is... unfortunate." She swallowed hard.

Andrew drew in a long, labored breath. "Yes. I would like to propose that we don't give the rumor mills any fuel."

Her knees quaked. "That would be advisable."

He gave a small smile. "Exactly. It might be advisable if we kept our activities... secret. I do look forward to our morning rides." His smile brightened.

She gave a much-practiced curtsey. "I concur. I bid you a good afternoon."

Andrew bowed deeply and as she walked away, a cloud gathered above her, turning her mood dark and brooding.

26

*L*aura giggled in excitement as she tugged at the folds of her dress. "My, my. You have grown up so much in the past few days. To think you were this scrawny, bruised girl when you arrived and now... Just look at you."

Exhaling slowly, Joy turned toward the mirror with her eyes closed. What if the person she saw in it made her different than she really was? Could she suddenly cease to be Joy, Farmer Richard's daughter, the tavern wench?

This would never be real.

What was happening in her heart, however, that was another problem all together. How could she be falling in love with someone like Andrew Lloyd-Foxx? He had two surnames, for crying out loud. He had estates, horses, money, power and prestige. She had... nothing.

As she contemplated that, she came to realize that she did have someone. God. He was with her right now, smiling down on her.

"Open your eyes, silly."

Slowly, Joy opened one, then the other and gasped softly. "Oh..."

The bell-shaped lavender dress was beautiful. The talented seamstress had added ruffles and lace in layers. The bodice was snug.

"I hope I won't faint again," she whispered as Laura curled her hair.

The maid snickered. "You wouldn't be the first or the last."

She took the curling iron, heating it in the fire and twisted the ends of her hair around the tongue. The first curl snaked down her face bouncing up and down as it was released.

"There you are," Laura said softly and stepped back an hour later.

Joy touched the bouncing curls that shaped her face. "I... I don't know who that is."

Laura lowered herself to her level. "It's still you in there, you know. Just because you are all primped and prettied doesn't mean that you stop existing. You don't have to become one of those socialites just because you put on a pretty dress and have your hair done up. Be yourself."

Joy took a deep breath and held it for a long time. When she finally released it, it came out in an explosion.

"You see what I mean?" Giggling, Laura patted her shoulder. "You look like you belong here, Joy."

Joy blushed.

Laura handed her perfectly white gloves that would reach her elbows. "Go out there, turn some heads, break some hearts." Her friend and maid winked at her.

Joy's face turned almost the same color of her dress. "I couldn't do that."

"Oh! The moment you step into that ballroom, every available male is going to fall in love with you. And the rest are going to look at you and wish they were available."

Joy swallowed and touched her bare neck. "I..." Her skin began to crawl.

Laura turned her back to her and busied herself with a small box.

"There is only one man down there who will truly be in love with you. And not because of what you look like, Joy. But because you have taken his heart. Because he knows the real you, and he is enchanted."

Laura stepped back toward her, holding a simple pink pearl necklace. She draped it around her neck.

"This isn't mine." Joy touched the smooth pearls with trembling fingers.

"No." Laura smiled at her softly. "This was Master Andrew's grandmother's. He sent it over earlier with his compliments. He wishes for you to wear it tonight."

A shiver went through her from her head to her toes. He wanted her to wear an heirloom. She wasn't worthy of this honor.

"Now go, my little butterfly. Fly away!" Laura flapped her arms dramatically and floated around the room.

Joy joined her, as best as she could in her ballgown, and soon both were floating around the room, giggling.

"Enough of this. Away with you." Laura clapped her hands.

Walking down the stairs, putting one foot in front of the other, the butterflies in her stomach awoke. Her breath, smelling fresh and minty, became raspy and labored.

At the bottom of the stairs, Joy drew in as much air as was possible. She glanced back up to see Laura watching her with a serene smile on her face.

Her plan had been to slip into the dining room unnoticed. But...

As soon as she entered, a hand touched her shoulder.

217

"Who knew that this old gown could look so spectacular on you?" Henrietta Billings gave her a honey-sweet smile, her words filled with vinegar.

She slipped her arm through Joy's as if the two were best friends, and began to direct her into the room. Tables were set up throughout, accommodating six people each.

"I believe you're sitting at our table. How fortunate. We can get to know each other." The tone was sweet, the meaning less so.

Joy had been around enough to know how to distinguish a friend from a foe. Henrietta was not a friend.

"See? And you are to sit at Andrew's left hand. How wonderful. You two must have so much to talk about after your exciting ride this morning. I heard it didn't go as planned."

Henrietta opened the fan and flapped it gracefully in front of her face as she sat down in her designated seat. Heat traveled to Joy's face. So much for keeping their friendship a secret.

"It was quite unexpected." Joy lifted the crystal goblet of water to her lips.

Henrietta gave her a somewhat sour expression and before she could say another word, Mrs. Lloyd-Foxx and Andrew entered the room.

The guests clapped enthusiastically and Andrew helped her mother to her seat. When he turned to his table, he gave a hint of a pause when he saw her, then resumed as if nothing had happened.

Henrietta wrapped both hands around his arm as soon as he sat down. "You must take me riding like you did Joy, Andrew. I insist. I would adore sitting on one of your beautiful horses."

He gave a slight nod. "I shall see to it."

218

Joy, who had been in the process of swallowing, choked ever so slightly and coughed delicately. When Henrietta gave her a smug look charged with heat, she knew.

She was being called out in a female duel. Her chest constricted and she held Henrietta's gaze. The two were locked in some sort of wordless battle, until Henrietta's eyelids fluttered and she looked away for a split second.

Oh, I won.

Then Henrietta's chin went up in the air and she narrowed her eyes. The woman hadn't capitulated yet.

"... to the marshes. It's a nice, calm ride and the horses are usually well behaved. We could go after the races, tomorrow." Andrew sounded about as excited as if he were scheduled for a tooth extraction.

Henrietta flashed Andrew a coy smile. "I would love that," she breathed and fluttered her fan.

Joy's world shrunk. The elation she had felt earlier had been snatched away.

She had made it through the four course dinner with only one small, unnoticed foible. Her dinner partner was a delightful Mr. Chase, a breeder from New York. He was approximately her father's age, with beady eyes, a receding hairline, and a pouch that told her he liked his food.

At the conclusion, Mrs. Lloyd-Foxx rose and bid everyone to enjoy the dancing soon to be commenced in the ballroom.

"You were such a charming dinner partner. May I have a dance?" Mr. Chase peered at her beseechingly.

219

There was only one person she really wanted to dance with, and he was occupied with the enemy.

"Of course. It would be my pleasure."

As if he had been granted his greatest wish, he signed her dance card.

After that, Joy found her dance card filling with alarming speed. It was flattering how many young men sought her out. After somehow stumbling her way through the first dance with Mr. Chase, who bowed politely when he led her to the side of the ballroom, she felt mortified.

How many times had she stepped on his feet?

"I believe you owe me a dance." A tall, roguishly handsome gentleman with light brown hair and dark, brooding eyes bowed in front of her. She gave her best curtsey and accepted his hand.

"Tim O'Riley, hailing from Boston." He brushed his lips over her knuckles, spreading a chill up and down her arm.

"Joy Richards. From Connecticut."

He allowed his eyes to travel up and down her. "Charmed. My horse, Prancer in the Sun, is racing tomorrow. You've heard of him?"

The music began to play and Mr. O'Riley held her firmly.

"I'm not familiar."

A smug grin spread over his face. "He's the one who's going to put the Lloyd-Foxx's Minuteman to shame."

Joy had the urge to slap the smile off his face, but felt that Mrs. Lloyd-Foxx might find her reaction too harsh and banish her forever for assaulting one of her guests.

Thankfully, the song ended before she could step on his toes too many times. And it was not for lack of trying. The man had an uncanny ability to save his feet from being trounced.

Like a leaf blown in the wind, Joy had no break in between dances. While dancing with a gentleman from New Hampshire, who was naming off the accomplishments of his horses, she spotted him.

Andrew was dancing with his mother. Instantly, Joy wished she were in his arms. He looked so utterly handsome, so sure of himself. She missed his company. She missed the way his eyes turned into a mischievous grin when he knew he was about to do something outrageous.

Would Henrietta see it the same way? Or would she scoff at him?

She would never find out because as soon as the races were over, she was on her way home.

27

With the excuse to use the retiring room, Joy found herself with a much needed reprieve. The dance floor was once again crowded, giving her a chance to escape to the outdoors.

As she passed the veranda, where several guests were lounged on the settees and chairs, Mrs. Lloyd-Foxx caught her attention and motioned her close. She separated herself from the group of her friends.

"I've been meaning to tell you, dear. You look lovely this evening. And you are quite the talk." A mischievous twinkle appeared in her eyes and faded when her gaze slipped to her neck. "Oh..."

Joy wrapped her arms around herself and waited for a tongue lashing. It never came. Instead, the expression became wistful and Mrs. Lloyd-Foxx threaded her arm through hers.

"I... It wasn't my idea," Joy whispered and touched the pears that had drawn her employer's attention.

"I know. It looks lovely on you, as if they were meant to be."

A tremor ran through Joy. Mrs. Lloyd-Foxx must have sensed it because she patted her hand.

"There are people I insist you meet, dear. Very dear friends of ours."

Once out on the lawn, where lanterns provided soft lighting and music of the cellist soothed her nerves, they approached a group of guests.

Andrew was among them. His expressions became guarded as they approached, returning to the conversation with a man roughly his own age without skipping a beat.

"And you think you can still win tomorrow?" The man next to Andrew laughed.

Andrew puffed out a breath. "No. Both horses exerted themselves beyond their capabilities today. Minuteman tried to show off. And Ladiesman called him on it."

The man laughed and clapped Andrew on the shoulder. A longing to stand next to him, to be truly part of his world gripped Joy fiercely. And she didn't fail to notice that Henrietta was nowhere in sight.

"Joy, dear." Mrs. Lloyd-Foxx motioned her toward a tall, slim woman, whose hair, piled up high with ornamental pins and combs, must have weighed a ton. She turned toward them stiffly.

"This is my dearest friend, Mrs. Campbell-Black."

Why did these people have hyphenated last names?

Joy curtseyed deeply, lowering her eyes demurely upon the woman's hard scrutiny.

"A pleasure to meet you," Joy said softly.

It was as though she had been introduced to the queen herself. The woman inclined her head.

"Are you certain you are ready for another companion, Camille? After all, they don't stay with you very long."

Mrs. Lloyd-Foxx put her arm around Joy. "I have a feeling this one is going to be with us for a while."

Mrs. Campbell-Black glanced at Joy down her long aquiline nose. "I think you are mistaken. This one is going to fly away quicker than any of the others."

Her words were like a punch to the stomach. She had spoken nothing but the truth. Joy was planning on leaving Sunday morning. But nobody knew about the decision she had to make. There were so many reasons not to stay and one of them was watching her through hooded eyes from across the way.

After introductions were made, she found herself standing next to Andrew and his friends. He bowed gallantly, taking her hand in his only to let go immediately. That miniscule touch affected Joy like she had never been before. Tendrils of warmth charged through her.

"Miss Richards," he said formally. Hearing him address her so formally had a chilling effect. "This is my very good friend Jefferson Campbell-Black and his sister Marie."

Again she curtseyed, meeting more scrutiny.

"A pleasure to meet you, Miss Richards. Andrew was explaining to us what happened on your ride this morning. You must be quite an accomplished rider to be able to stay on a horse running at high speeds."

Joy met his gaze, an unvoiced question in her own eyes. They were supposed to keep their association secret. No rumors. She didn't like the way Jeff Campbell-Black grinned at his friend as if he was aware of something Andrew wasn't.

"No, I am not as accomplished as most."

"And she's modest," Miss Campbell-Black laughed. "Wherever did you find her?"

224

Joy's eyes widened in horror. She wasn't ready to have everyone know about her sullied past.

Andrew's answer was a charming grin. "Wouldn't you like to know."

"And before you two try to get out of it, you are both to take me for a dance. Jeff is first, then Andrew." Miss Campbell-Black glanced at her dance card, then gave both of them a sweet smile.

Her brother didn't manage to bite back the groan and he was rewarded with a firm tap of her fan on his chest. Andrew bowed gallantly.

"I count the minutes."

Miss Campbell-Black grinned.

He needed a distraction from her. It was as if her mere presence prevented him from forming a simple thought or taking a full breath. The dress accented her in ways that had left him feeling out of sorts.

As he tried not to watch her too closely, he became aware of Jeff's too obvious examination. As if Joy was some piece of meat his friend was planning on devouring. That didn't go over well with him.

"Miss Richards, I'm sure there isn't much room on your dance card, but would you permit me the pleasure of a dance?" Jeff asked.

I don't think so! Andrew stood up straighter, fighting the scowl he was about to send toward his friend. He had *not* just asked her.

Joy blushed and glanced at the paper on her wrist. "It's full, but I'm sure I don't mind."

Of course she wouldn't mind a dance with him. He would charm her right out of that dress and...

225

Andrew blinked away the thoughts and shook out the image settling in his head. Before he could say anything else, Marie unknowingly came to his rescue. She swatted her brother with the fan again.

"Jeff! The dance is almost over by now."

She was exaggerating. Couples were still forming. Jeff grumbled when he took his sister's hand.

"Perhaps another time." His smile was warm and Andrew was hard pressed not to wipe it off with his fist.

Just then, Tim O'Riley bowed before Joy. He glanced at Andrew, a slick expression on his swarthy face. As Andrew had to stand by helplessly, she was swept away to the dance floor.

Tim O'Riley? Figured that Tim had snagged the prettiest girl at the ball right out from under his nose.

Andrew balled his hands into fists, then he took in a breath. What was wrong with him tonight? First he had a problem with Jeff asking Joy to dance, now he was ready to start a brawl with O'Riley.

It began to dawn on him that Joy may not be available for a dance with him. That thought turned his mood surly.

Hiding out by the punch table, he could do nothing more than to watch gentleman after gentleman claim her for a dance. It took much strength to keep himself from charging into the midst to demand a dance.

And that would start the tongues wagging in no time.

Her cheeks were flushed with exertion. Her laugh sounded weak and forced. Andrew pushed through the crowd in time to see a new dance partner approach her, bow, and take her hand. He pushed through the remainder of the guests and put a hand on the newest suitor's shoulder.

"I believe Miss Richards is in need of refreshments."

Joy released a hand to take the cup of punch he held out for her.

"Thank you, Mr. Lloyd-Foxx."

It did something to his surly mood to hear her address him in such a formal manner. He bowed, then turned toward her dance partner standing by her side.

"I'm waiting for a dance."

Andrew glowered at him. Realizing that he may have met his match, the man huffed in frustration when he walked away.

Even though he had committed a major faux pas, for which he would have to apologize later, he now saw his chance.

"May I?" he asked and extended his hand to her.

Joy took a step away. "You want to dance with me?"

"It would be my pleasure. I have waited all night, you know."

As they approached the dance floor, the conductor was announcing the next dance.

"I don't know this dance," she whispered.

Andrew inclined his head toward her. "Just follow me. I'll lead you." He held her gaze.

Her lips parted, then closed again immediately.

As soon as the music started, he felt as though he was riding down a road – fog all around. All he knew was that Joy was in his arms, swaying and moving to the music. The scent from her hair saturated his senses, the feel of her hand in his overpowering him. Nothing compared to this moment. He felt the hand of the Lord on him, directing his every step.

Thank You, Lord.

The music was quite lively and Joy winced every time she placed her foot squarely onto Andrew's.

"I'm so sorry," she whispered as she did it again.

He tried to be a gentleman but winced. "I haven't felt a thing. Wait. Was that a fly?"

Joy rolled her eyes. "Andrew!"

They danced a few more steps until she landed on his right foot with full force.

"Mmm..." he grunted.

She stopped. "Please, can we stop? I'm in need of a rest anyway. You'd be doing me a great favor."

Andrew led her toward the veranda, which was as crowded as the dance floor, with couples talking and watching the dancers.

"How about some fresh air?" he asked and heard her exhale in relief.

Compared to the heat of the house, the garden was frigid. A chill ran through her

"Are you cold?"

She couldn't shake the timbre of his low, soft voice.

"No. It's quite a temperature change. But I welcome it."

After all, how could she possibly be cold? Her hand, clasped tightly in his, felt like it was going to melt any moment now.

Silently, Andrew led them toward the edge of the lawn where marble benches stood among a blooming flower garden. Lanterns glowed, casting soft lighting on everything.

Her breath caught. She felt like Cinderella at the dance, well aware that this was all fleeting and would end at the stroke of midnight.

"Won't you please sit?"

She sank down on the bench, her dress billowing out like a cloud. She nearly burst into laughter at the thought of poking it with a needle. Would it explode? Or would the air just *poof* out as it did now.

Andrew sat stiffly next to her, his gaze kept straight ahead and his hands resting on his thighs. It felt as if they were separated by miles and miles.

"Are you enjoying the ball?"

"May I be honest?" she asked and tipped her head up toward him.

His lips twitched in the corners, that mischievous twinkle reappearing in his eyes. "Of course. After all, you know my deepest secret."

Joy nibbled on her bottom lip and hooked a curl over her ear. She froze, remembering how much time Laura had taken to get the hair just right. She pulled it back, very gently.

When she glanced back at him, Andrew was watching her very closely. His gray eyes had darkened to a charcoal.

"If I could choose, I would rather be out there on Ladiesman, galloping at full speed, getting pelted with mud from the horse in front of me."

Andrew's mouth opened. "Ah..."

Joy laughed softly. "You didn't expect that, did you?"

Andrew cleared his throat. "I suppose I should have known that you would prefer riding a horse above wearing a ballgown. Are you aware that it's nearly midnight?"

Joy chuckled. "The fairy tale?"

"Indeed. Aren't you Cinderella?"

The smile slipped off Joy's face. Her heart thumped in her chest.

"And you are?"

Andrew palmed her cheek tenderly. "Why, the prince, of course. What did you expect? Cinderella has to have her prince... Joy."

She gave a soft gasp.

His thumb brushed across the skin of her neck. Touching the string of pearls softly, he smiled. Leaning forward, he captured her lips with his, hesitantly at first then becoming more bold.

An explosion went off inside Joy's heart. The emotions that she had stored up there of all her fears, her pain, her anger, all exploded and was replaced by something so deep, she couldn't quite name it.

Abruptly, he broke the spell his kiss had cast on her.

"I'm so sorry," he whispered against her lips.

28

*J*oy's eyes few open. One moment she had been floating in the sweetness of their kiss, and now... Someone had taken a very pointy pitchfork and plunged it, hard, right into the middle of her heart. Her breath came out as an explosion. Her vision blurred.

I'm so sorry.

His whispered words bounced around in her head and she pushed herself away from him as far as she could. The air around them crackled with heat and tension. Then the swishing of a skirt announced that they weren't alone anymore.

"There you are, Andrew. I have been looking for you for some time. Remember, you owe me a dance."

Blinking away the haze, and knowing who was approaching, Joy grappled for a semblance of composure.

Henrietta stood in front of them, shooting him a glance filled with fire. Andrew's face turned a deep, ruddy red. Joy jumped up, forgetting to lift her skirt and caught the hem of her petticoat. She heard a rip and her eyes widened in horror.

Andrew pushed himself off the bench and bowed.

"Of course, Henrietta. How could I forget?"

Andrew turned toward Joy, his eyes still charcoal gray, anger now simmering underneath the thick eyelashes. He bowed stiffly.

"Miss Richards."

She suppressed a groan and caught a gleam of satisfaction in Henrietta's eyes. Andrew took Henrietta's arm to steer her toward the crowded house, leaving Joy standing by the bench, the hem of her dress hanging loosely down. She was gasping for breath, fighting to stay standing upright. The tears blinded her.

When she finally couldn't hold them in, she picked up her tattered dress and bolted toward the servants entrance at the back of the house. Tears now streamed down her face. The old, wooden stairs creaked as her feet flew across, her breath coming in sharp, painful gasps. Her chest burned, her heart... Her heart was barely functioning.

Joy burst into her room and collapsed onto her bed, hiding her face deep in the pillow. She was able to muffle the sound of her sobs and agony. It was then that she heard the chiming of the clock. She sat up among her rumpled bed sheets, counting along with the old grandfather clock. When the count reached twelve, she flung herself back into the pillow and allowed the tears to come again.

Cinderella had not gotten her prince, after all.

It seemed that time didn't stand still, even though her heart was slowly shattering inside. She had never felt such pain in her life. Joy thought before that her heart had been broken when she had been a slave. It was nothing compared to the excruciating pain she experienced now. It was a hot, searing pain that spread all over her body. She curled into a ball, covering her head with her pillow again.

If she suffocated, she welcomed death. Was this what Juliette felt when she knew her Romeo was lost to her?

Except Romeo hadn't told Juliette that he was sorry when he kissed her. She moaned, forcing the thought from her brain and finding she may as well try to move a mountain.

One moment she was floating in bliss and the next... stabbed through the heart!

"What are you doing here?" Laura entered, bringing with her fresh linen and towels. "Oh, Joy."

Joy found herself enveloped in her friend's soft arms. Laura mumbled something into her ear and started to help her to her feet.

"What happened with the hem?"

"I tripped," she whispered weakly.

"Is that why you are crying up here? Last I saw of you, you were wearing a bright grin on your face as you were dancing with yet another gentleman. Didn't I tell you that you were going to be a very popular girl tonight?"

The tears started to spill again and Laura frowned.

"What is going on with you, honey? Didn't you have a good time?"

Joy nodded her head emphatically, her curls bouncing around her face. She reached for the offered handkerchief and sniffed. She didn't have the guts to tell her friend how humiliated she had been.

"Joy, tell me. You must tell someone about what happened to make you cry like that. Only someone whose heart has been broken... Oh. What did he do?" A scowl crossed her face. "Shall I kill him?"

She blinked away the tears, the statement making her smile. But she also felt incredibly loved. God was with her, even in this. Master Andrew had every right to choose a mate more suitable for his station. She was a former barmaid and daughter of a farmer.

She didn't belong into his fancy life. Henrietta, on the other hand, did.

"It wasn't like that," she whispered.

Laura's eyebrow arched perfectly.

Haltingly, Joy told her about the many dances she'd had. Laura grinned, satisfied.

"Then Andrew, ugh Master Andrew, asked me to dance. I stepped on his feet five times in the first few seconds."

Laura giggled. "Oh. I don't need to kill him, then. Is this why you're so upset?"

Joy covered her face in her hands. "No," she wailed.

Laura removed her hands and gathered her into her arms again.

"Tell me, child. Tell me."

Being called child by her was laughable. They were merely a few years apart in age.

But it also soothed the ache in Joy's heart.

"We went outside and talked... for a bit," she sniffled. "We joked about the ball. He... he kissed me."

Laura squealed. "Then what are you crying about? I knew it."

Tears burst forth from her eyes. "And said... he was... sorry. Then he went off to dance with Miss Henrietta."

Laura stared at her, holding her hands. "He... did... *what?*" Her face had twisted into something hard, ugly and… terrifying.

Joy looked pleadingly at her friend and shook her head.

"Please don't make me say it again."

Laura jumped to her feet as if a lion was hard on her tail. "I'm gonna go down there and give him something to be sorry about!" She

234

headed to the door, her Boston accent thick. It would have been funny in any other circumstance.

Joy sat up rapidly. "No! I'm humiliated enough. Please, just let it go."

"That boy needs to learn how to treat a girl." Muttering, Laura paced back and forth. "His momma would be horrified if she knew."

"I can't face any of them, Laura. Not again. Please just keep this to yourself."

Laura sank back down on the bed and pulled Joy into her lap like a child, rocking her.

"I have half a mind to go down there and to... I don't know what I want to do, but it promises to be painful. What was he thinking? Does he think he can just treat you like that? Well, he's got another think coming. I've never heard anything like this! How dare he?" Laura stroked her hair roughly as her anger came out.

They sat quietly and soon Laura's strokes became soothing again.

"But, Joy. It's so not like him. What has come over him? I don't understand. He treats everyone with dignity and kindness. He would never..."

Joy's tears spilled anew all over Laura's crisp white apron.

"I'm not worthy of his affection."

Laura tapped her head sharply. "Never. There is more to this than we can see, Joy."

"I can't bear it any longer. I've made a fool of myself over and over again while I've been here. It's time to leave. I can't face any of them again."

"The missus is going to wonder where you are."

Joy could barely keep her eyes open. She closed them now.

235

"I will leave a note for her."

Laura continued to stroke her hair.

"Henrietta has won," Joy whispered. "She practically challenged me to a duel at the beginning of the evening. She wants Andrew. And he's better off with her. I have a feeling that she knew what had happened, and it gave her pleasure to take Andrew away from me."

"Oh, Joy." Laura sighed deeply.

Andrew had lost any pleasure in the ball. After wishing his guests a good night, he walked back outside, wandering around aimlessly.

How could I do that to her? Kissing her like she was a street girl...

He should have declared his intentions, showing her respect. Instead, he had treated her with no regard to her dignity, treating her without kindness and love.

And going off with Henrietta had nailed her coffin shut. He himself had added the first spade of dirt.

Andrew sat down on a chair, expelling a long breath. He roughed his hands over his face. Swallowing hard, he glanced up at the house, where the light was still shining in Joy's room, an arrow straight to his heart. The right thing to do would be to climb up the old lattice on which red roses trailed up the side of the house, to beg her forgiveness.

There was just one problem. He wasn't sure the rickety trellis would support his weight. Upon much closer inspection, he confirmed his suspicions when a thin rung broke off when he pulled on it.

He walked away, moodily kicking at the grass. Tonight could have been a perfect night for him and Joy. If only he hadn't put the cart before the horse, kissing her without asking her permission.

What kind of cad was he?

Why am I getting all worked up about a woman?

Andrew rammed his fingers through his thick hair.

She's like all the others.

His breath caught in his throat and came out as a long, soft groan. Joy was nothing of the sort.

His gut churned with sudden guilt.

Women were nothing like he was trying to tell himself. His mother had always been funny and strong, directing people with much aplomb. She excelled at this, showing her love in this way and yet...

He had treated her the same way he had treated Joy tonight.

He inhaled sharply at this revelation.

Ever since his brother's death, he had treated her terribly, telling himself that she was only a woman who used the men in her life for her own gain.

Andrew rested his forehead in his hand and groaned.

He pretended to treat everyone with equality and here he was, plowing over those he loved the most. He cared more for the unknown slave than he cared for his mother.

He treated her with disdain, holding her responsible for his brother's death and consequently the demise of his own dream. He couldn't see beyond his own nose.

And his poor sister-in-law, who was dead and buried. She had nothing to do with the death of his brother, yet he was holding her responsible for something she herself was a victim of.

Andrew closed his eyes.

He, Andrew Francis Lloyd-Foxx, the wonderful, benevolent caretaker of so many people, was a fraud. There was only one way to remedy this.

My Lord, my Savior. I know that You want me to repent for the way I have held a grudge against my mother. I pray You would forgive me for treating her and Joy, who is a gift from You, less than they deserve. I love my mother, and I love Joy. Please help me to make it up to both of them. In Your precious name I pray, amen.

As it always happened to him when he approached the King of Kings, peace flooded him. Andrew knew he had hurt Joy tonight. He left the resolution in Christ's hand, because he knew that he would just mess up the situation if he tried to fix it. The Lord, who set his feet firmly on the ground, was going to be his supply, no matter what happened.

He reclined onto the lawn, watching a shooting star streak across the night sky and wishing Joy were by his side.

29

*M*other." He strolled toward where she was sitting in a settee, watching the same night sky he had been. She lifted her face, a tired smile appearing.

Before she could answer him, he wrapped his arms around the woman who had shown him love all his life. His father hadn't been the only one, whose kindness to others had been an example.

"What was that for, son?" She was clearly taken aback by his gesture.

Andrew shrugged his shoulders. "I have not treated you like you deserve, Mother. I want to apologize for that."

His mother put a cool hand to his cheek. "You were always a good boy, Andrew. I knew that you would eventually come to your senses. I hoped it would be before my demise and so... I am thankful. I know that the last six years have been hard on you too, son."

They sat down in the lawn chairs on the terrace. Andrew glanced up at Joy's window. Her light still shone, drawing him fiercely.

"Andrew Francis Lloyd-Foxx. What happened tonight?"

Andrew swallowed hard. "Mother?"

"I was watching, you know. I may be old, but I'm not blind. I saw you and Joy. You looked so... blissful. I want you to be happy, Andrew. Joy is your match."

Andrew shifted uncomfortably. "I made a mess of it tonight."

"I would say that I have to agree with you."

It was fine for him to admit it, but she didn't have to rub salt into his wound.

"Mother, that's no way to encourage me."

She snorted unladylike. "You want a pat on your back? I saw how you left poor Joy in the dust after Henrietta came. That is no way to treat a girl you just... well, you know what I mean." His mother blushed delicately. "And that Henrietta. I'm so glad you are not marrying that girl. She is just too much of a manipulating little-"

"Mother, I always thought you expected me to marry her."

His mother's face contorted in disgust. "Henrietta Billings is a spoiled brat. I never ever wanted you or your brother to have anything to do with her."

He stared at her, his mind working on that tidbit of information.

"What are you going to do about Joy? She loves you, you know. Your father and I didn't teach you to treat a girl like you did Joy tonight. Your father would approve of her."

Andrew's lips lifted in the corners at the mention of his father. Moments like these made his loss more apparent. He rubbed his hands over his face.

"I am going to eat some humble pie, apologize profusely, and hope that she doesn't run away again."

"I would be very put off with you if she did, Andrew. And I would blame you. And then I would disown you."

Andrew sucked in a sharp breath. "You would?"

She patted his shoulder gently. "In a heartbeat, my boy. If you let that girl walk out of your life, you may as well start packing."

Andrew's eyes twitched. "You would do that to your only son?"

His mother leaned over and kissed his cheek. "Of course. Us girls must stick together. And she has been so entertaining. Now, go and start groveling. The night is young. And she is still awake, no doubt planning your demise."

"Planning my-" He snapped his lips shut before he said something that might get him into more trouble.

"Be the good boy I know you are, Andrew." His mother locked eyes with him. His own eyes, steely gray stared back at him.

She nodded to him and walked toward the house.

Let the groveling begin.

Andrew glanced at the window, illuminated by the soft glow of a lamp. What, if anything, were Joy and Laura up to? Were they truly hatching a dastardly plan that would end with his head on a platter?

Is she making ready to run away again?

His heart lurched unpleasantly at this thought. How could he have gone from not knowing her less than a week ago to... He loved her.

He was finally willing to admit that to himself. As he stood directly underneath her window, his mother's warning bounced around in his head. He needed to make this right not for her but for himself.

Joy deserved more than he had given her earlier. She was an amazing woman and he was about to show her how much she meant to him. With more determination and courage than he ever felt, he breathed a quick prayer and picked up several smooth pebbles from the walkway he was standing on.

Lord, help my aim to be true.

With that thought in mind, he gauged the distance between where he was standing and Joy's open window. Considering that Henrietta occupied the room next to hers, he had better not miss. It would make everything so much more complicated.

With much zeal, he tossed his first pebble, sending it soaring over the top of the roof.

Andrew paced back and forth, rubbing his hands together and blowing into them.

Very well. It didn't hit Henrietta's window. So far so good.

The next rock went sailing right through the open windowpane. He performed a silent victory dance while he waited. When nothing happened, his heart thumped hard against his ribs.

What if Joy had already taken off?

Joy had been asleep in Laura's arms when a pebble soared through the window and smacked her in the leg. She jumped up, confused, a sharp stinging sensation rising through her left leg. Seeing the sharp stone on the floor, she frowned. Her mind was still foggy from sleep when she walked closer to the window to investigate.

I'm not beat yet.

Flapping his arms about as if he were about to go on a prolonged run, he chose another rock. This one was perfectly round and smooth. Tossing it once or twice in his hand to judge how much force he should apply to the throw, he took his stance. As soon as it left his hand, he knew this one would hit its mark. It too sailed through the window, where it would land on the wood floor with a tiny clunk. While he waited for her to stick her head out, he picked his final stone.

This is it. She's either fast asleep or she's bolted.

Retaking his throwing stance, and even digging into the ground slightly with his foot so he could put all his force behind it, he let loose.

It went sailing in a perfect arch through the air. At the peak of its flight, Joy's face appeared in the window. She spotted him standing on the path below and her mouth opened.

"Andrew?"

Andrew's mouth opened and closed without a sound coming out. He watched as his pebble completed its arch through the air and hit her square in the forehead. A stunned expression slipped onto her face as her head snapped back on impact. She disappeared from view.

She's dead. She's dead. I've killed her. Not only did I insult her, I killed her like David did Goliath. Not that she's a giant.

"Joy!" His feet moved closer. "JOY!"

She reappeared after what seemed a very long time with a befuddled look on her face, and a perfectly round mark in the middle of her forehead.

Clamping down his lips as hard as he could, he breathed through his nose. It took some time for him to fight for control.

"I... need to talk... to you. Please come down."

Joy's eyes opened wide as his request began to make sense.

He wants me to do what? Has he completely lost his mind?

Laura rubbed the sleep out of her eyes and sat up slowly. Her lips twitched comically as she spotted the stones littering the floor.

"Did you... hear that?" Joy's voice cracked.

Laura coughed discretely and lifted her hand to her lips. "I suggest you do as he asks. It is a lovely night out there."

Joy's eyes narrowed dangerously. "Have you lost your mind?"

Laura snorted violently and clapped both hands over her mouth.

Ignoring her maid, Joy turned back to the window where she cautiously peered out. Andrew stood in the middle of the path wearing a smug look on his face and she almost raced out the door. But... She did have pride.

She lifted her nose high into the air when she addressed him sternly.

"I will not come down, Mr. Lloyd-Foxx. I have retired for the night. The way we left things tonight, you have no right to ask anything of me."

Down below, Andrew began muttering to himself and pacing back and forth. When he stopped to address her, she drew in a surprised breath. His glance packed so much heat, she found it hard to breathe.

"You stubborn woman! If you're not down here by the time I count to ten, I'm coming up to get you!"

She nailed him with a glance of her own. "You wouldn't dare. I'm in my nightgown."

"You think that's going to stop me? I've seen you wear far less."

Her jaw went slack and she lowered the window so forcefully that she feared she had cracked the pane. Turning to Laura, her friend busied herself with straightening her sheets and arranging her robe for easy access.

"I'm going to retire. The servants have an earlier day than the rest of the house."

Joy squealed with indignation. "You're going to let me deal with this on my own? I... I need you."

Laura patted her cheek tenderly. "You'll have to fend him off by yourself. I'm not coming in between you and Master Andrew. I like my job too much."

"Please don't go." A chill traveled up her spine. Joy attributed it to the panic she was sure to feel. Except, it really wasn't quite that.

Joy blocked the door as Laura tried to open it. "At least give me a key to lock myself in here."

"Oh honey, there is no key that could stop him tonight. You had better go, because I think your time is up." Laura glanced innocently at the clock on the mantle as if it could tell her.

The shiver now passing over her arms, Joy yelped, threw on a soft robe, and tied the belt around her tightly. If he was going to be such a pigheaded, insistent, obstinate, stubborn...

She threw the door open and bolted toward the back door.

"...ten." Andrew rested comfortably on the grass, his arms tucked behind his head. He rose slowly, holding her gaze. "You made just in time."

30

$\mathcal{P}$anting hard, she faced him. His gaze traveled from her eyes to the middle of her forehead, where the tiny, red mark was still stinging. He lifted his hand and let if fall back to his side when he considered the thunderous expression in her eyes.

"How... dare... you?" she hissed.

He took her hand and tugged her toward the maple tree in the middle of the yard. She planted her feet firmly on the ground and snatched her hand from him. Squaring her shoulders, her eyes narrowed, and she lifted her chin in defiance.

"I'm not going anywhere with you."

A low growl escaped from deep in his chest. Before she had any time to think, he grabbed her around her knees and slung her unceremoniously over his shoulder. Joy squealed as the blood rushed to her head and her hair dangled toward the ground.

"Put me down!"

She slapped his back hard. Then she grabbed a fistful of his jacket when he pretended to drop her.

"Try that again, would you?"

Undaunted, he continued to stalk toward the tree. As soon as he got there he plunked her onto the cool grass as if she were an armful of hay he was feeding his horses. Batting the hair that had fallen into her face over her shoulder, she met his gaze with the deadliest scowl she could muster.

"Just who do you think you are?"

His lips formed a tight, thin line. "If you weren't so stubborn, you'd see that I only wanted to talk to you." He leaned against the tree, his arms crossed tightly over his chest. The scowl on his face matched hers.

Staring at each other, both breathing heavily, neither said a word. Joy was the first to break the silence. Her ire was slowly ebbing out.

"I have nothing left to say to you. Your actions earlier told me that I mean very little to you. You regret meeting me. You wish you had left me with the tavern owner. You find me less attractive than that nasty Henrietta. You would rather-"

"Are you done?" he snapped.

"Not even close, *sir,*" she bit back.

"Very well. You leave me no option but to do this."

Andrew leaned in and covered her mouth with his large hand. Joy's eyes opened in surprise before they turned into slits. Fire shot out of them.

"Youch!" He quickly withdrew his hand, shaking it.

Joy crossed her arms tightly over her chest, a smug expression on her face.

"You bit me!" He had a perfect impression of her teeth on one of his fingers.

Joy nibbled on her bottom lip and lifted her chin, daring him to go on.

"Stop being such a baby. I didn't even draw blood."

Andrew's eyes widened before the thunderous expression on his face melted. He threw his head back, laughter bursting from his lips. Joy held onto the last strand of her anger with fierce determination until she lost the fight.

"What do you want, Master Andrew?" She hiccuped a giggle.

He wiped his hand over his face.

"Are you ever going to let me apologize?" he asked weakly.

"If dragging me out in my nightgown in the middle of the night so I can catch my death from chill is your idea of an apology, you are not doing well, sir."

He held her gaze again and a tremor traveled up her spine.

"Tonight didn't go well at all. But it was your fault. Why did you have to show up looking all..." He flung his hands helplessly into the air. "I had to do something. Whereas I truly regret that I treated you without respect by kissing you without asking your permission or informing you of my intentions toward you, I am not quite sorry that I kissed you."

Heat traveled to her cheeks and she turned to walk away.

"Hear me out, will you?"

Thunder returned to Joy's eyes. "How naïve do you take me? I know what your intentions are. Your whole explanation of *I will be your prince* made that quite clear. Do you think I'm some stupid farm girl, who can't put two and two together? You continue to insult me, sir."

"No, I didn't-"

"I knew very well what your intentions were, Mr. Lloyd-Foxx. I've changed my mind about you. You made your choice when you went off with that... Henrietta." Her nose scrunched up in disgust.

Andrew snickered and brushed a hand over his face. "I'm sorry, Joy." He held her gaze. "Henrietta was a mistake."

Joy poked him hard in the chest, causing him to stumble backward a step and wince. "One moment, *Mr.* Lloyd-Foxx. I am not Joy to you. My name is *Miss* Richards, as you so well know. Please address me as such."

He rubbed his chest.

"I don't think so. I'm Andrew." He pointed to himself and then to her. "You are Joy. That is how we will address each other from now on. I shall not wish to call you Miss Richards when we are old and tottering. You will always be *my* Joy." His eyes lost most of the intensity and softened, holding her absolutely captive.

With those two words, *my Joy,* he had taken the sting out of the humiliation of the evening.

A smug grin passed over his features as he comfortably leaned against the tree.

"Have you nothing to say to that? I shall have to make a note of this. I am sorry for the way things happened tonight."

Joy opened her mouth to say that no man owned her when he pressed his hand against it. He must have thought better of it because he removed it right away.

"I'm not finished yet," he whispered darkly. "You are not a simple farm girl. My intentions were to ask if I could court you."

Joy's breath caught in her throat.

"*You* want to court *me*?" Her eyes widened. "Not... own me?"

He stepped closer. "I do. You mean so much more to me than Henrietta or anyone else. It's not the pretty dress you wear. It's your inner joy that comes out when you're galloping recklessly beside me. I wanted you to know that. And, of course, things didn't exactly go my way. I care deeply for you, Joy." *Coward. Tell her the truth.*

Feeling his breath on her cheek, she drew back to regain control.

"I don't know what to make of all this," she whispered and felt the burning of tears. Sniffling, she lowered her head.

Andrew cupped her face with his hands and drew a thumb across her cheek.

"We both seem to have a history of running. Tonight it was my turn."

His touch sent tendrils of heat throughout her and she felt drawn to him like a horsefly to a horse. Decreasing the distance ever so slowly, she found herself lost in his gaze.

"Please say you forgive me." His voice was soft, a mere whisper on the evening breeze, his lips near hers.

Heart pounding in her throat, all she could do was nod. Andrew ran his hands up and down her arms.

"Good."

As he inclined his head, a moment of panic took over her mind. She wasn't sure she was ready for this.

"I ruined a perfectly good petticoat because of you."

He paused and drew away. His gaze became probing when he laughed.

"I will never be able to live that down, will I?" His arms snaked around her waist to draw her close. "I want to court you, Joy. The other night, the night you were running away, I prayed about what to do about you. Then you showed up. You're part of the equation. It's like you balance me out. I can't explain it. And you make me do foolish things I'd never, ever dare to do on my own. I like it."

His gaze slipped to her lips for a blink of time, then refocused on her eyes. It made her feel as if she were sitting on the back of Ladiesman again, going fast and completely out of control. It was exciting and terrifying at the same time.

Joy touched his cheek tenderly and hesitantly.

"I cried out for help for the first time in a long time when you appeared on the doorstep of the tavern. You looked so out of place and yet, you didn't judge me. You helped me. The other day, when I watched you with your horses, I wanted to be one of them. They had your attention completely and I..." She gave a shy laugh. "I wanted it. When you walked away with Henrietta tonight, it was as if someone had ripped my heart out."

"I will live to make it up to you. If it takes the rest of my life, I promise you."

He lowered his head towards hers and caught her lips with his. Emotions exploded in her heart, made her breathless. She slipped her hands around his neck, drawing him closer still and forcing him to deepen the kiss.

He drew away and rested his cheek against hers. Something magical pulsed through her body and she sighed deeply, melting into his embrace.

"I am... not... sorry."

Joy poked him hard in the side.

31

The noise of plates and cups rattling on a tray, the scent of baked goods woke Joy the next morning. Awareness came to her in a flood, her cheeks warming like a brazier in the winter.

Passing the tip of her tongue over her lips, she recalled everything.

"Good morning, sleepyhead." Laura placed the tray noisily on the nightstand next to her. "It is gone eight o'clock and you are still abed on race day?" She propped her hands on her hips and pursed her lips. "Why?"

With her face feeling as if it had been lit on fire, Joy tried to cover it up by hiding it in her soft, fluffy pillow. Too late. Laura had seen it and bent closer, a devious sparkle in her eyes.

"I take it I need not send Ben out there to find a newly dug shallow grave?" She wrinkled her nose. "Huh?"

A giggle exploded out of Joy's mouth before she could stop. Jumping to her feet, she threw her arms around Laura.

"You need not."

Laura grinned devilishly when she let go of her. "Tell me, Joy. I want the gory details."

Joy snorted and averted her gaze. "I... can't tell you everything."

More heat rushed to her face, which made Laura smile in a way a cat would, had it a juicy mouse in between its teeth.

"I only need to know the decadent parts. Such as, how he begged for mercy."

Joy smoothed down a strand of still-curly hair. "There wasn't much begging he needed to do. He fought hard and valiantly. I had to capitulate in the end."

"And how were the negotiations sealed?" Laura's eyes shone.

Instead of answering, Joy's response was to involuntarily bite her bottom lip.

Laura squeezed her arm. "I'm glad. I like working here. The Master is a wonderful man. I have three meals a day and a warm bed to crawl into at the end of the day."

Joy shook her head. "You have too much of an overgrown imagination."

Laura winked and proceeded to prod Joy into action.

"The races will start soon, child. You'll want to be present, won't you?"

In an attempt to not seem too eager, Joy allowed the primping to get ready for the race.

"We want the Master to not be able to focus on his horses when he sees you," Laura whispered evilly.

In the end, her attire nearly bettered that of the night past. Her hair twisted into ringlets and curls, which Laura attached beautifully to her head.

"Laura..." Joy couldn't help but stare at the reflection in the mirror.

Her maid gave a satisfied grunt and stepped away. "That color becomes you even more."

The sleeveless gown she had chosen for Joy to wear today was of a sea-green color. Lace adorned the snug bodice, ruffles of soft material gave the skirt more volume.

"Mm-hm." Laura stood back and handed her white gloves. "And here's your hat, my lady."

A laugh broke out from Joy's lips before she could stop it. "My lad-"

The look Laura gave her showed her sincerity, making a shiver travel down Joy's spine.

"I'm no-"

"Shush!"

After pinning the hat in a jaunty position, Laura gave her a nod.

"Well, go on."

Her stomach all aflutter, Joy walked out the door.

How was it possible that he didn't hear a word that came out of his best friend's mouth? He was standing right in front of him, and yet... All Andrew heard was a jumble. It caused him to shake his head in an attempt to clear out whatever prevented the meaning to get through to him.

It turned out to be a useless endeavor.

When Jeff's lips stopped moving, Andrew's gaze traveled up to his eyes, which bore into him with a question. It caused a lump to form in his throat, which he couldn't dislodge, no matter how he tried.

"Andrew!" Jeff punched his arm hard. "Have you not heard a word I said? Where's your head this morning? Did you stay out too long last night?"

A very curious sensation of heat traveled up his neck and before it could spread all across his face, Andrew turned away.

"Don't be ridiculous! I have horses running this morning."

His friend's stare only intensified and he felt it prodding him for more information. When he didn't offer any, Jeff gave a soft huff of disgust.

Andrew drew a hand over his face as he turned toward the string of horses. Minuteman regarded him with utter calmness as the groom wrapped his legs in preparation for the race.

"I would have loved to see you win today, my friend. For your sire's memory."

The stallion's ears twitched easily and if Andrew hadn't known better, he imagined that the horse was trying to reassure him.

Jeff stood next to him and tried to scratch Ladiesman, which seemed to offend the horse terribly because he tried to take a bite out of his arm.

"Did I see you with Miss Richards after hours last night?"

A very uncomfortable jab could be felt in his gut. "Say what?" His voice squeaked.

Jeff noted the tremor in his reply and leaned closer. "I couldn't be sure, but I thought I saw you two out on the front lawn last night."

Andrew swallowed loudly. "Couldn't have been."

Jeff waved a hand dismissively. "You're right. She looked quite friendly with whomever she was having a midnight tryst."

Andrew groaned and rubbed the back of his neck, which suddenly itched as if he had rolled in poison ivy. "It wasn't like that, Jeff."

His friend snickered softly. "Of course not. It never is."

"Jeff! Don't! We're... She's... It's terribly personal."

Jeff now threw his head back in a roaring laugh. "Yes, it usually is."

Before he could punch him in the jaw, thus making it impossible for Jeff to say another word, Ladiesman lifted his head and gave a soft nicker. As Andrew turned in the direction his stallion was looking, his tongue stuck to the roof of his mouth, which had gone dry as a brook in the middle of summer.

Miss Richards, Joy, looked absolutely stunning as she glided toward him. Her eyes sparkled with an extra bit of mischief – or was it something else? Something poked him sharply into his ribs.

"Breathe, man. You look like you're going to faint dead away."

Jeff's lips lifted into a charming smile as Joy was near enough and Andrew found himself wishing his best friend would disappear.

"Good morning, Miss." Jeff reached for her gloved hand first and brought it to his lips, brushing a kiss over the knuckles.

Joy's cheeks turned a delightful shade of light pink. She turned her attention toward him and his horses immediately.

"Mr. Lloyd-Fox. What a glorious morning. The horses look fit."

Andrew inclined his head. "Miss Richards. Most of them, except for two, are ready to give it their all."

Her face lit in a smile and Andrew's heart stopped beating. It was as if someone had directed a bolt of lightning directly to his heart, causing it to falter. It made him breathless and slightly surly.

As Joy walked down the line of horses getting made ready for their races, Jeff leaned closer to him.

"She's definitely worth another look. I wish I had had a chance to ask her to dance last night. Perhaps, as she's now your mother's companion, it will afford me some time to get to know her better," he whispered into Andrew's ear.

Grinding his teeth hard together, Andrew turned away.

"She's not your type, Jeff." It pained him to fall for such a cheesy and obvious bait.

"You think? What's she like, Drew? Do tell me!"

Andrew lowered his eyes in an attempt to conceal how much this bothered him. He failed to notice how his hands had clenched into tight fists. It didn't pass Jeff by because his upper lip curled.

"Drop it, Jeff. You are playing with fire."

For a moment, they squared off. Jeff, tall and gaunt and a few fingers taller, and Andrew, whose days in the saddle and out of doors had built his physique.

When Jeff threw his head back to laugh, Andrew allowed air back into his lungs. He would have hated to let a woman come between what had been a lifelong friendship and much mischief. They had started to drift apart since his brother's death, but the history between them still gave them a strong bond.

"She looks like a nice woman," Jeff said softly enough so nobody heard their conversation over the clamber of readying the runners. "I'm glad for you. I wish my mother's companions were young and pretty. I may find myself married after all."

"Married?" Andrew snorted. "What are you talking about? I'm not getting married."

"We'll talk in a year."

Slapping him across the back, nearly sending him stumbling into Ladiesman who once again took offense, Jeff walked away, whistling happily.

Joy hadn't anticipated the reaction her body had given her when she had seen him again. Had last night been a beautiful dream? A figment of her active imagination?

When his gaze caressed her, she knew.

It had not. Being near him made her breathless and unable to form a coherent thought, so she wandered down the line of stalls, filled with horses and their grooms to get her mind off him.

"Good morning, Andrew."

The loud commanding voice of her employer made her turn around. Mrs. Lloyd-Foxx strode their way, an ornate hat perched on top of her head as if it were a royal crown.

"Joy, dear." She folded both hands around Joy's and beamed at her. "I take it you slept well?"

Avoiding a glance toward her son, Joy nodded and swallowed past the sudden dry spot in her throat.

"Splendid." Slipping her arm through that of Joy's, Mrs. Lloyd-Foxx strolled toward the racetrack. "And I take it you enjoyed your first ball?"

More swallowing was necessary.

"I did, ma'am. Thank you very much."

It occurred to her, as Mrs. Lloyd-Foxx gave her a long, penetrating glance, that perhaps the woman was aware of what happened between Andrew and her? The thought gave her cause to tremble.

"Good, dear. I wanted you to have a good time."

The way Mrs. Lloyd-Foxx's eyes bored into her, seemingly prodding deep into her heart, was terrifying. Joy was tempted to fiddle with her gloves or with the lace on her dress when the older woman's voice boomed in her mind.

A woman never fidgets when in mixed company.

"I wanted you to have a memorable night so as to keep you from returning to your home."

"Oh..."

Another deep glance. "Was I successful?"

Joy couldn't keep her eyes from wandering toward where Andrew inspected the legs of one of the first runners. Mrs. Lloyd-Foxx noticed it and her lips curled into a happy smile.

Swallowing with her mouth dry proved difficult. "I..." Her lips quivered. "I need to leave. Every time I think of my family, I feel a weight right here." She placed a hand over her heart. "And it's crushing me."

Mrs. Lloyd-Foxx sighed and closed her eyes.

"I was afraid of that," she whispered. "You are running away from us, aren't you? I wanted you to make your home here, among us. If Andrew hadn't been such a brute, would you have stayed?"

Joy gasped softly as her face brightened with embarrassment. So she *did* know what had transpired between the two of them.

"Ma'am. It has nothing to do with your son. I need to see them. Sending a letter isn't enough at this time. So much has happened and it wouldn't be right to put it all onto paper only. Once I've made sure all is well, I promise you, I'll return."

"Thank the Lord!" Her eyes once again softened and adopted a motherly, gentle look. "We would miss you if you didn't return. Now, as to my son's behavior toward you last night-"

Joy's cheeks heated and she touched her belly protectively.

"He's never allowed a woman into his heart, you know. Men can do such stupid things, as can we. He'll make someone a good husband some day, when the right woman comes around. I believe it to be you."

Swallowing loudly, Joy averted her glance. "I-I..."

Was there anything this woman didn't know? Before she could say anything else, Mrs. Lloyd-Foxx directed her toward the house.

"I can see that perhaps, he made up for his mistake." A heatwave slammed into Joy. "Would you join us on the top of the house? We have a wonderful vantage point from there."

Joy hesitated. She longed to be where the action was, where she could feel the thunder of hooves, smell the sweat from the horses. And most of all, she wanted to be near Andrew. How her life had changed in a matter of days, ever since he had rescued her out of that place!

Was it gratitude she felt for him? Did she mistake falling in love for something that wasn't there? What if she stayed? Would their relationship go from the beginning of love to something deeper, more permanent?

Even though he said he wanted to court her, how could he?

He was from a long line of aristocrats, and she was a farmer's daughter and former barmaid. He needed to marry a virtuous woman, not one spoiled by too many men.

He could never marry her. Even if his mother seemed all for it, society wouldn't accept her.

"... you."

How much of the conversation had she missed? Since this wasn't the first time she had done that, she nodded politely, agreeing with whatever Mrs. Lloyd-Foxx had said. But then she removed her hand from the woman's arm.

"If you don't mind, ma'am, I would prefer to be close to the horses." She grinned. "I so enjoy them."

Mrs. Lloyd-Foxx' gaze caressed her face. "This is why you are good for my Andrew." She patted her gloved hand. "Of course you may stay. Enjoy. Join us after the races for supper on the roof. I'm sure Andrew will be famished by then."

Perhaps it was best not to elaborate further or to encourage her.

"Thank you, ma'am." With a quick curtsey, Joy walked toward the race track.

32

*O*nce at the track, the air was thick with noise. It virtually thrummed with the thrill of expectation. Joy's own heart beat rapidly as she made her way through the throng of people in their Sunday best. Even the farmers and their families were adorned in their finest, although Joy could spot them because their clothes were slightly less fancy, the cloth more rough than that of the upper crust.

Her own dress set her apart from them. She was still playing a part she wasn't comfortable with. Could it be that God was trying to get her ready for a new life?

Her heart gave a quick flutter of anticipation.

To be married to Andrew, to be part of this for the rest of her life was – not going to happen. Already the memory of the night before began to fade and she wondered, had it really happened?

Andrew was the first man she had *allowed* to kiss her. He was the first man she felt such a deep attraction to. The crush she once had on her friend Jonah was nothing compared to the strong pull she felt toward Andrew.

What am I supposed to do, God?

Asking advice from the Almighty was comforting. She remembered how good God really was. Her life wasn't going exactly as she planned, but He was still there. He cared for her well-being.

Sometimes, she needed to fall flat on her face to know that God would be there to lift her up.

It was a freeing thought and as the crowd pushed and shoved, trying to get to the best vantage point, she thanked God for all He had done.

"Andrew!"

He had the sensation of falling. Then he realized that it was not just a sensation. He was falling – out of his chair! Andrew's head hit the ground, while his feet were still propped up on his desk.

Ough...

He sat up again and rubbed his sore head. Then he stared bleary-eyed at Ben, who stood in the doorway.

"Ben. What is it?" he croaked.

"The horses are ready. They're about to call the first race!"

"Oh..."

Andrew pushed himself off the floor and hurried to the door. Ben caught his shoulder.

"You may want to..." He pointed to his dusty pants and jacket.

What is wrong with me?

Andrew grabbed a body brush, one that had just been used on Ladiesman, who stood in his stall, ready for action. He ran it over his own clothes. Tiny chestnut hairs now clung to his jacket and pants.

"What is wrong with you?" Ben shook his head, giving him a slightly pitying look, while he brushed the dark horse hairs off his employer.

"Thank you, Ben," he murmured.

263

Was it lack of sleep or something else that made him so sluggish?

He grabbed the top-hat from the hook and inspected the horses being led around the warm-up area. Their eyes were bright with excitement, their bodies taut and ready to race down the dirt track at high speeds.

Grandpop, a tall black stallion, would be the first of Andrew's horses to run. He looked about with intelligent eyes, his nostrils flaring in excitement. He was a good horse, but hadn't come into himself yet. Andrew hoped that the following year would be his year. For now, he hadn't quite grown into his legs yet, too gangly to produce any real speed.

After patting his horse, he made his way to the track. So many people had come out to see this race. Excitement and the thrum of voices hung in the air. Somebody was selling peanuts – something Andrew had allowed the year before. It was a perfect race day, with excellent running conditions. The track was fast today, and the horses would gain exceptional speeds.

As he moved to the starting line, acquaintances and neighbors stopped him and greeted him. As he chatted, aware that he needed to start the race, he began to search the crowd for a particular face.

Was she with the rest of his guests on the rooftop? Or had she decided to stay where the action was? He expected to see her in the crowd, her pink cheeks aglow with excitement.

It suddenly occurred to him that he wanted to watch the races by her side. Her excitement was so contagious, he wanted to feel what she felt, experience the race through her eyes.

When he didn't see her in the crowd, he couldn't explain why he felt so lonely all of a sudden. Had she really become so important to him in such a short time?

After last night, he couldn't imagine spending a day without her. She was smart, brave, funny. She could ride better than many men and had no fear on horseback. She was his perfect match.

Except... she was far below him in station.

Were he in England, she could be his mistress at most. But there were no such limitations on him in this country. He was free to court whomever he wished, even a lowly farmer's daughter.

They won't accept her.

The thought that was whispered into his heart by the breeze was completely unwelcome.

She's not a virtuous maiden you are expected to wed.

He ground his molars at these distracting persuasions. He didn't care what her past was. Last night she had acted as if she had been in love with him. The kisses they had shared had been sweet yet cautious.

Would his mother approve?

Andrew knew the answer before he had asked the question. His mother was completely in agreement that he should wed Joy when the time was right.

She was the one God had picked out for him. Yet, the soft whispers planted doubt in his mind.

When he spotted her, none of them mattered anymore. She had secured a spot by the railing. It was unusual for a woman to be so close to the track. Most of them were gathering in groups farther away, while their husbands eagerly awaited the beginning of the race.

He pushed through the crowd to stand behind her.

"Miss Richards."

He longed to put his arm around her slender waist, feel the touch of her lips on his, her heart thudding into his chest. She spun around. When she recognized him, her cheeks became the color of an apple in the early fall.

"Would you like to follow me to my special spot from which to watch the race?"

She nibbled her bottom lip. "This is perfectly fine, sir. I like it here."

Someone bumped into his back and sent him stumbling forward right into her. He reached around her to prevent himself from falling. Her gaze lifted to his, her eyes became as deep as the ocean. Her lips parted in surprise and all Andrew could think of was that one kiss that had started it all.

People jostled them closer and Andrew attempted to draw away.

"Come with me, Joy," he whispered and took her hand. "Trust me. I know an even better spot."

A mischievous grin spread over her face, one whose effect he felt down in his toes.

How could she possibly not be the one God had in mind for him?

He led her to a rise, in perfect sight of the finish line. Although he could see she was slightly disappointed, she didn't say anything.

"How are you this morning, Joy?"

Her lips twitched into a smile. "It's not exactly morning anymore, Andrew."

He blinked and glanced at his pocket watch.

"I say. You may be right."

Further conversation was stilled as the first race was called with grand fanfare and pageantry. The huntsman and bugler rode out in front of the prancing and head-tossing young horses, as they made their way halfway around the track. Then the horses picked up speed in a leisurely gallop to the start. There, they shuffled and postured, pinning ears at each other. The riders were trying to intimidate the horses of the competition. It was all part of it, but Andrew didn't approve of the practice. His jockeys always had strict instructions to keep his horses out of the fray.

A thrum of excitement vibrated through the crowd.

"Are any of your horses racing in this one?"

"No. I don't have one in the first race. I thought I would give the others a sporting chance to win." Andrew said it in a clipped, nasally voice, looking bored and unaffected.

"That is so big of you," she grinned.

"Tim O'Riley needs something to boast about," he mumbled.

"I see. You know he was the first gentleman to ask me to dance." Joy watched as his face did something unpleasant.

"Yes, and he's going to pay for that."

"Andrew! That's not nice."

"I don't feel like being nice today." He slipped his arm around her waist and pulled her to him. Joy's breath caught in her throat. "I hope you aren't offended."

Mutely, she shook her head.

"Good!"

Andrew held her close as they watched the race start. Tim O'Riley's horse, a large bay, shot out first and everyone cheered him on. Halfway around the track the horse ran out of steam and fell behind, coming in dead last.

"Mm, I wouldn't want to be that rider right now. Tim isn't going to be very happy with either the horse or the jockey."

"That's a shame. Pretty horse."

"Both horse and rider are inexperienced, both young."

Everyone clapped politely as the winner slowly cantered toward the winner's circle.

"I need to do my thing. Would you please come with me?"

Joy's eyebrows puckered into a frown. "What for?"

"I'm afraid that if I leave you alone for a moment, someone is going to snatch you up." His breath moved the fly-away hairs near her ear just enough to produce a tiny shiver down her neck.

Oh, my.

"I'm perfectly capable of taking care of myself." Her reply sounded weak even to herself.

"Please."

There was something about the way he said it ever so softly. Joy's breath stalled and she lifted her gaze to his slowly, as if afraid of what she would find.

It slammed into her full force. Love.

He loved her.

She nodded, her throat too tight to form words and they walked to the winner's circle. The prancing horse was given a ribbon and the owner of the horse was presented with a check as well as a chalice with the name of the race and date engraved.

Back on their private knoll, someone had taken the time to put two chairs out for them.

"I have a horse in the next race."

"Is that so? Which one?"

Joy's attention focused on him and with that her eyes. Once again, for no good reason, their softness made him feel as if he were in a free-fall into a vast ocean.

Andrew cleared his throat and his thoughts. "M-my horse Grandpop, the tall black, is running. He's not quite ready for this, but I thought I should give him a chance. He's been coming in the middle of the field since his first start this year. He'll be a decent runner, nothing spectacular."

The bugle was blown again, announcing the next race. The jockeys swung aboard their mounts and walked past the crowd onto the track where they cantered to the starting line.

Andrew took her hand as both turned their attention on the horses. It was done so smoothly and warmth spread through her fingers and up her arm in a steady pulsing throb. She'd never felt like this before.

The horses shot off as the starting shot sounded and his grip on her hand tightened. The tall, black horse was bogged down in the middle of the pack and seemed to settle there comfortably.

Then, as if he shook himself, the horse sprang forward and untangled himself from the crowd.

"Go!" Andrew shouted and jumped out of the seat. Joy found herself on her feet, shouting at the horses.

Grandpop flattened his ears as he and the leading animal approached the home stretch. Four horse lengths separated him from Tim O'Riley's horse.

"You brilliant horse! Get him! Extra oats for you tonight!" Andrew jumped up and down, his voice swallowed up by the roar of the crowd.

Grandpop seemed to have heard him because he flattened his whole body out in front of his jockey and gave another burst of speed. As the pair battled for the finish line, the black horse seemed to become longer and faster. In the end, O'Riley's horse gave a burst of speed at the very last second, beating Grandpop by a nose.

Andrew laughed and threw his arms around Joy.

"What a good boy!" He shouted hoarsely.

It was a little difficult to concentrate on the race while she was still embraced by strong arms. But it made everything so much more exciting.

"I beg your pardon." Andrew released her quickly. "I wasn't thinking. How inappropriate of me."

She gave him a glance that packed heat but it seemed to have no effect on him. He did reach for her hand and tucked it into the crook of his arm.

"He almost had him. That was his best race to date. That horse may just turn out a good runner after all. And he'll get extra oats tonight." He gave her one of those charming, melt your bones, kind of grins.

They reached the cooling off area in the field, where the horses and jockeys walked around. Grandpop wore a smug look on his face. His ears twitched about excitedly. He was lathered up with sweat and his nostrils were bright red.

"Well done, John. What happened?" Andrew clapped the short rider on the back as he dismounted.

"He's never pulled like that before. It was as though something clicked in his head. He was strong out there."

Joy patted the black horse's neck.

"Good boy," Andrew whispered into his ears. "Very good boy."

The stallion pricked his ears and lifted his head, as if he agreed.

"He brought in a good purse today. Not too shabby!" Andrew grinned triumphantly and watched as O'Riley's horse pranced around in the winner's enclosure, stepping on Tim's feet left and right.

"Ouch. Nothing like a thousand pound horse dancing on your toes," he laughed softly.

Joy turned to him, a mischievous look on her face. "About as much as me stepping on your feet?"

Andrew brought her hand to his lips and looked her in the eyes. "Nothing can compare to you stepping on my feet. It was a pleasure."

She snorted.

"Truly. A pleasure." Andrew repeated and winced as Grandpop almost stepped onto his feet.

33

$\mathcal{I}$t was as if his horses knew something, or felt his excitement. His next horse to run was Ladiesman. He was flashy with his coppery golden coat gleaming in the late morning sun, prancing around the parade ring, throwing his head as if he was ready to give everything. At the start, he got into a slight scuffle with another horse. Andrew gritted his teeth, determining to speak to the jockey after.

Ladiesman seemed to throw out his chest as they waited to line up in a relatively calm line for the next race. His ears were pricked, his muscles rippling with tension.

He was a very handsome horse and today he knew it.

Andrew expected him to try, because that's what he did. When briefing his jockey earlier, he had told him that he expected the stallion to give a fast start but then be spent. At least he'd set a fast race.

"That horse looks like he has something to prove, Andrew."

He gave his stallion another look. There was something about him today.

"No. He's being Ladiesman. I can't see how he or Minuteman can give more than a good, fast start. Although..." He cocked his head, then shook it. "No. He's a showman."

And the horses were off. Joy's fingers curled into his arm, holding tighter and tighter.

"Andrew! Look!"

As expected, Ladiesman separated from the crowd early on and set a breathtakingly fast pace. He wouldn't be able to keep it up for long. Already another horse was gaining on him and they hadn't reached the home-stretch yet.

As if sensing the other horse's challenge, Ladiesman increased in speed instead of slowing down. He left the rest of the field behind him, eating his dust as he crossed the finish line unchallenged.

Andrew stood speechless while Joy laughed.

"That was-"

"Unbelievable," he murmured and dabbed his white handkerchief to his forehead.

"He did it!" He wanted to draw her near again but knew that would not be possible. There were rules to this thing called courtship. At least in public. And he hadn't announced it yet, so for now he had to behave.

"Come along. I want you right next to me when I accept this prize."

Joy's eyes grew wide and round. "No." She stepped back a pace. "I'm fine right here."

It would get the tongues wagging and he practically begged someone to say something.

"I wish to share this moment with you, Joy. It would mean a lot."

She nibbled her thumbnail and lowered her hands quickly as if remembering that a lady never nibbled any body parts.

"What would people say?" she whispered.

Andrew tucked her arm under his. "That's on them. This moment belongs to both of us."

Joy gasped softly but had no time to say anything else as they walked to the winner's circle. On the way he had to stop to shake numerous hands and accept congratulations. People glanced at Joy as if wondering who exactly she was. He never said a word about it, only introducing her as *Miss Richards.*

Ladiesman pranced and snorted, acting as if he hadn't run all out. He proudly walked up to Andrew with a look on his face that seem to say, *Don't you ever doubt me again.*

Owner and horse seemed to have a silent conversation, then Andrew lifted his hand and cupped his horse's nostril, caressing it softly.

"Good boy. Very good boy."

Ladiesman shook his head regally.

With only a few races left, Joy was going out of her mind. She'd never expected to feel or experience such excitement. Being in the winner's circle made her feel like she belonged. She liked it, but warmed herself not to get too used to it.

Once back on their private knoll, Andrew's oldest friend joined them. It wasn't that she didn't like him. She craved that private moment they spent together. She wanted more of it, to be assured that perhaps she did belong here and that he did care for her more than she ever could have imagined.

"That horse of yours was full of fire today, Drew. Any more surprises waiting for us?" Jefferson Campbell-Black asked, a smirk on his face.

Andrew threw his hands in the air. "Anything seems to be possible today. I gave instructions not to push him. He won't have it in him."

"Wouldn't it be glorious if he gave more than you expected of him?" Joy asked.

Andrew heaved a deep breath and nodded. "Yes, but highly unlikely."

Minuteman plodded along with the other horses, his head low, ears flicking front to back as if he were bored with the whole thing. He looked more like a lowly plow horse than the fast thoroughbred.

"You see, Miss Richards?" Sighing, he pointed to his horse, who looked like he was about to fall down with exhaustion from the canter to the start.

"Oh..."

The horses lined up with less shuffling than in the previous race. O'Riley's horse *Flotsam* tried to intimidate Minuteman, but his jockey steered the stallion away. When the starting shot sounded, the field was off, clumping in one mass.

Andrew groaned and pinched the bridge of his nose.

Minuteman was stuck in the middle and gave no attempt to shake the others. About halfway through, the burgundy and gray colors of Andrew's stable moved up, and up, and up until Minuteman was hard on the heels of O'Riley's runner. Joy could only watch, slack-mouthed, as he gained. When Minuteman soared past him and onto the finish line, it sounded like the whole racetrack was roaring in excitement.

Only Andrew stood by silently to watch his horse shoot ahead of his rival only to win it by five lengths.

Joy bounced up and down, clasping onto his arm and screaming at the top of her lungs. Jefferson seemed to have shouted himself hoarse as well.

"He did it!"

This time Joy wanted to be the one who threw her arms around Andrew. Instead, she politely gave him a smile. He returned it, though she imagined his knees were quaking terribly.

"I would say he deserves extra oats too," she whispered.

A thin smile appeared on his face. "I'm too old for this."

Jefferson laughed and slapped his shoulders hardily. "Well done, Andrew."

Minuteman met him in the winner's circle, his eyes on him unwavering. He snorted and pushed toward him. Andrew grinned and put a tremulous hand on the stallion's sweaty neck. Minuteman shoved into him, softly blowing into his face. Andrew framed the horse's cheeks with his hands.

"How did you pull that off, boy?" he asked. The stallion just looked at him, his eyes full of pride and excitement.

If he never won another race in his life, this was the moment Andrew would forever remember. His heart swelled with pride. Two amazing horses had given everything to him today. They had gone above and beyond. And he couldn't fathom why they would do that.

The rest of the day was less stressful for him. One of his horses, *Justletme,* a sweet animal, came up lame because of a scuffle with Tim O'Rileys' horse. Andrew was ready to bring hellfire down on the man. But he wasn't going to lower himself to his level. He saw the look in Joy's eyes and feared she was going to see it done. With a loud puff that sent several strands of hair flying, she let it go.

He respected and loved her even more for it.

As the last race finished, he mulled that thought over. How could he love someone whom he had only known for so short a time? Someone out of his social class? Yet, she was so much more than he. He didn't know what it was about her, but she impressed him more and more.

She loves horses as much as I do.

As that thought settled in his heart, he found himself wondering if it would be enough.

The afternoon ended and as guests began to get ready to leave, she drew into the background, soaking it all in. This would be her last night for a while with these good people. She would miss them terribly. She longed to pick up a quill and parchment to write to her family that she was well, had found her match, and was happy.

It seemed wrong.

Her family deserved more.

She found Mrs. Lloyd-Foxx on the veranda, sipping a glass of lemonade. Her eyes turned to a twinkle when Joy approached her.

"Joy, my dear. What an exciting afternoon. I enjoyed every race and-" She leaned closer – "I even placed a wager and came back with a good purse."She giggled like a child about to eat the Christmas pudding.

"Ma'am. I'm so happy for you. And it was a splendid day. I shall always remember it."

277

Her employer's face fell. "I see. You *are* leaving us." She sighed.

"Yes, ma'am. My family-"

Mrs. Lloyd-Foxx lifted her hand. "I completely understand. However, I don't want you traveling by yourself. You'll take Laura."

Joy's breath hitched in her throat. "Pardon me?"

"You two seem to have forged a fast bond. I won't have a companion of mine traveling by herself. It's unseemly, Joy. You now represent this family." She took another sip. "And furthermore, when you are finished with your parents, you will return my maid to me. In person."

There was a tiny edge to her voice and Joy swallowed hard.

"But-"

Again, the woman interrupted with a raised hand. "No buts. It is my wish, and we all know I get what I want."

Inhaling deeply, Joy nodded. "Then I hope it will be so."

Shrewd gray eyes searched her face. "What about my son? Have you informed him of your plans?"

"No, ma'am. I... I don't know how to tell him."

"He cares deeply for you, child. It would break his heart if you didn't return."

There was nothing else she could say. She knew it in her heart.

"But we aren't socially matched, ma'am. I don't see how this could be to his advantage. I'm so much below his station."

The older woman turned to her and grasped both hands in hers.

"You have something to give that no one has ever given. I see the way my Andrew looks at you, Joy. You have made him happier than I've ever seen him. That is more important to me than money or social standing."

Her jaw went slack. She had never expected to come here a former slave and leave... with so much. A place to return to, a man who wanted her. A mother-in-law who saw that her worth was so much more.

Warmth enveloped Joy.

"Thank you," she whispered.

"As for your wages, I suggest you see Andrew for that. Also, you will need traveling money. I won't have you stay in questionable taverns along the way."

Joy argued and tried her best to refuse the offer. In the end, Mrs. Lloyd-Foxx glared at her.

Mrs. Lloyd-Foxx hugged her. "I will not discuss this any further! You hurry along and get back quickly. We'll be waiting for you."

She belonged.

She knew what needed to be done. Laura couldn't accompany her. Her friend was getting married in less than two weeks and Joy wasn't sure how long she would be away. It would be best to steal away in the night without anyone knowing. Money would come in handy, but besides that, Joy would make her way home alone.

This was her responsibility, no one else's.

As she entered her room, she found Laura packing a satchel.

"How... What are you doing?"

Laura gave her a pained look. "Packing your bags, silly. Isn't it obvious?"

She hugged her. "Thank you. But you're getting married and need to prepare. I can't ask you to come with me."

"You didn't. The mistress did. I obey her. I could never look the master in the eye if I didn't do this. I have to protect his treasure." She winked cheekily.

Joy sputtered, heat traveling to her cheeks. How could she possibly rid herself of Laura? Her friend would be furious with her, yes. But in the end, she'd see that Joy had her best interests in mind.

"Pack light. I only need one dress. I can wear my old ones once I am home."

Laura murmured something about Joy being so naïve and not knowing what was good for her. Listening to her made Joy smile. Her heart tightened at the thought of not being present for her wedding, of missing a day with her.

Her mind was made up, however.

"We should probably retire early," Joy said.

Laura nodded. "Are you going to tell Master Andrew? I would think that he has a thing or two to discuss with you."

"I..."

Just then a *tink* startled her. Laura and Joy looked at each other in confusion and searched the room for what could have made the sound. She walked to the window, when a tiny pebble came sailing through. It glanced off her sleeve and fell to her feet.

Laura saw it and immediately flattened her lips. Cheeks turning red, her friend hurried to the door.

"Methinks you have been summoned." A loud snort escaped Laura's lips.

Joy swallowed the laugh. "But what if he hits me in the forehead again?"

Laura paused before she exited. Her shoulders were trembling as she stripped off her white apron.

"Perhaps this will help."

The strain must have been to much for her because as the door closed Joy heard loud, hilarious laughter.

34

$\mathscr{T}$he apron was a clever touch. Andrew laughed despite himself. Ever since his mother had pulled him off to the side to inform him that Joy was leaving, his jubilant mood had turned – foul. What had him in such a terrible mood when he should be celebrating?

She was leaving. And she hadn't told him. Was she running away again without letting him know?

Joy's head appeared in the window, hesitatingly.

"Don't hit me."

"Nice flag. Come down. I need to speak to you."

Her eyes widened and she seemed to draw in a deep breath.

"Get down here!" he repeated, his voice low and threatening, when she seemed to hesitate.

Her face disappeared and moments later, she poked around the door to the back kitchen. He would miss her like crazy but he also knew that he had to let her go.

A caged bird is never going to be happy until it realizes that it is safer where it is. He didn't want to keep Joy captive. She was free to go, and yet – he wanted her to know how much she meant to him.

She stopped in front of him, her arms twisted tightly around herself as if protecting herself.

"Have you something to tell me?"

She shuffled and glanced at the ground. "I meant to tell you but it was a busy day. And many congratulations."

"Yes. I know. Were you planning on telling me at all?"

She gasped. "Of course I was going to."

His eyes narrowed. "Well?"

"Andrew. I'm leaving tomorrow," she said softly.

"Mmm. I was informed by my mother to give you your wages and some traveling money."

She smiled weakly. "I don't want the traveling money. I don't even deserve any wages. Your mother played dress-up with me. How much work was that?"

He cocked his head and she groaned.

"Very well. It was excruciating. But I was able to spend time with you and get to know you."

He touched the side of her cheek tenderly. "Go, and tend to your family's needs. I hope you have plans of returning. I may have to travel to Connecticut to drag you back here if you don't."

Her eyes lit as moonlight graced her face. "I'll be back. I promise."

He took her hand and steered her across the dew-covered grass toward the stable. She followed hesitatingly.

"Where are we going?"

"I'm going to make sure you hurry back."

The horses were resting. Even if they hadn't run in a race earlier, the day had been exciting as their routine was disturbed. Andrew passed one dozing horse after another. Some blinked sleepily as he passed the soft light from the oil lantern he carried over them.

She was leaving all this behind tomorrow. For the first time in her life, she had all she wanted. Why couldn't she stay and send a letter instead? She would never have to leave his side again.

"Joy."

His soft voice sent tendrils of warmth zapping through her. She lifted her face to him. His steely gray eyes softened. Breath stalling, she tugged a strand of hair over her ear.

"Andrew?" Her voice was tiny, as if she were a mouse. It came out like a squeak and caused a smile to appear on his lips.

He cupped her cheek. "I want to give you something before you leave me. Think of it as a reminder that I exist and that I care for you."

His gaze trailed her face and settled on her lips.

He wishes to kiss me again.

Her heart sped to a rapid pace and she closed the distance.

"I know how much you care of me," she managed to whisper.

He brushed his lips over hers. Joy's bones melted into something resembling oatmeal, and she leaned into him. Catching his face in her hands, her response seemed to encourage him. He deepened the kiss, his hands dropping down her back and to her hips. Greedily, as if she feared he would withdraw, she returned the kiss, losing herself in it.

"I want to give you this before you leave."

His breath swept over her lips, caused a chill to pass down her neck and across her shoulders. Joy's eyelids fluttered open and she found herself gazing into his soft eyes.

"Wh-at?" Her own voice was barely above a whisper.

Andrew swallowed hard, never letting go of her. Her body pressed to his, he nodded toward the horse in the stall. She was sleeping on her feet, as horses tend to do, her lower lip hanging, her hips cocked so she could rest one of her hind legs. Her ears twitched in their direction.

"What are you saying?"

"When you return, this will be your horse," he murmured, his lips so near her ears his breath tickled the hairs over it.

Her eyes widened. "You're... you're giving me a horse?"

He grinned lopsidedly. "That's not all." He took her hand and placed it over his chest where his heart was beating. "I want you to remember that this belongs to you, Joy, waiting for you. I know you have to go. You and Laura have rules to follow on your trip."

"Rules?" Her brows furrowed as her eyes traveled back and forth between Andrew and Mommy. "What kind of rules? I'm not a child, you know."

He waved his free hand dismissively. "No matter. You will stay in reputable inns along the way. No traveling at night. And as soon as you reach home, you will send a missive."

"What if I can't write?" she asked teasingly.

Andrew's eyes darkened. "Then put an x on the page. I'll know it's from you," he growled.

Before they parted, he reminded her again that he wanted her to return.

She came to the conclusion that he cared.

It sent a jolt into her heart and made what she was about to do even worse. Would he ever forgive her for deceiving him?

He cannot.

Nobody in his station would forgive her for what she was about to do.

The night was muggy and still, sticky heat hovering, enveloping her like a feather-stuffed blanket. Sweat traveled down her back and between her shoulder blades. Her face was slick with it and she had only traveled down the employee stairs bathed in almost complete darkness. Her fingers had become her eyes.

The back door squeaked loudly, the sound bursting into the still night. Joy leaned into the wall of the house, pressing her back hard against the brick. Her heart thudded loudly in her ears, the sound of her breath threatening to wake the dead.

Still, nothing stirred.

The moon was hidden behind thick clouds, the trees stood dark and silent – as if they were waiting for her next move and disapproved severely. Her heart clenched sharply and she puffed out another breath, blowing away a few strands of hair from her face. As the staccato rhythm of her heart increased, she dared to step out of the shadows and into the night.

The first step was the hardest. Slowly, as if her body had been glued to the wall, she stepped away. Her feet sank into the grass. The second step felt even worse. Everything in her wanted to stay, to wait for the morning and for Laura to accompany her.

It would make the journey so much more enjoyable to have someone along with her. Except, how could she ask this of her friend? This was her task to do, nobody else's. She had to see her family. She needed to assure herself her sister was safe and taken care of. She longed to walk across the familiar fields to the house. Going alone gave her a squirrely feeling in the pit of her stomach.

On the path to the stable, as she sneaked along like a thief in the night, she drew courage where there was none. Upon stepping into the stable, her mind was at ease as much as it could be.

Lighting a small lantern to help her saddle a slumbering Mommy, she strapped the small satchel containing one of her new dresses and a purse of money Andrew had given her before they parted.

Tears fell when she trotted out of the stable-yard.

Lord, grant me the wish to return. And make Andrew see that I had no choice but to leave alone.

Her prayer stayed with her as she urged the mare into a canter once they reached the main road, leaving the estate behind quickly.

Andrew knew something was off the moment he lifted his head off the pillow. It was even before that when he heard the clomping of heavy work-boots on the stairs, agitated and raised voices in front of his door. When his man entered only a second later, bearing a tray of coffee and eggs and toast, he was followed by Ben.

"I'm sorry to catch you abed but something has happened, Andrew."

Swallowing a groan, Andrew sat up and kicked the sheets off. With his left hand he reached for his cup of coffee, while his right hand roughed through his sleep-tousled hair.

"Let me guess." He took a very necessary sip. "Mommy is gone."

Ben's jaw slackened and his eyes widened. "How'd you..."

Andrew swallowed a groan. "I gifted her to Joy last night in hopes to entice her into coming back. No need to call the constable. She took her own horse. Did Laura take one, too? I thought they'd take the carriage."

Ben shuffled from foot to foot and balled up his cap in his hands.

"It was the plan. I was getting it ready for her, the coachman was instructed to leave after breakfast. And then Laura came to the stable. Alone."

The coffee he was drinking now churned in his stomach as a ball of fire gathered.

"What do you mean, alone. Isn't Laura with Joy?"

Ben shook his head. "Joy's gone."

He dashed to the door, unaware that he was still in his nightclothes and went running down the stairs, only to bump into his mother.

"Oh, dear! Have you heard? She's left without anyone." Her face was twisted up in fear and agony. Andrew pressed her shoulder gently.

He wanted to find Joy and... And what?

She had made a decision to leave on her own, after all they had done for her. Anger roiled fiercely in his gut. He blew out a long breath, hoping it would ease the pain he felt in his heart.

"Mother. Joy has decided to go on her own. We can't..." His voice faltered.

"Andrew! It is a two day journey at least and she's a woman. She is bound to fall prey to vagabonds or all sorts of men of ill repute."

Someone might as well have poked him with a red hot poker, he felt seared in his heart. Turning away before his mother saw the pain in his expression, he squeezed her shoulder again.

"You have to go after her, son."

Of course, he needed to go after her. She was weak and would be vulnerable to all sorts of riffraff out there. And yet, why had she left alone? It wasn't the first time she had tried to run away. He had given her a horse and now, she was able to fulfill her plans. She didn't need *him* anymore.

A twitch started in the corner of his left eye. Soon his insides twisted as he became aware of how she had spurned him. After all he had been to her, she had taken off anyway.

"No. She's made her choice. She doesn't need our help, my help. She's on her own."

He turned around and went back up the stairs.

"Andre-"

His door shut out the sound of his mother's voice. It was his own silent voice he couldn't stop.

Go after her before she gets herself into trouble.

No!

He sat on the edge of his bed and put on his shirt, pants, and boots, ignoring the cravat. He didn't even bother to run a brush through his hair.

"Sir, may I assist you with your-"

Andrew gave his man a look that stopped the words.

"I'll leave you to it," he murmured as he backed out of his room.

That stubborn woman!

How could he possibly protect her if she wasn't willing to follow the plan he had so carefully come up with? His mother had been kind enough to give up her carriage until it had returned from dropping the women off. Laura had been willing to wait on her wedding until they returned. He had shown her that he cared, had gone out of his way to keep her safe, and she had thumbed her nose at it.

Stomping and grumbling to himself, he exited the back door. On the way through the kitchen, he had caught a snippet of conversation the maids were having. As he entered, the room became silent.

"You think she planned it all along?" He rounded on one of the newer women who was a bit of a gossip.

She cowered and lowered her head. "No, sir. Of course not, sir."

Slamming the door didn't help his anger much.

As he entered the stable, the grooms quieted and greeted him with nods or grunts. Everyone knew what had happened. She had made him look like a fool on top of everything else. He didn't even check on his horses but walked straight to his office, closing the door carefully behind it.

Did she not care for him?

Andrew sat wearily in the chair and glanced out the window into the stable, where his horses were being taken in and out of their stalls.

For the life of me, I'll never comprehend the female mind. Why didn't she take the hand we offered her?

35

*H*er grand scheme had seemed so simple, and yet now that she was hours from the estate, she knew she had hurt the only man she would ever love. He would be furious at her, his pride shattered.

Mommy snorted and drew her back to the present. It had been hours since she had left the estate and her heart still ached. Sweat coated the horse's sleek coat. Joy wiped her arm across her own moist forehead. It was time to take a rest. Her stomach growled and she willed it to stop.

They plodded through a small village. A general store beckoned her, so she pulled up the horse and hitched her to the post.

"Morning." An old voice greeted her as she stepped inside.

It was relatively cool inside, the various wares neatly arranged on shelves. Her stomach growled again while she turned to the proprietor behind the cash register. The man's eyes widened.

"I'm hungry," she said with a smile. "Do you have any baked goods?"

The man nodded silently and pointed to a small counter, where a peach pie, cherry pie and a tray of blueberry muffins made her mouth water.

"I'll have a muffin and a piece of peach pie, please."

She inwardly thanked Mrs. Lloyd-Foxx and Andrew for the money, missing them both immediately. As she exited the store, her breakfast wrapped carefully in wax paper, Mommy greeted her with a soft nicker.

Moments later, Joy swung back into the saddle to continue her journey home. Outside the town they came upon a meadow and brook. It was time to take a break.

Andrew dozed with his chair teetering on the two back legs. His chin rested on his chest and he caught himself snoring softly now and then.

They were flying toward the lighthouse at incredible speeds. Her laughter rang in his ears. He turned his head to see the look on her face. Her blue eyes sparkled with joy, her cheeks rosy. Her hair escaped from her pins, trailing behind her. He could reach out and touch her any moment now-

"Andrew?"

His head popped up violently and the chair toppled over backward, spilling him onto the floor. Rapping the back of his head against the floor caused stars to sprinkle his vision. He sat up and cradled his head.

"I'm so sorry. I didn't mean to startle you."

His mother stood in the door, a somber look on her face. He rose, rubbing the back of his smarting head.

"Mother. What can I do for you?" He straightened out the chair.

"Why are you still here?"

He blinked rapidly. "Pardon, Mother?"

She took him by the shoulders and shook him. "Why are you still here? Have you lost your good mind, finally? You can't let her go alone. Go after her!"

He opened his mouth, though no sound escaped.

"You are going to regret letting her go on her own. She gave us the slip, yes. You know you love her! Now go after her!"

"I-"

She propelled him toward the door as if he were a naughty boy who had been caught with his fingers in the cookie jar.

"If you're not on your horse in three minutes, I'll saddle it myself and throw you up there. I read an article in the paper only moments ago, warning travelers of brigands who masquerade as injured. It said that it was a band of three men, and they manage to halt a carriage under the guise of having broken down. They have robbed numerous innocents this way. Do you want Joy to end up robbed? Or worse?"

His internal struggle lasted only as long as Ben appeared out of nowhere with Minuteman all tacked up for him.

"Get on that horse and ride like you've never ridden before. Forget your pride, son."

He swallowed the last lingering anger he held onto since she left and heaved himself onto his prancing stallion. They galloped out the stable yard, something he usually frowned upon.

God, help me find Joy before it's too late.

After taking a longer than expected rest by the side of the road in the meadow, Joy and Mommy resumed their long journey. Plodding along now, Mommy looked more like a dusty old mare on her last leg than the proud mother of fine thoroughbreds. A sunburn spread over Joy's face and hands.

I really didn't think this through, did I?

293

Her intentions had been pure. The execution... flawless. The result was to be seen, if she ever made it home.

And if Andrew would ever talk to her again.

She rounded a bend in the road and saw the wreckage right in the middle. Drawing in a sharp breath, Joy dismounted and left Mommy standing by herself. The mare found some grass to nibble on, while Joy approached what seemed to have been a nasty spill. Large barrels, smelling slightly of fish oil, had fallen from the carriage. One of them was leaking its contents into the dirt.

A twinge ran through her as she approached cautiously. She found the unconscious driver by the side of the wreckage with a nasty cut on his forehead. The horses were nowhere to be seen.

Ignoring the tingling of nerves on the back of her neck, she touched him gingerly.

"Sir?"

The man didn't twitch a muscle. The hairs on her arms stood in attention as she considered the situation. She was the only one who could lend a hand at this moment. Her medical expertise was limited to curing the common cold, if that.

"Sir. Can you hear me?"

When she bent down to shift the unconscious driver off the main road, something wrapped around her wrist and held her fast. As if on cue, the man in the road rose. His face turned into a sleazy sneer that sent chills up and down her back and all throughout her.

As she looked up, she saw what – or more importantly, who – was holding her. A big man with a dangerous but triumphant leer held onto her wrist.

And this would be how I get myself into trouble.

Wrenching her arm away only made him increase his hold. His fingers dug into her skin and Joy felt her fingertips throbbing with lack of blood.

"What an unexpected surprise." The *injured* man's gaze grazed her. "You're trav'lin' alone, dearie?"

Trembling on the inside, Joy saw the opportunity. "No. My husband is coming. We stopped a little while ago and he asked me to go on without him."

Another man came from the bushes, swinging a nasty-looking bat of sorts.

"Ain't that quaint. Why don't we sit ourselves down here and wait for him."

The man who had been holding onto her dragged her to the side of the road and grinned. Injured man fetched Mommy.

"Look at this here horse. That's quality, that."

They pushed her along in front of them, into the patchy woods by the side of the road. Once they were hidden from the road, they tied up Mommy to a tree. Injured man unhooked her satchel and threw it to the third man, who seemed to be the leader.

His eyes widened as he drew out her dress. He threw his head back in laughter. "If only I had me a wife who could wear this."

It was followed by a round of raucous laughter that gave her the creeps.

God, please help me get out of this alive.

He then hefted her leather purse, opened it. His grin brightened and revealed teeth that were in need of care, stained dark from chewing tobacco. He took a bow.

"An' we thank you for this."

He threw the leather purse into the air and caught it.

"That's mine!" she growled. "I've earned it."

The three men laughed nastily.

"Now it's ours. We've earned it too. Where's that husband of yours? Was he far behind?" The man who still held her wrist shook her. "Don't try anything with us. You'll lose a lot more than that fancy dress, the horse, and that sweet purse if you do."

Joy once again tried to wrench out of his grip. This time, she was forced onto her knees.

"What we gonna do with her?"

Leader came to stand in front of her. He roughly tipped her chin this way and that, forced her mouth open, examined her hair.

"She'll fetch a good price on the market."

No! Never again.

Joy jumped to her feet, not caring when she entangled with the hem of her skirt, ripping it. She managed to evade the hands that groped for her.

"Come back here," the bulky man hissed and dove at her.

Though he was big and strong, he was slow. She had always been fast on her feet. With lightning speed, she avoided his grasp. They seemed to be playing a game of tag until one of the other men interfered and stepped in, catching her hair.

Pain rushed from her scalp through her shoulders into her fingertips.

"Enough of this!" *Bulky* yelled.

Without regard of how much pain it was causing her to be dragged by her hair, the man twisted her arm behind her back. Then, he leaned in, dousing her with breath that had long turned putrid. Joy barely managed to swallow the bits of undigested muffin that came up.

"What to do with this one?"

They seemed to enjoy their taunting, all the while counting her money. Joy slumped against a tree, feeling wretched. Her arm felt numb from how hard he had twisted it.

How was she going to get herself out of this?

A little help, God. Your will, but... I'd rather not end up back where I started.

36

*I*t was getting late in the afternoon and the bandits had begun to make a makeshift camp. One of them kept an eye on her at all times, leering.

"Where's your husband?" The one they called Owen asked. "Gettin' late."

The way he looked at her sent tendrils of fear cursing through her. He was the quiet one, the one who had appeared injured.

"She don't have one." Leader, they called him Jack, taunted. "She's all alone. We have time, gents. No need to worry about anyone comin' to 'er rescue. She's ours to do with as we please." The smile on his face sent chills up and down her body.

"Mighty fine dress she's got, though. Think she's one of them hoity-toities from Boston? They gots lots of money." Bulky, his real name was Murph, sneered. "If we keep her..."

Soft, dangerous chuckles followed.

"We can have some fun and could be set for life."

"Women are trouble, gents."

Everyone jumped at the sound of the new, lazy voice. The men grabbed whatever weapons they had. The bat, a knife, a sharp pitchfork.

Joy's gaze snapped to the new man and her heart leapt.

"Who are you?"

Andrew stepped into the camp, his hands raised. "I'm not going to make trouble. I'm a businessman, like yourself. Would you like to do some real business or would you rather keep her at hand? If I could give you some advice. Get rid of her at the earliest time. She'll make you regret that you even caught her. Women are pests. They'll destroy your whole crop."

Ouch. I think he's mad at me.

Joy hadn't felt so happy to see someone as she did to see him this very moment. His voice did have a trace of bitterness and she didn't think he was acting.

"What do you offer?" Jack asked. His face was scrunched up in a sneer. "Or perhaps you're her husband. Maybe she told the truth."

Andrew threw his head back and laughed. "Being married would be a some sort of torture for me. No. Thank you. I pass. Are you willing to sit down, man to man to man? And man, of course." He looked at each of them as if he was sitting across from legitimate business partners.

The brigands looked at each other and turned to huddle together. Andrew shot Joy a warning glance and she didn't have to be told to keep her mouth shut. What was he planning?

"Right. What are ya offerin'?" Jack glared at Andrew.

Oh, God, please let us get out of here!

"I'll take her off your hands. I know some people who are in need of her." A slow smile played on his lips. He was very good at this. Almost too good.

Joy shivered involuntarily.

"How much?" Owen asked, licking his lips.

"I think, $10 will be enough."

Ten dollars? Was he out of his mind? Did he have that kind of money on him?

The men conferred in a huddle again.

Andrew flashed her a look and cocked his head toward Mommy. She noticed – for the first time – that he had slowly inched closer to the mare. He was now within reach and as the men discussed the lucrative option he had given them, he sprang into the saddle, whipped the horse around, and kicked her into a gallop.

"Reach up!" he yelled as he passed her.

This would only work once. To jump on a fast moving steed, after sitting still for hours, was not as easy as it sounded. Joy reached for his hand and gave a yell of triumph when she caught it. Her arm was nearly wrenched out of its socket and she yelped in pain. The momentum of the running horse pushed her up and she found herself – through some miracle – sitting behind Andrew.

Gravity still worked and she struggled to keep her position.

"Hold on!"

He lowered himself against Mommy's neck as they approached a particularly large fallen tree.

"Andrew, stop!" Her voice trembled.

Her seat wasn't secure. She was sure to fall right off on the other side. And then they would both be caught because the gang was right on their tail by the sound of their furious voices.

"Just hold on," Andrew repeated.

Mommy leapt over the tree. Joy dug her knees into the mare's sides, grabbed hold of as much material from Andrew's shirt as she could. As the horse landed and sped on, Joy knew she was going down.

"I got you."

His arm came around her and helped her regain her seat. Mommy raced through the brush and small trees, as agile as a foal. Now and then a branch slapped Joy's cheek, leaving a sting and the warmth of blood slipping down her face. They gained the road and the voices behind them became distant.

After a while, Andrew urged the horse back into the trees to where Minuteman stood tied up. Joy slid off the back and fell onto the soft, spongy ground. Groaning, she rolled onto her back and stared at the darkening sky.

"Joy. We need to put more distance between us and them."

A small whimper broke through her lips. "I'm sorry."

Andrew lifted her to her feet. "Not now. We'll talk later."

That sounded ominous and she dreaded their discussion. It took her a few times to manage to get her foot into the stirrup and swing into the saddle. Her legs trembled from the exhaustion but she was loath to show her weakness.

Andrew pressed Minuteman in to a fast trot. This time, Mommy seemed content to linger at his haunches, but kept up with him nonetheless.

After what seemed like forever, he finally slowed to a walk. He turned toward her and in the twilight it was hard to discern his mood. Joy rehearsed her words in her head.

"What were you thinking?"

That was not the way she had envisioned herself starting this conversation. She lowered her head, her long dark hair obscuring her face.

"I'm sorry." It was that simple. Could he forgive her?

Andrew drew in a long breath. "You didn't answer me." His voice, though not cold, unfeeling – far from the tender way he assured her that he would wait for her.

She kept her face averted. "I didn't want Laura to delay her wedding to Ben. She seemed so excited whenever she talked about it. She still had to finish sewing her dress and there were so many things to consider."

Andrew gave a nasally laugh. "That's very convenient, you know. I had a feeling you might use that excuse."

"It wasn't an excuse," she said, her teeth gritted tightly. "I wouldn't be her friend if I made her go with me."

"Instead you allow her to wonder what has happened to you? Which is more cruel?"

She sucked in a quick breath. "I... That's not..."

Andrew lifted a hand. "The less we talk, the better for the both of us. I suggest we start looking for a place for the night. And you wouldn't have any money left, would you?"

She shook her head, her stomach knotting tightly.

"I didn't think so. I left in a bit of a hurry. Thus, I took no purse."

Her mouth opened. "No... money? But how are we going to get home?"

He gave her a superior look. "We'll manage. I'm sure we can find a kind farmer who would allow us to sleep in his hayloft."

The thought of sleeping in a stable wasn't overly appealing, yet Joy felt a sense of giddiness. She glanced at her traveling companion. He rode silently, his lips pressed into a firm line. Anger poured out from him and yet Joy wouldn't want to be anywhere else.

"How did you find me?" she finally asked.

He flinched as if he had forgotten that she was there. Then he shrugged his shoulders. "I don't know. I heard something off in the woods and decided to investigate. I did come across the broken carriage and knew instantly something was afoot. But I hoped it didn't involve you." He smirked. "It did."

"Fine acting back there."

He pursed his lips. "I wasn't acting."

"Andrew, I-"

He held up a hand. "I don't want to talk. The sooner I deliver you home, the sooner I can return to my home."

Tears burned her eyes. His voice was harsh and pierced her heart deeper than she ever expected.

"Very well."

37

"We need to rest," she groaned. Mommy seemed to agree as she snorted and shook her head. Minuteman seemed as tired as his dam.

Her rear end burned. Her heart ached for the loss. Andrew hadn't said another word all afternoon. They had stopped along a brook only to allow the horses to rest. He had curled up against a young aspen tree and fallen asleep, leaving her mind spinning in circles.

She had lost his love as she knew she would.

What about God? She hadn't turned her back on Him, hadn't tried to bargain with Him. But she had sneaked out. Was He angry with her too? Was that why she had been robbed? Was that why she had lost Andrew's love?

Every action has a consequence. She had decided to deceive Andrew. God didn't like falsity.

They had ridden many more miles and it was getting dark.

"How are we going to find a place to spend the night?" she asked softly, hoping not to raise his ire.

Andrew's brows furrowed deeply and he narrowed his eyes. "I didn't have time to think about packing a bag, Joy. My mother threatened me that if I didn't follow you, she would do me bodily harm. I left with only what I had on my person. Pardon me for trying to do the right thing."

He had come after her and somehow found her. She hoped, prayed, that he would eventually forgive her for leaving in the dead of night.

Help us find a place, Lord, was all she could come up with.

"We should dismount for a while." He graced her with a mischievous grin. "You're wearing suitable footwear this time, are you not?"

She bit her lower lip. "I am, thanks to your generosity."

Andrew's face tightened. "Never mind. Let's try to find a place. The horses need rest."

"Not only the horses," she mumbled and stumbled.

Andrew shot an arm out to steady her. For a moment, they stood in the road, facing each other. He was the first to turn away, tugging on Minuteman's reins to move him along.

Oh, God. I've lost him. I'll do anything to get him ba- She was back to bargaining. With a silent sigh that sounded almost like a whimper, she gave in. *No more demands. You're in control. If You meant it to be, he'll come to see I didn't mean to deceive him.*

No instant peace followed. Joy did find that she was able to let go of her worry.

The sun was setting behind the horizon. Joy was sore of feet, hungry, and tired. Sweat clung to her dress and made her hair stick to her face. Both horses looked dusty, the dirt from the road sticking to their sweaty fur.

It was becoming difficult to see the ruts in the road and Joy stumbled again and again.

"There is something familiar about all this." Andrew lifted her to her feet. She smiled up into his face.

305

"This is old hat to us."

His jaw tightened at the mention of *us*. He turned away and continued trudging down the road. Houses lined the road now and again. They needed a barn for their horses. Although, perhaps they would be sleeping under the stars tonight.

If it weren't for her growling stomach, she would have dropped along the side of the road. As the twilight stretched into evening, it seemed that they would have to sleep with empty stomachs.

"We could stop over yonder." Andrew pointed to a small meadow. "I hope there is water."

There wasn't. They trudged on, flatfooted. Joy winced at the new blisters forming on her newly healed feet. The sky was now the dark purple of night and no possible farm was within reach. Until-

"There's a light." A splash of hope crept through Joy as she pointed to the house surrounded by fields and ramshackle buildings that might be barns.

"Let's pray they let us stay." Andrew passed a worried gaze over both horses. "They are not used to all this."

Joy nodded and they silently approached the house. It was small, no larger than the schoolhouse Joy had attended back home. An addition had been added to the back. It's unpainted siding looked old and weathered, with cracks and moss growing on the lower boards. A large bush grew on the side and by its scent it was lilac. Beyond was a small, empty pasture.

Andrew stepped to the door and knocked. A hollow sound disturbed the chirping of the peepers in the pond by the pasture.

"What is it?"

Joy drew back at the harshness of the voice and blinked when the door opened a crack.

"What do you want?" an old crackly voice demanded.

Andrew drew himself up. "I'm sorry to disturb you, but we are travelers who have been robbed a few miles down the road. They took our money and provisions. Might we ask to sleep in your barn for a night? I promise we'll be on our way first thing in the morning."

Old watery-blue eyes sized him up, then they wavered to Joy, and finally to the dusty horses. They widened slightly, then the door closed.

Andrew turned to her, puzzlement written across his face. "What did I say?"

"I don't think it was what you said, but how you look."

"Mm..." He drew a hand through his hair and brushed off the dust on his once crisp shirt.

"You also have a spot of dirt right there." She pointed to his very opinionated chin, her lips quivering dangerously. "But other than that, you look the gentleman you are."

He cocked his head and lifted his hand. "You still have blood on your cheek."

She drew in a breath when he touched her. His fingers grazed over the scratch then lowered back to his side.

The door was wrenched open again and a wizened man stood framed by the light of an oil lamp. In his right hand he held a very ominous looking pistol. Andrew lifted one hand and put the other protectively around Joy's shoulder.

"We mean you no harm, sir. My name is Andrew Lloyd-Foxx. I own a thoroughbred stud farm near Boston. This is Miss Joy Richards, en

307

route to Hartford. We need a place to stay the night and perhaps some bread and cheese, if you can spare it. We lost-"

"Ya said so. Did ya steal the horses?" The old man pointed to both.

Andrew bristled visibly. "No, sir! That is my stallion Minuteman and his dam."

"They look well-bred." Their possible host poised his lips. "You were robbed, you say?"

"Yes, sir. They took our money and provisions. We have a bit of a ride to get to where we're going."

"Looks like they roughed you up."

Joy flinched as the farmer pointed to her. "No. I'm fine. It was a branch that snapped my face while we were trying to get away."

"Oh, for heaven's sake, Earl. Let them in. Can't you see they are dead on their feet?" A new voice, female this time, came through the door.

Earl growled something over his shoulder and he was pushed out of the way by a tiny woman. Like her husband, her hair had long turned pure white. Her face, like his, was wrinkled and both wore the marks of a rough life spent on the farm. Where his eyes were the blue of a winter sky, hers were almost black.

"Come in, dears. I have some bread and cheese we don't mind sharing with you."

"Thank you, ma'am. I must ask if I may see to our horses first. They've had a long day."

Murmuring something that sounded like disgruntled approval, the old farmer motioned for Andrew to follow him.

"Come on in, dearie. Let the boys take care of the horses."

The thought that her husband was a boy made Joy smile. "Thank you so much. You have no idea how grateful we are. I thought we'd have to bed down in a field. It was so dark out we couldn't make out the road anymore."

The woman, bent over and shuffling forward, nodded. She took Joy's hand and led her into the house. It was one large kitchen with a sitting room to the side. It reminded her of home, with its simple furniture and evidence of hard living. After spending time living in luxury, it gave her a jolt to have almost forgotten how the other folks lived. She blinked against the pressure building up behind her eyes.

"It looks like you had a hard time of it, dearie." The woman's voice drew her out of her musing. She went to the cupboard and took out a tin container. Pouring something into a simple wooden goblet, she handed it to her.

"Fresh this evening. It'll do you some good."

Thirsty beyond measure, Joy drained her goblet of milk in a few gulps. It left a mustache on her upper lip and she wiped it on a dress that had seen better days.

"Thank you."

Suddenly, her limbs felt heavy and sluggish. A wooden plate of cheese and bread was placed in front of her. Her stomach growled softly and the old woman smiled, deepening the wrinkles in her weathered face.

"Eat, child. I'm afraid you and your companion will have to make do with the hayloft tonight. We only have the one bed in the other room, and my husband's rheumatism was acting up today. We'll have weather soon. And the hay needs bringing in." A sigh followed when she shuffled back.

The front door opened and the men entered.

"Edith. This young bloke has offered help to bring in the hay. He said he'd send a letter home to send for his men. All for a night's lodging in the loft and some food."

Andrew shrugged his shoulders. "It's the least I can do." He ate the food set in front of him with great enthusiasm.

"We are so grateful, young man. It would help much. Earl can't do it all by himself and there are only a few boys who are available to help this time around."

As they finished eating, the only sound in the room was the ticking of the clock. Andrew rose and stretched.

"'Till morning, then."

"This is awkward."

Andrew stared at the one sheet he carried up to the hayloft. After having looked in on the horses, who were happily chewing their hay in their stalls, they had climbed the ladder.

Edith and Earl were poor, as evidence that they could only spare one blanket and one sheet.

"You take the sheet. I'll make do with the blanket." Joy took the scratchy, threadbare woolen cover from him.

Her nose twitched with the familiar scent of farm and animal. How many times had she enticed her sister to spend the night in the barn, to tell scary stories, and to sleep among the animals?

Now, the thought of the pieces of straw poking her all night long, leaving her red and itchy in the morning, was unwelcome. She had become spoiled by sweetly scented sheets, delectable warm baths, three square meals a day, not to mention a maid who dressed her every morning.

Andrew groaned as he spread the sheet over a patch of older hay. It was very obvious that they were running low and were in need of harvest. He avoided glancing at Joy, who was curling up on her blanket, her back to the rafters. Her blue eyes pierced into his for only a second, then she looked away.

He crossed his arms behind his head, staring at the cobwebs covering the ceiling. He turned his head and came face to face with a hen, who had decided to bed down in the hay next to him. Although she startled him like no tomorrow, he began to snicker.

"Andrew?"

He turned to his side, using his hands as pillows. "I'm going to sleep next to a chicken."

Soft, melodic sound of laughter come from her. If only she hadn't deceived him, making him remember that all women were cunning, looking only to make a good match.

"The joy of living on a farm," she said, sounding sleepy. She turned to face him, her hands tucked under her head as his were. "Are you going to talk to me at all? Remember, you said you want to court me."

Of course she would bring that up now. "That was then, this is now." He closed his eyes and willed himself to find sleep.

A deep, hiccup of a sigh came from her. "I didn't think, Andrew. I wanted to spare Laura. I care for her and it was my way of expressing it."

"It doesn't matter anymore."

311

She sat up, the moon shining through the opening in the loft casting her face in shadows.

"You aren't going to forgive me? I thought better of you." Disappointment drenched her voice and he found that it slammed him in the heart, making it skip a beat or two.

"Stop talking. It's been a long day. We need sleep."

He turned his back to her.

"How many times would you have me say I'm sorry?"

He exhaled long and softly, keeping his answer to himself.

Hay was poking him through the sheet. Sleep would be difficult to come by. His thoughts were running around and around in circles. Desiring her on one side and despising her for her deceit on the other. Her actions had hurt him more deeply than he ever thought was possible.

Why?

What was it about her actions that affected him so overtly?

Andrew turned back to face her. When he did, it was like scales came off his eyes. It was in his power to forgive. He ought to do it before he fell asleep, and yet, it was hard not to take her action as a personal affront to him.

He needed to choose to forgive. It wouldn't be handed to him.

"Joy?"

He rose and softly padded to where she lay curled up in a ball under her thin blanket. She stirred sleepily, yet when she saw how near he was, her eyes snapped open and she sat up rapidly, drawing her cover to her chin.

"Wh-at?" Her voice filled with panic.

He reached out to touch her face, caressing it gently. Hearing her suck in a sharp breath, he leaned in closer. She pressed a hand to his chest, stopping him.

"What?" she repeated.

He exhaled with a huff, drawing her into his arms. As she became stiff as a board, he pressed his lips to her forehead.

"I'm glad I found you in time. I'm sorry I was so... difficult. There is nothing to forgive." Tipping her chin up, he let himself be taken for a ride in her gaze. When he lowered his face to hers, she drew away.

"Just like that? You forgive me so quickly and all is well between us? And now you're going to kiss me?"

"W-ell. Yes." He tried his charming smile on her, knowing he would win her over instantly.

Joy pushed herself away from him. "I'm sorry, Andrew. I can't... You barely spoke to me moments ago and now you want us to go back to where we were?" Tears glistened in her dark eyes.

He swallowed loudly. "What's wrong with that?"

She rose and moved away. "I'm not some mistress who is at your beck and call. I won't be treated thus. I know I acted out of turn, but you should have believed me. Instead, you decided to think the worst of me. That I was only after your money after all."

He hissed softly and averted his gaze.

"I can see I'm right." Her voice crackled. "I think we both are in need of some sleep."

She took her blanket and moved as far away from him as possible.

Well, that went well, he thought as he crawled back to where he had made his bed. Trying to sleep on the scratchy hay was impossible, so

313

Andrew stared out the open loft door and watched the stars come out one by one.

God, please help me make this right.

38

*H*e didn't wake because of the animals stirring. He didn't even stir to the sound of the rooster crowing. He woke because every inch of him itched like there was no tomorrow.

He rose from his bed and found Joy in the process of getting up. She looked at him and averted her face.

"Good morning," he said, his voice sounding rough from sleep.

"Yes."

He certainly had his work cut out for him. Had he believed that a simple prayer would change her heart over night? It could have, but perhaps God had a journey for him that involved more than simply praying and being delivered.

"I'm so itchy!" he groaned and scratched a tiny welt on his elbow.

Joy came to stand in front of him, scratching her own welts. "I'm covered in bites," she whimpered. Then she sank down on her haunches, her eyes becoming as round as two saucers. "Those aren't mosquito bites, Andrew. It's poison ivy."

He sat up. He'd never been allergic. His brother, on the other hand, had only to look at it to have been afflicted.

"I don't-"

She snatched his hand. "Don't! You'll just make it worse."

The itching was driving him mad already. "Well, what do you suggest I do?" he ground out between clenched teeth.

She gave a soft snicker, then pressed her lips into a tight line.

"Let's see if our hosts will allow you to bathe in oatmeal."

He made a gagging sound. "I refuse to-"

"It's either that or you can suffer all day long. I suspect it's going to be agony to sit in the saddle, itchy and sweaty."

He shot a heated glare in her direction. "Fine!"

It turned out that breakfast was a large meal. The farmer seemed to have very productive chickens, who blessed him with many eggs. They were also offered bacon and bread, along with a cup of watery coffee. When asked if they had some oatmeal to spare, Edith looked at him in pity.

"You poor dear. I'll see what I have. We can heat some water on the stove and you may bathe in the old tub in the barn."

"Sounds lovely," he managed to reply.

Joy, on the other hand, seemed completely at home here. Then again, she had grown up like this. The difference between them slammed into him, gave him more fodder to wonder if...

Had God really picked her as his mate?

Perhaps he had been so enchanted with her uniqueness that he hadn't heard the Lord right. They had such a difference to gap, would it be possible?

As it was, Joy barely looked his way during breakfast. When he and Earl went into the barn to tend the animals, she stayed behind to help with the cleaning of the dishes. As he left the house, he heard her chatting with Edith as if she had known her all her life.

"Thank you for your hospitality," he managed stiffly, as he tried not to jar his welts.

Minuteman seemed overly happy to see him and knocked him about with his head. Grunting with every move, Andrew hurried through the feeding. The horses needed a good brush but he was in no shape to deliver it today.

"What are your plans, son?"

Son??? He bristled at the familiarity of the farmer's language.

What is going on with me? When had he become an entitled snob?

"Er. We'll leave as soon as possible and ride as long as we can. Then we'll hope to find another kind farmer such as yourself, who won't mind giving us his hayloft to sleep in."

The thought of spending another night on the scratchy surface sounded about as attractive at the moment as a visit to the dentist.

"Mmm..."

Earl was a man of few words and they worked side by side to feed and care for the animals, which consisted of two cows, numerous chicken – who fluttered about the barn freely – and a litter of piglets with Momma pig suspiciously watching every move they made.

"Are you ready for a bath?"

Joy appeared, carrying two heavy buckets. Water sloshed over the edge and onto her skirt. Feeling like he should offer, he dashed over to her.

"Allow me."

She laughed caustically. "Do you think I can't handle a bit of water? This is what I do, Andrew."

Earl pointed to the tub. "You can bathe in there."

Did the old farmer actually snicker softly?

"Oh..."

Words couldn't describe how he felt. The 'tub' an old wooden crate, standing underneath a spout to catch the rain water. Presently, a few spiders had decided to spin their web across the top. Joy leaned closer, a smirk spreading over her face. She was enjoying herself.

"It's worse than it looks."

He turned to her and gave a half grunt, half laugh. "I'm sure I'll enjoy it thoroughly."

"I could only heat up a few buckets on the stove. It would have taken all day. I'd rather get on the road, so... I'll get the rest of the water from the well," Joy snickered.

That didn't sound so bad. At least it was clean-ish.

A part of her felt sorry for him, and the other part wanted him to suffer. Why was he making her feel like this? What about him was bringing out a part of her she was unfamiliar with?

Andrew dumped another bucket of chilled water and gazed forlornly at the 'tub', looking completely pathetic. Red, oozing welts had sprung up all over his arms. She even spotted some on his neck. He was going to be in tremendous pain and yet she secretly enjoyed it.

You are sick! Where is your compassion? He was kind to you.

And he also ripped her heart out and stepped on it.

She poured another bucketful into the tub and added some oatmeal. It wasn't much, but it was all Edith had been able to spare.

"Your bath is ready." She gave a grand bow. Then she said, kindly, "At least it'll ease some of the itching, Andrew."

He grunted and gazed around. "I'm supposed to get undressed and..." He pointed to the surroundings. "For all the world to see?"

Joy bit her bottom lip. "I'll get the sheet and... hold it up."

"Joy!" He groaned. "Don't be silly. Just... go inside and warn everyone, or something. Although, a towel would be nice."

She shook her head. "No towel. It's coarse and would hurt you in your... delicate... state." She clamped her lips tightly.

"Mm..."

Andrew looked at the tub, then back at her. With a sigh, he motioned for her to disappear. She turned quickly, hoping he didn't hear her laughter as she entered the house.

An hour later, the sun still low in the morning sky, they were on the road again. The horses were fresher than either had expected, eager to be on the road. A good night's rest had done wonders for either of them. If only their human companions felt the same.

With every jar, every step, Andrew pressed his lips together, biting back a grunt or groan. The oatmeal he had bathed in had dried on his skin. Joy fared much better, although her hind end was beginning to feel the strain of too many hours in the saddle. When they stopped to rest the horses before noon, both exhaled in relief.

"I'll take care of the horses," she said as Andrew dismounted.

"No. I'll take care of my own."

She lifted her chin. "As you wish, my lord," she said icily.

319

Andrew paused. "I didn't mean..."

"I know what you didn't mean, Andrew." She swallowed hard. "*Master* Andrew."

Her eyes burned as she quickly turned to lead Mommy to a brook in the woods just off the road. Andrew followed behind.

"Joy. Don't do that."

She snapped around. "Why not, sir? You've made it clear what you meant. When we reach my family's farm, you are free to return with Mommy."

"She was a gift," he ground out.

"I don't deserve her. I thank you." She continued her angry stomping walk through the woods.

"Don't be childish." His hand on her arm drew her around.

Her anger had become palpable.

"Forgive me," he said softly.

She scrunched up her nose and stared at him. The oatmeal had left a film all over him and had cracked in places as it dried. It had to itch worse than the welts on his arms, which were oozing freely now.

All the disappointment she felt for him evaporated.

"I... forgive you," she whispered. "But I won't be your mistress or your on again off again love interest."

39

$\mathcal{H}$e held her gaze for a long time. Then he turned without a word to lead Minuteman to the brook and allowed his horse to drink. Feeling like her world was tumbling head over heels and not knowing how to handle the emotions that were roiling inside her, she followed. Both horses drank greedily.

They didn't speak until they rested in a meadow, shade from large maple and oak trees making it an attractive spot to rest for a while. They removed the horses' saddles and tied them to a tree, allowing them to graze.

Settling on the ground, Andrew pulled out the sandwiches Edith had made for them. The couple had been a godsend, after all, providing them with shelter and provisions.

"We should be home by evening," she said, uncomfortable with the silence between them.

Andrew brushed crumbs from his rumpled shirt and took a swig from the water skin they had been given. He once again held her gaze for far too long that she felt heat travel to her cheeks.

"Do I have something on my face?" she finally inquired.

He gave a weak smile and was about to scratch a spot on his neck when he thought against it.

"May I tell you a favorite memory of my parents?" he asked, picking a blade of grass and slowly shredding it.

"Why?"

He gave a grim smile. "Because you already know my secret of helping runaways. Now I want you to know this part of me."

"It wouldn't be wise since we'll be parting ways soon." A sharp wrenching of her heart felt as if a piece had broken off.

He gave a long sigh and leaned carefully against Minuteman's saddle. "Let's not jump to conclusions, shall we?"

"You've made it clear that you don't intend-"

"I have made nothing clear," he growled. "You are drawing conclusions and perhaps this story will help me express my wishes to you. I have failed. I – Andrew Lloyd-Foxx – benevolent rescuer of those less fortunate, have once again stepped into a giant hole and made a mess of it. I seem to do that often with you around. Allow me to elaborate further, Joy."

She narrowed her eyes and leaned on her elbows. "As you wish, Master Andrew."

He nailed her with a heated glare. "Would you please stop that? Are you going to punish me every time we quarrel by calling me that? I believe we'll have our fair share of disagreements, Joy."

She stared at him moodily and stuffed another small chunk of cheese into the corner of her mouth. The left side of his lips twitched. Then he leaned back, the muscles in his jaw convulsing, and closed his eyes.

"I loved my father. He was a man of integrity and honor, doing the right thing even when it was not popular. It didn't make him any friends, but he never seemed to mind. My grandfather, on the other hand, was steeped in tradition. He believed that it was his right to have slaves, even though he treated them very well and tried to keep families together as much as possible. When my father took over the estate, the first thing he did was

322

give them their freedom. Many stayed on as servants. His father also had several mistresses over time. One of them bore him children."

She gulped at air. "I don't want to know."

His lips twitched again, yet he never opened his eyes. "I was twelve when my brother and I were playing hide and seek. It was a cold, rainy day, and we were driving my mother insane. My father was with us at the estate, preparing the defense of a Negro accused of beating a white man. He had already threatened to use the belt on us if we didn't find something quiet to amuse ourselves with. Both Peter and I knew it was an empty threat.

"It was my turn to hide and I had found a perfect spot across the hall from the parlor where my parents were taking tea together. We had moved a fortnight before and all was still so new and exciting. My father being there was a rare treat as his law practice kept him in Boston during the week and most weekends.

"I could hear their soft conversation and I knew that my mother was sad for some reason. I'd never seen her cry in front of us, but now I could see that she seemed to have been crying. *I suppose with me and the children in the country, it makes it easier for you to have a mistress in Boston, Tom. Someone ought to be beside you when you are hosting a party,* she said to him and I could hear her teacup clatter against the saucer.

"My father became very still. He turned toward me, although he didn't see me. I saw the hurt in his eyes. Then he turned back to my mother and said in a very bored tone, *Madam, I cannot handle the one wife God has given me. What in the world would possess me to try to keep more than one woman in line? When I entertain the partners or anyone else, I would want nobody beside me but you.*"

Joy gasped softly.

"It was the first time I ever heard my mother giggle. She rose from her chair and kissed my father's cheek, another thing she never did. My father hugged her and held her for a long time.

"Peter came crashing through the door, looking for me, and ruined the moment. But I'll never forget what I heard and saw that afternoon. My parents weren't outwardly affectionate with each other. It wasn't done. But once in a while I'd catch my father's gaze when my mother walked in and I remembered that conversation.

"My father knew what a mistress had done to his parent's marriage. I have an uncle and aunt somewhere. We don't acknowledge them, but they are there. They came for the holidays, they were part of the extended family celebrations. The mistress always lingered in the background, causing angry outbursts from my grandmother." He peered at Joy through halfway opened eyes. "I will not do that to anyone."

Joy sniffed and shifted her attention to the horses. "Why are you telling me this?" she whispered, her voice barely loud enough to be heard.

"Because, even though my parent's marriage started off as an arrangement, they loved each other. When I marry, it'll not be for financial gain, or social status. It's going to be one person. I was hoping I had found that person when I met you."

Her gaze drifted back to him and she wished her heart would stop beating so rapidly that it made her breathless.

"You are unique, different from the women I've socialized with. I felt God moving me to court you." He sat up and kept his steely-gray eyes fastened on her. "I want to be sure. I don't want to break your heart if it isn't meant to be."

Too late. Another wrench in her chest confirmed it.

"We don't know each other well and thus we do not trust each other. I would like to remedy that. I meant it when I said I would like to court you. When we arrive at your house, I will ask your father for permission."

She swallowed loudly.

"It won't be easy to blend into my world, Joy. We will be looked down upon. You will have to learn which fork does what-"

She snickered. "I already know that."

He grinned. "You do. See, you have already learned in a week what took me a lifetime to learn."

"I'm game. Are you?"

His gin deepened. "I think so. I'm sorry for what I said."

She shifted closer. "And I'm sorry for running off by myself again. And thank you for coming to my rescue. Again."

His arms slipped around her waist, drawing her to him. "It was my pleasure. Third time's the charm?"

She allowed the smile that had been teasing to break free. "I hope it's the last time."

He gave an bored yawn. "Me too. I find this hero business very tiring."

Her laugh was cut off by a kiss.

The sun was hovering over the horizon when they crossed the Connecticut river by ferry. Another hour and she would be home. Already, the air tasted familiar, the sights were like long lost friends. Since their reprieve at noon they had pushed the horses hard, stopping only to water them.

"I used to swim with my friends in this brook." She pointed to the side of the road.

Everything was familiar. Even the birds sounded like old pals. Joy laughed.

"I'm almost home."

Andrew nodded. "And thank the Lord for it. I hope you have a proper tub. I think I have a splinter from that old..."

"We do have a tub and I'm sure my mother has an herbal remedy to help your itch."

He shifted uncomfortably in the saddle. "I don't need help to itch, I need it to stop."

She giggled. "My mother will help *stop* the itch."

A wry smile appeared on his face. "I hope so. This is maddening. I want to rip my skin off."

She cocked her head. "Please don't."

They were riding through a small farming town. On the left was a post office and Andrew let out a happy laugh.

"I can send a letter to my mother to wire me some money. And to send help to Earl and Edith."

"Yes. But you still have no money to send the missive with." She gave him a smug look. "I'm sure my parents can spot you the penny or two."

"Do you think you could convince them that I'm good for it?"

She drew her bottom lip between her teeth and gave him a coy look. "I'll do my best. But you really don't look like the wealthy gentleman who rescued me from the tavern. I may have problems convincing them."

"Your father will know the moment he sees the horses."

"They don't exactly look like the shiny racehorses from the track either."

He gave a puff of air that sent the hair covering his forehead flying up. "Woman. Confound it." He looked flustered, yet couldn't hide the slight smirk.

Farther down the road beyond the town center, she pulled Mommy to a sudden stop.

"What?"

"Home," she breathed and pointed to a spread on the left.

The saltbox house had once been red with crisp white trim. Now the color had faded, the clapboard shingles worn and cracked. The shutters on the small farmhouse sagged. One banged against the house in the slight evening breeze. A sagging porch hugged the front, its roof missing shingles to allow the sun to poke through.

Off to the side stood a rickety barn, leaning precariously to one side. He wouldn't consider it fit to stable his horses for the night. The fields beyond were overgrown with grass easily reaching his hips, the fence posts rotting out. More shingles lay shattered on the ground near the dilapidated building.

"Oh." Joy's voice strangled. "It looks worse than before."

An eerie silence hung over the place. No animals wandered around in the yard or pasture. Her mother's garden, however, looked as though it had been planted and tended. Snap peas and beans, as well as other plants, grew on tall vines and thick bushes. Potato plants seemed to be thriving. At least something was alive.

"You... grew up here?"

His question caused her stomach to clench tightly. "It used to look so much better before my father's accident. I told you. We fell on hard times."

The breeze tickled her neck and caused the hairs on her arms to stand up. Or was it more than a sudden chill due to the sinking sun?

Where was her mother?

At this time in the afternoon she usually sat on the front porch, doing her mending. And that was another thing that was missing. No clothes had been strung out on the line between the barn and the side of the house.

"I... think... something isn't right," she stammered.

Andrew's eyebrows rose in an arch.

"Something is off."

She kicked Mommy into a canter and halted her in the yard in a cloud of dust. Not trusting the posts of the porch to hold the mare, she let her wander the lawn and snack on the overgrown grass. Andrew careened to a halt next to her.

"What do you mean?"

She shook her head and raced up the steps to the front porch, Her foot went through the rotten wood in the top stair and she let out a sharp yelp as splinters pricked through her boot.

And then she stepped inside. The door to the small breezeway complained loudly.

Andrew caught her wrist. "Be careful. The house looks like it is about to collapse."

She brushed him off. "It's fine."

As soon as she entered, Joy could smell it. Something rotten stunk up the whole house. Her mother kept a neat and tidy home, even if they didn't have much.

Andrew bumped into her and sent her stumbling into the main room of the house. On the left side was a small sitting area around an oft-used potbelly stove. Dust motes danced a lazy dance in the light of the sun coming in from one of the windows.

The stench made it hard to concentrate.

"You're right. Something is wrong."

In the center of the living room/kitchen was a hallway with two doors opposite each other. One of these doors was ajar. The kitchen was a mess. Shattered plates lay on the worn wood floor. Jars of her mother's precious jams lay smashed among them. A chair had been overturned, its legs broken and splintered and-

A strangled cry escaped her as she dove to the prone figure on the floor by the large kitchen table.

"Mom!"

The woman who had birthed her was bleeding all over the scuffed up floorboards from a wound in her gut, the hilt of knife sticking up.

40

*T*his was not the way he had pictured delivering Joy home to her family. He hadn't expected the chaos around him, the stench of something long gone, nor the woman bleeding all over the floor. He lowered himself to his haunches, swallowing the bile that rose in his throat and checked for a pulse. He leaned back on his heels when he found one.

"She's alive. We... should stop the bleeding," he said, his voice trembling. "I-I think-"

Joy dashed to the cupboard and wrenched a drawer open, nearly spilling its contents on the floor. When she knelt back by his side, she looked at him with big eyes.

"We need to take it out." Pointed to the knife.

He shook his head. "No. She'll bleed out. We need to secure the hilt and bandage around it."

Her fingers trembled terribly and her face had a green, near translucent shine to it.

"Where's your father?" he asked.

Joy's gaze lifted down the corridor and the partially opened door.

"He's..." She swallowed loudly. "He's back there. I should check on him."

Andrew nodded, continuing to wrap the clean dish towel around the wound.. A scream wrenched the silence. A moment later, Joy rushed past him, out the front door where she leaned over the porch railing, retching. His own stomach did a curious flip, causing him to feel nauseous. He rose and stood behind Joy as she bent over again, bringing up more contents of her stomach. He rubbed his hand over her back and kept the hair from tumbling into her face.

She slumped against the creaking post, burying her face in her arms. Shoulders trembled and shook as sobs took hold of her body. He didn't need to ask why. The stench in the house now made sense.

He swallowed more bile and wrapped his arm around Joy's shoulders.

"How?" His voice cracked.

"Shot in the head," she whimpered. "There's blood all over his... and the flies." She gagged and pressed a tremulous hand against her lips.

Air whooshed out of his lungs. This certainly was a terrible homecoming.

"My sister." Joy's head snapped up. "What if they took Hope?"

He squeezed her arm. "First things first. Your mother is alive. You know where the doctor is. Go get him. And the sheriff. Hurry. I'll take care of her wound as well as I can. She's lost a lot of blood."

Joy sniffed and wiped her sleeve across her nose. "Right."

"Take Minuteman. He's faster and younger."

She nodded and hurried to where the stallion was grazing. Andrew hurried back inside, all too aware now of the reason for the stench. If he focused on her mother, perhaps he could ignore the images in his mind. The scent of blood permeated everything.

Joy's mother groaned softly, making him focus on her.

"Ma'am. We are getting the doctor."

God, please give Minuteman wings and help Joy to fetch help swiftly. Give this woman strength to pull through. And help Joy deal with the painful loss of a parent, perhaps both. I pray for her sister to be safe.

The rag in his hands was saturated with blood, staining his own hands. Andrew swallowed loudly.

Joy's vision was blurred as she urged greater speed from the horse underneath her. She knew he had it in him and he delivered. The town came into view sooner than expected. She galloped through the center of the sleepy town and down one of the side streets.

God, please let him be there. God, please let him be there.

She repeated this prayer until she stopped at the third house on the right, a modest red brick building with the physician's shingle above the door. Minuteman's legs were covered in dust as she pulled him to a stop right outside the door and tied him up hurriedly. He panted hard, but she had no time to see to him.

Bursting through the front door, she entered into the waiting room that smelled of cleaning solutions. A woman in a white apron sat at a desk, knitting something Joy didn't have the energy to identify. She looked up and her wrinkled face crinkled in confusion.

"Joy? Joy Richards? It's about time you came back home. Where on earth have you been? Your parents have been worried sick about you-"

"Mrs. McClourd. There's been a horrible... disaster at the house. M-my p-parents are..." She hiccuped. "My m-mother is bleeding. We need the doctor and the sheriff. Someone sh-shot my d-dad."

Her limbs trembled like aspen leaves in the gale storm.

Mrs. McClourd, the physician's wife, stared at her. "Child! What are you babbling on about?"

"Help, please. Where is your husband? My mother is dying."

The older woman's knitting clattered to the ground. "He's out at the Thompson's farm at the moment. Mrs. Thompson is having her ninth baby and there are complications."

Joy didn't even stop to bid her a good day. The Thompsons owned a large dairy farm clear across town.

"Please get the sheriff to my house," she shouted as she ran back to the waiting stallion.

And they were off again at speeds so fast, it would have made her laugh in pleasure. But she didn't. Her mother was bleeding to death and her father-

Tears burned in her eyes, blurring her vision completely.

Please, God...

Andrew counted the times the woman's chest rose and fell ever so slightly. That it still did so was good, very good. It meant he didn't have to tell Joy that her other parent had died. He had gone to her father's room and seen what had happened.

It would be one image he wouldn't be able to rid himself of for a long time. The unseeing eyes that stared at heaven so much like Joy's in color. The blood. The stench of decaying flesh.

The woman in front of him moaned again and this time her eyelids fluttered. He leaned closer.

"Can you hear me, Mrs. Richards?"

She lay still again, only the sound of her raged and laborious breath filling the room. It seemed like hours until the sound of wagon wheels could be heard in front of the house. The door to the room opened and banged shut. A tall, elderly man strode purposefully into the kitchen, a physician's bag clutched in his hand.

He drew in a sharp breath when he took a whiff of the air and focused on the prone figure on the floor.

"Dr. McClourd, family physician."

Andrew exhaled slowly and eased out of the way to let the more qualified man take over.

"She's lost a lot of blood. Has she regained consciousness since you've been here?" The doctor checked his watch as he examined her pulse.

"No, sir. She's moved but hasn't awakened."

"Mm." He tenderly probed her head. "She received a nasty knock on the head. This wound needs to be stitched up. Are you up to assisting?"

He had decided not to pursue becoming a physician because... Once again, Andrew's stomach dipped and swirled.

"Of course."

"Mm..." The man looked him up and down, then turned his attention to the door, which banged open.

Joy rushed in. Her hair had been blown about, tears had made clear lines down her dusty face. Her dress hung off her as if she had worn it for days. Gone was the refined woman he held in his arms not long ago.

Somehow, he felt more attracted to her than ever.

She skidded to a halt next to him and fell to her knees. "How is she?"

Her blue eyes beseeched the doctor to say something, anything to assure her.

"She's lost a lot of blood. This wound needs stitching and she may be bleeding internally."

She gasped, her face turning deathly pale under all the layers of dirt.

"Your companion has kindly offered to assist."

Andrew swallowed visibly and gave a crooked grin. "Remember, I do have some medical training."

Joy shook her head. "This is my job, Dr. McCloud."

"Joy!" Andrew felt the need to voice a protest. She was a woman. The thought of her assisting the doctor caused his stomach to twist at even greater magnitude.

"Andrew. Could you see to the horses? I... need to do this. The sheriff is on his way. I passed him in town. After, would you and he move my father's body." Tears darkened her eyes.

He nodded. "I'll do whatever you need me to do."

Joy's gut churned violently as she tried to focus on the doctor's equipment. Blood spilled slowly from her mother and soaked into the sheets of Joy's bed. While the the knife was being removed, her mother had arched her back and howled in pain.

Her mother hadn't gained consciousness but her breath labored as the doctor stitched her up. Joy tried to go into her imagination to cut out the horror around her. For the first time in her life she was unsuccessful. The voices of the other men in the house prevented her from escaping.

"It was clearly a robbery," the sheriff was saying. "We've been having a wave of it around the area. Now, we can add murder to it."

The door to what had been Joy and her sister's bedroom stood partially open. Andrew and the doctor had carefully laid her mother into Joy's bed for the surgery. The scent of blood was everywhere, the stench of decay clung to everything. Death was all around.

Not wanting to disturb the doctor's concentration, she longed to inquire about her sister. Her bed looked as if she hadn't occupied it in a long time, her things had been cleared out. Where had she gone?

"Ah..."

Joy averted her eyes, focusing on the braided rug on the floor, avoiding looking at her mother's head. She felt beyond sick.

"Do you have any suspects?" Andrew asked.

"Not at the moment. I'm sorry, Mr. Lloyd-Foxx."

"I'm willing to offer a substantial reward for anyone to help find those who did this."

"Of course, sir. Is there anything I could do for you?"

"Now that you mention it..." The men moved out of hearing. Joy watched a fly land on her dusty boot.

"It's done, Joy. Would you please take these instruments and wash them in clean, hot water?"

Her mother's blood was on the scalpel and the needle that had been used to stitch up the wound.

"W-will she make it?" she asked, her voice weak and tremulous.

Dr. McClourd gave a grimace. "Time and prayer. And keeping the wound clean. That is of utmost importance. I will show you how. I will stay until I'm called back to the Thompsons'."

336

Prayer.

Joy sat in the chair, her mother's hand in hers. She tenderly rubbed her thumb over the top of wrinkled, cool skin.

God. This shouldn't have happened. Please heal my mother. I'm so sad that I didn't get to say good-bye to my father. Please, let me find my sister unharmed. Bless Andrew and... Bless Andrew and his family.

Her father's body had been moved yet the house still reeked of death.

"I need to clean my parent's room."

Dr. McClourd nodded earnestly. "Indeed. Cleanliness will help speed your mother's recovery. But Joy. We will see how she fares. If she survives tonight..."

Once again tears clouded her eyes. "Thank you for all you've done."

She walked to the front door, which stood open as did every window in the house. Andrew was still talking to the sheriff and a group of men who had come with him.

"I'll send for the undertaker," one of the men was saying and jumped onto a buckboard. He whipped the pair of draft horses into a trot. As they drove toward town, she saw the shrouded body in the back.

Suddenly it all hit Joy as if she had slammed into a stone wall. The world spun around her at a fast pace and she groped for something to hold her up before she came crashing down. The railing was steady enough to slow her descent. Joy sank slowly onto the worn boards of the porch.

Her father was dead. Her mother might soon follow. Her sister was unaccounted for.

Jesus. My sister... my baby sister...

337

Words couldn't describe how she felt. Her mind was incapable of stringing syllables together to make sense of how her heart felt as if it was being wrenched out of her chest. Her head felt like it was ready to pop off her body.

I hear your cry, My daughter. I heard it before you even uttered a thought. Do not be dismayed. I am near.

Her heart stuttered. Had she heard those thoughts correctly? Could it be that she really was heard and understood? She felt the truth in her heart of hearts.

"Joy."

It was too difficult to raise her gaze. She knew Andrew stood next to her. It was too arduous to acknowledge him.

The boards creaked ominously as he lowered himself next to her.

"I'm so sorry," he whispered and wrapped his arms around her tightly. He smoothed a hand over the back of her head.

She let herself be held, allowed herself to draw strength from him when she didn't have any.

"I'll take care of your father's mattress," he said after what seemed an eternity, "and all the funeral arrangements. I don't want you and your family to have to worry about it. I'll also pay for the doctor and a nurse to tend to your mother."

"I want to take care of her," she mumbled, her voice muffled by his arms.

"Let me have the doctor send for the best nurse there is in this area. Your mother deserves that much. You can tend her but allow me to put an experienced nurse in charge."

Joy finally found the strength to lift her head. She traced his jaw, rough from the lack of shaving. "You're a good man, Andrew. My family is in your debt."

He grinned sheepishly. "Good. I could use the extra points when I ask her for your hand in marriage."

She drew away slightly. "We can't. There's the mourning period to consider. And should you really marry a woman who... I... I've been defiled." A chill passed through her. She couldn't quite meet his eyes.

Andrew gathered her against him and pressed his lips to her forehead. "God looks to the heart, Joy. He deems you beautiful and who am I to question Him? You have been made pure by Christ's sacrifice. It's good enough for me."

"Andrew." Her voice was but a whisper against his cheek. The world tilted and began to fade as he lowered his lips to hers, his gaze never leaving her eyes until they came together.

41

*I*t was much later when the doctor entered the kitchen. Joy had spent the remainder of the afternoon unsuccessfully scrubbing the floor to get rid of the stain of blood. Every window was open and slowly the stench of decay had been replaced by the sweet odor of various flowers Joy had picked and placed in jars around the house.

Andrew had gotten rid of the mattress soaked with her father's blood. Thankfully, he had carried it out the back door and had buried it somewhere. Joy didn't even ask. He had taken care of the horses and had pumped water into the tub in the hut they used for bathing in the summer.

He hadn't complained once about his poison ivy, which looked like it had to be itching him like crazy. Joy had found some oatmeal and gave it to him to soak in. He had given a sigh of relief and walked off.

The horses had been tied up outside, nibbling the tall grass. Andrew had also come across the cow, Bessie, wandering around the pasture with a very full udder. Joy would milk her later on when things in the house had been set to order.

Her mother loved a tidy house. They didn't have much, but she expected it neat and trim.

She rose to her feet as Dr. McClourd entered.

"How is my mother?"

340

He placed a hand on her shoulder. "She's still breathing, her pulse is steady. Mr. Lloyd-Foxx asked me to send for the best nurse in the area. I will take the liberty to do so this evening when I return to town. She should arrive tomorrow. Can I ask you to care for your mother until then?"

She wasn't a nurse. Joy didn't hesitate one second.

"Yes."

"That's my girl." A twinkle appeared in the doctor's eyes as he rummaged around in his large bag. He came up with a purple lollipop. "You may have this since you were a good girl."

She giggled and gave the man who had delivered her into this world her best curtsey.

"Why don't you fetch Mrs. Fleming? I'm convinced she'll want to help her best friend. And ask her to bring some of that broth of hers. Your mother will need it."

Her mother's best friend. Yes, it was a good plan.

"I will go right away.'"

She wasn't going to disturb Andrew while he was taking a bath, so Joy saddled Mommy and trotted toward the Fleming homestead. It lay about three miles from town and was a very big spread. Mr. Fleming, Uncle Paul, as he was known to her and her sister, had been a solicitor before he took over the farm. He had done very well for himself.

Aunt Penny, his wife, had been her mother's best friend since they had attended the one room schoolhouse. They both had married and their friendship lasted.

The large farmhouse with the well-trimmed front lawn and extensive flower bed soon came into view. It was as if Joy hadn't left at all. Everything was the same. Cheerful checkered curtains flapped through the open windows, the scent of homemade baking tickled her nose and made her stomach growl. It occurred to her that she hadn't eaten much beyond the cheese and bread Eliza had given them.

The front door opened as soon as Mommy came to a halt at the hitching post.

"Joy?"

Her stomach gave a squeeze as she turned toward the woman who had practically been her second mother.

"Oh, Joy!"

Warm, tender arms wrapped around her. The aroma of home cooking clung to the spindly woman. She held her at arm's length and gave her a long scrupulous inspection. When she seemed satisfied, she gave a sharp huff.

"You're much too thin, honey. And whatever happened to you in Boston? Why didn't you keep in touch with-"

Joy held up her hand. "It's a very, very long story and I don't have time to tell you now. My... I need your help." Tears burned again and she blinked rapidly. "Mom needs you. She was attacked and is in bad shape. The doctor is with her right now."

Penny Fleming sucked in a sharp breath and shook the flour off her apron.

"What about your father? He was feeling poorly last week and your mother had a bout of the cold. She asked me to look in on him from time to time. I-"

342

Joy swiped a finger under her eye, catching the tear that had begun to flow. "He's dead." It hurt to say.

Penny's eyes widened. "How?"

"There must have been a robbery. They stabbed Mom and-" She swallowed loudly – "sh-shot Dad."

"Oh, Joy!"

"I need you to help me nurse Mom."

Penny Fleming spun around on her heel. "I'll be over right away. Is there anything else I can do for you?"

Joy shuffled from foot to foot. "We don't have food. Dr. McClourd asked if you could bring some of your broth for Mom. Would you have some to spare?"

Penny smiled sweetly and squeezed Joy's arm. "I'll bring some of my famous stew and some bread and cheese. And, yes. I'll fetch the broth."

Joy kissed her cheek. "Thank you, Aunt Penny."

As she turned to hurry back to Mommy, she remembered something very important. Aunt Penny would know.

"Do you know where Hope is? I don't think she's been home for a long time."

Her mother's best friend snickered. "Of course I know where Hope is. She's with her husband. My Jonah."

Joy drew back. "Hope married Jonah?"

Penny Fleming nodded. "I'll send Paul to fetch her. We'll come as soon as we can."

Joy nodded. "Hurry. I don't know how long Mom can hold on."

Andrew winced as he dried off as well as he could. It felt good to take the oatmeal bath. He felt like a new man, until everything dried and he would once again be tempted to scratch his skin off.

Joy trotted into the yard and slipped off Mommy. She walked her to where Minuteman had been tied up to a pick line and attached her next to him. Both horses were able to lie down, eat grass to their heart's content, and rest after the strenuous ride.

"Did you find what you were looking for?"

Joy looked at the ramshackle house, sighed, then looked back at him. "She's coming and bringing help. My sister, Hope."

"You found her? That's a good thing, then."

Joy leaned wearily against him and he tried not to think about how itchy he already was. He folded her into his arms and kissed her forehead.

"She's married." Her voice sounded funny – off.

"Nice. That's one bit of good news, then."

Joy lifted her head and gave him a somewhat weak smile. "Yes. Of course. I need to see to my mother."

He stepped away and let her go. Something was definitely not right here. But they had both been through a lot in the span of an afternoon and they were both feeling weary. Her eyes shone darkly, sparkling as if a thousand candles had been lit across a canvas of deep blue sky. Finding himself falling into their depths, he welcomed it. He caught her back to him, cupped her cheek with the palm of his hand.

"Let me take care of you," he whispered.

She pressed into him and blinked rapidly. "I wish you would," she breathed.

A tear slipped down her cheek before Andrew caught it with his thumb, leaning in to capture her lips. She yielded to him, a soft sigh slipping from her mouth. He deepened the kiss, the desire of more now rushing through him like an avalanche. Her lips were soft and welcoming, and he wanted-

"We shouldn't..."

Joy drew away. Her hand resting against his chest spread an incredible amount of heat and he found himself longing for more – so much more. His mind told him that she was right.

That they couldn't go any further.

That they had already exceeded the limit of what was allowed for a courtship.

His thumping, pulsing heart wanted none of the limits.

Andrew's jaw tensed as he fought to regain control. Joy's forehead rested against his, her unique scent of horse, sweat, hay and desire dragged him back to a place he knew he shouldn't – couldn't – go.

Nevertheless, to avoid fornication, let every man have his own wife, and let every woman have her own husband...

Andrew's mind engaged and he drew farther from her upon this reminder. If he allowed himself this pleasure – something he did not usually indulge – he would destroy her trust.

"You're right. We shouldn't," he rasped.

Joy's gaze fastened on him, drew him back into that place he shouldn't allow himself to go. It was then that the creaking of wagon wheels drew both their attention to the road. The softest of groans escaped her lips as she turned toward it.

Andrew stepped away and let Joy go. She ran toward the newcomers, while he turned to tend his horses.

The reunion wasn't what Joy had pictured. Hope was all grown up. Her honey-colored hair was neatly braided, she wore a lovely dress. The smile on her face was tentative – shy. The hug she gave was too.

"I've missed you. We feared something terrible had become of you."

Joy forced her lips into a smile. "We'll talk about it later. First, we need to tend to Mom."

Hope hitched her skirts and handed Joy a basket filled with food.

"I'm here to help. What can I do?"

The three women walked into the house. Since she had been outside for hours, the scent of blood and death was like a wall she had been slammed into.

Her mother's face was pale, near translucent. The bandage that surrounded her mother's wound was stained red. Dr. McClourd had shown her to clean the wound with wine, then soak the bandage with an alcohol solution, then secure it. He had also left some laudanum, instructing her to give one teaspoon when needed for the pain.

She hated the stuff.

Her father used to scream at them if he didn't have his dose of this medicine. She suspected that he had become addicted to it. Aunt Penny helped her, while Hope soaked the bandages.

"She's in good hands until a professional nurse arrives."

Once the women were done, they settled onto chairs. Silence was oppressive, the only sound the slow, regular breathing coming from her mother.

In all of this craze, Joy suddenly realized that she wasn't all that worried. Why was it that she could look at her mother with some peace, not knowing what would become of her?

She suddenly realized that in this storm of life, she was safe. The outcome was not sure, but God was with her. For the first time in her life, she felt divine arms surrounding her. Tears gathered in her eyes again, this time not because she had no strength or was terrified of the outcome.

God is with me.

Her heart filled with thankfulness.

"Joy," her sister gasped.

She had completely forgotten that she wasn't alone. The peace she felt was unworldly. It was, until she turned to where Hope was pointing to her mother. Her breath caught in her throat.

Her green eyes were open, darting around the room in fear. When they came to rest on her, they widened and her mother whimpered softly.

"Mommy." Hope reached for her hand.

"J-oy?" She whispered her name so softly that it could have been mistaken for a whimper.

"I'm here, Mom."

Auntie Penny moved into view and doled out the teaspoon of laudanum. Her mother's eyelids fluttered and closed. Soon she was breathing slowly again, sleep beginning its healing.

Hope motioned for her to follow her into the kitchen. Once there, she faced her sister.

347

"It's so good to see you, Joy." Her pale green eyes sparkled as if they had been dipped in diamonds. "We feared the worst. Where have you been all this time?"

She wasn't ready to tell all. "Things didn't go the way we had thought they would. I didn't end up working for a family. It was all a ruse. I... will tell it when the time is right. I'm so happy to see you, Hope. I worried that something may have happened to you." She hugged her sister tightly and could feel her tense.

"I... married Jonah."

Joy forced a smile. Why did it bother her so much that her sister was happily married to him? "That's wonderful. He's taking good care of you?"

Hope pressed a hand to her belly. "We're expecting our first child in seven months, or thereabouts." She giggled and her cheeks turned a becoming pink.

Confounded. Hope has it all! What do I have? Nothing.

Her heart gave a slight lurch when she realized how wrong she was. She had more. So much more. God's peace could not be taken from her. His joy remained with her, no matter how hard life would be.

The front door opened and Andrew walked in. Her heart did more than thump loudly. Not only that but a flock of butterflies burst into flight in the center of her gut. The fluttering traveled up her spine, across her shoulders.

And then he grinned at her.

42

*A*untie Penny stepped into the kitchen and focused immediately on Andrew, who remained near the door.

"Who are you and what do you want?"

Joy flinched at her terse tone and jumped in with an explanation.

"He's... he's with me. We're... I work for his mother and Andrew... was kind enough... to come with me."

Obviously she had omitted quite a few important details and Andrew's aristocratic brow rose into a very impressive arch. It seemed that Auntie Penny and Hope both smelled a rat as their faces turned to her as if waiting for more. Finally, Andrew stepped forward.

"Andrew Lloyd-Foxx. It's a pleasure to meet you. You must be Hope." He kissed her sister's knuckles in the most charming manner. "I've heard much about you."

Hope blushed bright red. Auntie Penny's eyes narrowed suspiciously and she crossed her arms over her ample chest.

"That's quite a mouthful, sir. What do we call you? Mr. Lloyd? Or Mr. Foxx?"

Hope snorted and covered it with a cough.

Andrew's lips twitched. "How about Andrew?" He reached out his hand.

"Mmm..." Her mother's best friend relented and shook it.

Joy greedily sucked in the air as she had forgotten to breathe during this exchange.

"Exactly what do you require Joy to do for your mother?"

Andrew rested his hip against the wall as if he were completely at home in this kitchen, as if he wasn't an outsider.

"She's her companion. It's a relatively new position and we're in the process of negotiating the length of her employ."

Joy snorted and covered it up with a quick cough. When everyone turned to her, she mumbled something like, "Sorry. Swallowed a dust mite. Tickled my throat."

Auntie Penny once again turned toward Andrew, giving him one of her scrupulous examinations. He didn't even flinch.

"And what does your family do? Where do you live?"

Andrew shifted slightly. "We live near Boston on an estate. Although we do have a residence in the city, where my mother enjoys to spend the fall and winter to take in the society events. I oversee the breeding, training, and running of our racehorses, and supervise our other various enterprises."

Auntie Penny's mouth scrunched up. "You make your living by turning people to gambling on horses." She gave a disgusted snort. "I see what sort of enterprise you have."

"Auntie Penny! Andrew and his mother are wonderful people. We wouldn't be here if it weren't for them. They have become my friends." She swallowed hard. "I have felt very welcome at their estate."

"Joy. Your father will be mortified about-" It was as if Penny realized that the girl's father had recently passed away in a very violent manner and her lips snapped shut with a loud pop. "I'm sorry."

Silence clung to those words.

"How is your mother?" Andrew asked, breaking the stillness.

Grateful that his interrogation had been interrupted, Joy said in a slightly hurried manner, "She woke up just now. We gave her laudanum and she's sleeping more peacefully."

Andrew nodded. "I want you to spare no expense in her medical treatment. I'm very eager to make sure your mother is taken care of. I believe the doctor is sending for an expert nurse. I can make some more inquiries, if you feel the need to have more than one nurse attending her. I will also ask mother if she could spare some help around the house. You don't need to care for your mother and run this house at the same time."

"That's very generous, Mr. Andrew. But we can take care of our own," Auntie Penny replied somewhat caustically. "And where will you be staying tonight?"

Now he shuffled from foot to foot. "I believe the girls should not be here alone, not with thieves and murderers running around town. I'll sleep outside on the porch."

Joy gasped. He was used to the softest of feather beds, his sheets the finest linen money could buy. He could not sleep on the partially rotten floor on the porch.

But he had slept in the hay.

And now look at him – covered in a poison ivy rash.

"There is no need for you to stay, Mr. Andrew. Hope's husband will attend the girls tonight."

It was like watching a sparring match of wills. Joy's eyes popped from one person to the other. Andrew was in for a hard time.

"I would feel more assured if I did."

Hope looked like she was about to crawl into the crack on the floor.

"As I said, my Jonah will come. Perhaps you should be on your way back to your estate. I'm sure a man in your position has many responsibilities that can't wait."

Andrew gave a smile that never reached his eyes. "I assure you, ma'am. A man in my position has others who can do the job for me. I'm very content to stay and see that the girl's mother is recovering well."

"Andrew." Joy couldn't stand it much longer. "I didn't groom Mommy after I rode her into town. Could you..."

His right eyebrow inched up slightly, then he bowed. "Yes. I'll take care of it. I'll also milk that poor cow we found wandering around."

"Have you... ever milked a cow before?" Her voice sounded strangely strangled. "I don't think it's such a good idea."

Andrew blew a breath out his nose and waved a hand. "How difficult can it be?"

She cocked her head.

"I will take care of it. And tomorrow I'll start on the roof of that barn."

Her stomach lurched at the thought of him on a ladder. As he strode purposefully toward the door, Joy caught him.

"Have you ever replaced a roof before?" she whispered.

He patted her shoulder. "You take care of your mother. I am a man with many qualities. I'll take care of it."

Joy blushed. "I know you have many talents, but none have to do with roofing a barn."

He leaned close, the scent of outdoor, horse, hay and masculinity tickling her nose. Her insides took a tumble, rearranging themselves in a most disagreeable manner. Not only that but she found herself in short supply of air. He seemed to know the effect he was having on her and grinned devilishly.

Both Auntie Penny and Hope stared at her when she joined them by her mother's side.

"Your *friend* is an interesting man." Auntie Penny picked up a knitting needle and started on a lovely blanket. Hope settled back and took out some shirts she was mending. Her eyes darted to and from their mother's best friend and Joy.

Hope was sweet. She had always been innocent, kind, child-like. She never engaged in arguments and avoided conflict like the smallpox. Her whole nature was to be compliant.

Jonah had married a perfect wife.

The thought didn't settle on Joy well. Hope was married. She was expecting a child. She was settled.

What about me?

"Joy? Mr. Andrew is interesting. How did you meet?"

Oh... "He came and took me away from the place I worked before," she babbled and felt the heat rise to her cheeks.

"Where was that? The family in Boston? Your mother was so proud of you, child. But after the first month she became concerned that she hadn't heard from you. We began to wonder." Dark brown eyes, the color of coffee with a touch of cream, narrowed.

Joy swallowed down the dread. "There was no family, Auntie," she whispered. "It was all a falsehood."

Hope's eyes filled with tears and Auntie Penny stilled. The old woman flinched.

"Where have you been for two years, girl?"

Shame as thick as her aunt's stew sloshed over her and she couldn't help but lower her head. Her cheeks now burned with heat and her stomach churned nervously.

"I was passed from person to person until I ended up as a barmaid in a sordid tavern. That's where Andrew found me and rescued me. So you see, Aunt Penny. He's a good man."

"Joy," Hope whispered and reached for her hand. "I'm sorry. So sorry. I should have gone with you."

Joy shook her head rapidly. "No. You wouldn't have survived. Not that you're weak. You are the sweetest person I've ever met. It would have destroyed you. I'm glad you didn't... I'm glad you're married." She smiled, this time meaning it with every fiber of her being. "I worried about you the whole time. Thinking of you in the places I ended up in... It was horrible." Her vision blurred.

Hope jumped up and wrapped her arms around her neck. "When Auntie came to tell me, I was afraid you would be angry at me for marrying Jonah," she whispered.

Joy grinned wryly, casting a quick glance at Penny, whose ears seemed to have grown in an attempt to hear the whispered conversation.

"How can I be upset with you? You and Jonah are happy." Joy squeezed her sister's arm.

Joy walked toward the barn, where she saw Bessie had been corralled in one of the runs right outside. The posts hadn't all rotted away. Mommy and Minuteman were munching on grass in the same enclosure. Andrew was seated on the tree-legged milking stool. His sleeves were rolled up and he patted Bessie's bony rump.

"Now, cow. Please be kind. I've never done this before and I don't like to be made a fool of." He sighed and leaned forward. "How hard can this be?"

Bessie, although seemingly docile, had an ornery streak and she didn't appreciate men milking her. The only ones who had taken such liberty with her had been the women of the family. At eight years of age, she wasn't about to let that change. She waited for the milk to start flowing until she kicked the bucket to send it flying. It sloshed over Andrew, his once expensive shirt hanging listlessly off him, soaked with milk.

"I say..."

He tried again, and the bucket sloshed over him once more, covering him from head to toe. Joy giggled and he turned.

"How long have you been watching?" His expression was thunderous.

"Long enough to know you shouldn't be milking Bessie. She likes it done in a certain way."

He bristled and shook the liquid from his hair. "This is *not* how I imagined it."

He stepped away and motioned for her to take a seat. The cow was thoroughly put out, her tail swishing at Andrew. It whipped him in the rear end and he yelped.

"What have I done to deserve this?"

Joy grinned. "Nothing. She doesn't like men."

He stared. "You could have warned me."

She gave him a honey-sweet glance. "Would you have listened?"

He glowered and glared at the cow, who seemed to settle down after Joy cooed softly to her, her cheek resting on the animal's flank.

"You make it look so easy."

"It is. But they also say that milk is very good for your skin, Sir Poison Ivy."

He arched an eyebrow and leaned closer. "I will make you regret that, Joy Richards."

She giggled and concentrated on the cow, not on the man behind her.

The sun was sinking low on the horizon. They had eaten the stew Auntie Penny had brought and waited for their mother to wake again. It hadn't happened. The doctor had been by and declared that he was pleased that she had woken once already.

Andrew appeared, dressed in one of their father's clothes. He was approximately his height, although the pants were slightly short. Seeing him wear the worn pants, the homespun shirt, caused something to loosen inside Joy.

When he had eaten his bowl of stew, he had turned to Auntie Penny.

"I must say, madam, this is the tastiest stew I've ever had the pleasure of consuming." He even smacked his lips together as he scraped the last morsel onto his spoon. Auntie Penny looked quite mollified and even went so far as to blush.

"My husband went hunting last month and shot a particularly large buck. We've been enjoying the spoils."

Andrew nodded appreciatively. "Mm... It's delicious. Thank you so much. Now I shall take care of the animals."

"One moment, *Mister* Andrew. What are your intentions toward Joy? Why are you here?"

Andrew exchanged a quick glance with Joy. "She's been a great encouragement to my mother, and I love, eh, like her enthusiasm when it comes to horses."

Both Hope and Auntie Penny stared. Joy decided to pick up the empty dishes, lowering her head so the hair fell across her face pulsing with heat.

She had hoped to avoid this subject until her mother was better. Her wish that Andrew meet her father had... failed.

"That tells us nothing." Auntie Penny crossed her arms tightly over her chest and squared her shoulders. Andrew drew himself to his full height.

"I believe that this is a discussion I will be having with Joy's mother, all due respect to you. I will wait until she's well enough to hear me. In the meantime, I wish to be useful to this family."

Oh Andrew, you wonderful, deluded man. Auntie Penny is going to eat you for breakfast.

43

*A*s Andrew and the older woman were about to square off in a verbal duel, the sound of creaking wagon wheels interrupted them. Andrew strode to the door just in time to see a tall man in neat, yet simple clothing set the brake and jump down from the seat. He stopped as he saw the horses and took a closer look.

When Andrew stepped onto the porch, the newcomer focused on him. A puzzled look passed over his face and he brushed his wheat-colored hair from his forehead, securing it under a hat. Then he marched toward Andrew.

"Good evening."

Andrew nodded. "And who might you be?"

"Jonah!" Hope stepped out and went to her husband, who wrapped his arms around her.

Ah, the son has arrived.

Andrew retreated into the house, giving the couple a moment to linger outside.

"Is that Jonah?" Auntie Penny asked, her face beaming as if the sun was shining inside the home.

"Yes, ma'am. He's talking to his wife."

Joy leaned against the frame of the door to her room. She avoided his gaze but kept her eyes peeled on the front door. There was something she wasn't telling him. That something had to do with her sister's husband. Andrew didn't like how he suddenly felt the urge to challenge Jonah to a duel.

He wasn't a jealous man. But right now, he didn't exactly like Jonah, even though he seemed to be a family favorite.

Jonah coming threw her for a time loop.

It took her back to when she and Jonah were sitting in the hayloft, watching the dancers below. That night seemed like another lifetime ago. She'd had one dream. To carry on her father's business and perhaps marry the handsome son of her mother's best friend one day. That night, it seemed like something might come of it as they sat so close that their legs brushed together, their hands touched on occasion. He had never promised anything, even after that. But something had shifted between them, giving her hope.

What would have happened if he had asked her to marry him three years ago? She would be the one expecting a child now. She would be the one tending a small homestead. She would be...

A ripple of a terrifying memory passed through her. It was dark in her small cubby of a space. The night was nearly spent and still. She heard the creaking of footfalls on the stairs, across the floor. Soon he would be on her, hurting her, taking from her what she wasn't willing to give.

Joy shook herself out of the memory and concentrated on the present. If she hadn't been through all those horrible things, she would never have met Andrew.

She would have missed the opportunity to ride amazing horses.

She shifted her attention to where Andrew was sitting on the old, cracked kitchen chair. He ground his teeth and raised a hand to a patch of the rash on his forearm. Thinking better of it, he lowered his hand and caught her gaze and held it. Warmth spilled into her from a glance that enveloped her. She was completely at his mercy and found herself drawing instinctively nearer. Her feet loosened from the ground and carried her to where he was sitting completely still, watching her like a hawk. A calculating, devilishly charming smile slowly tipped his lips up, causing a slight chill to replace the warmth.

It made her feel out of control and reckless, ready to abandon anything if only he would ask her to.

It also wiped out every ounce of regret she might have felt. The peace she had felt earlier still lingered, though she had to search around in her heart for it.

Jonah removed his hat when he entered. Their gazes locked. Joy felt nothing for the boy she had hoped to spend the rest of her life with. Smiling a welcome, she stepped toward him.

"Jonah. It's good to see you."

Joy reached both hands out to him. Jonah nodded and shuffled his feet back and forth.

"I'm sorry about your father. I will help in any way, shape or form I can."

"Thank you. That's very kind of you. Congratulations on your marriage. You are a blessed man." Joy turned toward Andrew. "This is Andrew Lloyd-Foxx, a friend. He accompanied me here."

Jonah narrowed his eyes, nodded, and shook hands with Andrew. It was all very civil. The men seemed to suspect something about each other, yet none had threatened the other for a duel.

"We worried when we stopped hearing from you, Joy."

She waved her hand as if swatting at a lazy fly. "It's no matter. I'm here now."

Auntie Penny left soon after supper to tend to her own family. She still had two strapping boys to feed as well as her husband. She threw a warning glance in Andrew's direction.

"If I hear of any funny business going on... This isn't Boston, you know. We do have standards."

It seemed to amuse Andrew. Not so Joy. She couldn't push her out the front door fast enough. Then she joined her sister, sitting vigil over her mother.

It was past midnight, both girls were falling asleep, when Joy nudged Hope.

"Why don't you go home tonight, Hope. I can take over the nursing for tonight. Come back tomorrow morning."

"I don't think so, Joy. Jonah can sleep in the hayloft with Mr. Andrew."

Joy flinched. "I don't know if that will go over so well. He did catch poison ivy last time he tried that." She snickered. "I think he wants to sleep on the porch."

Hope smiled. "Very well, then. Let's tell them."

Both walked out into the darkened kitchen. A candle stood in the window by the wash basin, giving enough light to see the dark outlines of the furniture. Joy could traverse this small house with her hands behind her back and her eyes closed.

When they reached the partially open front door, the sound of snoring reached their ears. Hope turned to her, her big eyes growing even bigger. The men had stretched out across the front porch, their snoring making the shingles on the roof tremble.

"I don't think they care," Hope whispered, her voice sounding slightly strangled.

Joy nodded, pressing her hand into her mouth to prevent herself from bursting into laughter.

It was early in the morning, the pre-dawn light illuminating the room enough to start making out the details. Joy had been awake, sitting by her mother's bedside, praying.

Lord, please heal my mother's body and mind. Give the nurse wisdom. Help me to-

Her mother's eyes opened.

"Mom," Joy whispered and leaned forward.

Her mother's pupils enlarged, making her eyes appear black.

"Joy? A dream?"

Joy covered her hand with her own. "I'm here, Mom. I'll take care of you. Everything will work out in the end."

Brows puckered and a moan slipped through cracked lips.

"Thirsty."

Carefully, Joy spooned broth into her mother's parched throat. Much of it spilled down her cheeks and chin. When it was done, her mother closed her eyes.

"What... Pain."

A deep furrow had formed between her eyebrows.

"I'll give you something."

A dose of laudanum settled her mother back into sleep. This became a routine much throughout the morning and into the afternoon. Between Joy and her sister, her mother was never alone. God's presence was palpable. It had been all night. It was as if the heavy, humid air of summer night had become saturated with God.

By the afternoon, her mother's body was threatening to pull itself apart with chills that came from a fever. Her teeth chattered together, threatening to shatter them all. Jonah was sent to fetch the doctor, who arrived with a young woman, perhaps a year or so older than Joy.

Nurse Marion had arrived. Tall, slender, raven-black hair tucked into a no-nonsense bun, piercingly blue eyes quickly assessing the situation, she took over in a matter of moments and began to order the girls around like a matron in a hospital ward.

Andrew and Jonah kept to the barn. There was enough work to be done there and neither felt the need to get in the way of the women.

"How do you think it's going in there?" Andrew asked, taking a sip of water from the pitcher.

The men had been working on tarring the roof of the barn. It was thirsty work and Andrew's poison ivy rash was itching him like crazy.

Jonah scratched his scruffy jaw. "I would say that Hope is probably trying to help Nurse Marion without query. Joy is probably questioning every decision the poor woman makes." His lips twitched into a grin.

Andrew's lips formed a line. "I suspect you are right. She does have a tendency to make you explain yourself."

"Mm. She does that. It's quite tiring. Wouldn't you agree?" Jonah took a sip.

"I think it makes her more interesting. She speaks her mind, even when it might not be welcome." Andrew snickered.

Jonah gave him a thorough inspection. "You mean to court her properly, I suppose? And marry her?"

Andrew's throat had dried out enough for him to not be able to answer this question at the time, so he nodded.

"But you're of high social standing. How could you marry a simple farm girl? Wouldn't that cause trouble within the ranks?"

"You let me worry about that," Andrew said. "I know what I'm doing. Besides, this is the ninteenth century."

Jonah stepped toward him, his brown eyes narrowed. "Don't hurt that girl, you hear. I'll hunt you down."

"My intentions are honorable. You have my word."

They returned to their hot work, the sun beating down their backs all afternoon. At quitting time, their relationship had thawed enough so they could jest with each other.

44

*M*iss Richard! I assure you that this is quite normal. Your mother will wake up. She's doing remarkably well. I know what I'm doing."

Joy glared. The woman annoyed her with her nose up in the air as if she was better than everyone. Her mother had longer periods of wakefulness, which were filled with delusional babbling.

"Her fever is breaking," Nurse Marion said slightly kinder. "She'll get better."

Her mother had lingered near death for three days now. Her father had been buried the day before. Joy found herself in a bubble where she was practically numb to all feelings. Was this God's way of having her deal with it? Would she always be unable to feel?

Over breakfast of eggs and bread, Andrew had told her that the barn was almost suitable for inhabitants again. She hadn't seen neither him nor Jonah all day, sitting with her mother as she was.

"I need to stretch."

Joy found Hope stretched out on the divan in the front room. It had been an heirloom from her father's parents, given to them when they were married. It had been patched and patched again, although her mother always kept it neat. Hope lifted her head and rubbed the sleep from her eyes.

"I didn't mean to startle you," Joy whispered.

Hope massaged her belly tenderly. "Come sit with me. The nurse seems to have it all under control. I like Andrew. He and Jonah have worked so hard in the last couple of days. He's a good man. But... is he right for you?" Hope took her hand and drew a thumb over the top.

A group of spiders had been set loose inside her stomach and crawled all around.

"I think he is. He's rescued me from myself several times. He doesn't care that I'm a farmer's daughter. In fact, he called me a snob when I pointed it out to him several times." She gave a soft laugh. "His mother is wonderful and manipulative. She's a regular matchmaker. And there is a maid by the name of Laura."

Joy proceeded to tell her sister all about her new home at the estate.

"You love it there. They've become family to you." Hope's eyes filled with tears.

"As Jonah has for you, Hope."

Her sister blushed. "I hoped you wouldn't hate me too much for marrying him."

Once again, her gaze traveled outside. The men were coming in from the pump, having washed off the grime as well as they could. They were talking and laughing with each other.

"He was never meant for me," she said softly. "I thought, wished, it for a time but God had other plans. It seems that His are much more perfect for me."

Hope hugged her. "An estate with horses. You'll be running the household and the servants." Her baby sister looked at her in awe.

"Well... it runs itself," Joy stammered.

"You always were meant for something greater." Hope kissed her cheek.

Joy gasped.

"I'm going to see Mother. Get some rest, Joy."

Andrew shifted on the hay, trying to find a comfortable spot. His poison ivy rash was going away, thanks to Nurse Marion's home remedy. The woman seemed a very capable nurse.

It was a sweltering hot night in the hayloft and he wasn't going to get any sleep. Rising from the pile of hay he had been resting on, he groaned. He felt the ache of muscles he hadn't known existed and he considered himself a fit man.

Minuteman snorted softly as he walked past him. He scratched his velvety nose and continued out the barn door. A light breeze tickled his cheek, fluffed his hair. It felt good. He almost missed sleeping on the rickety porch.

He strolled away from the house, toward the small pond out back. Perhaps a swim would rinse off the grime on his body. He quickly stripped off his shirt and submerged into the water. It felt glorious to be clean after a day of hard work.

Coming out, he reached for his shirt when he spotted a lone figure sitting by the freshly dug grave in the family graveyard. His heart started to tap out an irregular pattern.

Joy.

Quietly, hoping not to disturb her, he came to stand next to her. With a start she jumped, and he regretted his stealth.

"It's you," she whispered and tucked a strand of her dark hair behind her ear.

"Yes. May I?" He pointed to a patch of grass next to her.

She didn't say anything, just smiled. Andrew picked at a blade of grass, tucking it between his teeth. Joy ran her hand over the top of the grass that hadn't been trampled by the mourners the day before.

"It was a very beautiful service."

She nodded. "My mother missed it. She doesn't even know he's gone."

They sat silently until Joy sniffled softly. He turned to her and caught her chin.

"I'm sorry."

She swallowed audibly. "Thank you. It means so much that you are here with me now."

"I seem to recall a time when you were at my side when I suffered a great loss. Not that a horse can be compared to a father."

"Both are heavy to bear."

More silence followed as Andrew quietly slipped his arm around her shoulders. She rested her head against it and returned to her vigil.

"May I tell you about him?"

The moon rose, larger than normal, casting a silver, dreamy light about them.

"I'd be honored."

"In many ways he was a hard man. He was never overly loving. He never just came into our room to tell us he loved us. He demonstrated it, when he could. The pair of boots I told you about, I was so proud of them. The look he would give me when a horse I had been training received high

368

praises from the owner. Those were the things that showed me how much he loved me."

"How about Jonah?" Although the men had an easy relationship, it was a question that lingered in the back of his mind.

Joy stiffened just a little, then relaxed. "We were comfortable together. It was as though we would just slip conveniently into marriage. But he never asked. And then I went away. I'm glad. Hope and Jonah are a much better match then we ever would have been. And then there is you." She traced his scruffy jaw with her fingertips, igniting a flame inside him.

"There is me." He lingered on her face, memorizing every inch of it. "And it's a good thing?"

Her face lit like the rising sun. "What do you think?"

He leaned close and covered her lips with his, mindful that the desire to go too far was lingering underneath the surface. When they drew apart, something had cemented in his heart.

He would never let her go.

"I should go inside."

He rose and assisted her to her feet. They walked toward the barn, hand in hand. Feeling reluctant to let her go, he drew her to him one last time.

"I love you, Joy Richards."

Her eyes widened and she inhaled sharply. Resting her forehead against his, she held his gaze.

"I love you too, Andrew Lloyd-Foxx."

Her mother woke up the next morning, slightly dazed yet more lucid than before. She answered Nurse Marion's simple question, then allowed her daughters to feed her some more of the broth Auntie Penny had brought over earlier. When the nurse excused herself – after checking on the wound and pronouncing it well – the girls gathered around her.

"Sweet Hope," her mother whispered and held her younger daughter's gaze.

Tears stung Joy's eyes when she turned to her.

"And you're back." Her voice was barely strong enough to be heard.

"I..."

"She brought her beau with her," Hope giggled.

The eyes widened and she cocked her head.

"It's not what it seems."

Hope's laugh became louder. "That's not what Nurse Marion said. She saw you two by the barn last night. It looked cozy, according to our witness."

Joy grappled for something to say, to defend herself. Her mother only smiled and closed her eyes. She didn't go back to sleep because she returned her gaze to her eldest not seconds later. A question lingered in their depth.

"He's a respectable gentleman from outside of Boston. His family have been breeding – oh Mom, you are going to love this – descendants of the Godolphin Arabian." The words flowed out with such force, like the floodgates of heaven had been opened. "And he gave me one of them. I saw

370

a race, and I danced at a ball, and I... I was able to ride his horses. One of them tossed me like I was a sack of potatoes. Dad would have been so-"

She stilled. Her mother didn't know her husband had died.

"Mom-"

"I know." Tears pooled in her eyes and splashed down her temples onto the pillow. "I could feel it in my heart."

Joy felt her heart break for her mother. Even though her father had been a hard man, her parents had loved each other. Her mother had nursed him after his accident. What would her mother do now?

"He's finally at peace now."

A heavy silence settled on everyone.

"Tell me more about the gentleman."

Her mother was awake long enough to hear about how he had rescued her from the abusive tavern owner, had given her a new start.

"When you're better, I'll introduce you to Mommy. She's my horse." Joy continued to talk about the time she and Mommy had given Ladiesman a run for his money. Her mother smiled when she retold about the impromptu race the day before the actual race.

"I want you to meet Andrew. He and Jonah are working hard to fix things up." *And he's very handy at that too.*

Her mother nodded wearily. "I will. Now I need to rest."

Joy slept until early morning. When she woke, the house was silent. It gave her a moment to pray and think. It occurred to her then that no matter what happened with her mother, God could take her at any moment. It made her mindful of what she had, thankful of the fragments of time they were spending together.

371

Joy scooted into a sitting position and stared at the predawn light coming through the small window. One of the window panes was cracked. Andrew was right, her mother could not stay here for the winter.

Her mother would need nursing far beyond tomorrow, and Hope had her husband to care for now along with a baby. She had made a promise to return to Massachusetts. Her desire was to go back with Andrew but the reality was that her mother would need her.

Instead of fretting, Joy put her new found trust in God to use.

Father. I'm in Your hands. I will not rant or rave, bargain or throw a fit. I pray for my mother, that she'll gain her strength back and that she suffers no ill effect from this. I am your maidservant. I'll go wherever You send me. I wish to return with Andrew, start a life with him. But You know what's down the road for me. I rely on You, Jesus. Please guide me.

With Nurse Marion stirring in the room across from hers, she wanted to be out of the woman's space. When she entered the barn, the cow greeted her with a bellow and Mommy's nostrils quivered. Andrew must have gotten up early to feed them because their manger was filled with hay.

Her gaze traveled to the empty stall next to Mommy.

"Andrew?"

Her voice was absorbed by the walls. Nobody answered her.

Her heart dropped into the pit of her stomach.

The only sound was the crunching of animal's teeth on their breakfast. Where was he?

She swallowed hard against the pressure on the back of her throat. What if he had left her? What if he had enough of this meager living?

The fear she had given over to God rose in her chest. Why had he left in the middle of the night without saying good-bye?

What goes around comes around, Joy Richards. Why wouldn't he leave? There was nothing to keep him here.

She closed her mind off to those disturbing thoughts. She knew better. Andrew wouldn't leave without giving her a heads up. He loved her. He had given her a horse.

He loves me.

She tried to focus on milking Bessie. Her mind was whirling.

What about joy? Where did that go?

Joy ground her teeth hard.

Her 'joy' had been swept away by the onset of fear. When she thought about her situation, she realized she didn't have enough information. Andrew may have left.

And if he did, what are you going to do?

She would manage. If Andrew had left, there had to be a reason. Her hope couldn't be in Andrew. It couldn't be in her mother surviving. It had to have a deeper route. Her hope had to come through Christ.

With a start she realized she had found what Andrew had talked about in the beginning when they met. She had found joy.

All her life she may have trusted God in everything, but in practice it was so much harder than she thought. She closed her eyes and turned her attention toward her heart.

I have to be joyful in this too, she thought and prayed. *I have to know that whatever You have for me, is good for me, even though I may not see the goodness in it. In the end, it will come out right. If Andrew left, there was a reason for it. And I will be alright without him. I have to be alright without him. There is no guarantee that our life together will be long, or short.*

She was leaning against the barn door, taking a deep breath of the humid air, when she heard it.

Muffled thuds from the hooves came from the direction of the road. Moments later, Minuteman trotted into the yard. Andrew slipped off his back and grinned when he saw her.

"Good morning."

She cleared her throat. "Where have you been?"

He frowned and walked his horse into his stall to untack him.

"He needed a run. He was acting like he had ants in his hooves. So I took him."

Her smile faltered.

"You thought I had taken off?"

Andrew drew close to her. The scent of horse and hay tickled her nose.

"I... may have."

He tipped her chin up so he could peer into her eyes. "I'm not going anywhere. I told you, Joy. I love you. You're stuck with me."

Warmth vibrated through her whole body.

"Can you tell me that again?" she asked.

Andrew grinned in that charming manner and folded his arms around her.

"Miss Richards. I love you. I want to spend the rest of my life with you." He kissed her forehead.

Her joy, although not dependent of this circumstance, was complete.

45

*F*ixing the roof on the house was difficult work. The sun beat down on both their backs and Andrew contemplated taking off his shirt. But Jonah's mother was in the kitchen and she continued to glare at him whenever they met.

She's not a fan.

Jonah handed him another bunch of shingles. The men had driven into town early in the morning and had ordered enough supply to fix up the house so that Joy's mother wouldn't need to worry about the repairs. There was a long list of things that needed replacing.

"Getting tired, city-boy?"

Jonah's teasing was pleasant. It reminded him of his brother. Andrew swallowed a lump produced by that thought. He honestly couldn't remember his brother's voice.

"I'll show you, farm-boy."

They laughed and Andrew found his attention wavering. Joy had stepped out of the house. Since her mother had woken up two days ago, she seemed to be less weary and burdened. Her cheeks had turned a healthy pink during the time they had come to stay here. She walked with a bounce in her steps, passing the ladder he and Jonah were using.

Her eyes sparkled when she looked up at him. He saw a flash of mischief and found himself quite drawn to her. Jonah elbowed him, bringing him back to reality.

"Are you just going to stare at us like that or are you here to lend a hand?"

Her eyes flashed. Challenge accepted.

"Are you suggesting, sir, that I come up there and show you how it's done?"

Andrew grinned, then climbed down the rickety ladder.

"You going to show me how it's done, Miss Richards?"

She cocked her head to the side, measuring him up. "I can do that with my eyes closed."

"Of course you can, madam." Andrew handed her the hammer. He motioned to the ladder. "Enjoy. Jonah and I were getting tired. It's hot out here today."

Joy stared at the hammer in her hand and tipped her chin into the air.

"I won't even dignify that with a response."

She turned on her heel and, after placing the plate full of sandwiches and cups of mint tea on the railing, returned to the house.

Jonah had come down from the roof and gave him an awkward grin. "See what I mean? She's trouble."

Andrew chuckled. "Just the kind I like. I train thoroughbreds."

Jonah chuckled and turned to climb back up the ladder. Andrew was about to follow along, when his attention was snagged on the sound of a carriage coming toward them.

His head snapped around when the team of horses stopped in front of the house. He recognized the rig as well as the animals pulling it. Even the driver had a familiar look about him. The man jumped from his seat as soon as he had secured the vehicle. He placed a step next to the door and opened it.

Andrew drew in a breath as his stomach flipped. Trying to blend into the shade of the post, he knew it was too late.

"Andrew Patrick Lloyd-Foxx! Don't even think of hiding from your mother!"

He squared his shoulders and stepped toward the carriage.

"Mother. What a surprise. I didn't know you were coming."

His mother held out her cheek for him to dutifully peck. As he did so, Laura stepped out. She wore a sheepish smile and kept her face averted.

"We decided that after your letter, that it would be best if I came and saw things for myself. How is Joy's mother? Is she being attended by a physician?" She gave him a look from top to bottom. "What are you wearing, son?"

He shuffled from foot to foot. "Mother. May I introduce Jonah Fleming, Joy's brother-in-law. Joy is inside, seeing to her mother. You just missed the doctor, who is very capable. A nurse is attending Mrs. Richards. Welcome to you and Laura. And as to my attire, this is perfectly comfortable."

"Is that poison ivy all over you?"

He groaned inwardly.

"Has the doctor given you something for it? How did you get it? And what are you doing?" She looked at the ladder leaning against the porch and at Jonah peering down from the roof.

"Mother..." he grunted. "I'm helping where I can. I caught poison ivy on my way here. It's getting better."

Sleeping in the hayloft was not something he was going to explain to his mother. She would have a spell of the vapors.

"Oh my." She sniffled disgustedly. "You are doing manual labor."

"Swinging a hammer is quite therapeutic. You should try it once or twice." He offered the tool he was carrying to his mother, who gasped ladylike and tipped her nose in the air.

"I wish to see Joy and her mother."

He bowed and offered her his arm.

Her mother sipped the broth Joy had given her. Every hour, she regained her strength more and more. Hope had stayed home today because she wasn't feeling well. Aunt Penny stayed with her.

"What's on your mind, child. I can practically... see the thoughts... tumbling around."

"I'm worried, Mom. I don't want to leave you here by yourself."

"What..." Her mother touched her temple as if in pain. She released her breath very slowly.

"Do you need more medicine?"

Her mother shook her head very slowly. "It will make me fuzzy in the head. You mentioned something earlier about leaving again. Your home is with me now."

Tears obscured Joy's vision. "I can't stay. I gave my word that I would return to the estate. Mrs. Lloyd-Foxx is counting on me. She pays well, Mom. I can support you with my income."

Her mother sighed. "I suppose… I could stay here alone. Jonah and Hope are close. With your income, we might make it."

Joy nodded and took her mother's hand in hers, watching her fall back asleep.

Andrew hoped his mother wouldn't faint when they stepped into the house. Although Joy and her sister, along with Jonah's mother, had cleaned every inch and the scent of death had disappeared, it was such a simple home. His mother had never set foot into a house like this.

"Oh."

She sniffed and lifted her chin.

"Joy grew up here?" she whispered to him.

Andrew nodded. "They are farmers, Mother. Don't judge."

She squared her jaw. "I wouldn't, Andrew! I was merely saying… I want to help."

His expression softened. "I know. It's been hard for them."

He steered her toward the hallway and knocked on the door to the bedroom. Joy opened and froze.

"Mrs. Lloyd-Foxx," she breathed, looking as if a boulder had dropped on her toes. "Wh-at are you doing-"

His mother wrapped her arms around Joy.

"I'm sorry for your loss, child. I came to help."

Joy looked at him with horror in her eyes.

"Eh… There isn't much you can do right now."

"Please come in," a weak voice called from within.

379

Joy hadn't expected her mother to perk up so quickly. She had asked Nurse Marion to help her sit up and had made sure that the sheets were arranged just so. Mrs. Lloyd-Foxx had looked uncomfortable at first but soon she was talking as if the two of them had been friends all their lives.

Andrew, on the other hand, was received in a cooler manner. It was as if her mother was trying to figure out if he was worth her daughter's affections. He quietly sat there as the women talked.

"Andrew and Jonah have been working hard on fixing up the barn and porch roof." Joy finally had enough of his silence.

Her mother nodded. "Thank you, Mr. Lloyd-Foxx."

"Please. I'm Andrew, Mrs. Richards. It was my pleasure." He smiled that charming grin.

Her mother's taut features relaxed. "So, you're my Joy's beau, then? I supposed she could do worse. A man who knows how to swing the hammer and isn't afraid of hard work is worth his weight in gold."

Andrew's tanned cheeks deepened to a crimson.

When her mother's eyes drifted closed, they all ushered out of the room quietly, leaving only the nurse to attend her.

"She cannot possibly stay here."

Joy's attention was diverted to where Laura sat very stiffly on the old sofa. When their gazes met, Joy saw the hurt of betrayal there.

"You're right, Mother. What do you suggest?"

Mrs. Lloyd-Foxx began to pace. "As soon as she is well enough, we'll bring her to the estate. We'll have the best physicians this side of Boston attend her."

"No," Joy stated quietly. "This is her home. She's not going to want to leave it. Especially with my sister expecting."

Andrew stepped close and placed a hand on her shoulder. "Look around, Joy. This is not a place to convalescence. The window panes are cracked, the roof is close to leak-"

Joy drew herself to her full height and faced him and his mother.

"I appreciate both of your kindness." She swallowed the anger their suggestion had begun to fan inside. "You can't tell me or my family what is right for us. We've taken care of things for a long time. Hope and I will handle it."

Mrs. Lloyd-Foxx swallowed loudly. "I never intended to offend you, Joy. We can provide a comfortable home for your mother, dear. She'll be well taken care of."

"No, thank you."

After a few more attempts to convince her, Andrew ushered Laura and his mother outside.

It was later on in the afternoon when she came outside in search of Andrew. Her temper had cooled. When she spotted him tamping down the ground, she approached tentatively. Would he speak to her after she had shot him down like that?

He looked up and gave her a crooked grin.

"I came to apologize for my outburst. I know you meant well, but-"

He stepped towards her and shook his head. "We are the ones to apologize. My mother and I are used to taking charge and we like to help. Whatever you decide, Joy, I support you. Even though I'd hoped to return to the estate soon."

She cupped his cheeks with her hands. "You and your mother ought to return. I can't. I have to see to it that my mother is well."

"My mother will return. I will stay. You can't get rid of me that easily." He smirked.

"I don't want to. I love you, remember?"

He snickered.

Laura and Mrs. Lloyd-Foxx returned to the house next morning. They had found lodging in town. Joy was finishing milking Bessie when they arrived. Andrew was grooming Minuteman. Once the women alighted from their carriage, Joy greeted them.

"Thank you so much, Mrs. Lloyd-Foxx. You know I appreciate-"

"I wish to visit with your mother. I've brought some reading material. I could sit with her for some time."

Joy drew in a long breath. "That's not necc-"

"I will determine what is necessary, Joy."

The woman swooped past her, leaving Joy and Laura standing in the front room. Joy gave a tentative smile.

"How was your wedding?"

Laura crossed her arms over her chest. "We postponed. Master Andrew was going to preside over the ceremony, since he is an ordained minister."

"He is?"

Laura gave a cool grin. "Yes. I'm surprised you weren't aware."

Joy swallowed past the lump in her throat. "I'm sorry, Laura. I didn't want to interfere with your plans. I knew you and Ben were so excited."

Eyes narrowed. "I would have postponed it until we returned. You matter to me, to all of us. But you had to run off in the middle of the night, like a thief."

She felt the pressure building behind her eyes. "Please forgive me," Joy whispered.

"It might take me a bit. And I'll subject you to more torture when you return to the estate."

Joy snickered. "What torture did you have in mind? I'll do anything."

Laura nodded coolly. "I will think of something. Perhaps a whole week of beauty treatment and baths."

Joy managed not to groan.

"Then I'll forgive you."

Andrew leaned his head against the side of the house. Jonah and Hope had left for the day. The men had been working hard on tarring the roof. He sipped a cool glass of water with a leaf of peppermint adding some taste. His body ached from all the work they had done in the last couple of days. His heart ached for Joy's mother.

She had lost her husband in an instant. It made him think. What would he do if his mother were attacked and killed?

The door opened and his mother stepped onto the rickety porch. She sighed and sat down next to him, facing the barn.

"You've worked hard, Andrew."

He nodded. "Mother. I want you to know that I love you. What you did for Mrs. Richards is very kind."

She waved a hand and dabbed her handkerchief against her forehead. "I did it for myself, son. What am I going to do when you off and marry my companion, hm?"

Andrew let that one settle. Then laughter rumbled through his chest. "What is it with this family and companions?"

His mother giggled and patted his cheek affectionately. "It must be our good blood? Or the women have good taste."

He grinned devilishly. "That they do indeed."

46

*H*appy laughter came from the room Joy's mother had been occupying for the past two weeks. It was so good to hear her like that. She sounded tired, yet carefree.

Joy listened to the sound of the women talking. Mrs. Lloyd-Foxx's laugh was a light tingle of raindrops on the tin roof. Both women were becoming fast friends. Perhaps they would go with Andrew and his mother to the estate. Mrs. Lloyd-Foxx was leaving this afternoon to return. Andrew was not.

It made Joy want to hug him in front of everyone. But such a display of affection was best left for when they took their evening ride, as they had started to do several days ago.

"Joy?"

She snapped back to the present upon hearing her mother call her name. When she entered, both women were grinning as if they had something up their puffy sleeves.

"Camille and I have been discussing the future."

Oh-oh.

Camille, Mrs. Lloyd-Foxx, gave a smile that dripped with sweet innocence. "Your mother is of the opinion that perhaps her convalescence would proceed faster if she came to the estate. I have assured her that she won't be in the way. In fact, I rather enjoy her company."

"But Hope's baby, Mom. She would want you to be at hand when the time comes. It is her first."

Her mother patted her arm. "I'll be here. The little one isn't due until late spring. I'll travel back early spring. Hope and I have discussed this. Penny is at hand. She's had plenty of experience."

Mrs. Lloyd-Foxx nodded. "And we can send the best obstetrician to attend her. If... if the need arises."

"Have you discussed this with Hope?"

Both women nodded solemnly, like two peas in a pod. Both smiled in a way that made Joy cautious.

"As soon as the doctor has given his consent, I can travel to the estate."

"And I'll send the carriage for you so you can travel in comfort."

"I don't mind riding," Joy mumbled. "Why are you doing this, Mom?"

Her mother sighed and reached for her hand. "It's all arranged. No need to discuss why, child."

When Andrew and Joy took their evening ride later on, she mentioned their mothers' plan. He nodded and pulled Minuteman to a halt on a slight hill overlooking the valley below.

"I'm happy that your mother has agreed to come and stay at the estate once the doctor has given her the go-ahead. My mother seems to quite enjoy her company."

"I feel like I'm missing something." Joy smoothed her hand over Mommy's sleek neck.

Andrew grinned. "No. I'm sure you're not." His grin widened while he reached into his pocket to pull out a licorice stick. Joy's eyes brightened.

"For me?"

He didn't flinch when she took one candy and stuck it into her mouth.

Andrew slipped off his horse and assisted her out of the saddle. It wasn't as if she needed any help. With his arms around her, his eyes searched her face closely.

"As you know, I care greatly for you. With your father's passing, I will approach your mother and ask for your hand in marriage."

"Andrew, it's a year until-"

"You can marry. Yes. One year from now, you and I will walk down the aisle and declare our love and commitment to each other before God and family."

She swallowed loudly and almost dropped her licorice.

"Wh-at?"

Andrew inched closer. "I wish to marry you as soon as your mourning period is complete. It's going to be a very long year," he said ruefully and rolled his eyes dramatically.

Joy found once again that her life was complete in this moment. There would be more times like this. There would be others also, where she would have to rely on God completely. But there would always be joy in her heart, no matter the circumstances.

"Before you make any grand plans in that department I want you tell me that you will share your work with the runaway slaves with me. No secrets."

He drew away slightly. "I can't do that. It's too dangerous for a woman."

She cuffed him hard on his forearm. "Please tell me you didn't just say that."

He gave her a sheepish grin. "I don't want you to get hurt."

She lifted her chin. "I can do it, Andrew. We're to share the hard things in life. And I want to give back. You rescued me, I want to help you rescue more like me, or so much worse."

Andrew kissed her forehead and gave in. He told her how the slaves from down south would arrive without warning, stay a night or two to regain strength and nourishment. Then, they would be ferried onward toward safety in Canada.

"You and I will help them together," he said softly.

She bit her bottom lip as a smile appeared on her face. "In that case I accept, Mr. Lloyd-Foxx."

Andrew kissed her tenderly, making her forget temporarily all about the cares of the world.

Epilogue

*C*ould her heart pound any harder? Her stomach clenched nervously as the soft summer breeze teased a strand of hair from its pin.

"You ready?" Andrew gave her a cheeky grin, one that sent more butterflies bursting into flight in the center of her gut.

"Mr. Lloyd-Foxx. Are you really sure you're up for this? After all, I'm quite sure it didn't end well for you last time."

Andrew checked the girth on Minuteman's saddle. "Mrs. Lloyd-Foxx. I'm sure I don't know what you mean. It is time we show this young upstart a thing or two."

His stallion tossed his head in excitement, flipping white foam onto Andrew's heretofore spotless riding coat.

Mrs. Lloyd-Foxx.

She hadn't quite gotten used to the sound of her married name. Rightly so, since they had only been married a week. One glorious, exciting, lovely, wonderful...

"Are you with me?" Andrew poked at her waist.

"Yes," she giggled and didn't wait for him to announce the beginning of the rematch between Minuteman and Ladiesman.

She squeezed her horse past Minuteman, who pinned his ears at this act of defiance. Ladiesman was eager and keen to show off to the older stallion. By the time Andrew realized what was happening, Ladiesman was already going full speed.

"Cheater!" her husband shouted from behind her.

Joy let out a loud war whoop. She fought the urge to toss the delicate hat Laura had forced her to wear into the air. Looking over her shoulder, she saw that Andrew was gaining on them.

"Come on, boy," she whispered to the stallion – who apparently didn't need to be told twice.

They approached the lighthouse at breakneck speed, Minuteman panting at Ladiesman's flanks. Every time the older stallion would try to get past her horse, Ladiesman would accelerate just a bit more.

In the end, her horse reached the imaginary finish line a nose ahead of Minuteman.

"You cheated," Andrew panted while the horses slowed to a walk.

She turned to him with a smile dripping with honey. "I would never, my husband. You accuse me of such atrocities."

He dismounted and reached up to her. Joy cocked her head.

"Let me help you down."

"I can do it myself, thank you." She flung her leg over the back of the stallion only to find herself caught up in Andrew's arms. His eyes darkened to appear charcoal. Joy's heart burst into flight when his lips touched hers.

She had not only found her joy, she had found someone she was blessed to spend the rest of her life with.

Author's note

Thank you for coming along with me and my characters. This story really began when my son and I were reading about the abolitionists before the Civil War, men of God. William Lloyd Garrison, Lyman Beecher, Charles Finney were all men who fought – using their God-given talents – for the rights of slaves. I started to think about what it would be like if someone rescued a slave.

I researched horse racing before the Civil War. I don't know why. I love horses. I've had the pleasure of owning a beautiful retired racehorse called Justwouldificould, or Grace as she was known. She was the sweetest horse I'd ever met and I suppose I fashioned Mommy in her likeness. I pictured Ladiesman much more like my ornery gelding, Thunder – or Twice Shy, and I am not going to comment on why I ended up giving him this show name. I think you can figure it out. Horses have been an integral part of my life for a long, long time. I came across a breeder of Godolphin Arabians somewhere in the south. I got so caught up in the history of the estate that I began to imagine what it would look like in New England.

Thus, the Downs was born. Now, it was an actual race track near Boston. The estate is made up.

As with any historical fiction, we don't envision things the way they really were back then. I had to re-research when the first bathroom was put into use. It happened to be in 1833, but the first bathroom was installed in a mansion in New York. Thus, even Andrew and his mother didn't have a bathroom yet.

The horse part was not difficult at all. I included a few personal experiences. Having ridden retired Arabian racehorses, I have experienced the immense power and the rush of speed when they want to go. I've also tasted dirt when gravity was tested. I wanted Joy to fall off at the end of the initial race between Mommy and the gelding, but I figured everyone would think that she's not a very good rider. In reality, everyone who is a horseman/woman has fallen off so many times, we've lost count.

I loved writing about the horses. The most touching scene for me was when Lad was dying and waited for Andrew to give him the 'permission'. Horses are such amazing animals, I had to demonstrate the bond between owner and horse.

The hardest part was picturing the travel and the journey back to CT. Highways back then were nothing more than rutted roads and they were very dangerous to traverse. Thus, the attack on Joy. In reality, the ride home would probably have taken longer than two days. But I needed to make it fit the time-line. I'm sorry for fudging it. I hope you forgive me.

The most important part for me is not getting the history right, although this is very important. It's to get the spiritual component correct. I feel that every novel I work on, I have a very important mission. To share God with you all. The component of living with joy is so important. As humans we tend to look at the circumstance and begin to doubt God.

I do it all the time. *Did God really...* is a frequent question I ask myself, especially when it comes to writing. I wanted Joy to experience joy beyond her circumstances. I hope you have enjoyed her journey.

I really hope you enjoyed it as much as I enjoyed writing it. If you want to leave me a review on any of the online sources, I'd be so very excited.

In His service,

Anne

Acknowledgments

There are many people I have to thank when it comes to the writing of any book. First of all, God has to direct me. If He's not in a story, I get lost and it becomes a chore. So, thank You, to Jesus, my Savior for so much more than the writing process

A special thanks goes to my husband, who puts up with my writing. It's tough when you've spent the day working and come home only to find that your wife isn't around. She's lost in some adventure and has forgotten to make dinner. It's a good thing there's take-out.

My daughter Natasha deserves a special shout-out. I love how talented she is and how she has the ability to produce covers that convey the story in one picture. What I love more is sharing the process with her. I mean, how blessed am I to share my passion with my daughter?

Logan, my baby – though he now is taller than all of us. I love reading to him and wonder when he'll finish his. He's quite imaginative and I can't wait for the day when I read a book written by him.

Sean, the oldest, encourages remotely. He's no longer available for pity parties, so we do them over the Internet. I'm proud of the man he has become and the husband he is to his lovely wife.

Lisa, oh editor. I acknowledged her in the beginning since I felt it was appropriate at this time. She's stuck with me for most of my writing journey and has become a wonderful friend. I love talking books with her.

Chrissy, my critique partner for this book. I'm so thankful that she took the time to read this story. She is, after all, super busy with her own writing.

Patricia is one of those people I can chew the ear off and she'll still listen to me. She's my writing mentor and I am so blessed that God put her into my path. I have learned a lot from her.

My readers. I always put them last, but they are incredibly important. I don't know most of them personally and that bothers me. I love to engage with people (which makes me a very unique writer, I'm sure). So feel free to reach out through social media. I'd love to hear from you. And I'm always thankful for a review.

Thank you, everyone.

Contact information:

Facebook: @intothelightfiction
Website: intothelightfiction.weebly.com
Twitter:
Instagram: www.instagram.com/anne.perreault.92/
Bookbub: www.bookbub.com/authors/anne-perreault

Newsletter: https://mailchi.mp/25f04fba2cfb/httpsmailchimpintothelightfiction

About the Author

Anne Perreault was born and raised in Germany. By the time she was 14 years old, the family moved to Dubai, UAE. While living in this exotic place, she traveled extensively to various countries around the world. After graduating from an American boarding school in Austria, she attended college in England, where she met her husband. She graduated from New England College with a degree in biology, and settled down in Connecticut. Anne became a horseback riding instructor as well as a certified therapeutic riding instructor. She and a group of friends started a therapeutic riding center in Bristol, CT. During that time, Anne also received a masters degree in secondary education. While raising their three children, she began to write an inspirational story primarily for her daughter. The family recently moved to Southern Vermont, where they are building their home, something that is a huge adventure. Besides writing, she is busy homeschooling her youngest son.

Made in the USA
Middletown, DE
22 September 2019